CALC

D1016400

Praise for Maureen Child's
Other Novels

"Sassy repartee . . . humor and warmth . . . a frothy delight."
—*Publishers Weekly*

"Maureen Child infuses her writing with the perfect blend of laughter, tears, and romance . . . well-crafted characters. . . . Her novels [are] a treat to be savored."
—Jill Marie Landis, *New York Times*
bestselling author of *Homecoming*

"Absolutely wonderful . . . a delightful blend of humor and emotion . . . . This sexy love story will definitely keep readers turning the pages."
—Kristin Hannah, *New York Times* bestselling author
of *Firefly Lane*

continued . . .

Bedeviled

A Queen of the Otherworld Novel

MAUREEN CHILD

A SIGNET ECLIPSE BOOK

SIGNET ECLIPSE
Published by New American Library, a division of
Penguin Group (USA) Inc., 375 Hudson Street,
New York, New York 10014, USA
Penguin Group (Canada), 90 Eglinton Avenue East, Suite 700, Toronto,
Ontario M4P 2Y3, Canada (a division of Pearson Penguin Canada Inc.)
Penguin Books Ltd., 80 Strand, London WC2R 0RL, England
Penguin Ireland, 25 St. Stephen's Green, Dublin 2,
Ireland (a division of Penguin Books Ltd.)
Penguin Group (Australia), 250 Camberwell Road, Camberwell, Victoria 3124,
Australia (a division of Pearson Australia Group Pty. Ltd.)
Penguin Books India Pvt. Ltd., 11 Community Centre, Panchsheel Park,
New Delhi - 110 017, India
Penguin Group (NZ), 67 Apollo Drive, Rosedale, North Shore 0632,
New Zealand (a division of Pearson New Zealand Ltd.)
Penguin Books (South Africa) (Pty.) Ltd., 24 Sturdee Avenue,
Rosebank, Johannesburg 2196, South Africa

Penguin Books Ltd., Registered Offices:
80 Strand, London WC2R 0RL, England

First published by Signet Eclipse, an imprint of New American Library,
a division of Penguin Group (USA) Inc.

First Printing, January 2009
10 9 8 7 6 5 4 3 2 1

For my mom, Sallye Carberry

Thanks for all the trips to the libraries and bookstores.
You gave me a love of reading and you taught me to dream.
I love you.

Prologue

"'Fifty ways to leave your lover' my ass," Maggie Donovan muttered, and turned off the stereo. "Not one decent example of how to dump a guy you *know* needs dumping."

Well, since she was getting no help from the universe, she'd have to go with her standard *Sorry, this just isn't working out* when she had a little we-have-to-talk conversation with her soon-to-be-ex, Joe. Unoriginal but to the point. "And so ends another sad chapter in the Maggie Donovan love chronicles. Pitiful, Mags. Simply pitiful."

Decision made, she stood up and walked across the living room, stepping over her always-sleeping dog on her way to the front door. She'd just take a little walk to the Quick Mart a couple of blocks away for a pint of Häagen-Dazs Caramel Cone ice cream. Always a good plan.

Outside, a cold wind blew in off the ocean, rattling the leaves in the trees until it sounded like hundreds of whispers from an invisible crowd. Lights blazed from neighborhood windows, a game-show host shouted from her next-door neighbor's TV and the soft whine of traffic from the nearby highway hummed in the background.

Maggie took the porch steps in two long strides, hit the lawn, then stopped dead.

A man stood in the shadows at the edge of her yard.

"Whoa." Where the hell had he come from? And why did he seem . . . familiar somehow? It wasn't likely she'd have forgotten meeting someone like this before.

He was tall, with shoulder-length black hair that whipped around his head in the wind. His green eyes were so pale, so clear, they shone like a cat's eyes in the darkness. He was big and looked tough and just a little scary. *And,* she told herself helplessly, *so sexy he should be illegal.*

Oh, good one. Be attracted to a lurking stranger.

"Who are you?" Maggie asked, taking one slow, tiny step backward toward the safety of her house.

"Who I am doesn't matter," he said. His voice was so deep, it seemed to rumble through the air like a freight train. "Who *you* are is all that matters."

"Okay, well, I already know who I am."

"No, you don't," he said, his clear, powerful gaze locked on her. "Not yet. But you will. Soon."

"Okeydokey."

He frowned, and Maggie swallowed hard, figured she could live without Häagen-Dazs for one night and took another step closer to home. "Look, it's been fun, but I'm going inside and—"

She didn't see him move, but suddenly he was standing right in front of her. How? What? Maggie took a shaky breath and told herself that this was not happening. People don't move like that. Can't move like that.

Then his gaze caught hers and she thought she saw the pale green color of his eyes swirl silver. But of course she didn't. That would have been nuts.

Heat from his body seemed to reach out for her, and Maggie came really close to leaning in toward him. What was up with that? A gorgeous stranger stares at her with his amazing eyes and she turns all hot and trembly?

He smiled as if he knew what she was thinking—and approved.

"You are . . . more than I imagined," he said, his voice whispering up and down her spine like the soft touch of fingertips.

"Uh . . . uh . . ." God, she couldn't even *think* let alone talk. Then it hit her. *More than he imagined?* "You know me?"

"Not as well as I will."

"Oh boy." She really should be screaming right about now. Or running. Or throwing herself into his arms. No, scratch that.

"Your time's coming," he told her, his voice so low that it was almost lost in the sigh of the wind.

"Time? Time for what? No. You know what? Never mind." She shook her head, held up one hand and warned, "Back off, buddy, or I'll scream so loud it'll shatter glass."

"No, you won't."

He smiled then, and she thought that he probably meant it to be reassuring. But it wasn't. His expression was too wicked and too . . . *confident* for that.

"Just as you won't remember this meeting."

Right. Like she could forget a guy who looked like *him*. Maggie opened her mouth to deafen him with a scream the likes of which he'd never heard before. But before she could pull in the breath to manage it, he disappeared.

One minute, he was there.

The next, *poof*.

Frowning, she glanced idly around the yard, her mind wandering back to thoughts of ice cream. Right. That's why she'd come outside. To satisfy her need for something cold and drenched in chocolate.

Mrs. Hardy, her neighbor, who had to be at least 150

years old, opened her door and shouted, "Maggie? Who was that young man?"

"Huh? What man?" She looked at the older woman, whose gray hair was snug to her scalp, held down in tight pin curls by a thousand bobby pins.

"That man you were talking to."

Maggie rolled her eyes. Mrs. Hardy was always seeing burglars and aliens and imaginary FBI agents skulking in the neighborhood. Now, apparently, she was spotting them having chats with Maggie.

"Uh, he's nobody," Maggie assured her. *Just a figment of your imagination, you nosy old lady.*

Honestly. Some people were just nuts.

Chapter One

With a little 20/20 hindsight, Maggie Donovan never would have gone to see her ex-almost-fiancé that morning. Unfortunately, just like anybody else in the world, Maggie didn't know something hideous was going to happen until she was in the middle of the freaking nightmare.

Dressed for work in her faded blue jeans, paint-spattered tennis shoes and a T-shirt that read DO IT IN PAINT, Maggie had had a simple enough plan: Take a box of Joe Ericson's left-behind junk—including ABBA CDs, for God's sake—to his office, drop it off and put him out of her life for good.

He wasn't a bad guy, really. But she'd finally had enough. She just hadn't been able to deal with the idea of spending one more night watching his DVD collection of the original *Star Trek* TV show and discussing over and over again how Kirk was a much better captain of the *Enterprise* than Picard.

So anyway, her plan was simple—until she walked into Joe's office and found him being *eaten*. Not in a sexual way, either.

"Holy shit!" Maggie staggered back, eyes wide and locked on the icky scene in front of her.

The naked female sitting astride Joe wasn't human—

the long tail whipping around in the air was a dead giveaway, not to mention that she was currently devouring Joe. Wearing only a huge round gold-and-crystal pendant that glittered and sparkled with a weird inner light, the naked creature was so busy gulping her food, she didn't even hear Maggie's shriek.

Eyes bugging out of her head, Maggie dropped Joe's box o' crap and, with some delusional idea of somehow saving her ex-honey, grabbed hold of the tote bag slung across her shoulder with both hands. Her purse was always heavy. But today it carried an extra punch, what with the five new jars of tempera paint she'd just picked up at the art-supply store.

What the hell was happening? Was that really a *tail*? She'd heard of man-eating women, but she hadn't really thought they actually *ate* the man!

The creature still hadn't even glanced at her, and Maggie knew she should be turning around and running for her life. After all, once the beast finished off Joe, what was to stop her from having Maggie for dessert? But how could she leave Joe to be gulped down like a Hostess Ding Dong? Sure, she'd broken up with him, but only because he was boring. That didn't mean she thought he qualified as Creature Chow.

She supposed she should have been more scared than she was, but freaked-out and furious won the day. Racing toward the desk and what little was left of Joe, Maggie swung her purse in a wide arc, smacking it into the creature's head hard enough to interrupt her "meal."

Instantly the naked diner turned on her with a snarl that displayed rows and rows of what looked like very sharp teeth. Her dark red eyes burned, and the pendant hanging between her high, perky breasts seemed to glow even brighter.

The creature swung one arm out at Maggie, knocking her ass-over-teakettle, toppling the single chair drawn up in front of Joe's desk to fall on the floor. She landed on her butt, though, which, sadly, had plenty of padding. Still clutching the purse that contained her life, Maggie jolted to her feet in time to see the naked whatever push away from Joe and head toward her.

It took only a very quick look to let Maggie know that there was no saving Joe. By this time he was barely more than a stain on his faux-leather desk chair. The nondescript office seemed to shrink around her as the creature smiled—which was somehow even more terrifying—and leaped at her.

"Yow!" Maggie scrambled out of the way, still swinging her purse, but this time the naked snacker avoided getting smacked, and the momentum of the swinging bag pulled Maggie off balance until she stumbled right into the whatever-she-was.

"Isn't this nice?" the thing crooned with its mouth full. "Someone ordered food delivered."

Up close and personal, the female looked even scarier. Those red eyes were like uncovered manholes into hell, and when she grabbed hold of Maggie and threw her to the desk, Maggie knew she was in trouble. Not only did the thing have some serious chomping power, but she was strong, too.

"Back off," Maggie shouted, knowing it was no use. No way was this thing going to quit.

"You have to die; you've seen too much." She smiled, displaying those shiny, sharp teeth to excellent advantage.

"Don't remember a thing," Maggie assured her, struggling for all she was worth. "Honest. Can't see without my glasses, anyway." She blinked furiously, pretending to need glasses, trying to convince the hideous female that she was one step up from Mr. Magoo.

"I don't believe you," she said, laughing as blood ran down her chin to her neck.

Oh, God. Maggie swallowed hard and struggled to

find something on the creature to grab. But she'd never been much of a hair puller, and since the damn thing was naked, there weren't a lot of other choices she was willing to make. Boobs or tail? *No, thank you.* "You don't have to kill me," she argued frantically. "Honestly, I won't say a thing. Who would believe me if I did?"

"Idiot human."

"No reason to be insulting," Maggie said, her mind racing in tandem with the rapid beat of her heart. How was she going to get out of this? That shining pendant the creature wore swung down close to her, and Maggie curled her fingers around it and yanked. It took a couple of tries, while the female on top of her was screaming and howling and trying to pry herself loose, but Maggie hung on and finally wrenched the gold chain the pendant hung from strongly enough to snap one of the links.

"Nooo!" The howl coming from that "woman" lifted every hair on Maggie's body straight up and brought goose bumps to every square inch of her skin.

Taking advantage of the creature's momentary distraction, Maggie reared up and back, planted one foot in the female's belly and kicked out, giving herself just enough room to spring up off Joe's desk and charge. She had zero idea what she was going to do now, but she was just so darn mad, she wasn't really thinking. Besides, her opponent was looking a little worried, which evened out the playing field a bit.

Swinging that pendant as if she were aiming for a home run in Dodger Stadium, Maggie cracked the heavy gold-and-crystal bauble into the creature's head again and again. Fury was riding along with terror, but clearly her rage was still in the driver's seat. The wildest part, though, was that instead of fighting back, the creature was cowering in a corner, her tail wrapped around her body. Like she was afraid of the very necklace she'd been wearing only a minute or two ago.

"What the hell is wrong with you? You can't just go around eating people!" Maggie shouted. She knew she wasn't making much sense, but then, she was willing to bet that not a lot of people would have been at their best in this situation.

"No, stop!" The naked female raised both hands, trying to ward off the pendant, but by this time Maggie was just too pissed to care. "Don't. You ignorant human, you'll kill us all."

"Oh, please, like I'm going to believe something that wanted to eat me!"

Still swinging that pendant, Maggie reminded herself that this thing had turned Joe into an all-you-can-eat buffet and had planned to do the same thing to *her.* So no guilt here. Just righteous indignation and a hell of an ache in the arm that was still swinging that heavy pendant.

The creature was whimpering now, moaning, and Maggie's fury was starting to fizzle out—though she kept swinging that heavy pendant—when the *next* weird thing happened.

The crystal front on the pendant shattered, and a whirling tornado of golden light spilled from it. The minitwister seemed to grow and expand, almost like it was alive and breathing. There was a swishing sort of sound as what looked like spinning gold dust lifted up and down in the still air, and Maggie backed up. She looked at the broken piece of jewelry and then to the tornado that was wrapping itself around the now-screaming, naked whatever.

"Oh, crap," she whispered, looking around the room as if searching for help that wasn't coming. "Out of the frying pan and straight into the bonfire."

That naked female curled itself up into a ball of keening wimpiness—all of her teeth-baring aggression was gone now as she tried to make herself so small that the golden tornado wouldn't find her. Maggie knew just how she felt. She grabbed up her purse and clutched it to her like it was a shield. She should have been running—she knew that—but somehow she couldn't make herself stop watching. Horrified, she saw the whirling gold cloud settle over what had eaten Joe and, in an instant, reduce whatever it had been to a pile of lint on the floor.

"Ohmigod." One word, because she was just too freaked for three. That gold whirlwind spiraled up toward the ceiling, then did a quick about-face. It was moving away from the lint pile and headed toward Maggie. "God. So I'm not going to be eaten; I'm going to be a dust bunny instead. This cannot be happening."

But it was. She dodged to the left and the vortex moved with her. She leaped right and the damn thing kept pace.

Her tennis shoes slid in something slimy that she so didn't want to identify. Heartbeat thundering hard in her chest, she bolted around the edge of the desk, headed for the door. She didn't even come close.

The whirlwind hit her and felt like what she imagined getting slammed into by a train might. Pain. Lots of pain. She staggered, dropped her purse and fell to all fours while the golden cloud settled down over her, sinking into her skin, sliding through her body. She felt it merging with her, traveling through her system, giving her what felt like the fever of the century. Soon, she thought wildly, she'd be lint.

Maggie thought about her sister, her niece. She wouldn't see them again. Wouldn't ever find a guy incapable of boring her to death. Wouldn't become a famous artist and live in Paris. Hell, she wouldn't even get to see the next Harry Potter movie. Game over.

Groaning, Maggie hung her head, stared down at the floor and realized she couldn't see it, which was probably not a good sign. She couldn't breathe, either.

Was this what that . . . *thing* had felt? Gagging, coughing, eyes streaming tears, Maggie would have thought she'd been Maced, but as it turned out, this was so much worse.

Visions spilled through her mind: Of a city she'd never seen before, filled with shining crystal buildings and floating people. Huge, ancient trees with windows cut into their trunks lined streets that shone brightly in the sunlight. Fields of flowers stretched out for miles and then blurred into a wash of vibrant color. Then those images faded and other, less pleasant pictures showed up. Creatures like the one who'd just died, and so many others that looked far scarier.

Maggie shook her head, trying to dislodge the images; then she groaned, coughed and struggled to breathe. Slowly the visions faded until there was only one last picture rising up in her mind.

A pair of eyes.

Familiar. Pale green.

Staring right through her.

And then it was over.

She could almost see again, and breathing was easier. She wasn't dead, and even the nausea was fading, so Maggie gratefully sucked in air like a drowned person after CPR. She felt ragged, like she'd been beaten up by experts.

"Crap," she muttered to no one, since Joe was gone and the female was dust. "What the hell was *that*?"

Naturally she got no answer, so she collapsed onto the floor, letting her face slap into Joe's ugly, industrial beige carpeting that somehow smelled like sulfur. Her whole body ached like she'd been at the gym—which was why she avoided most exercise.

But there was a strange sensation of power settling into her, which she could not explain at all. Along with the aches and pains she felt, there was a kind of strength beginning to build inside her that just made absolutely no sense. Still, what about the last fifteen minutes could she possibly explain?

She needed to get away from here. Fast. Before anything else bizarre could happen.

"You gotta get up, Mags," she told herself. "Get up and get out of here."

Her vision was still a little wonky, but only at the edges, and who needed peripheral vision anyway? She pulled in a shaky deep breath and told herself again to get a move on. Who knew what else might show up in Joe's little office of the damned?

That thought was apparently enough to engage all of her engines. Reaching up, she laid one hand on the edge of Joe's desk to pull herself to her feet. But when she yanked the heavy wood snapped in two. She sat there for a second, staring at the hunk of oak in her hand, then tossed it aside, muttered, "Termites," and got up on her own.

A little wobbly, but considering what she'd just been through, not too bad. "This is *not* happening," she told herself, avoiding looking at Joe's desk chair. "It's all a weird dream brought on by too much wine and ice cream last night. That's all it is. I'll wake up any minute now and promise never to sin like that again. All good."

Joe wasn't gone. There wasn't a dead whatever sprinkled across the floor, and Maggie hadn't just killed it. Things like that simply didn't happen. Feeling better the farther into the land of Denial she went, Maggie reached down to pick up her purse and that's when she noticed it. Her fingertips were glowing. Like the pendant had been. Her skin actually looked as if it were lit from within.

"Vision's still bad, that's all." She shoved one hand through her shoulder-length, dark auburn hair, took in a long, deep breath and tried to steady the wobble in her knees. Slinging her purse up and over her shoulder, she curled her fingers into her palms and made a break for Joe's door.

If this was a dream, she was perfectly safe. She never died in her own dreams, even if it looked a little iffy now and then. If this *wasn't* a dream? Then she needed to get gone before some other hungry something showed up.

What was that thing? Some kind of mutant? An animal of some kind? But that didn't make sense. No animal she'd ever heard of had the body of a woman and the tail of a lizard.

"Oh, God." That freaked-out feeling rose up inside her again, and she moved even faster, headed for the stairwell that would take her down to the street, where she'd parked her PT Cruiser.

Her steps on the cement stairs sounded like a frantic heartbeat echoing around her as she took them two at a time. Going down stairs was always easier than up, and who had the time or patience to wait for an elevator? She couldn't stand still now, anyway. If something hideous and ugly didn't show up, someone else might. And how would she explain the glowing fingers, let alone what had to be her wild eyes and heavy breathing? Not to mention that if she had to tell someone she'd been in to see Joe, then she'd have to explain that nasty stain on Joe's chair—oh, God. How could she possibly do that?

She hit the bottom level, charged the door and stepped into sunlight. *Thank God.* She raced to her car and hopped inside, locking herself in. Glancing into her rearview mirror, she caught the look of shock in her own blue eyes and knew she was still feeling the effects of whatever had just happened. And something had definitely happened. She was out of breath, her fingers were still glowing and she still had the stink of sulfur up her nose.

Scanning the area, she saw only the everyday: people scrambling for parking places, shoppers marching down the sidewalk determinedly swinging full shopping bags, bright splotches of chrysanthemums blooming in the pots attached to light posts.

The world looked so . . . normal. It was the world she knew. The world she *wanted*. She wished, desperately, that she could be as ignorant of what had just happened as all of these other people were. This side street in Castle Bay, California, was crowded with too many cars and pedestrians. She couldn't have a meltdown here. Someone would see her, and then what?

Letting her head fall against the seat back, Maggie blew out a breath. She didn't know what to do. *Call the police* was her first thought, but she pooh-poohed that one right away. What could she possibly report? Yes, Joe was dead, but there was no body. And the thing that had killed him was gone, too. Besides, did she really want to call the police and open the conversation with, *Hello, I just killed a monster. Who do I talk to*?

Good for one free ticket to a luxurious stay at the nearest rubber room.

"Go get a mocha, Maggie. Starbucks. Where we head during a rough day. Yep. Mocha. Maybe a doughnut," she told herself firmly. "Then go home. Where nothing weird ever happens."

Good plan.

She grabbed the steering wheel with her still-glowing fingers and it snapped in two. She wanted to cry. "That's just great. Great."

Then, carefully holding on to what was left of her steering wheel, she fired up the engine and got the hell outta Dodge.

Culhane entered the small, old home with a blur of movement that would have been undetected by any human. If there'd been one around. But he knew the moment he shifted that he was alone in the place.

His long black hair fell to his shoulders, and he swung it back and out of his way as he moved silently through the house, cataloging every room in his mind.

There was a creative spirit alive in the room where canvases leaned against an easel and droplets of paint splashed the walls. He looked through the stacked paintings, feeding his curiosity. Most of them centered on the sea or the lighthouse. Misty wisps of fog crowded around fishing boats that looked like toys dropped into a sea so big it could swallow them. There was life here. And talent in good measure. But then, he'd expected no less.

He moved on. The next room was where she slept and dreamed. Her scent surrounded him as he noted the clothing dropped on the floors and chairs, as if she'd simply been too busy to pick them up. Sunlight filtered through the lacy curtains hanging at the windows as he left her room, her scent following him, tempting him. It seeped into his mind, his soul, and stirred something Culhane deliberately ignored.

He walked on, opening doors, exploring rooms that were empty yet pulsed with the memories of lives lived. Now she was imprinted on this place. *She* lived here. The one who had been foretold. The one he'd waited centuries for. Finally, today, it had begun. He'd felt the burst of power and sensed Maggie Donovan take her first step into his world.

He was tall, even for a Fenian, standing almost six feet, five inches. His legs were long, his arms muscular and the harsh planes of his face rarely twisted into a smile. He'd lived too long, fought too hard to find much worth smiling about.

And now, when the time of change had finally arrived, he would be forced to deal with a human woman to accomplish his goals.

"Human," he muttered darkly, his gaze sweeping over the small rooms, crowded with what those of her kind no doubt believed to be necessities. Soft chairs, warm rugs, pillows on beds and in her kitchen, food enough to feed a clan of warriors.

Culhane prowled the house again, this time looking for hints into what kind of woman Maggie Donovan had become. He would need all the information he could gather for when he faced her to tell her of her destiny.

Maggie was supposed to be at the local hardware store, painting an idyllic holiday scene on the wide front windows. Yes, all that training and studying in art school had really paid off. Her hand-painted displays of clearance signs, going-out-of-business placards and Christmas scenes were the best in the state.

But at the moment she simply wasn't in the mood to deal with painting smiling snowmen, dancing elves and holiday wreaths. Besides, she thought, who knew if she could hold a damn paintbrush without it snapping into kindling in her grip?

Her steering wheel was only a half circle now, thanks to the glow that hadn't quite left her fingertips, so now probably wasn't the best time to mingle with people who wouldn't understand her sudden freakish strength any more than she did.

Fear was a small knot of misery in the pit of her stomach. She had to figure out what was happening to her. But for now what she had to do was pick up her niece at middle school.

A couple of years ago Maggie's older sister, Nora, got a divorce and moved back to California with her daughter, Eileen. Now the two of them lived in the guesthouse behind Maggie's place, and it had worked out well for everyone. At the moment Nora was in New Mexico at some drum-banging festival to get her chakras or some damn thing realigned, so Eileen was staying with Maggie.

At twelve, the youngest Donovan was tall and thin and blessed (or cursed, depending on your point of view), with the Donovan coloring: dark red hair, pale blue eyes and milky white skin. And just like her mother and aunt, if Eileen spent longer than fifteen minutes in direct sunlight, freckles dotted her skin until she looked as though she'd been sprinkled with gold paint.

No, she'd never get a tan, but there were compensations. All those cute blondes tanning to a luscious brown would one day have skin that looked like beef jerky. True, not much compensation when you were a pale twelve-year-old, but it was at least something to look forward to.

Maggie parked outside the school, watched the crowds of kids exploding from the old brick building and felt her tension sliding away. All it took was a few minutes here to bring her world back into its normal focus again.

This was real life. This was so far removed from the bizarre nightmare scene in Joe's office, it was like a ray of sunshine spearing down out of a black sky.

Here she knew the rules: Don't block the driveway, ignore the PTA psychos who were directing traffic and, most important, never hug Eileen in front of her friends.

Maggie scanned the herd of hundreds of kids for Eileen's telltale height and distinctive hair. When she spotted her, Maggie grinned and reached across the seat to carefully open the car door.

"Hi," Eileen said when she dropped into the passenger seat and shoved her backpack onto the floor at her feet. "You'll never believe what happened. My best friend, Amber, was talking to Justin, who said Dennis told him that Grant said that he kind of liked me." Her eyes were bright as stars. "Isn't that cool? Amazing. Grant Carter likes *me*."

Hmm.

Romance in the seventh grade. *God.* First Joe getting eaten, and now she had to worry about Eileen getting interested in boys. Nora should be here doing this.

"Uh, how old is Grant?"

Eileen hugged herself, then buckled her seat belt. "Oh, he's already *thirteen.*"

Safe then, Maggie told herself. Or if not safe, then not exactly an emergency. If her niece had said this amazing, wonderful, supercool Grant Carter was fifteen, then Maggie would have had to lock her in a closet.

"Do you think Mom will let me wear makeup?"

"As soon as you're twenty," Maggie assured her, and started the car engine.

"That's so rank."

"It's a hard, hard life."

"It's so not fair. Amber wears makeup," Eileen pointed out. "*Her* mom cares about how Amber looks."

"Hmm. Let's call Amber's mom. Maybe she'll adopt you."

"Ha-ha." Eileen slumped down into her seat so low she could barely look out the windshield. Nobody pouted better than a Donovan.

Maggie steered the car toward Pacific Coast Highway and tried to ignore the deep sighs of depression coming from alongside her.

"How was school?"

"Same as always," Eileen said with a dramatic groan. "Big building filled with boredom."

"Good to know some things don't change." Maggie narrowly avoided a near collision with a delivery truck whose driver was text-messaging someone—she hoped it was a driving school—and said, "Do you have your cell phone with you?"

"Am I breathing?" Eileen dug the small dark red phone out of the pocket of her jeans and turned it on. "Why?"

Maggie kept her gaze on traffic and headed for home. "I need you to call Sam's Hardware. Get the number from Information. I have to reschedule the paint job."

"Thought you were doing it this morning."

"Something came up." Understatement of the century.

Eileen shrugged, got the number and dialed it, then handed Maggie the phone. She held it gingerly, half expecting it to shatter, as her steering wheel had.

"Hardware," a deep voice announced.

"Hey, Sam? Maggie."

"Where were you?" he demanded. "Weren't you supposed to be here this morning?"

She winced, moved into the left lane and hit her blinker. "I know, I know, and I'm sorry, but something came up unexpectedly."

Had it ever.

"It's almost Thanksgiving, Maggie," Sam announced, as if he were telling her something she didn't know. "If I don't get my Christmas scenes up soon, I'll be the only shop on Main Street looking like the damn Grinch."

She rolled her eyes. "Would I let that happen to you?"

"What's wrong with your steering wheel?" Eileen asked.

She glanced at her niece. "Nothing. An accident."

"You had an accident?" Sam blurted. "Are you okay?"

"I'm fine." Sure, fine. She saw people getting eaten every day. She was good. Maggie pulled into the driveway of her house and turned off the engine. "Look, Sam, I'll be there tomorrow morning for sure. Snowmen, elves, candles and wreaths, all designed to make you look like Father Christmas."

"Good, 'cause you know people won't come in here and spend money unless I'm a nice guy, God damn it."

Maggie shook her head. Sam was grouchy, demanding and irritating, and everyone in town knew it. He also was the only hardware store for miles, since Castle Bay, California, was way too small to attract one of those giant home stores.

But if Sam wanted to think of himself as a sweetheart, she was willing to play into his delusions. Painting the wide bank of windows on his store was a two-hundred-dollar job.

"Right, Got it. I'll be there." She hung up, gingerly handed the phone to Eileen and gently pulled up the emergency brake.

"So who broke the steering wheel?"

"Me," she said. "And before you ask, I don't know how. It just . . . happened."

"Well, that's pretty weird." Eileen picked up her backpack, opened her car door and got out, still talking. "You know, the average adult female uses only twenty percent of her body muscle mass."

Maggie sighed. Eileen loved a good statistic and was forever quoting some obscure data. She claimed to get most of her information off the Internet, like any other good cyber-friendly preteen, but Maggie thought she made up most of them. Climbing out of her car, she followed Eileen down the shaded drive to the back of the house.

Normalcy seeped into her system as she listened to the everyday sounds of her neighborhood. The narrow street was crowded with trees so old they were tearing up the sidewalks. But every time the city tried to rip up the offending trees, the locals came out with lawn chairs, parked themselves beneath the giant maples and refused to move.

The shade was thick, the lawns were tidy and the houses were old.

Maggie's place was almost a hundred years old. Her family had lived in the house for nearly sixty of those years, and her grandfather had done some pretty quirky remodeling. For example, the front door looked perfectly fine from the outside. Except for the fact that it didn't open. Her grandfather had paneled right over the opening nearly twenty years ago. Why? Good question. One he'd never answered, along with why he'd thought turning his house into a miniature Winchester Mystery House was a good plan.

But Grandpa had liked working with wood, and Grandma always said it kept him out of her hair.

The house itself was wood-framed, California bungalow style, with a stone porch and wide windows. Ancient maple and oak trees studded the front and backyards and shaded both the main house and the guesthouse her grandfather built so that he could leave Grandma and still be around. He'd filled the guesthouse and the main house with what he always called "whimsy."

Maggie smiled to herself. *Whimsy* didn't even come close. There were doors that opened into walls. A tiny staircase that went nowhere. Windows that didn't open and secret passages that led from bedrooms to kitchens to living rooms. As kids, she and Nora had loved living here. There was always a new mystery to be uncovered, and they had spent hours discovering hidey-holes.

Eileen handed Maggie her backpack. "I'm gonna go get my sweatshirt from home; then I'll be right back." She stopped, looked over her shoulder and said, "We do have cookies, right?"

Maggie laughed. "Am I alive?"

Eileen nodded and raced across the yard.

"Hey," Maggie yelled. "Want hot chocolate?"

"With cookies?"

"Of course!" Maggie shook her head. When had she not had cookies? She unlocked her back door, stepped into the quiet of her kitchen and took a breath. The room was cozy, with plenty of space. This was the one place in either house that Grandpa hadn't been allowed to putter in. So the counters, cabinets and floors were all just as they should be—no surprises.

There was a pedestal table in the center of the room and four chairs drawn up to it. The walls were a bright yellow that made even a dark day like today seem a little brighter. Maggie smiled to herself and felt a calm begin to seep into her bones. Good to be home. With Eileen. Dealing with hot chocolate and cookies.

If she just kept moving and didn't stop to think, maybe she could stop remembering that scene in Joe's office. Glancing down at her fingers she noticed that the glow thing was fading, and she hoped that when it went it took the memories along with it. Dropping her purse onto the pedestal table, she headed for the refrigerator to get the milk for hot chocolate.

That was when she felt it.

She wasn't alone.

Chapter Two

$\mathcal{F}$ear grabbed the base of Maggie's throat, and she took in the cold air drifting from the fridge in small, desperate gulps. The back door hadn't opened, so she knew it wasn't Eileen in the room with her. God, she didn't want to look behind her. What if it was another one of those *things*?

What if something had followed her?

God. What if it planned to eat her and then get Eileen?

No way.

Nobody was going to mess with her niece. Poor old boring Joe was one thing. But Eileen was just a kid— and, until Nora got home, *hers* to protect.

She couldn't just stand here in front of an open refrigerator for the rest of her life, Maggie told herself firmly. Eileen notwithstanding, it was damn cold. So she did the only thing she could think of: She reached in, grabbed the brand-new, unopened gallon jug of milk and spun around abruptly, ready to swing that heavy jug at . . . a *hunk*?

"Holy hot guy, Batman."

"What?"

She'd scream in a minute or so, but first . . . wow. Even his deep voice was gorgeous. His gaze met hers, and Maggie felt something almost electric zap through her like a lightning bolt. Then it was gone again, as though somebody had turned off her switch. Just as well. She really didn't need another man at the moment. Especially one who looked like a pirate right off the cover of a romance novel. And, let's not forget . . . a *burglar*.

"Get out," she ordered, but her voice came out in a strangled whisper.

He frowned at her, and even frowning, he was the kind of guy women probably tossed their bras and panties at. Her hormones did a quick two-step before she smacked them back into line. It wasn't easy.

He was tall enough that his head nearly hit the ceiling. His long black hair framed a face that looked tough and mean and sort of familiar somehow. Which was weird, because if she'd ever run into this guy before, she sooo would have remembered. He was wearing a dark green shirt tucked into brown suede pants. His knee-high, dark brown leather boots were flat soled and were stitched with what looked like gold thread. Around his waist there was a wide leather belt with a *knife* sheathed in a scabbard.

Okay, gorgeous and clearly dangerous.

But it was his eyes that grabbed her. They were pale, pale green. The eyes she'd seen when those visions had raced through her mind earlier.

"What the hell is going on with me today?"

"Maggie Donovan?"

"How do you know me? How'd you get in here?" Cold air was still wafting out from behind her, sending a chill over her backside that seeped right down into her bones. Weird, because there was a wall of heat coming from her gorgeous intruder that was blasting her from the front.

Could she simultaneously combust and freeze?

"We must talk," he told her. "It's your time."

"My time? My time for what? No, never mind. Don't want to know. Just get out. I have a dog. . . ." Just where the hell was her dog, anyway? "She doesn't like intruders. She'll bite your ass." *Hmm.* Hormone issues again. Her grip on the milk jug tightened, and she really hoped she didn't break it before she could use it like a weapon.

"You talk too much."

"Thanks so much for your input. Maybe you didn't hear me tell you to get out. I've got a silent alarm that goes directly to the police station." Yes, a lie, but Maggie wasn't very concerned about playing fair with an intruder. "They're probably on the way right now, so don't even try to hurt me."

"I'm not here to hurt you. I'm here to help you."

"Oh, I bet you tell that to all your victims."

"Can't you be silent?"

"Why should I be? It's my house, and you're awfully snotty for a pretty burglar."

"Snotty?" He snarled the word. "Do you know who I *am*?"

"No. That's the point. I don't know who the hell you are, or why you're in my house or even why my dog isn't here chewing on you!"

"I've never known a female like you."

"Am I supposed to care?" she snapped. Her gaze whipped around the kitchen as she wondered if the walls were somehow shrinking. He seemed to be taking up a lot of space. "You need to get the hell out of my house."

He planted both hands on his hips and braced those incredibly long legs of his wide apart. *Damn.*

"I felt the power shift this morning. It's finally happened, and it's time for you to accept your destiny."

She shook her head. "Are you serious? A burglar wants to talk about my destiny? I don't have a destiny. I'm pretty much a destiny-free zone."

"Burglar?" he repeated, fury filling his features with a dark red flush that only made his eyes look paler, more haunting. "You believe I'm a thief?"

"What'm I supposed to think? I didn't invite you in. Yet here you are, and you're carrying a *knife*." Maybe she shouldn't have brought that up.

"You insult me."

"Oh, I insulted *you*?" Maggie muttered, then told herself to stop talking to the man. Did she really want to go out of her way to anger an armed intruder? Was that really the wise choice here?

"You try me, Maggie Donovan."

"No, thanks."

He frowned again, and she noticed how easily his features shifted into that expression.

"I will start again. I've come to talk to you. It's your time, and you must—"

"The only *must* around here is you leaving. I don't have to talk to you. Who the hell are you?"

"I am—"

"And what do you mean, my time?" Her arm was starting to hurt with the weight of the gallon milk jug dragging on her. But she couldn't put it down. *Some* kind of weapon was better than nothing.

"If you could stop talking for a moment, I could explain—"

"Explain what? How I wandered into the Twilight Zone? I don't think so. You're a part of this screwy mess somehow, aren't you? So why would I listen to you? And by the way, why do you have a knife, and how did you get in here anyway? What the *hell* is happening to me?"

"Maggie?" Eileen's voice.

Instantly the gorgeous giant spun around, going into a deep crouch and pulling the knife at his belt free all in one fluid motion.

Maggie saw light glitter dangerously on the silver

blade and did the first thing that popped into her mind: She swung the milk jug in a wide arc and slammed it into the back of the guy's head.

He dropped like a stone. Milk erupted into a geyser as the plastic shattered, and the white wave coated her, him, and splashed across Eileen's face as well.

"Wow," her niece said, smiling at her with pride as she wiped milk from her face. "That was amazing. Who's he?"

"I don't know." But now that he was unconscious, Maggie took her first steady breath in quite a while. Still, she had to admit that even out cold and covered in milk, he was quite the honey. Too bad he was some kind of criminal.

Maggie was still shaking when her less-than-alert "watchdog," Sheba, a golden retriever who'd never met a snack she didn't want, sauntered into the room, walked up to the fallen giant and began to lick the milk off his face.

"Oh," Maggie told her, "thanks so much for your help."

&

Culhane woke up to find himself tied into a chair, with Maggie Donovan and a child looking down at him. A yellow dog was stretched out atop his feet.

He couldn't even recall the last time he'd been taken down in a battle. And yet this one mortal woman had done just that. Not only had she caught him unaware, but she'd knocked him out and tied him up. She was definitely ready to answer the call of fate.

Taking a breath, he shook his still-wet hair back from his face and accused, "You hit me."

"You pulled a knife on my niece! Not to mention the whole breaking-and-entering thing," she pointed out, dropping one arm around the girl, who'd come to the door behind him unnoticed.

Bad enough that he'd been so distracted by this woman that he hadn't heard the child's approach. But to have this female insinuate that he would have harmed the girl was an insult he would not accept.

Culhane glared at her. "I am a Fenian warrior for the Fae of Otherworld. I do *not* harm children."

She blinked at him. "You're a *what* for *who*?"

"Fae," the girl said, nudging her aunt with an elbow even as she looked at Culhane with sharper interest. "Isn't that like Faeries?"

"Oh," Maggie murmured, looking at him a little differently. "Now, that's a shame."

Culhane muttered a curse.

"What's a Fenian, though?"

"We don't care," Maggie told her.

Still feeling the insult and the humiliation of his situation, Culhane ignored the interplay between the two females and looked at the girl. Her eyes were wide and interested, but there was more there, too, he thought. A stillness. A watchfulness. And temper, along with a courage that outmatched her years. That he understood and admired. He met that young gaze and gave her a formal nod. "I wouldn't have harmed you."

She studied him for a long moment or two, and Culhane waited for her to make up her mind about him. Finally she shrugged and said, "It's okay. I believe you."

"Well, I don't," her aunt said, and Culhane's gaze slid back to the woman who was the reason for his presence in this place.

There was temper in her eyes, as well. He found it less admirable in her than in her niece.

"You try my patience," he said, glaring at Maggie.

"Hah! You're the intruder here, Sparky."

"Are you really a Faery?" the girl asked.

"Fae. I am Fae," he said.

"Picky, picky . . ."

He scowled at Maggie again.

"Then I'm kind of sorry I called the police," the child said, and he shifted his glance to her. The younger Donovan seemed much more reasonable than her aunt. Besides, he admired strength wherever he found it, so he nodded at the girl.

"Don't be. You did what you should."

"They'll be here any minute," Maggie told him.

"I won't be here when they arrive." He let his gaze move up and down the length of the woman who was foretold to be the hope of Otherworld and felt something quicken inside him. Her clothing didn't exactly mark her as the savior of a race. Her jeans were paint spattered, but clung to her long legs and hugged every curve. Her shirt was ridiculous, but he enjoyed the way it displayed her full breasts. Her hair was a deep red with threads of gold brightening the darkness. Her eyes were blue, her mouth was full and, at the moment, curled into a sneer that he found offensive. Yet there was more here. He felt the crackle of energy in the air and wondered if she did, too—or was she still too human?

Despite what his body might want, though, he wasn't here for sex. She was the promised one, gods help him.

To think it had come to this: a Fae warrior requiring the help of a mortal female. It was almost enough to convince him that perhaps prophecies weren't all they were supposed to be. But even as that thought formed, he reminded himself that she'd shown him no fear. She had strength, courage. Everything she would need.

The fact that he could spring from these ropes in an instant was meaningless. She had bested him. For the moment.

She had actually managed to not only incapacitate him, however briefly, but surprise him as well, humiliating as it was to admit.

The sneer she was giving him intensified, and Culhane felt his chest swell with indignation. Who was she to look at him as though he were no better than a good-for-nothing pixie? He was an elite warrior of the Fae, and no one in centuries had treated him with so little respect. She might be the hope of Otherworld, but without his assistance she was only fodder for the enemies she didn't even know existed yet.

"Won't be here, huh? Just how were you planning to get out of those ropes?" Maggie tipped her head to one side and let her sugary sweet tone and self-satisfied smile tell him what she thought of him. "Eileen tied them, and she learned knots from the Girl Scouts. Trust me when I say those girls know a little something about—"

"Enough of this." Culhane shifted while she was speaking, sliding his body from one dimension to another and back again. With the shift, the ropes binding him came loose and dropped to the floor. He stood up, nudged the sleeping dog off his feet and looked at the woman who was at the heart of his troubles. "Ropes can't hold me."

"Well, shit." She stopped, glanced at the child and corrected herself. "Shoot."

"That was very cool." The girl was looking at Culhane with renewed interest. "Like magic or something."

"Back up, Eileen. Stay away from this guy." Maggie tried to shove the girl behind her, but Eileen wasn't going willingly.

"I've told you I won't harm you or the child," Culhane said again.

"Well, sure, if a burglar gives you his word, why wouldn't you believe him? Forgive me for not trusting the guy who broke into my house."

"I didn't break in," he told her. "I shifted. Just as you saw."

"Really?" Eileen prompted. "You can go through walls and stuff?"

"I can."

"Whoa."

The wail of sirens sounded in the distance, and irritation crowded Culhane's chest until he could hardly draw a breath. This was not how their meeting was to have gone. The woman was too distracted to listen to him. Her world was crowded and noisy, and apparently she had yet to come to terms with what had happened to her today.

Now, with the human authorities arriving, Culhane was forced to leave before anything had been settled. Yet more irritation. "I have no time for your police."

"They'll probably want you to make time." Maggie kept a tight grip on the girl.

Eileen was still shaking her head in awe. "Did you see that, Maggie? He, like, poofed right in front of us. And the knots are still tied. That was so great. Way cooler than that magician we watched on TV last month."

"Do you still have the pendant?" Culhane ignored the child and concentrated instead on the woman he'd come to see. As he watched, the blood drained from her face and her eyes became a dark, deep, troubled blue.

"What do you know about that?"

"What pendant?" Eileen demanded.

"Do you have it?"

"No," she said. "It was broken. I left it."

"What pendant?" Eileen repeated. "And where'd you leave it?"

The dog began to snore.

"The pendant's owner?"

Maggie cringed a little, glanced at the girl beside her and hedged, "Gone."

"According to prophecy."

"What prophecy?" Eileen's voice was getting louder in response to being ignored.

"It was an accident, sort of," Maggie told him.

"Doesn't matter. It happened as it was meant to. The dust touched you."

"There was dust in the pendant?" Eileen tugged on Maggie's arm, but her aunt didn't tear her gaze from Culhane's.

"Um . . . yeah. It did."

"I feel the power," he said, taking one step closer to her, keeping their gazes locked. "Even now it's taking you over."

"What is?" Eileen wanted to know. "Dust? How does dust take you over? Over into what? And what pendant?"

"No, it's not," Maggie argued, holding up one hand to show him what was left of the faint glow in her fingertips. "It's fading."

So much she didn't know. So much she had to learn. "No, it's not fading. It's becoming a part of you. Becoming stronger."

Her jaw dropped and her eyes looked even wider than before. If she became much paler she would simply blend in with the white cabinets behind her. "What?"

"Aunt Maggie . . ."

"Not now, sweetie." Maggie looked at her hands, then at him, and Culhane felt her fear. Good. She should be afraid. Gods knew he wasn't looking forward to this any more than she was.

"Look, this is all some kind of mistake." Maggie held her niece close to her side. "I'm sure we can work something out. Maybe I could go get the pendant and have it fixed."

"It wouldn't change anything."

"You know," she said, as if her fear were slowly being replaced by a sense of outrage, "I've had a really crappy day. And I'm done talking about all of this. So unless you want to take a fun ride in a squad car with some nice officers, I suggest you hit the road."

"You're telling me to leave?" He couldn't believe her audacity. "I leave when I decide to, and I return the same way. As much as you would wish to ignore everything that's happened today, there is no going back now, Maggie Donovan. You can't undo what happened any more than I can." He stepped into a pale wash of light sliding through the kitchen window. Outside, clouds filled the skies and a storm built its fury.

Inside, a storm of another kind was building.

"You're the one." Culhane stood tall and straight, looking down into her eyes, willing her to feel the inevitability of this moment. He drew on his centuries of power, of strength of command, to impart to her the gravity of the situation they all found themselves in. "This is immutable. I've waited. Watched. But that is over now. Your time of destiny has arrived."

She looked from him to the girl and back again. Then she smiled. "Sure it has."

He sighed.

Pulling Eileen even closer to her, she wrapped both arms around the girl and glared at him. "I don't know what you're trying to pull, but the cops are almost here, so if you're planning a stealthy escape you might want to work on that."

"I'll be back," he told her as the sirens outside abruptly cut off.

"Nice Arnold imitation."

"Arnold?"

"Never mind."

Culhane took a step closer as pounding sounded from the front of the house. The human police were here, demanding entry. "There's much to explain—without the child involved."

"Excuse me," the young one interrupted. "I'm not a child. I'm almost thirteen. Well, I will be in ten months."

Culhane held up one hand for silence, and Maggie

looked dumbfounded when he got it. From the front of the house came the frantic pounding of fists and the explosive shouts of the police. He fought a fresh burst of impatience. None of this was going as he had planned. But then, dealing with mortals was always fraught with exasperation.

"When your police have left, I'll return." Then he shifted again and couldn't stop himself from smiling— just a bit—when he heard the child say, "So cool."

By the time the police were gone, Maggie figured she'd had a full enough day for anybody. Instead of trying to cook, she picked up the phone, ordered pizza for her and Eileen and tried to forget about everything that had happened.

Not easy to do when your brand-new, surprisingly annoying superstrength kept intruding. Sure, it had come in handy when she opened a bottle of wine. But snapping the doorknob off in her hand was a pain in the ass, and she didn't want to think about having to replace the showerhead. *Hmm.* Although . . . maybe she'd get one of those water-massage things this time.

With the way her luck with men was going, a shower-massage orgasm sounded like way less trouble.

Just the thought of the word *orgasm* had Maggie twitching uncomfortably on the couch, which upset Sheba, asleep beside her on the cushions, so much that it actually forced the dog to roll over. "Sorry," Maggie muttered, stroking one hand down her lazy dog's back.

Sheba wouldn't understand about the orgasm thing anyway. She'd been spayed at six months. But for Maggie, it had been so long since she'd had a good, solid, earth-shaking orgasm, she could hardly remember what it felt like. Joe had not only been boring, but surprisingly untalented in certain areas—not that she wanted to speak ill of the eaten. Then up popped this burglar in suede pants and leather boots, and all of a sudden Maggie was imagining all sorts of interesting things.

Her body was clenched, and she had to will it into submission. "Get a grip, Maggie. Not only did the guy disa-freaking-ppear right in front of you, but he's some kind of nut, too."

But then, how had he known about the pendant? About what had happened to her earlier? Had he been following her? Did he know what that thing in Joe's office was?

Frowning, she pushed Culhane the weird from her mind and shouted out, "Hey, kiddo, you finished with your homework?"

"Almost. Want to help me with my math?"

Maggie laughed, half turned on the couch and waited for Eileen to poke her head around the hallway door. They both knew all too well that Maggie's relationship with math was sketchy at best. "Did you really ask me that?"

The girl grinned. "Just kidding."

God, having Eileen here with her was really turning into a gift. No better way to avoid thinking about a certain annoying male than to focus on the kid you were babysitting. "I figured. Did you call your mom?"

"Not yet. I will, though, before I go to bed."

"Okay." Maggie checked the clock on the wall. "You've got a half hour before lights-out."

"Got it." Eileen smiled. "Unless, of course, you want to be a totally cool aunt and let me stay up to watch *Supernatural*."

"Nice try," Maggie told her, remembering Nora's strict instructions on TV time and bedtimes. The woman would have made a great general. Nora might be a little flaky about her own life, but she ran Eileen's with discipline and structure. "I'll tape it for you, though, and you can watch it tomorrow."

Eileen's narrow shoulders slumped. "Fine. But I'll be the only one in school tomorrow who doesn't know what happened. Your only niece, the one who loves you, will be completely left out of the discussions about Jensen Ackles. I'll be ostracized by my peers, but don't let that worry you. I'll probably get over it after years of therapy. . . ."

Maggie grinned. "Any seventh grader who can use the word *ostracize* in a sentence is already standing out in a crowd. I'll risk it."

"Fine." How Eileen managed to look disappointed and haughty all at once was a mystery, but she managed. When she slammed her bedroom door for emphasis, Maggie just chuckled.

"God, 'normal' is such a great thing," Maggie murmured.

Determined to push Culhane and everything else out of her mind, Maggie focused on some stupid reality show playing on television. As she paid attention, she told herself that TV was really sinking to a new low. Had they completely run out of ideas? This show was supposed to be about a woman choosing her mate from a group of gorgeous *demons*.

"Oh, please. What a stupid gimmick. Demons? Who believes this shit?" She punched the button on the remote and stabbed it so hard the damn thing splintered in her hand. "Perfect." Now she was stuck watching the show because she was too lazy to get up and change the channel by hand.

But after a few minutes even Maggie was interested. Apparently set in La Sombra, a town in northern California, the show featured some truly gorgeous "demons." As she watched, her mind started wandering back to earlier that day. If these guys were demons, then maybe what she'd seen in Joe's office was one, too. Seriously challenged on the attractiveness meter, but . . .

Was it possible? Were there actually demons out there?

A second or two later she laughed at herself. "Come on, Maggie, demons? What's next? Bachelor vampires?"

"Vampires wouldn't show up on television."

"Yow!"

The air rippled in front of her, blurring her view of the television set. Before she had time to worry that she was being struck blind, though, the blurry effect ended and Culhane was standing there in all his leather-covered glory. *So much for normal.*

"We will talk now."

"You have *got* to stop doing that." Maggie jumped off the couch, but instead of landing she just kept on going up and up and . . . "Hey!"

She looked down and saw that she was actually floating. "Ohmigod." Already a few feet off the floor, she pinwheeled her arms frantically, trying to get back down where she belonged. That didn't work, though, and she probably looked like she was doing the backstroke or something. Stomach churning, throat tight, her gaze flashed to her own personal pain in the butt. He was smiling.

The bastard.

"Are you doing this to me? Because if you are, this is not funny."

"I'm not the one doing it." One jet-black eyebrow lifted. "Your power is growing."

"Power? This isn't power. This is floating. I don't want to float. I want to stand." Not entirely true. What she wanted to do was lie down with an ice bag on her head and a glass of wine close at hand.

Instead she was still rising. This couldn't be good. Looking down at Culhane, her sleeping dog and the living room, she idly noted that she really needed to vacuum. And dust. Especially the top of the entertainment center. *Good God.*

"Get me down from here."

"I think not," he said, sitting on the couch, where she'd been only a moment before. Stretching out his incredibly long legs, he rested them on the coffee table and crossed his feet at the ankles. Beside him Sheba the Wonder Dog slept on.

Maggie looked around desperately for something to grab onto so she could lower herself to the floor. But she'd waited too long. Now there was nothing within reach, and as her head bumped the ceiling, she winced and glared down at the man below her.

"If you're ready to listen to me, I'll help you down." He folded his hands atop his flat abdomen and looked comfortable enough to stay there all night.

"Help me down first. How can I listen to you when I'm *floating*?" She braced her hands on the ceiling and shoved. For a second it worked. Her body lowered a little, but then she bobbed back up to the ceiling again. Weird to know how those giant balloon animals in the Macy's parade must feel.

Now if only she could get someone to tether her ankle and pull her the hell down!

"Come on, *help*."

Frowning, Culhane pushed himself to his feet and walked a few steps until he was standing directly beneath her. Which, of course, was when Maggie remembered that she was wearing her nightgown, and he was no doubt staring straight up at her personal space.

"Close your eyes," she ordered.

He actually laughed, and the change in his features was breathtaking. The man went from gorgeous to flat-out *amazing*. Only the fact that he was laughing at her made it possible for Maggie to keep from drooling.

While she bounced around on the ceiling like an escaped helium balloon, she tried to hold the hem of her short nightgown close to her legs, which wasn't easy.

"Are you *sure* you're not doing this to me?"

"No, the trapped Fae dust from the pendant is doing this to you."

"Fabulous," she muttered, twisting her head this way and that, still looking for a way out. But there was nothing. No long, dangling chain holding up a chandelier. No handy floor-to-ceiling pole lamp. Just cobwebs. Lots and lots of cobwebs. She really had to do more housework.

"Are you going to help me down or not?"

"Will you listen?"

"*Yes*, all right? I'll listen. If you want to sing some songs, I'll listen. You want to read the phone book, I'm your audience. Just get me off the damn ceiling!"

"Aunt Maggie?" Eileen's voice came, calling from the hallway. "Who's here?"

"Go back to bed!" Maggie shouted. The last thing she needed was one more person seeing her rolling around on the ceiling.

"Are you never alone?" Culhane asked.

"Was wondering the same thing myself." Her gaze shot to the hall as Eileen naturally ignored the order to go to bed and walked down the zigzag stairway Grandpa had built. Over thirty stairs to go up about two feet.

The man had really had too much time on his hands.

"Maggie, how come you're on the ceiling?"

"Her power grows," Culhane said.

"Cool," Eileen added.

"Go to *bed*!" Maggie shouted.

"I knew you'd come back." Eileen had transferred her attention from her floating aunt to the tall, dark warrior standing in the middle of the room. The girl was really taking all of this much better than Maggie was. But then, Eileen wasn't bumping her head on wooden beams, was she? "I went on the Internet to do some checking after you left, and—"

"Hello?" Maggie spoke up, her voice as filled with sarcasm as she could make it. "If you two don't mind, maybe you could chat later . . . when I'm on the *floor*?"

"I was talking." Eileen threw herself onto the couch with enough energy that Sheba woke at last. Looking up, the dog spotted Maggie, whined piteously, then dove under the coffee table, where she shivered so hard, Maggie's forgotten wineglass trembled in response.

"And I'm still floating."

"I have never experienced so much trouble dealing with one mortal woman," Culhane grumbled, his voice deep and dark, rumbling through the small living room like a runaway freight train.

"Two," Eileen reminded him.

"Yes, of course." He merely glanced at the girl, then waved one hand and she was silent, her eyes still fixed on him but with an empty, vacant stare.

"What was that?" Maggie slapped one hand to the ceiling, gave herself a shove and came really close to being within slapping distance of Culhane. Then she was bobbing back up again like a cork in water. If she weren't so mad, she'd be really freaked out right about now. "What did you do to her? Eileen's never quiet or still—"

"I silenced the child."

"You did *what*?" Okay, gorgeous or not, this guy had to go.

"It's only momentary. She's unharmed."

"She'd better be, buster, or when I finally get down from here I'm gonna make you sorry you ever *heard* of Maggie Donovan."

"Believe me, I already am."

"Well, that's really nice!" She looked at Eileen again and worried. But she didn't look injured. She just looked . . . stunned. Who *was* this guy? "I didn't *ask* you here, you know. You're the one who keeps popping up out of nowhere. I've had a completely crappy day, and instead of helping me, you look up my nightgown like a perv, put some kind of spell on my niece and scare my dog."

"*You* scared your dog."

She huffed out an impatient breath. "Fine. I'll give you that one."

"You are the most irritating woman I have ever known."

"Don't I feel special?" She stuck her tongue out at him.

"Hard to believe that *you* are the prophesied one."

"Can we have this conversation when I'm on the floor?"

Without another word Culhane rose up, floating effortlessly and with a lot less flailing about than Maggie had. His long black hair ruffled in the slight breeze his motion created. His gaze was fixed on Maggie, his mouth set in a grim, straight line. He hung in the air beside her for a long moment, and Maggie couldn't help but notice that he seemed to get better-looking the closer he got to her. Which really wasn't the point at the moment.

"Your destiny has arrived," he said, "and I am here to see that you accept it. I am a warrior of the Fae, and you are the chosen one. The one who will defeat Queen Mab and free the males of the Otherworld."

Maggie's head thumped into a beam on the ceiling. "Uh-huh. Chosen one. Like Buffy. Sure." Scrambling to push herself down off the ceiling, she at last admitted, "Okay, I give you that something completely weird is going on. Obviously I'm floating, so yeah. Problem. But, chosen one? Come on."

"You don't believe."

"Is that what you need to help me out here? Because if it is, then okay. I believe you," she assured him.

Culhane studied her for a long moment, then shook his head in disgust.

"Give me your hand." Not a request. An order.

She'd have held hands with the devil himself if it would have gotten her back on the ground. Maggie held out one hand, and when Culhane's fingers closed over hers, heat suffused her body. From the tips of her toes to the top of her head, what felt like fire rushed through her veins, bubbling under her skin, and she had to wonder if holding hands with the devil wasn't exactly what she was doing.

Chapter Three

*O*nce safely on the floor again, she sat on the couch and held on to the arm to anchor herself. Her eyes were wide, and when the dog crawled into her lap looking for comfort, Maggie transferred her tight-fingered grip to the animal. "It's okay, sweetie, I was scared, too."

"Your dog is a pitiful source of protection." Culhane looked at the dog with disdain.

"She's sensitive."

"And a coward." Sheba was sprawled across Maggie's lap and looking pleased with herself. As Maggie's fingers dug into the golden fur, Culhane almost envied the animal. Not a thought he enjoyed entertaining. Maggie was luscious and tempting and more infuriating than anyone he'd ever known. And she stirred something inside him. Something he preferred to ignore.

"Wake Eileen up," she commanded.

Both black eyebrows lifted in surprise that she would think to order him to do anything. "In a moment."

"Now. No more talking until I see for myself that she's all right."

Rather than drag this meeting out even further, he blew out a breath, waved one hand over the girl, and instantly she was back with them.

"How'd you get down, Maggie? When did Sheba come out from under the table and—"

"Go to bed, honey." Maggie sounded tired now, and Culhane felt a moment's sympathy for her. He had been waiting an eternity for this night. She was waking up to a world she'd never suspected existed. He must give her enough time to become used to the idea. To come to see that she was indeed destined to lead.

It would require patience. Diligence. Tolerance.

"Who's Mab?" Maggie's gaze was on his as if she were attempting to stare directly into his brain and pluck out the answer for herself.

"I know!" Eileen called out from the stairway. "I was trying to tell you before that I looked up Fae on the Internet, and on Wikipedia it has all kinds of great information, and I was reading up on the warriors and all of that stuff—"

Culhane sighed. He'd never been fond of children, and this one in particular, though brave, seemed to constantly be interrupting. Did no one teach children to be quiet anymore?

Maggie grunted, shoved the heavy dog to one side and turned to glare over the top of the couch. "Hey, information girl, you know you're not supposed to go on the Internet unless I'm around."

"Please. Mom is soooo overdoing the whole look-out-for-child-molesters-on-the-Internet thing. I'm not an idiot, you know."

Culhane rolled his eyes and waited—as he had all day. Already it seemed as if this day had lasted an aeon. If this was the hope of the Otherworld, then his people were in for a disappointment. The woman's mind couldn't stay focused on any one thing for longer than a heartbeat.

"Not an idiot, but still a kid."

"Teenager—"

"Not yet." Maggie had a tight grip on the couch, but

even so, her legs lifted off the cushion a bit. "Besides, you know the rules."

Eileen gave a dramatic sigh and pouted for good measure. "Yes, but this was an emergency, and we needed information—and you should be grateful, because I found out about Mab and about *him*." She stabbed her index finger at Culhane.

He didn't want the girl telling Maggie anything until she'd heard it from him. Besides, who knew what this Wikipedia was saying about him and his people?

"Want me to tell your mom?" Maggie smiled.

Eileen huffed out a breath. "That's just mean," she said as she started up the zigzag stairs again, clearly realizing she'd been beaten. Her head was down, shoulders slumped, and as her bare feet clomped up the ridiculous flight of steps, she muttered under her breath.

"If you're finished . . ." Culhane shifted his gaze from the now empty hallway to the woman glowering at him.

"Oh, excuse me," she snapped, not actually asking pardon at all. "Have you been put out? Are you having a bad day? Feeling crabby now, are you? I'm so sorry to hear it."

"We have—"

"Not your turn yet," she said, and groaned when the dog threw herself across her lap again. "You will never, ever do that to my niece again; you understand me?"

His insides rippled with anger, and power tingled through his system. To be dressed down by a woman who was younger than him by centuries was more annoying than he could say. Culhane lifted his head, squared his shoulders and looked down at her with all the fierceness of his bloodlines. "I will do—"

"Nothing to her," she interrupted. "Ever." The dog whimpered, and Maggie grunted and groaned as she shoved the hairy beast onto the couch cushions. Standing up, she folded her arms beneath her breasts, tossed her hair back and warned him, "You do anything to her again and I'll . . ." She paused, tipped her head to one side while she thought about it, then sighed. "Fine. Can't come up with a good threat, so never mind. My point is, Eileen's not a part of this . . . whatever the hell it is, and you're going to leave her alone, got it?"

His anger at the insult of her tone was immediate and instinctive, but not permanent. It couldn't be. He needed her, damn the gods for sending her to him. Though he fought to restrain his fury, a part of him stood back and applauded her ferocious defense of one she loved. Looking into her eyes, he saw that fighting her on this would only make things more difficult. So he inclined his head in a nod.

"I give you my word that no harm of any kind will come to the child."

"Damn right it won't. Okay, good." She smiled a little, her mouth curving up at one corner, and Culhane watched the motion with a hungry gaze. Ridiculous to be attracted to a woman who had given him nothing but trouble from their first meeting.

"Glad that's settled." Maggie started floating again, but this time Culhane reached out, grabbed her and pulled her back down.

"You must focus. Concentrate on standing still."

"I have to *concentrate* to keep from floating? What kind of dumb-ass power is that? And why am I suddenly going all antigravity, anyway? What the hell is going on?"

Patience, he reminded himself, and wished that he had a larger supply of that virtue to draw on. Most certainly he was going to need it. "I've been trying to explain. There's much to tell you. Much you have to learn."

"Yeah, probably." Her fingers curled over his forearm as she frowned and fought to keep from lifting off her feet. "How about we start with why this is happening to me?"

The lights in the room were soft and dim. The sound from the television was an annoyance that was easily taken care of. Culhane waved his hand and the set shut off, its now dark screen like a blind eye staring into the room.

"Will you quit doing that?" She looked at the TV. "Now how will I know which bachelor demon gets picked?"

"Demons." Culhane hissed the word.

She sighed. "Well, they're not *really* demons. It's some bigwig's idea for a gimmick, that's all. Unless . . ."

He laughed shortly as the truth dawned on her. "Of course it is real. Demons are real. Fae are real. And the power overtaking you now is *real*."

She shook her head, hitching her folded arms high enough that the tops of her breasts peeped out of the neckline of her nightgown. He'd already seen much of her. Enough to make him hard and hot for her. But that time would come, and he could wait. First he had to make her see and accept her destiny.

"This is really a lot to take in, you know? I mean, sure. Weird shit is happening, but—"

"You killed a demon today," he said, and watched her eyes darken at the memory.

"She was a demon?" Maggie took in air desperately. "I was trying earlier to figure out what that thing had been, but I never thought of . . . See, the word *demon* doesn't really spring to mind, generally. But your saying it so matter-of-factly, it's hard to argue with. Of course she was a demon. What else would she be? All those teeth, the tail. What she was doing . . ." She took another breath. "And I killed . . ."

The hand on his forearm tightened until he could feel the bite of her short fingernails through his coat. "Oh, God. Yes. I killed her. It. Whatever." Her gaze lifted to his. "I didn't mean to; it just happened, and if I hadn't she would have eaten me just like she did Joe, so I can't really be blamed for—"

"The pendant," his voice boomed out, interrupting the incessant flow of words from the woman. "The demon you killed wore the pendant. It carried the dust of slain Fae."

"That tornado of gold dust was dead Faeries? Ohmigod." Her eyes went wide and horrified. "It was all over me. I was breathing it and . . ."

She wobbled, and he gave her a nudge that sent her falling backward onto her couch.

"I think I'm gonna be sick."

"You won't." He dropped into a crouch in front of her. Her hair was a wild coronet around her head. Her eyes looked glassy, and her skin looked as pale as porcelain. Culhane laid one hand on her knee, felt the sting of electricity flow between them, but ignored it and stared into her eyes. "As a descendant of Fae, the Faery power is taking hold of you quickly." He waited while she accepted that much before adding, "You're destined to become a Fae warrior, and it's my job to help you defeat Queen Mab. Once you've done that, *you* will be queen."

Since looking into a possible future and seeing Maggie on the Otherworld throne, Culhane had been keeping watch over her, biding his time. Centuries of battle had honed his skills for strategic thinking. And, he realized, he would need all of those skills to deal with this one woman. She must accept her destiny. Must fight and defeat Mab. Everything depended on it. A human female, though trouble, was more malleable than her Faery sisters. A fact Culhane was counting on. When the battles were over and Mab deposed, with Maggie on the throne, Culhane planned to rule Otherworld himself as her consort.

With that thought firmly in mind, he trapped her gaze with his. "This is your destiny. Accept it."

"Easier said," she pointed out, still working her mouth as if swallowing back nausea. "Okay, being a queen doesn't sound so bad, but please. Me? A warrior? I can't even get myself off the ceiling!"

"It takes time."

"I don't *have* time." Maggie picked up his hand and lifted it from her leg. "Sorry to disappoint, but it's November and I've got *tons* of work lined up. I'm way too busy to have a destiny."

A now familiar feeling of irritation swept through him. "I offer you a future and you turn it down to . . . paint pictures on glass?"

"You don't get to knock what I do for a living, Culhane. I happen to be the best glass painter in the county."

"It does not compare to what I offer you."

"You know, my life's just as important to me as yours is to you, so why don't you back off a little there, Lord of the Rings?"

"Lord of . . ." Culhane shook his head, muttered a Faery curse under his breath and reminded himself fiercely that this woman was the one hope of Otherworld.

"I mean," she was saying as she scooted to the side and off the couch, "I'm glad to know why this is happening, so thanks for that, but seriously, it's like some weird-ass dream, and I'd just as soon wake up and go paint Sam's Hardware in the morning."

"You must—"

"The only thing I *must* do is remember not to float," she said, then grinned. "I'm doing it. Guess I can concentrate after— Damn it!" Sheba whimpered. Maggie frowned, then slowly sank back to the floor. "Okay. Better. I can do this."

"There is more to it than floating."

"You're probably right, and I'm really sorry to hear you're having trouble in Faeryland—"

"Otherworld," he ground out through clenched teeth.

"Right. But the thing is, I've got a job already. And a house. And a dog." Sheba lifted her head. "And a niece I'm watching until my sister's finished getting her chakras lined up. I just don't have time to be queen, but thanks for asking."

Could she really be turning him down? After all these long years of waiting for Maggie Donovan to come into her powers, was he going to be disappointed because a mortal woman wasn't interested? No. Culhane refused to accept defeat. Since the time of the last Ard-Ri of Ireland, he'd defended his people and never surrendered. He would be damned to perdition before he would start now.

"You're becoming Fae," he said, his voice a low rumble of disapproval that had her dark red eyebrows lifting in response. "You have no choice."

"There's always a choice." She fisted her hands at her hips, and his view of her breasts disappeared. "I'll figure out this floating thing, and if any other powers crop up . . ." She blew out a breath. "I'll worry about that when it happens. So, thanks for thinking of me, but no, thanks. Really, I'm good—"

"Your powers," he said, interrupting her again, because what choice did he have if he didn't want to stand in this room for an eternity, "will continue to grow and manifest. You'll need my guidance to learn to use them."

Her feet left the floor again, and, muttering in disgust, she squeezed her eyes shut and focused her mind. Though he'd been tried beyond all reason, Culhane respected the fact that she was learning so quickly to contain the power charging through her.

An instant later Maggie dropped back to the floor. Then she opened her eyes, met his gaze and said, "All I really need at the moment is an anchor. And maybe a glass of wine before going to sleep and waking up tomorrow to find out all of this is just some twisted nightmare."

"Ignoring this won't change what is."

She gave him a brilliant, albeit forced smile. "Worth a try, though!"

As she scooted past him her breasts brushed against his chest, and for one split second they were both caught, swept up into a frenzied wash of need that seemed to thread cords around their bodies, tightening with every breath. Maggie swayed a little, looked up at him and accused, "Are you doing that?"

"I'm not." Culhane stepped back and away from her, breaking whatever bonds had temporarily linked them. He wasn't interested in developing an attachment to her. All he wanted from her was the right to rule the Fae as her consort. And he would do what needed doing to accomplish that.

With the bond severed her breathing came easier, and the flush of heat that had filled her cheeks drained away. "Good, because you may be a hottie, but I'm not looking for another man at the moment. Especially one who floats and refuses to peel me off the ceiling when I need him to."

His green eyes fixed on her face, Culhane felt her fear, her hesitation, as surely as if they were living beings swirling around them in the too-small room. He'd given her enough to think about tonight. Better that he return again later, when her powers were manifesting and she was more likely to accept his help.

Dark brows lowered over narrowed eyes, he said quietly, "You can't fight destiny, Maggie Donovan. When you accept that, I'll be back."

He seemed to blur for a second; then he was gone.

Maggie looked around the room, half expecting him to leap out from behind the furniture or something. But there was nothing. Just the scent of him still lingering in the air. Something foresty, clean and a little—okay, a *lot*—tantalizing.

"Talk about your impressive exits."

*

Maggie painted Sam's Hardware first thing in the morning. It was good to be back doing something normal. Something she was good at. The fact that she kept floating off her small stepladder was just a minor irritation.

The brief storm had passed, the morning sun was already hot and they were heading for at least eighty-five degrees. Nothing like painting snow and trying to get all the paint on before the heat dried it up on the glass.

Her arm was aching, so she took a break, half turned on the ladder and looked up and down Pacific Coast Highway. Castle Bay was a small town by anyone's standards. Supposedly at one point in its history it had been a stagecoach stop, and really, it hadn't gotten much bigger since then.

These days it was more or less a pit stop for people exiting the freeway looking for gas or food or a bathroom break. Sometimes they'd spend a few dollars at the boutique shops or the half dozen art galleries before continuing on to Monterey, Carmel, and all of the other tourist traps lining the West Coast. Castle Bay's only real claim to fame was the haunted lighthouse on a spit of land jutting out from Smuggler's Cove. Every Halloween the town was crowded with paranormal seekers and just plain weirdos. But other than that life was quiet, simple, uncomplicated.

At least, it had been for Maggie.

Up until yesterday.

"Not a dream," she told herself as she remembered trying to brush her teeth that morning while bouncing around the bathroom like a crazed SuperBall. She pushed one hand through her hair, remembered too late the splash of white tempera paint across her palm and sighed. A soft wind blew up from the nearby sea, cooling the sweat on her forehead as Maggie went back to what she knew. Snow. On glass. *Merry Christmas*.

She'd painted these windows the year before and the year before that. She'd done the same for most of the businesses in Castle Bay. Just as, after the holidays, she'd be packing her paintbrushes around town to announce sales, clearances and moves to new locations.

The problem was, Maggie was all too ready for a jolt in her life. Okay, the floating was a little disturbing, but at least it was *different*. The sad truth was, she was stuck in a rut. A comfortable one, to be sure, with her house and her family and her job—but still a rut. Everything happened every day just like the previous one.

There was no excitement in her life.

Well, until yesterday.

"Poor Joe," she murmured, remembering her latest ex-boyfriend. She'd broken up with him because he was boring. But the fact was, she was *just* as boring. Otherwise she never would have gone out with him in the first place.

He'd been like her last four boyfriends. Safe. Dependable. It was like dating a grown-up Boy Scout. Her sister, Nora, had always been the adventurous one, romance-wise. She led with her heart, took risks and chances. . . . *And see where that has gotten her?* Maggie's brain whispered. A husband who cheated on her, then left her for the family babysitter.

After seeing her sister so crushed by love, Maggie had carefully selected only the straight-and-narrow guys to date. To protect her heart? Or because she was a coward?

And why was she now wishing for a little . . . excitement?

Instantly Culhane's image rushed into her mind. The mental picture of him was so strong, so . . . *great*, she almost fell off the stupid ladder. Yes, he was dictatorial and pushy and probably crazy, since he insisted on this Fae business. But he was also sexy, interesting and so far from boring that his name couldn't even be said in the same sentence with the word.

Still, boyfriend material? Not likely. One-night-stand material? Absolutely. "If only I were," she mumbled. But there was enough Catholic-schoolgirl guilt left swimming around in her bloodstream to keep her from indulging in one-night stands that were headed nowhere.

So where did that leave her? No boring guys. No Culhane. No choice. That settled it. She reached out and swiped a brush filled with blue paint across a snowman's hat. The minute she was through painting the hardware store windows, she was going inside to buy a shower massager. Screw men—Joe, poor bastard, Culhane and all the rest of the Y chromosomes in Castle Bay—no, make that California.

She'd just be on her own. Who needed a man, anyway? She was good. Nothing wrong with a well-developed rut.

Now she was even thinking in circles. What she really could have used at the moment was a little one-on-one time with an understanding female ear. Nice timing that both her sister *and* her best friend for more than ten years, Claire MacDonald, were out of town.

How long was it going to take Nora to get her chakras aligned, anyway? And why was it so important that Claire rush home for a holiday visit? "Don't they know I *need* them?"

Maybe what she really needed was more friends.

When the new cell phone she'd bought only that morning to replace the one she'd crushed rang, Maggie stuck her paintbrush into her mouth and dug one-handed into her jeans pocket. " 'Lo."

"Maggie?"

Think of the chakra. "Nora, hi," she said once the brush was out of her mouth. She climbed off the ladder and leaned against the wall so she'd have something to hold on to in case she started floating again. "I was just thinking about you. How's it going in Santa Fe?"

"I have met the most incredible man. . . ."

"Man?"

"He's . . . too good for words, so I'll wait and let you meet him."

Maggie stiffened. Nora goes away for a five-day trip, finds a man and brings him home with her? Adventurous. Maggie felt more plodding than ever. "He's coming home with you?"

"*Yes.* He wants to meet Eileen and see where I live. Oh, Maggie, I think he could be the one. His name is Quinn, and he's gorgeous, and ohmigod, the sex is planet-shifting wonderful!"

"*Sex*? You've already had sex with him?" A woman dragging a screaming toddler behind her stopped dead and stared at Maggie. "I wasn't talking to you," she snapped, and went back to her sister, the romantic risk taker. "I can't believe you, Nora. You hardly know this guy. Taking chances is one thing, but—"

"Our souls recognized each other."

"Nora . . ."

"Honestly, Maggie, you've got to crawl out from under your rock once in a while."

She'd been thinking the same thing herself a few minutes ago, but now . . .

"No more about Quinn," her sister said. "Trust me, you'll understand when you meet him. So anyway, the drum festival was amazing. We all sat out under the stars last night. Blistering cold, but it was gorgeous. And Quinn kept me warm."

Maggie rolled her neck on her shoulders, stretching while her sister kept talking.

"Weeping Buffalo—he's our guide for this trip—says that tonight there'll be an eclipse."

"Really? I hadn't heard that."

"Well, we won't actually *see* the eclipse. It's on another plane, but it's there and we'll feel its power."

"Uh-huh."

Nora laughed, and Maggie grinned at the sound. Her sister liked all of the woo-woo stuff in life, but even she didn't really buy it all.

"So how's my baby girl?"

"Eileen's fine." Maggie stepped back, looked at the hardware store window and then moved closer to add a touch of shading to the snow painted across the bottom of the glass. "Apparently a boy likes her."

"Oh, God. Tell me that's not starting already."

"With you as her mom? 'Fraid so. And he's an older man."

"What?"

Maggie laughed. "Thirteen."

"Oh. God. Are you trying to kill me?"

"Just keeping you on your toes." She clucked her tongue. "Damn snow isn't right."

"Is this snow on another plane with my eclipse?"

"No, wiseass. I'm painting Sam's Hardware."

"Okay, I won't keep you."

"No, it's okay," Maggie said quickly, not ready for her sister to hang up just yet. She looked up and saw a pair of elderly women walking toward her. Wearing polyester pants, sensible shoes and bright shirts covered in splashes of color, the two could have been sisters. Their gray hair was in tidy rolls of curls that had been sprayed into submission. Lipstick smiles creased their faces, so she smiled back and waited until they'd passed to say, "I wanted to talk to you, actually."

"There *is* something wrong with my girl. What is it? Tell me, Maggie."

"This isn't about Eileen. It's about . . ." What? She couldn't say she'd killed a demon and sucked in a lungful of Faery dust, could she? Instead she grabbed onto something Culhane had said the night before—about her being a descendant of the Fae. "Do you remember Gran's stories?"

"Of course I do. I'm the one who listened while you were out drawing pictures on sidewalks."

Maggie ducked her head, turned toward the window and stared into the hardware store. She didn't want anyone on the inside of the store reading her lips. But the only one watching was Sam, who lifted his left arm and pointed at his wristwatch, as if to remind her time was money and she was supposed to be painting, not talking.

She waved at him, then blurted, "Didn't she used to say that she had slept with a . . . um . . ."

"Faery. Yeah. Mom didn't want her telling us the stories, because she said they were inappropriate, but I loved hearing Gran talk about this stuff. And once we were living with Grandma and Grandpa, I had her telling me the stories over and over again. She said she was seventeen and met this great-looking guy and he kidnapped her to the Fae world. Said she was there for a long time, but when she came back home she'd been gone only overnight."

"And she was pregnant."

"Yep. Gran told me that we were special. That we're part Faery, and that's why I'm so small and you're so artistic."

"Uh-huh." Maggie's chin hit her chest, and a sinking feeling opened up in the pit of her stomach. *True, true, all true,* a voice was singsonging in her mind. *Oh, God.*

"Of course, Gran's folks looked all over for this guy," Nora was saying, and Maggie tuned back in. "But they never found him. Then Grandpa fell in love with her, they got married, he adopted Mom, end of story."

"Right. And so our mom was supposedly—"

"Half Fae. Yeah. She never believed it, of course, but I like thinking about it. And as much as Gran loved Grandpa, I don't think she ever really got over her Faery lover."

"Fabulous. That's just fabulous." Was that a cold ocean wind rippling along her spine, or the twisted finger of fate making her feel a chill right down to her bones?

"What's this about, anyway? You've never wanted to talk about this stuff before."

"Oh," Maggie hedged, "Eileen was on the Internet and she found—"

"You let her on the Internet? Were you there? Were you watching? Predators are online, you know. You have to—"

"Wow, look at the time." Maggie pulled the phone away from her ear to dilute her sister's screech, then slapped it back long enough to say, "Thanks for call-ing. I'll tell Eileen you love her. Have a good time with Crying Cow."

"Weeping Buffalo."

"Whatever!" She snapped her phone shut and, just in case, turned it off. No way did she need Nora calling back at the moment, since her mind was racing and her heart was frantically pounding in her chest.

Culhane hadn't been lying. She *was* descended from Fae. So . . . that led to another ugly question: Was Cul-hane right about the rest of it? Was she a destined queen?

The hardware store window was moving.

"Damn!" *She* was moving.

Through the window she watched as Sam's eyes got as big as dinner plates. Then she grabbed hold of the side of the building, waved at him and shoved herself over to the ladder.

She was not getting her day off to a good start.

Chapter Four

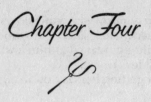

"*G*otta get my eyes checked."

"Jeez!" She wobbled on the ladder and grabbed at the top rung.

Sam was standing just below her, alternately rubbing his eyes and examining the spread of snowmen sliding downhill on shiny red sleds; Christmas trees; and the foot-high letters spelling out HAPPY HOLIDAYS!

He shook his head and muttered, "People don't float, for chrissakes. Gotta go to the eye doctor. Probably having a stroke. Damn customers."

Maggie felt a twinge of guilt that was immediately drowned in a sigh of relief that Sam figured *he* was the one with the problem.

"Good painting. This oughta convince everybody I got the Christmas spirit."

"Sure, Sam." Hey, he wanted to believe that holiday decorations made him less of a grumbling jerk? Who was she to tell him different?

"You're gonna put in more snow, though, right?" He waved one hand at the windows, touched a tree dotted with white paint before Maggie could tell him not to, and left fingerprints behind. "I mean, I want it to look *really* Christmassy," he added, rubbing the tips of his fingers together to get rid of the paint. "Nothing says Christmas like snow."

"Sure, Sam." Maggie was used to the critique. Every year Sam wanted more and more holiday for his buck. But let her try to raise her price and all thoughts of happy holidays and caroling children went out the window. "More white on the trees. You want wreaths on the door glass, too?"

His dark eyes narrowed on her. "Is that extra?"

She sighed. Father Christmas in person. "No."

"Then, yeah. Put 'em up. Something really big and splashy. Red ribbons and all that crap."

"Morning, Sam," someone called out, and the older man spun around to see a customer darting into his store.

"Gotta go keep an eye on her," he muttered. "She walked out with a pair of pliers last week. Can't prove it was her, but I know. You keep going. Lots of snow, now, remember."

"Right." Once he was gone Maggie relaxed her grip on the top rung of the ladder. No way had she wanted to risk floating again in front of Sam. Bad enough she'd done some floating in front of Eileen that morning at breakfast. Good times. Naturally, Eileen had jumped all over it.

"You're still floating," her niece pointed out.

"Apparently." And she had the headache to prove it. Why'd she have to be so tall, anyway? No, she was the Amazon in the family, and Nora was the petite one.

"So, are you a Faery now?" Eileen was watching her with interest, and Maggie had skillfully dodged that question.

She only wished she could ignore it entirely.

"Becoming a Faery?" Now she glanced down at her long legs, her paint-spattered jeans and her blue tank top with the words MAGGIE'S MURALS emblazoned across her less-than-petite boobs. "Yeah. That's me. A delicate little fairy."

Then she snorted and went back to work.

⌐

"You've got to be kidding me."

Culhane glanced at the pixie beside him, then shifted his gaze back to the woman across the street from them. "No, I'm not. That's her."

Bezel shook his head, sending his long, silvery hair flying. Here in the shadows of the alley lying between two stores on the main street of Castle Bay, the small, wrinkled-up creature looked even more horrifying than usual. Which was saying something, Culhane told himself. Even for a pixie, Bezel was ugly. His face had more furrows than a farmer's field, and his eyes were so pale a blue they looked like chips of ice glittering in the dim light.

As the pixie stroked the few straggly hairs on his pointed chin and considered Maggie Donovan with a less-than-approving gaze, Culhane found himself wanting to defend her. He frowned to himself at that notion and kept his silence. He didn't have to wait long to hear Bezel's opinion.

"This is trollshit and you know it, Culhane." The pixie turned his face up, spearing the other male with those cold eyes. "No way is that female able to go up against Mab and win."

"She will," he said firmly, and wondered whether he was trying to convince Bezel or himself. Didn't matter, really. The die was cast. Maggie Donovan would become who she was meant to be. Even if it killed Bezel. "You're going to train her."

Bezel's face wrinkled even further in distaste. "What am I? A miracle worker?"

"And you're going to do a damned good job of it."

The pixie snorted and waved one long-fingered

hand. "Oh, don't get your leathers in a bunch. I said I'd do it, didn't I? Save the mighty-warrior-of-the-Fae attitude, too. Not impressed. I've known you too long to be scared by you."

True. The Fae and pixies were more or less natural enemies, with the roots of that enmity going back to before Otherworld had come about. Each race had wanted to rule, and when the Fae had won that contest, hard feelings were born that carried on to this day. But somehow this small, annoying creature had become a friend. Of sorts. They'd known each other for centuries, and over those years a fragile, unexpected bond had grown between them.

Culhane turned his face into the cold ocean wind that sailed down the alleyway, sending papers skittering across the dirty pavement. The stench of the mortal world was all around him, and as his breath shortened, he thought that even his lungs were loath to take in great gulps of this air.

Yet here he was. He couldn't be in Otherworld until his plan was completely in motion. He'd done what he could so far, but . . .

Now that the older male had retreated back into his store, Maggie was standing precariously on a stepladder, working again. Going up on her toes, she reached out with her right hand to swipe a paint-laden brush across the glass. Culhane watched her turning a bare surface into a wintry scene and admired the talent behind that hand.

She had depths to her that she didn't share with others. He sensed it in her. Those depths revealed themselves in her painting, whether she knew it or not. He wondered, too, if she noticed that the silly painted creatures she created were all . . . lonely. Her snowmen were not standing in groups, but alone on hills. Sliding on sleds built for one. Decorating small Christmas trees by themselves.

Nowhere in these images did he find couples, friends,

solidarity. They were all singular creatures, and he felt a kinship with the painted faces. He understood the ease of *alone.* He knew what it was to keep to himself, to stand unaided in a world designed for mates. And he asked himself if Maggie, too, shared that sense of being an outsider, even among those she loved.

"Hah!"

Bezel's triumphant shout shattered his thoughts, and Culhane turned one unamused eye on him. "What?"

"Culhane the mighty is hungering after a mortal."

Irritated that the pixie had noticed what Culhane had thought he'd hidden, he muttered, "I hunger only for what she can do for Otherworld."

"Yeah, tell yourself that if you need to, Fenian. But I know what I see. Makes me wonder what Mab would think of this."

"Mab won't find out."

"You'd better hope not." The pixie's gaze shot back to Maggie as her feet began to lift off the top rung of the ladder. "For the love of the goddess . . . would you look at that? Not got the brains of a tree squirrel. She's going to get caught floating, and then what?"

His harsh statement still ringing in the air, Bezel kicked at an empty soda can, and as it careened down the alley it made a nearly musical clatter.

"She won't get caught. Look, she's already stopped it. Her concentration is improving."

"Damn well better or she won't be any use to us at all." Bezel laughed, and the sound was like nails scraping against iron. "Can't you see it? She challenges Mab, the queen strikes out and your idiot painter floats herself at her. Oh, that'll be great. I can see the victory parade now."

"It's your job to train her, so if she fails, it'll be *your* head."

Bezel swallowed hard and lifted one hand to his throat, as if checking that his head was still attached to his scrawny body. Satisfied, he bared a mouthful of teeth at Culhane, and the warrior wasn't sure whether it was a threat or an attempt at a smile. Either way, he didn't much care for it.

"I'll train her," the pixie said. "But I can't guarantee she'll listen. You know what dealing with mortals is like. Even Faeries are flummoxed by them."

Culhane frowned. "I am not."

Bezel rocked back and forth on his long, wide feet. "Yeah, you ought to try telling that to somebody who can't see you standing there with your tongue hanging out while you watch the part-Fae."

Culhane gave the little man a cold, hard stare. "If you value *your* tongue, you might want to try to restrain it."

"For the love of pixie children, why don't you just bed the female, get it out of your system and *then* worry about training her?"

"She's not here for my pleasure," Culhane warned, crouching until his gaze speared into the pixie's so the little man wouldn't make the mistake of not listening. "She's here for Otherworld. She's too important to us to risk scaring her off." A wheezy chuckle burst from his throat.

Bezel studied him, then curled his upper lip back to display even more of his jagged teeth. "If you don't want to scare her off, then maybe you ought to dial back the 'great warrior' crap and turn on some of that charm you're supposed to have."

Culhane grinned. "Charm, is it?"

"Don't quote me," Bezel told him. "I don't see any charm, trust me. But my wife says you could charm the pookas out of Ireland—though why anybody'd want to mess with a blasted pooka is beyond me."

"I knew Fontana liked me," Culhane said, and enjoyed seeing the displeasure ripple across the pixie's wrinkled face.

"Yeah, well. Never said my wife had taste."

"Obvious enough that she doesn't, since she married you."

"Ha-ha. Very funny. A comic warrior. What nobody should be without."

"You have a miserable disposition, Bezel. Did anyone besides me ever tell you that?"

"Only everyone in Otherworld. I'm a pixie. It's my job."

Irritating as he was, Bezel was right. They all had jobs to do. Duties to perform. And if Culhane didn't get his mind back to business, they'd never get Maggie to the place she needed to be. Standing up again, he braced his feet wide apart, lifted his chin to the chill of the wind and narrowed his gaze on the woman across from him.

Her jeans were too tight, straining across her bottom as she reached again, swiping red paint atop an already painted tree until it looked as though ribbons had been threaded through its branches. She bit her bottom lip, and just for a moment Culhane thought about biting it for her. Bezel was right about that, too.

He did want Maggie Donovan.

And sooner or later he'd have her.

But for now . . .

"So . . ." Bezel jabbed his pointy elbow into Culhane's knee to get his attention.

"What, you pestilential pixie?"

"Hey, don't matter one way or the other to me," Bezel said with a shrug. "I just wondered what you were planning to do about that Baranca demon sneaking up behind your girl there."

"What?" Culhane's gaze focused for a change not on Maggie, but on the tidily dressed "woman" coming up behind her as if to admire her painting. A human wouldn't notice anything amiss. But Otherworlders—and some Demon Dusters—would know the woman for what she really was: a Baranca demon disguising herself as human. And since she was, at the moment, sneaking up on Maggie, Culhane could only think the demon had sensed the raw Fae power shimmering inside Maggie and was after it for itself.

"By the halls of *Ifreann* . . ."

"Looks like your girl's not gonna last out the day."

"Oh, shut up." Culhane spared him a quick glare, then shifted with a swift, blurred motion. He reappeared behind the Baranca only long enough to sweep her away. Hopefully Maggie hadn't noticed a thing. It wouldn't do to have her think he was watching her. He wanted her to trust him, damn it, and being a Fae stalker wasn't going to get that done.

He reappeared in the alley an instant later with one arm wrapped around the throat of a furious Baranca demon.

"What'd you bring it *here* for?" Bezel shouted.

"Let me go; you have no right!" The demon disguised as a woman stabbed one of its high heels at Culhane's shin.

Culhane sidestepped, ignored the pixie, tossed the demon to the trash-strewn asphalt and braced himself when the Baranca rolled quickly to its feet. It straightened its shirt, smoothed its slacks and sneered, "The woman is mine."

"You're wrong." Culhane swept in low and fast, taking the demon's legs out from under it. It hit hard, but swiped out one clawed hand at his face. He dodged the blow, slipped his knife from the scabbard and stabbed it down into the center of the demon's chest. Then he blew a stream of gold-dusted air at the demon and stood back while it exploded with a shriek of outrage.

"Now I got demon dust all over my damn suit," Bezel complained. "Did you have to kill it here?"

Culhane wasn't looking at him, though. Instead his gaze was fixed on Maggie, still painting, unaware of what had just happened.

"Yeah." Bezel shook his head in disgust. "You're horny, and she's oblivious. This is gonna work out great."

$\mathcal{E}$

Eileen hopped in the car that afternoon with bright eyes and an excited smile.

"Good day, huh?"

"The best." The girl squirmed around in her seat, buckled her seat belt, then turned to face Maggie. "First, Grant sent me a note—"

"What'd it say?"

"Private, hello?"

Maggie didn't like the pleased gleam in her niece's eyes, but after the weekend it would be Nora's problem again. *Please, God, let nothing else happen between now and the weekend.* Was that too much to ask?

"Anyway, that's not the best part."

"Okay . . ." Maggie steered her car into traffic and headed for home. Her hands on the still-ruined steering wheel looked as festive as the coming season. She really lived her work. She had white, red, green and blue paint splashes all the way up her arms and collecting into dried clumps under her nails. A quick glance into the rearview mirror told her that her face hadn't come out much better. She had streaks of white paint in her hair, and the splashes of red paint on her cheeks made her look like she was crying blood. No wonder the barista at Starbucks had looked at her so oddly.

Sighing, she asked, "What else, then?"

"In study hall I went on the Internet to check on—"

"Excuse me?"

Dramatic sigh. "Please. They have so many child locks on the Internet connection, we can barely sign on."

"Good to know. Yay, PTA." *Hmm.* Child locks. Maybe that was a thought for their home computer. Maggie'd have to talk to Nora about that when she got back.

Please, God, let her come back soon. Maggie had far too much going on in her life right now: gorgeous Faeries and dead demons and golden tornadoes and floating feet and . . .

"Earth to Aunt Maggie!"

"Huh? Oh. sorry."

"*Anyway*," Eileen said pointedly before continuing, "I looked up *Fae* and *Fenian warrior* and *Otherworld* and everything else I could think of, and there's some really good stuff there."

Biting her lip, Maggie knew she shouldn't be encouraging Eileen to follow up on all of this weirdness. In fact, she should be pretending that none of it was happening. But on the other hand she could really use some information. "Did you print it out?"

"Duh."

"Right. So what's it say?"

"All kinds of things." Eileen bent over, unzipped her backpack and rummaged inside for a minute. When she straightened up she had a stack of papers clutched in her hand. "I told my teacher it was for a report, so I guess I'll have to write one."

Since Eileen actually liked writing and was really good at it already, Maggie didn't see how that would be a hardship.

As Eileen read, Maggie worked to concentrate on her driving. It wasn't easy. While one corner of your brain was cataloging Faeries and pixies and banshees, of all things, another was watching out for pedestrians and cars driven by people who clearly got their licenses from mail-order catalogs. "Oh, for God's sake, if you're afraid to step on the gas stay home and call a cab!"

Eileen snorted but, when Maggie glared at her, went back to her reading. "So the Otherworld is where the Fae went when they left our world."

"Then where exactly is this Otherworld?" She couldn't believe she'd just asked that.

"It's here—but not."

"Ah." Maggie nodded. "That's clear."

Eileen sighed. Was there anything more mortifying than having a kid take a patient tone with you? "It's, like, on a different plane of existence."

Maggie laughed as she pulled into a left-turn bay. "Now you sound like your mom."

"I know, but maybe she's right about this stuff. I mean, it would have to be here but not here or everyone would see Faeries, right? Not just us."

"We didn't . . ." Oh, what was the point? Eileen was too smart to try to fool. They'd both seen Culhane, and they both knew he was a little less—or more—than human. "What's it say in there about Mab?" The light turned green and she turned into the grocery store parking lot.

"Mab is queen." Eileen thumbed through her stack of papers, found the one she wanted and waved it like the Olympic torch. "Some people think she's also this kind of Faery thing called Mara."

"Huh?" Maggie stomped on the brake when a moron backed out of his parking place, apparently trusting in God to keep cars out of his way.

"It's another name for Mab, I guess. It says that Mara is a kind of 'malignant female wraith.'"

"That doesn't sound good." Maggie frowned and pulled into the now-empty parking spot.

"Really. Anyway, Mab is queen, and she, like . . . visits people when they're sleeping and gives them nightmares."

"Oh, very nice."

"Yeah. Guess she gets bored or something. Anyway, women are in charge in Otherworld. It's a completely matriarchal society, and the men are, like, second-class citizens, which isn't good, really, but think about women being in charge." She sighed. "I think it's totally cool, because if women were in charge here, things would be totally better than they are now, and—"

"Revolution later, information now."

Another sigh. "Okay."

Maggie turned off the engine, opened her car door and said, "Talk and shop."

Eileen followed her into the store and trailed behind as Maggie pushed a dark blue cart with a bad wheel. Over the *whacketa-whacketa* sound, Eileen continued.

"Mab's been queen for, like, forever, and they say that she's really powerful."

Maggie tossed two boxes of Double Stuf Oreos into the cart and seriously considered a third.

"The Fae warriors—like Culhane," Eileen explained, in case Maggie had forgotten about him, "fight the battles Mab wants them to, and spend most of their time protecting the other Fae."

"From what?" Maggie asked, and grabbed a box of Cheerios.

"From demons, mostly. But there are bad Fae that have to be taken care of, too."

"Bad Fae?" Maggie wondered which side of the coin Culhane fell on.

Eileen whipped through her stack of papers again. "Oh yeah. There's all kinds of things in Otherworld. I told you about banshees and pooka, and there're shape-shifters and demons and Gray men and dark men and demon brides—"

"I get it." The wheel on the cart got louder as Maggie moved faster, and she got a couple of baleful looks from other shoppers, like *she* was the one making all the noise. She reached for a gallon jug of milk, since she'd clocked Culhane with the one at home, then headed for the butcher department. "Lots of creepy-crawlies in this Otherworld."

Here, too, her mind whispered, reminding her of the thing that had eaten Joe.

"Oh, they don't stay in Otherworld," Eileen said solemnly. "They come and go all the time. And they

can make themselves look like us, so you don't know if
you're talking to a Faery or a pixie—"

"Wasn't Tinker Bell a pixie? I think I'd notice if I saw
a fluttery thing about four inches tall. . . ."

"Okay, but—"

"Spaghetti for dinner?" Maggie picked up some
hamburger and sweet sausage and tossed them into the
cart. She had pasta at home, so she didn't need more.
Wheeling the cart toward produce, she was forced to
stop when a man and his cart were blocking the aisle.
Men should not be allowed to grocery shop alone, she told
herself. They didn't know the rules. Worse, they didn't
care about the rules.

Behind her, Eileen read, " 'Demons who kill mem-
bers of the Fae capture their essence and use it to en-
hance their own strength. They must keep Faery dust
in a recept . . .' "

"Receptacle," Maggie murmured, still waiting as the
old guy in front of her studied bottles of salad dress-
ing. "Excuse me . . ."

He ignored her.

"Receptacle. Right. 'If Faery dust touches a demon,
the demon's destroyed.' Ooh."

Yeah. Ooh. Or ick. The memory of the Joe-eating demon was still fresh in Maggie's mind, and she really
didn't want to dredge it back up.

"Seriously?" Shaking her head, she spoke up just
in case the old guy in front of her was deaf as well as
rude. "Could you just move your cart to one side so I
can—"

Slowly the man swiveled his head to look at her, and
his eyes were narrowed slits of solid black in a time-
worn, weathered face. Evil pumped from him in what
felt like thick, dark syrup. Maggie jerked and instinctively tightened her grip on the cart handle. It snapped
in two, and the old guy smiled at her.

Not a happy smile, either.

"Uh-oh." Eileen sounded scared.

Maggie was, too. But her niece's worried voice was enough to jolt her into action. Pulling the girl behind her, she stared at the demon shopper and said, "Get out of my way."

"You reek of Fae power." His voice was a sly whisper that scraped across her raw nerve endings like sandpaper. "I could take it from you."

"You could try." *Oh, good bluff.* Could he actually *hear* her knees rattling? She backed up, dragging her *whacketa-whacketa* cart and Eileen with her. Keeping her gaze fixed on the man she now knew was an enemy, she watched as his eyes changed from an inky black to a watery gray, and only then did she begin to draw an easy breath.

He couldn't do anything to her here. In the middle of Albertsons? It wasn't as if he could kill her and get away with it. People wouldn't just announce, "Cleanup in aisle five" and let him go.

No, she was safe, and he knew it.

"Go on, then," he told her, still smiling that weirdly chilling smile. "I'll find you another day."

"Bring it on," she boasted, feeling the need to do a little intimidating of her own. "How do you think I got this power, huh? By watching one of your pals turn into dust bunnies, that's how. So maybe you should think about that."

His features creased into a worried frown, and Maggie felt a little better. Then she reached the end of the aisle and made a sharp right. "Screw the salad," she told Eileen. "We're going home."

Chapter Five

*B*y the following day Maggie was starting to get used to the whole power thing. Or maybe she was just delusional. She was still getting floaty at odd times, and she was strong enough that she had to remember to pick things up gently or all she was left with were shards of whatever she'd had before.

Her eyesight was now incredible, but her ears were starting to look a little pointy—so thank God her hair was long. But the best part so far? Faery power did a real number on her metabolism, so she could eat as much as she wanted without worrying about it. Apparently flying/floating really burned up the calories. And she was thinking about putting in a bid to paint the local law office's windows. Those fifteen-footers had intimidated her before, but now no window was too high—as long as she painted when there was no one around. Finally: good news. She hadn't seen Culhane in a while, but she didn't know whether to classify that as good or bad.

Her hormones were disappointed, but Maggie wasn't sure she agreed.

Dinner was over, and Maggie and Eileen did the dishes together. In the otherwise quiet house they listened to the wail of the wind as it swept in off the ocean and rattled the windowpanes. Outside, the night was thick, and as cold as it got on a Southern California winter evening. Inside, lamplight burned, and Eileen sat at the kitchen table to do her homework, much as her mother and Maggie had done when they were girls.

"I hate math."

"Who doesn't?" Maggie reached across, tapped her finger on Eileen's paper and said, "You forgot to divide that fraction first."

"How'd you know that? You don't do math, either."

"Some things you have to learn, whether you like it or not." *Hmm.* Hadn't she just told Culhane she wasn't interested in his version of education? Maybe she'd been wrong about that. Remembering that guy in the grocery store, she told herself that maybe this training was something she'd just have to do—at least until she found a way out of this mess. After all, if she could deal with numbers, how hard could training be?

Eileen lifted her gaze. "Why do I need to know this? Isn't that why people invented calculators?"

Maggie'd once wondered the same thing, but since opening her own business she'd found it helped to understand more about numbers than you found on a keypad. "Who do you think invented calculators?"

Eileen brightened. "Nerds?"

"Rich ones," Maggie pointed out with a grin. "Understanding math made them rich."

The girl blew out a single disgusted breath. "Fine, fine, but I'm going to be a writer, and we don't need math."

"Yeah? What about making sure people aren't stealing from you? And counting all your royalties? Knowing how much of your money you need for taxes and living and saving? And what about retirement?"

"I'm *twelve.*"

Maggie laughed. "Sorry. My worries. Not yours."

In the living room Sheba barked: three short, sharp bursts of sound that had Maggie leaping to her feet, with panic just a step behind taking hold of the base of her throat.

"Sheba never barks," Eileen whispered, turning her head slowly toward the open doorway to the living room.

"I know." Barking required energy, and all of Sheba's was usually used to roll over during naps. Swallowing hard, Maggie turned, opened the pantry door and said, "Go. Go to your room, and stay there until I call you."

"Maggie—"

"Eileen, *move*." This secret passage snaked through most of the house, and her niece knew every inch of it. "Now."

Sheba gave a low-throated snarl that wormed its way through the air.

Eileen scuttled through the pantry door and disappeared as Maggie closed it softly behind her.

Scanning the kitchen, Maggie thought, *Weapon, weapon, who has the weapon?* What did she have? Well, hell, she'd conked out Culhane with a gallon of milk, so just about anything would do. Quietly she moved to the closest drawer and pulled it open, hoping it wouldn't make that squealy sound it sometimes did.

She was lucky. Grabbing up the first knife handle she found, she drew it out to discover she'd instinctively grabbed a cleaver. "Nice." Not that she could see herself slicing and dicing anything, but she had to at least try. Eileen was her responsibility. And besides, this was *her* house.

Sheba's snarls cut off abruptly and became whimpers and then what sounded like doggy moaning. *Oh, God.*

Maggie crept to the doorway and peeked her head around the edge for a look at the lamplit room. Everything looked just as it should. Except for the tiny, ugly man who was bent over rubbing Sheba's belly.

"Sheba, you slut."

His head snapped up, and icy blue eyes pinned her in place as surely as if she'd been chained to the floor.

"About time you showed up," he snapped. "I'm not getting any younger."

"Or prettier," Maggie sniped right back. "What the hell are you?"

The homely little man straightened up and lifted his chin until he was nearly three feet tall. Wizened, wrinkled cheeks made his face look as though it were falling, but those eyes of his were sharp and clear. His long silvery white hair streamed down past his shoulders, and the suit he wore looked to be green velvet, of all things.

"Not *what*. *Who*. The name's Bezel. I'm a pixie, and Culhane sent me here to train you."

"Why?" Maggie was really getting sick of people popping in and out of her house like she was the local bus station or something.

"I owe him a favor, okay? And pixies pay their debts, despite what the Fae think."

"A pixie? How cool is *that*?"

Bezel spun in a tight circle, looking for the source of that voice, and then scowled when Eileen stepped out of a panel beside a bookcase.

"I told you—"

"I know, but he's a pixie," the girl said, walking closer. "They're nice."

"I am not," he argued.

"How come you don't have wings?" Eileen looked him over, as if trying to spot where he'd hidden them.

"*Wings*? What do you people read, anyway? Do I look like the kind of guy to have *wings*?"

"But you said you're a pixie."

"We don't know what he is," Maggie snapped, still

holding the cleaver as she moved to grab Eileen's arm and pull her up close. "Besides, does he look like Tinker Bell to you?"

"Tink." Bezel spat the name. "That sellout."

"Huh?" Was this happening? Was she really standing in her living room having a conversation with a pixie?

Sheba whined for his attention, and the pixie dipped his long, thin fingers into her fur again to scratch. "Tink wanted to be famous, so she used a glamour—"

"A what?"

"A spell," Eileen provided.

"Oh." Maggie stared at the girl. How did she know this stuff?

"Made that Disney guy think she was all tiny and pretty, when *I'm* prettier than she is."

Good God.

"So he puts her in his stupid cartoon movie, and pretty soon the only pixie anybody's ever heard of is Tink." He lifted his gaze. "She never lets us forget it, either. Always sprinkling pixie dust like we don't all shed the damn stuff ourselves . . ."

"Okay." Maggie kept a grip on Eileen. "You say Culhane sent you?"

"Why the hell else would I be here?" He glanced around the cluttered, homey room and shuddered. "Mortals. Always living in boxes. How do you stand it?"

"Where do you live?" Eileen asked.

"We don't care," Maggie told her before the little man could get started. "Where is Culhane?"

"Hell if I know. Think the 'mighty Fenian warrior' lets me in on his plans? Not."

"You're awfully crabby for a pixie," Eileen said.

"You're awfully mouthy for a kid."

"Teenager." She shrugged. "Almost."

"Well, that explains it."

A ripple of movement rolled through the room.

"Finally," Bezel said.

Culhane appeared out of nowhere to stand not a foot away from Maggie. She jumped a little, then smoothed herself out. *Honest to God.* Could her heart stand all this strain? "Did you really send this guy?"

"Bezel's here to train you." Culhane looked at the pixie. "Didn't you tell her?"

"Haven't had a chance. Just got here."

Shaking his head, Culhane turned his gaze on Maggie. "Bezel will explain your new powers, show you how to control them. He'll teach you what you need to know about the demons and how to protect yourself from them."

"Uh-huh." Maggie's grip on Eileen loosened as the girl maneuvered her way closer to Bezel the Ugly. "And what are *you* going to do? Just sit back and give orders?"

The pixie laughed, and it was a scary sound.

Culhane wrapped one hand around Maggie's upper arm, and instantly she felt a sizzle of something hot, delicious and just a little wicked dart up her arm and rocket around her chest like a crazed Ping-Pong ball. Then those sizzling sensations dipped lower, and everything inside her whooped with joy and expectation. *Sorry to disappoint,* she thought, and caught her breath as Culhane dragged her away from the others.

"I can't be here to train you myself." He looked past her to where Bezel and Eileen were having what sounded like a spirited conversation. "I have to stay mostly in Otherworld to keep Mab from finding out about you."

"Okay, that's probably good." She remembered all too well the things Eileen had found out on the Internet. Maggie was in no hurry to face a Faery queen. In fact, she was still looking for a way around all this destiny crapola.

"You must learn," he said, looming over her, fixing those pale green eyes on her face until Maggie could almost feel herself getting lost in them. "Listen to Bezel. I'll come when I can."

She shook her head to break whatever spell he held her in. "Just a minute. Look, I'm all for avoiding your queen, but it's not like I can spend every spare minute listening to your pixie. I've got a life to take care of. There are things I have to do. Money to make. Bills to pay."

"This is more important than you can imagine."

Behind them Maggie could hear Eileen peppering the pixie with questions, and she almost pitied him. Almost. Reaching out, she grabbed hold of the front of Culhane's shirt, pulled him down closer to her and caught the fresh, almost foresty scent of him. His face was just a breath away from hers, and for a second Maggie wasn't sure if she wanted to yell at him or just kiss him until she passed out. A moment later, though, she got her wild imagination under control and said, "Trust me when I say I know it's important. I saw a demon in the grocery store. He said something about taking my power."

"They sense it," he said, nodding. His eyes were solemn, his delicious-looking mouth flattened into a grim line. "This is why you must train. As time passes, more and more of them will come looking for you. Fae power strengthens a demon when he can capture it."

"Yeah," she muttered. "So I heard."

"The demon you killed had a mate who is vowing revenge. He's offering money to any demon who kills you."

She sucked in a gulp of air and fought the need to put her head between her knees. "Oh, God." Terror was ripe and rich inside her when a sudden, horrifying thought occurred. She shot a glance at her niece, still bothering the pixie, then dragged Culhane far enough away that she couldn't be overheard.

"What about Eileen?" she asked, keeping her voice as low as possible. "Is she safe with me? Should I send her somewhere? Where can I send her? I'll call Nora—"

"The child will be safe enough," Culhane interrupted her rushed flow of words. "Her Fae blood is so diluted she won't attract interest from demons, and it is one of the highest Fae laws that no child shall be harmed."

"Are all of the Fae law-abiding citizens?" she asked, wanting to be reassured, but still scared.

"Most," he said. "But even those that are not wouldn't harm a child. Even Mab herself would never condone a child's being harmed."

So in some respects Fae society was a lot better than human, she thought. "But if Eileen's with me, like today at the grocery store, won't they come after her to get to me?"

"The demons wouldn't bother," he said. "Easy enough to take the power from a recently turned human without involving a child and drawing unnecessary attention from the mortal police."

That was good to know, she thought, and her heartbeat settled down a little. At least Eileen was relatively safe. She, on the other hand . . . "Recently turned human. That's what I am?"

"Yes, that's why you must learn, Maggie—to protect yourself. To protect those who will need you." He lifted one hand to softly stroke her cheek with the tips of his fingers.

Was that magic she felt zooming around inside her? Or was it something more elemental? Whatever it was, she really liked it, and it was a great distraction from the all-encompassing *fear* threatening to overtake her.

Her body was humming and her mind was blurry. As she stared up at him, his mouth curved into a small smile that just barely tipped the corners of his lips. Funny, with him this close to her she forgot about danger, forgot about the misery that was currently her life. . . . She even managed to forget that her niece was just a few feet away from her. All she could think of was Culhane and what he did to her system with a simple glance out of those eyes. She swallowed hard and leaned in closer. He moved, too, and his scent wrapped itself around her, drawing her in, making her want. Need.

Then he disappeared in a ripple of motion, and Maggie's hopes dissolved along with her balance. She fell forward a step before she could catch herself, and only hoped no one noticed. When she turned around there was a smirk on the pixie's face, but he didn't say anything.

"You said you owed Culhane a favor," she said.

"Yeah." He looked disgusted by the admission, which only made Maggie more curious.

"What'd he do for you?"

Bezel stroked the straggly hairs on his chin. "He introduced me to my wife."

"Isn't that nice?" Eileen asked nobody.

"Your *wife*?" Maggie goggled at the hideous little man.

This mean little pixie had a wife? And Maggie couldn't find a man who wasn't a bum, a liar or a Happy Meal? That hardly seemed fair.

"You want to dial the shrieking down a notch?" He reached up and rubbed his ears. "I got sensitive hearing."

"Wow." Eileen was loving this.

"Great." Maggie slumped down to the couch and gave in to the urge to put her head between her knees at last. While she concentrated on her breathing, the pixie kept talking.

"Just so you know," he said in that scratchy voice, "pixies and Faeries don't really get along, so I don't want to be here any more than you want me to be."

"I'm not a Faery." Her voice was muffled.

"Not yet."

That got her head up fast. "What?"

"You're changing. Turning. Hell, don't you listen? Culhane just told you that. And as much as I hate most Faeries, they're still better than humans, so it's a good thing, as far as I can see."

"Gee, thanks."

"You're turning into a Faery?" Eileen's eyes went wild and wide as she looked at her. "This is so huge, Aunt Maggie! When you're a Faery can you make me one?"

"Oh, for . . ." Bezel shot the girl a glare, then fixed those chilling eyes on Maggie again. "Listen up, lady. I'm here to train you, and I will. But that doesn't mean I have to like you. So I'll teach, you listen, everything'll work out. Until some demon kills you."

Maggie just sat there staring at him.

"So where do I sleep? You got a good-size tree out back?"

"An oak," Eileen said.

"Show me."

The girl and the pixie left together, with Sheba right behind them. Maggie slumped onto the couch and didn't even try to fight it when she started floating.

Could her life suck any worse?

She closed her eyes as she hit the ceiling and bobbed there like a pool toy. "This is just fabulous," she muttered. "I've got the hots for a Faery warrior, a pixie with a grudge is here to teach me how to use powers he doesn't think I should have so I can fight a queen I don't want to fight. Oh, and a pissed-off demon husband wants me dead."

Good times.

⚓

"Wake *up*!"

"Huh? What?"

Nora Donovan shook her sister's shoulder again and gave her a pinch just for good measure.

"Hey!" Maggie's eyes flew open and she looked blearily up at her. "Nora? You're home early?"

"Of course I'm home early," she said, dropping onto the side of Maggie's bed. "Eileen texted me last night about what's been happening, and I cannot *believe* that you didn't tell me!"

"Um, uh, Nora . . ." Maggie pushed herself up on her elbows and frowned at the pale wash of light outside her window. "It's not even morning yet. God." She dropped back onto her pillow with a groan and closed her eyes again.

"No, you don't." Nora reached over, picked up a pillow and smacked her sister in the head with it. She'd hopped a plane as soon as she'd gotten Eileen's text, and she wasn't going to wait another minute to hear about what had happened in her absence.

Nora's dark red hair was the same shade as her sister's, but the similarities ended there. She wore her hair short and spiky, and her eyes, Donovan blue, were tipped up at the corners, contributing to her elfin look. At the moment her mouth had the same stubborn tilt that all Donovan women seemed to possess.

"Damn it, Maggie, wake up and talk to me." Nora felt as tight as the hide drawn across the top of Weeping Buffalo's drum. Ever since she got her daughter's text message about what had been happening at home, she'd been unable to think of anything else.

Now that she was here and could get some answers, she couldn't even wake up her younger sister. "Don't make me use Grandma's never-fail wake-up call. . . ."

Maggie slitted one eye open. "If you dump a glass of ice water in my face, I'll have to kill you."

"Yeah, but you'd be awake. Now talk to me. I've been traveling for *hours* to get home."

Maggie sighed, rubbed her eyes and muttered, "God, Nora, what did Eileen tell you, anyway?"

"Only what you should have told me. That you're turning into a *Faery*."

"Oh, crap."

"Is it true?"

"I don't know."

"How can you not know?" She wanted to pull her hair out, but then thought about yanking on Maggie's instead. Hers was longer, and this was all her fault anyway. "You are or you're not. This is not something you guess about."

"It is if you don't want to think about it." Maggie closed her eyes again.

"I'm not leaving until you've told me everything, so you can forget about going back to sleep, girl."

"You are such a pain."

"So I've been told. I've learned to live with it, and so should you. Talk already."

She did. And once she got going the words seemed to tumble out of her mouth in such a rush that Nora could hardly keep up. Her heart galloped in her chest and her stomach was spinning by the time Maggie finished speaking, and Nora realized that what she was feeling was fury.

"I can't believe this. This is so unfair." She pushed off the bed, walked three steps, then spun around and stabbed one finger at her sister in accusation. "How come *you're* the one with Faery power? I'm the one who's into this stuff. I'm the one who believes in everything that you've always laughed at." She threw her hands wide in complete exasperation. "I'm the one who was always begging Gran to tell me about the Fae! I even have a Faery tattoo on my butt!"

"Really?" Maggie lifted one eyebrow. "You never told me that."

Grumbling under her breath, Nora kicked one of Maggie's shoes out of her way as she started pacing again. "My tattoo isn't the point." She whirled around to look at her sister. "I don't even believe this is happening."

"Me neither."

The coming dawn slid into the room through the white lace curtains. The two women stared at each other, and Nora said, "You don't look any different, if you were wondering."

"Actually"—Maggie pulled her hair back on the right and said—"now that you mention it, are my ears starting to look a little pointy?"

Nora walked closer and leaned in for a better look. "No more than they already were. Don't you remember me telling you that Gran said the reason our ears were sort of tilted up is because of our Fae blood?"

"No, I don't remember that at all."

"Honest to God, this is just so unfair. I know all the stories and you get the Faery dust. How is this right?"

"Beats me." Maggie looked up at her. "Did Grandma say anything else I should know about? Like, did she ever mention Mab or a guy named Culhane?"

"Culhane?" Nora frowned. "Is he the one Eileen said is a hunk?"

"Hunk and a half," Maggie muttered, but she didn't sound happy about it. "He makes me so mad, and then the very next minute he's got me all hot and bothered and hoping he just tosses me onto the floor and—"

"Why do you have one hand tied to the bedpost?" Nora's eyes bugged out and her mouth dropped open as she slapped Maggie in the face with a pillow again. "You're not into weird stuff with this Culhane guy with *Eileen* in the house? Oh, my God, you Faery slut, you."

"No!" Maggie would have given anything for another hour or two of sleep, but that was for damn sure not going to happen. "God, it's too early for this. This isn't kinky, and there is no me and Culhane. I just . . . tend to . . . float if I'm not tied down."

"Float?" Nora's eyes were still bugging. And even so, she managed to look gorgeous. Talk about unfair. "You mean like flying? You can freaking *fly*?"

She shrugged. "Maybe."

Nora pushed a stack of clothes off a chair and dropped into it. Crossing her arms over her chest, she glared at her younger sister and muttered, "And this is all happening because you took Joe's stuff back to him."

"Basically. If I hadn't gone there I never would have run into that creepy thing and wouldn't have had to kill it and get submarined by a gold tornado. . . ." Something occurred to her, and Maggie smiled. "Which makes this sort of your fault. *You're* the one who said I should go see Joe. Clean break and all that shit."

"Well, if I'd known what would happen I would have gone for you."

The thought of tiny little Nora facing down that man-eating demon was enough to terrify Maggie. "No, you wouldn't," she said softly. "It was scary, Nor. Seriously scary, and this whole thing has me freaked out like you wouldn't believe. I've got this gorgeous Fae warrior popping in and out of my life—"

"Culhane."

"Yes."

"How gorgeous?

Maggie sighed. "The stuff dreams are made of."

"Wow . . ."

"And I've got a bunch of demons after me, and a pixie from hell who's snarkier than *we* are. . . ."

"Is that him sleeping in the oak out back? I thought I heard snoring when I came in."

"Bezel. Yep, that's him. He refused to sleep in a human's 'box.' " Maggie smiled wryly, remembering watching the pixie scramble up the tree with as much ease as a chimpanzee. He'd tucked himself onto a wide branch, then given her the evil eye and told her to leave him in peace.

Pushing up from the chair again, Nora walked to her sister's side. She shoved Maggie's legs over and sat down on the bed. "Man, I leave home for a few days, all hell breaks loose, and nobody even bothers to tell me about it until after the fact."

"I was going to tell you. . . ."

"No, you weren't." Nora gave her a look.

"No, I wasn't. I couldn't think of a way to tell you on the phone, and you sounded happy, damn it. I didn't want you to worry, and . . ." Scooting into a sitting position, Maggie pushed her hair back, scrubbed her hands over her face and admitted, "I knew you'd be bent out of shape about this."

Nora huffed out a breath. "Can you blame me?"

"Hey, it may look like a good time to you, but trust me, so far it hasn't been all happy, shiny party time, you know."

"Right, right." Nora blew out a breath. "I'm still jealous."

"Can't think why."

"I know. That just makes it worse." Then she shrugged. "I checked in on Eileen before I came to wake you."

"She's fine."

"Yeah, but I had to see for myself. She's really young to be dealing with Faeries and pixies."

"If it helps any, I think Bezel's afraid of her."

Nora laughed, and some of the tension in her body drained away. Maggie looked at her and knew that her sister was both excited and terrified. It felt good to know that someone else was experiencing the same kinds of emotions she herself was.

"After I got Eileen's text I went a little nuts," Nora

admitted. "I checked out of the motel, packed everything up and caught the first flight out. All I could think about was getting back here. Making sure you and Eileen were okay. I barely had time to say goodbye to Quinn before running to the airport."

"That's right," Maggie said. "Where is this new guy? Thought he was coming home with you."

"I left in such a hurry he couldn't come along. He said he had a few things to wrap up first."

"Hmm."

"I know what you're thinking," Nora said with a frown. "Not like I wasn't thinking the same thing the whole plane ride home. Is Quinn really going to come to me? Or was he just looking for a good thing while it lasted?"

"Nora—"

"He seems great, but I've been wrong about men before."

Case in point, Maggie thought silently, Nora's rotten-to-the-core ex-husband, who after seven years of marriage had left Nora for their babysitter, a nineteen-year-old bubblehead with an IQ to match her breast size.

"I know, I know," Nora said quickly, waving both hands as if dismissing this whole conversation. "I shouldn't fall so fast and so hard. But, Mags . . . when I met Quinn it was like this instant connection. I've never felt anything like that before. It was like we were supposed to meet. Like someone somewhere had set it all up for us. Like it was meant to be."

Crap. More destiny stuff. Though Nora's sounded much better than hers.

"So why are you worried that he's not going to show up?" Maggie's voice was a hush in the quiet, and for a moment Nora felt as though they'd slipped back in time and they were kids again, whispering in the dark so their Gran wouldn't hear them and know they were still awake.

"I'm trying not to be," she admitted.

"Tell me about him."

Nora smiled, and even in the pale light Maggie could see the shine in her sister's eyes. Nora always had led with her heart, and it looked like this time she was already more than half in love with her mystery man.

"His name's Quinn Terhune. He says he deals in futures." She shrugged and picked at a loose chenille thread on Maggie's pale green bedspread. "Stock market stuff, I guess. But oh, God, when he touches me I'm on fire."

"I know that feeling," Maggie said.

Nora's lips quirked. "Tell me it's not the tree-sleeping pixie."

She laughed. God, it was good to have Nora back. With everything else in her life so off-kilter, hearing her sister give her a hard time was enough to straighten things out a little.

"Definitely not Bezel. Culhane. Which is just as bad, if not worse. He's opinionated and bossy and annoying and wouldn't even peel me off the ceiling the first time I floated."

"But . . ." Nora scrambled over Maggie and took a seat on the other side of the bed.

"But," Maggie admitted on a sigh, "there's something there. I don't know what, but the man's hands are like electric or something. He touches me and I'm burning up."

"Wow." Nora scooted around until her back was against the headboard, too. "Sounds like what it's like with Quinn. Weird, huh? I swear, though, from the moment I met Quinn it was like . . . magic."

"Magic?" A tiny thread of worry spun out through Maggie's system as she thought about her sister's choice of words. What if there were more going on here than even she knew about? Culhane and Bezel both had warned her that there were demons and, heck, who knew what else out there gunning for her. What if one of them had found her sister and was planning on using Nora to get to Maggie?

Along with that thread of worry came a white-hot slide of anger, too. Eileen and Nora hadn't signed up for the Fae business. And damned if Maggie was going to allow her family to get dragged into this mess.

"Nora," Maggie said thoughtfully, "what are the odds that the two of us—with our lousy history with men—would each meet a guy like that? In the same week?"

Slowly Nora tuned her head to look at her sister. "You don't think—"

"I don't want to. But I think we ought to find out what exactly's going on. If your guy Quinn is a demon or something, we have to know."

Nora stiffened, her features tightening. "He's not."

"Hope you're right."

"But what if he is?" Nora straightened up. "Then I had sex with a *demon*, for God's sake, and invited him *home*, where he can get my daughter!"

"Nobody's going to get Eileen." Maggie patted her hand. "When Culhane shows up again, I'll ask him what's going on."

"And if Quinn gets here before Culhane comes back?"

"Well, then," Maggie said as she untied her wrist from the bedpost, "we'll just have to handle it our-selves."

Nora looked up at her. "That probably would have sounded more commanding if you weren't floating."

Chapter Six

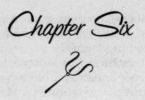

Culhane shifted a hard look down a side street in Castle Bay. He'd come through the portal to check up on Maggie Donovan, but instead he was here, tracking a demon.

The blasted things were all over this little town, and the humans didn't have any idea. How was it, he wondered, that mortals could be so oblivious to their surroundings? How had they survived all this time without being able to sense danger?

A glamour could alter a demon's—or a Fae's, for that matter—appearance. But the essence of who and what they were remained. Humans seemed to deliberately ignore any sign or hint of something out of the ordinary. If they felt watched, they put it down to paranoia. If something cold touched them, they told themselves they were imagining it.

They had no sense of self-preservation.

Culhane pushed away from the brick wall and moved through the crowd of pedestrians unseen. As much as these mortals baffled him, the fact that they were so unaware worked to his advantage most of the time. He moved among them, unseen unless he wished it different. Foolish humans were completely oblivious to the many and varied threats that moved among them.

Scents and sounds surrounded him, so different from home. Here the colors were harsh, the noise a cacophony. His footsteps, though, were sure as he moved swiftly down a crowded sidewalk, darting through the crowd, his purpose uppermost in his mind.

He'd been watching over Maggie and had seen the demon confront her in the grocery store. Though she hadn't risen to the creature's challenge, she'd found a way to escape it, so Culhane hadn't intervened. He might even have allowed the demon to live if the same creature hadn't been following her that morning. Clearly the demon still had plans to finish Maggie off and claim the Faery dust for itself.

That, Culhane would not allow.

Following the demon's trail was easy enough. Though it wore its human costume, the demon's underlying scent could not be hidden so easily. It went farther from the heart of the small town and moved closer to the harbor. Here the tang of the sea flavored the air. Here the buildings were older, dirtier, the streets narrower. The docks lay idle now but for a few pleasure craft, but the jetty that led to the old lighthouse was crowded with people wandering there and back as waves crashed and spray flew into the air.

Culhane closed the distance between him and his prey, and it was then that the demon finally became aware that it was being followed. One quick look over its shoulder and the creature began to sprint. Running, shoving its way through the crowd, the beast in human costume made a desperate bid for escape. It shoved one man into the street, and a car horn blasted even as the driver slammed on his brakes to avoid hitting it.

Culhane wasn't more than a step or two behind the creature, so when the demon threw a child down to the sidewalk, Culhane jumped over the small, crying boy with ease. Damned if he'd play games with the thing.

He had other business to take care of—such as turning a human female into a Fae warrior.

The demon darted down a side street, ran between the parked cars and into a squat brown building with faded paint and broken windows. Flower boxes holding the skeletons of blooms long dead lined the front steps, and the door hung open as if in welcome.

Culhane took the demon up on its invitation. Stepping into the building, he wrinkled his nose at the smells. The mortal world smelled badly enough, but this place was a true test of a warrior's resolve. The stench of something rotten curled in the stale air, and Culhane knew he'd found a demon nest.

Drawing his knife from the scabbard at his waist, he moved farther into the shadows, eyes sharp, checking every hole and darkened corner. "You hide from me? Are you really such a coward?"

"Coward?" The voice came from nowhere and everywhere. "You think you were following me? I *led* you here. You're in my house now, Fae. The rules are mine."

Culhane laughed and heard rustling. The demon was constantly moving—looking for a better angle of attack? Or a better hiding place? "And your rules are to hide and jump out at me from the darkness? What a brave demon you are. This must be why they chose you to go after the human woman."

"What do you know about her?" The voice was sly, the question careful.

The demon was still moving, shifting position in the house so that Culhane couldn't keep a lock on it. But Culhane's ears were attuned to every creak, every whisper, every slide of a foot against the floor. He knew precisely where the demon was now, but had no intention of giving that away.

"She's my charge," Culhane shouted, to make sure that any others hiding in this pest-hole heard him. Too much rested on Maggie Donovan. He would take no chances with her safety. He never had. "Under my protection."

"Why does a Fae warrior care what happens to a mortal?"

"Since when does a Fae warrior explain himself to a demon?" Culhane countered. The soft brush of cloth on wood told him where the demon was. Culhane tracked it without moving an inch.

"She killed one of us."

"To protect herself. The demon was feasting on a human and then attacked her."

"Word is, her mate's putting out a reward for the human bitch. You think I'm the only one who will be after her?"

"My protection," Culhane reminded it. His gaze moved carefully over the room, noting the torn furniture, the ripped carpet and the broken tables. Demons were all different, he knew. Some preferred opulent living here among the mortals. Some preferred anonymity. This one apparently leaned more toward a rathole.

"I saw you stalking her," Culhane said. "At the food store. You confronted her."

"Only a warning," the demon cooed, its voice coming now from behind Culhane. "Only having some fun. Not like I could have killed her in the grocery store."

"You were still stalking her today, but you won't kill her. She is beyond you." Or would be soon. When Maggie Donovan fulfilled her destiny, she would be a force to be reckoned with throughout the worlds.

"Because of the Fae power? Please." Disgust and humor both rang in the demon's voice. "She doesn't know how to use it yet. She'll be dead inside a month."

"Not by you or yours," Culhane promised quietly. Then he spun around, stretched one hand into the shadows and grabbed the demon trying to slither closer. Fingers closing tight around the creature's throat,

Culhane yanked it into the half-light. The demon's human mask had slipped, leaving behind only oily, dark green skin, red eyes and the hint of horns. "You should have stayed away from her."

"I didn't hurt her," the creature whined, pleading for mercy now that it had been caught.

"And you won't." Culhane drew his knife back, thrust it forward and delivered the killing blow so fast, the demon never saw him move. As he dropped the creature to the dirty floor he bent over it, blew a stream of Faery dust over the demon's body and watched as it exploded into dust.

Finished, Culhane lifted his gaze again for one last sweep around the interior of the building. He sensed the presence of others, though they were making no move to confront him. Just as well, he thought. He'd spent more than enough time in this place. But before he left he issued one last warning.

"I know there are more of you here. I could take the time to search you out and dispose of you as I have this one." He slid his blade back into its scabbard with a whisper of sound.

The house was silent, but Culhane knew they were still there. At least two more demons were hiding in the nest they'd built out of the humans' leavings. So he spoke again, to make himself clear.

"The woman has the protection of the Fae warriors. Leave her alone . . . or die. Your choice."

Then he turned, left the house and disappeared into the sunlight.

_&_

"Oh, my pixie ass! What part of the word *concentrate* do you not understand? Stop worrying about floating and flying and worry more about the enemies who'll be coming after you."

Maggie fixed a hard stare on the ugly little man who,

over the last two days, had become the bane of her existence. "I *am* concentrating—on not floating so high I'm whipping around through the treetops! How'm I supposed to concentrate on more than one thing at a time?"

"I thought women were supposed to be multitaskers."

Maggie's feet hit the ground and she laughed. "Where'd you hear that?"

"What?" He glowered at her, his silvery eyebrows drawing together over those weirdly pale blue eyes. "You think this world is the only one where women think they're better than the rest of us?"

"Man, I'd really love to meet your wife." Any female, pixie or human, who would intentionally put up with this little jerk should be, in Maggie's opinion, put up for sainthood.

"That ain't gonna happen," he muttered, and kicked Sheba's ball. Reluctantly the golden shuffled off after it. "She's not real happy with me at the moment."

Delighted to take a break from her "training," Maggie grabbed the change of subject and held on with both hands. "What'd you do? Drop pixie dust in the hallway?"

"Funny. If you want to know, she didn't want me coming here, helping Culhane."

Okay, that was surprising. Maggie reached up, lifted her hair off her neck and almost sighed as the cold wind buffeted her bare skin. "Why not?"

"Nosy, aren't you?"

"Yeah."

He sighed, and his scraggly chin whiskers ruffled in the breeze. "For one thing, Fontana's not real fond of humans. You guys are so big you make her nervous. But mostly she's afraid Mab'll find out and have me flayed."

Not what she was expecting to hear, for some reason. Her stomach jittered a little at the ugly picture his words had evoked. "Nice queen you got there."

"Yeah, she's Ms. Popularity in Otherworld."

"If everybody hates her, how come nobody's over-thrown her?"

His eyes narrowed on her. "Thought that's what you were going to do."

Her? A revolutionary? "Not my plan. Culhane's."

Just the mention of the Fae warrior's name had tiny pools of heat forming in her center. She really didn't want to admit that, even to herself, but it seemed that the longer he stayed away from her, the more she thought about him. *Damn it.* She even dreamed about him, long, tantalizing, sexual dreams where those magical hands of his stroked her body into a feverish pitch and she woke hot, needy and cranky.

Meanwhile, Culhane was probably off in Fae having a grand old time, not giving her a thought, while she was sweating and being insulted by his pixie.

"It's a good plan."

Her gaze shifted to Bezel, who was watching her with a steady, penetrating stare.

"You think I'm hopeless."

"Yeah, but I think all humans are hopeless. You're no worse than the rest of them."

"Wow, thanks." She stretched out on the grass and barely managed to stifle a groan as Sheba dropped her enormous body across Maggie's chest. At least now she didn't have to worry about floating.

The sky overhead was smoke gray, with clouds the color of fresh bruises piling up over the ocean, getting ready to rush to shore. The bare-branched trees were rattling in a cold wind that heralded a coming storm, and every muscle in her body ached like a bad tooth. She had demons and Faery queens who wanted her dead, and a pixie making her life a living hell.

How had she come to this?

Seriously? Maggie was beginning to think it might

be easier if she just let some demon eat her and have it over with.

"Feeling sorry for yourself?"

Maggie turned to look at the pixie as another frown crossed Bezel's features. She idly noted how comfortable he seemed to be with that particular expression.

"Maybe."

"Well, cut it out. You've got Fae blood in you, and the power, so it could work." He lifted one long, bony finger and pointed it at her. "But you've got to try harder. You don't exactly have a lot of time."

"I know, I know," Maggie said on a sigh. "Demons are after me."

"It's not just them you have to worry about. If Mab finds out about you . . . "

Oh, Maggie didn't even want a description of what would happen to her if Mab discovered her existence. If the queen would flay one of her own, there was just no telling how her imagination would run amok with Maggie.

"I get it. And trust me." Maggie pushed Sheba off her chest and sat up, ignoring the dog's whining. "I'm plenty worried about all of this."

"Then for the goddess's sake, pay attention." Bezel walked back and forth in front of her like a general inspecting his troops—and finding them lacking. Well, too bad. She hadn't *asked* to join this army, had she?

"I told you, Faery dust is fatal to demons."

Yeah, he had. As if she didn't know that for herself. Hadn't she had a front-row seat to watch a demon dissolve in a golden tornado? "But," she reminded him, not for the first time, as she pushed herself to her feet and concentrated on not leaving the ground, "I *got* this dust from a demon."

"Came from a damned pendant, though, didn't it?"

"Yes, but . . ."

Bezel inhaled sharply, then made a face at what he called "the stench of mortality." "You don't listen. I told Culhane this was pointless, but he insisted you be trained."

"Some training. What're you supposed to be teaching me? Shouldn't I be learning karate or judo or something? How to flip big, bad demons over my shoulder like Buffy?"

He snorted and looked her up and down dismissively. "You can't stand still without your feet leaving the ground. How in *Ifreann* can you learn to throw demons around?"

"*Ifreann?*"

Muttering, he said, "Think hell. Only it makes your version of hell look like a party." He shuddered, and the ripples of it sent his long hair swaying. "Besides, do I look big enough to teach you how to toss demons around?"

"Fine." Maggie was a little disappointed that she wasn't going to be trained to be a superhero or something. After all, she could almost fly. Why not fight? And hey, she wasn't even thinking about it and she wasn't floating, so good for her. She was getting the hang of this stuff, no matter what Bezel had to say about it. "Teach me. But answer me this: If Culhane's so concerned about my training, why isn't *he* doing it?"

Bezel snorted a laugh at that. "He's a Fae warrior. He can't stay away from Otherworld too long or the queen will wonder what the devil he's up to. Then where would we be?"

Maggie opened her mouth.

He cut her off. "I'll tell you where. Mab would slide into this world to check things out for herself, stir things up while she's here and probably kill you, just for starters."

"Okeydokey, then." Maggie swallowed hard, lifted her face into the cool sea wind and reminded herself not to ask a question if she didn't want the answer. Still, it was hard to imagine a Faery queen she didn't even know wanting her dead.

Bezel kicked her to get her attention. "If you're finished asking stupid questions, listen up, because I'm not going through this part of it again." His gaze narrowed on her. "Demons kill Faeries to capture their dust. Just having it on them gives them strength. But if the dust touches them they die. So it's a trade-off." He shrugged narrow shoulders. "Most of your demons are smart enough to leave Fae alone. But there are always some who want the power more than they fear death."

Great. That was just great.

"So they kill a Faery and trap the dust in something."

"Has to be gold. Or at least part gold," Bezel said, probably not for the first time, since he looked so disgusted.

Maggie didn't feel sorry for him. She had a lot going on at the moment. Kind of hard to concentrate.

"The purity of the gold is what holds the dust in place."

"So when I broke the crystal front on the pendant . . ."

"Demon go boom."

She gave him a tight smile. "That's lovely."

"Hey, I didn't kill it."

"I didn't know I was going to— never mind." She'd had to come to grips with the fact that she'd actually killed something, but she didn't want to spend a lot of time talking about it. "Why'd the demon have the damn thing in a pendant with a crystal front if it could be broken that easily?"

"What am I?" the pixie demanded, "a demon psychologist? How do I know?"

"God, you're annoying."

"Yeah?" His long hair whipped about his face, and he shook it clear of his eyes. "You're no vacation in Tamre yourself."

"What's Tamre?"

He screwed up his forehead as he thought about it. "Think Tahiti, only better."

"In Otherworld?"

"*No*," he sneered. "In this one. It's a secret country. Man, dealing with trolls is easier than this." He tugged at his chin whiskers. "Now, are you going to show me how you kill a demon or not?"

"I'll try."

"There is no try," he intoned slowly, pompously. "There's do or don't do."

Maggie laughed and goggled at him. Could her life get any weirder? "You're kidding me. You're giving me Yoda?"

His silvery eyebrows wiggled as he smiled, and his teeth looked bright and sharp. "Great flick."

"What kind of pixie are you?"

"You think we don't get over here to see movies?" He looked insulted. "I told you we come and go whenever the *Ifreann* we want to. Besides, *everybody's* seen *Star Wars*."

Stalking off a few paces, he spun around on his wide flat feet and glared at her from a distance. "Now, are you going to see if you can blow Faery dust or not?"

She'd slipped into a truly bizarre world, Maggie told herself as she straightened up and fought to concentrate. A world where pixies quoted Yoda, demons wore Faery dust as fashion accessories and she herself was being taught how to kill enemies she hadn't had until a few days ago, just by blowing on them.

Very strange indeed.

"Take a breath, damn you, and focus!"

She did as Bezel said, gathering herself, pulling together the power that continued to hum and buzz inside her, then blew a fine whisper of air from her lungs. Finally, when a shimmer of gold dust sparkled in that breath, her personal triumph was lost in the hopeless wish that Faery dust had the power to shut Bezel up.

E

Culhane found her in her studio.

The night was quiet, and an old clock somewhere in her house was chiming midnight when he shifted into being right behind her.

She sat at an easel, the painting before her glimmering softly in the glow of dozens of candles she had set about the room. Her features were luminous in the flickering light, and her dark blue eyes were fixed on the project at hand. There was fire in her hair, he thought, and fought the urge to touch, to bury his hands in the thick mass.

He hadn't counted on this. In the years he'd watched over her, there'd always been a distance between them. Time and worlds had kept them apart. Now, though, it was as if he were seeing her for the first time, and hunger for her had become his constant companion.

He sensed more than saw that she was aware of his presence, and the fact that she no longer jolted when he appeared pleased him.

"Just pop in to say howdy?" She didn't bother to turn and look at him, just kept painting, her hand steady with the fine brush she wielded.

Culhane lifted an eyebrow, then walked to her side and went into a crouch to study the painting as she worked. After a long moment he spoke quietly. "I thought to find you asleep."

At this, she did give him a look that he couldn't quite read. "Are you telling me you sneak into my house when I'm sleeping to watch me?"

He shrugged, a casual move that belied his interest in her. The fact that he had watched over her while she was sleeping more times than he wanted to count was an irritation to him. She was a means to an end. Nothing more.

Or so she should be.

"I've an interest in you, Maggie Donovan. It's up to me to see that you're safe."

"Hmm." She turned back to her work, leaned in closer to her painting and touched the tip of the brush to the edge of the lighthouse she was capturing on canvas with color.

On the canvas, its gray stone gleamed with the spray of a painted sea. Culhane almost thought his fingers would come away damp should he reach out and touch it. The ocean she'd created was wild and rough, whitecaps frothing on a bleak, dark surface. The painted sky was caught in a storm, with lightning hidden beneath banks of clouds until it was no more than a pale shimmer of a threat.

The beach the waves rushed toward was empty—as he'd already realized that most scenes in her paintings were. There was the sense again of loneliness. Of waiting. And again he wondered if she'd ever noticed that what was missing in her creations was people.

He shook his head to empty it of ramblings. "Did you think I'd trust in only a pixie to keep you safe?"

She laughed lightly, and the sound seemed to weave its way around him.

"Safe?" she asked. "Usually I get the feeling Bezel would be happy to see me keel over dead."

"It's his way."

"Doesn't make him a pleasant companion."

Now he laughed at the very notion. "Nothing about Bezel is pleasant, but he knows what he's doing, and he can help you stay alive."

"Good. I'm all for that." She leaned back, studied her canvas, then set the small brush aside, grabbed another and reached to a palette filled with splotches of colors.

The brush she wielded now looked like an open fan, and she pressed it into a shade of green blended with white. Then, carefully, she laid the tips of that loaded fan to the edges of the whitecaps on her canvas.

Though Culhane would have thought before that the water was complete, he saw now that she was making it even more alive, like a hungry beast waiting to swallow the unwary.

"Why is it," he wondered aloud, "that you waste your time painting foolish scenes on glass when you've this kind of talent inside you?"

Even in the dim glow of candlelight, he saw the flush of pleasure fill her cheeks, her eyes. In only a moment, though, that flush had passed, and she turned to look at him.

"I like eating," she said simply, with a shrug. "Artists don't make much of a living. So I use what talent I have to run my own business, and this I do for myself."

"A practical woman," he mused, and stood up, walking around her, looking at both her and the painting she was creating. "I wouldn't have thought so from our other conversations."

"Practical?" Her laughter faded into a chuckle, and still she shook her head at the notion.

"Why is that funny?"

"Because a practical woman wouldn't be sitting here in the near dark, painting at midnight, chatting with a Faery."

One corner of Culhane's mouth curved in a brief smile. Outside, the night crept closer to the windows, yet seemed to be held at bay by the candlelight. "I thought painters needed light. Any I've seen are always in the bright light of sun or in the glare of electricity."

She went back to lovingly bringing her ocean to life. "I used to need the extra light, too. But since . . . well, my vision's strong and clear enough now without it, and I like candlelight."

"It likes you as well." The moment the words were out, he thought of how he might pull them back in. But it was too late. She was already turning her head to look at him with curiosity.

"Was that a compliment?"

"It might have been," he admitted roughly. "Though it's not why I'm here."

"Figures." She sighed. "Why are you here, then?"

"To watch. To see. To learn."

"Why? Worried that I'm not your 'chosen one' after all?" She set her brush down, stood up and faced him, chin high and eyes flashing with something that was all female and all confusion to Culhane. "Think if you watch me close enough, you'll find out you picked the wrong woman?"

"No," he said, and thought he caught the brief shine of disappointment in her eyes before it was quickly gone again. "You're the one, Maggie. And I think, inside you now, you've admitted that truth, as well. I've known who you were your whole life. I only waited," he said, "for the day to come when you would know it, too."

She staggered a little, and in her eyes he saw the surprise of his words strike home.

"My whole life?" She worked on that for a bit, then asked, "So you watched me. All these years?"

"You're not that old," he pointed out with another brief, rare smile. Why was it, he wondered, that with this woman he could smile more than he had in hundreds of years? Why was it she who touched something in him he'd never thought he had? And why was he allowing himself to be drawn away from the point?

"You're only thirty, Maggie Donovan. Hardly more than a blink in the grand scheme of things."

"And yet, in all that time," she mused thoughtfully, "I never felt you. Saw you."

Now? Was the time right to tell her that she had seen him, felt him, long ago? He looked at her in the soft dance of the light and knew that it was now or never. She had to be aware of just how closely they were linked.

"You did."

The stunned disbelief on her face would have been funny had he not also seen the worry in her eyes. It took her only a moment to shake that off and snap, "You're nuts. I think I'd remember seeing a Faery pop up out of nowhere."

"Do you?" He walked toward her with quiet steps. His gaze locked on hers, when he reached her he lifted one hand, cupped her chin and turned her face gently toward the painting she'd forgotten all about. "Why is it, do you think, that you so often paint that lighthouse?"

She pulled away, and he didn't want to admit that he missed the touch of her.

"Why wouldn't I?" she asked, her voice deliberately light, unaffected. "Maybe because it's sitting out in the bay, big as life? Artists come from up and down the coast to paint that lighthouse. I've seen it my whole life. And it's haunted—well, supposedly."

"It is."

"Really?"

"Another time," he said abruptly, wanting her attention back on the painting. Back to where he was leading her memory. "There's another reason you're drawn to that lighthouse, isn't there, Maggie? Something personal happened there, near that lighthouse. Something that haunts you as much as the ghosts that swirl about in the fog."

She frowned, pushing one paint-stained hand through

her hair, and the fact that she had no care for vanity touched him, as well.

"All right, yes," she said, folding her arms over her chest, inadvertently tugging tight across her breasts the thin, stretchy fabric of the shirt she wore. "When I was a kid I nearly drowned there."

She looked at the painting, but the faraway glint in her eye told him she was looking back, just as he'd wanted.

Her voice went soft as the candlelight, and as she talked a sharp wind lifted outside and battered at the glass.

"I wasn't supposed to be out that day. There was a storm coming in, and I used to love to go to the beach and watch it blow across the ocean. My grandmother didn't mind that I went to the beach, but she made me promise to stay out of the water."

Maggie huffed out a rush of air, and Culhane wondered if she even noticed the hint of Faery dust that sparkled in her breath.

"Naturally," she was saying, a small smile curving her mouth, "I didn't listen. I was twelve, like Eileen is now, and I figured Gran was old and nervous."

"As most children do."

"I guess. Anyway, the water was choppy and the waves were slamming into each other. The wind was so strong it was blowing sand into my skin, and it stung, but I still didn't leave. It made me feel . . . powerful to be a part of it, you know?" She glanced at him, and he nodded. "I couldn't stand staying on the beach. I wanted to be out in it, and I knew I was a strong swimmer, so I wasn't scared. So I swam out and fought the water for every stroke."

Maggie stared down at the painting, seeing that storm in her memory, as she'd tried to re-create it on canvas, and she couldn't believe she'd done something so foolish.

"I was headed for the jetty that leads out to the lighthouse. But a rogue wave caught me and tossed me farther out." She wrapped her arms around herself now as the memory took hold and made her feel again the slap and pull of the cold water. "I was so scared, and thinking maybe Gran wasn't so dumb after all. I even remember wondering if she'd be mad when she found out I drowned.

"The water was rough and the spray so thick I couldn't draw a breath when I surfaced without taking in gulps of water with it. I was cold and tired, and my arms ached and my leg was cramped from kicking so hard and there was no one around to yell to for help." Her voice was coming fast now, and she couldn't seem to stop it. Strange, she hadn't thought about that day in years. Had buried it deeply enough that she was able to go into the ocean again without feeling that bone-deep fear she had once felt so long ago.

She tore her gaze from the painting and looked up at Culhane instead. His gaze was locked on hers, and his sharply carved features were as still as a statue carved by the hand of a generous god. He was so near she could have reached out to touch him. The candlelight in the room threw shifting shadows over his face and danced across his eyes. But he only stood still, watching her. Waiting.

"I was a good swimmer," she told him, "but it was too hard, and I started sinking. The waves pulled me under, and it was so dark I didn't know which way was up. I remember thinking that dying wasn't so bad, because by then I was more exhausted than scared. I even thought, *Now I'll get to see Mom and Dad again,* because they'd died a couple of years before. That's why Nora and I were living here with Gran and Grandpa."

"Tell me," he said, his voice soft and nearly lyrical, with the hint of an accent she couldn't quite place.

She pulled in another breath to steady herself for the

end and said it in a rush. "I was underwater. I opened
my eyes, and everything was dark and still, like it
wasn't on the surface. There was no sound, nothing.
And then . . ." Maggie laughed a little, almost embar-
rassed to confess this part of her experience. "This is
the craziest part, so hang on."

"I'm hanging," he said, "as long as you need."

Maggie nodded and continued before she could pull
back. "I heard a voice with music in it." She looked up,
waiting for him to laugh at her, but his features were
still, his gaze fixed on hers. "This voice, it told me to
kick again, to push myself out of the dark. It was so
strong, it was inside my head and outside, too, rippling
in the water around me. And I did it. I don't know how,
but tired as I was, I kicked as hard as I could, and the
surface was there, and as soon as I made it there were
hands waiting for me. Hands that pulled me up and
out of the water to the rocks under the lighthouse."

She scrubbed her own hands up and down her arms,
as if searching to find that solid, warm grip again. "I
don't remember much after that, but—"

"But what?"

"Eyes," she said quietly. "There were pale green eyes
watching me, making sure I was all right. I never told
anyone that part." She stopped talking, stared at Culhane, and as the truth clicked in her mind, slid into her
system with a surety she'd never known before, her
suddenly crazy-ass world began making sense.

"It was you," she said, and her voice was filled with
more than surprise, more than wonder. "You were
there. It was you who told me to swim. You who pulled
me out of the water. You who saved me."

"You saved yourself," he said, cupping her face between his palms so that heat filled her, seeping into
all the cold, lonely places she hid even from herself.
"There are laws. I couldn't go into the water to pull
you out. You had to make the decision to survive for

yourself. But once you'd decided to fight, I was able to help you to safety."

"It was real," she murmured. "It wasn't a dream."

"Not a dream, no. I told you: Your destiny is set, Maggie Donovan. And I'm here, always, to see that you're safe. That you fulfill that which I've waited centuries for."

His eyes shone with the glow of candle flames, and the quiet of the room, the rush of the wind lay between them. His thumbs on her cheekbones sparked fires beneath her skin, and still Maggie was lost. "I don't even know what to say to that."

"And maybe that's best." He let her go and took a step back. "You've a temper on you I've seen too often already."

"Temper?" She, too, stepped away, as if needing the comfort of more than an emotional distance. The fact that she'd just discovered that her mystery savior was a man who could turn her inside out with a single look was a hard thing to swallow. So instead she reacted to his last statement.

"Who wouldn't have a temper? I see my ex get eaten. I start glowing. I've got a pixie sleeping in my tree and a pushy Faery always telling me what to do."

"For your own good."

"Oh, well, that makes it all right." Needing something to hold, she reached to the side, grabbed a paintbrush and tightened her fist around it. "Who are you to know what's good for me?"

"After remembering what happened when you were a child, you can ask me that?"

Fine. She sounded like an ungrateful bitch. But damn it, how was she supposed to feel? Sure, she was glad he'd saved her ass when she was a kid. But now that she was grown, did that give him the right to endanger her?

"Culhane, I don't know how to fight. How'm I supposed to defeat a queen?"

"You'll learn," he said, moving up behind her until the heat of his body washed over her like a sigh.

"What if I can't?"

"You will."

"Why is this so important to you?"

"Do you know what it is to be no more than a servant?" he demanded, turning her in his arms so that he could look down into her eyes. "The males of my race have been treated as less than that for millennia. The warriors are different. We're needed. To fight. To kill. But Fae women don't share power, Maggie. They cling to it like a lover and will do anything to protect it. Mab is the worst of them all."

"But why me?"

"Your strength will defeat her, Maggie."

"Right. I'm a tough one."

"This isn't about your fists or your skills. This is about inner strength. You have it within you to best Mab. Otherwise none of this would be happening."

"God."

"This was written. You can't alter it. Neither can I. The difference is, I wouldn't even if I could."

"I don't like this." She pulled out of his arms, needing the space between them as she walked to the window and stared out at the wind-whipped night. "Any of it. I want my life back."

"You haven't lost your life," he argued. "Not then. Not now."

"Haven't I?" She whirled around to face him, only to find him already gone.

Maggie could still smell him in the room, though, that clean, tempting, foresty scent that seemed to cling to his hair, his clothes, his skin. She could feel his hands on her face and see his eyes as they stared watchfully down into hers.

"Damn Faery." She scraped her hands up and down her arms, glanced at the painting sitting on the easel and felt again the cold grip of the ocean when it had tried to end her life.

He'd saved her then.

But if he had to choose between her and Otherworld, would he save her now?

Chapter Seven

❧

The very next night Maggie had to admit that Quinn Terhune made quite the impression.

Hell, even Eileen liked him.

"Can I get you another glass of wine?" he asked, giving Maggie a bright, charming smile.

She wanted to like him, but after everything that had been going on in the last several days, her Spidey sense was tingling too loudly for her to blindly trust in anything. Maggie had to admit, though, that he was easy on the eyes.

He looked like a Viking—or what she imagined Vikings had looked like once upon a time—tall and broad chested, with a square, hard jaw, piercing blue eyes and long blond hair he kept pulled into a ponytail at the base of his neck. The black jeans and gray knit sweater he wore didn't distract from the image at all.

"Maggie?" Nora snapped her fingers in front of Maggie's nose. "Hello? Wine? Hmm. Maybe you've had enough."

"Not nearly," she managed to say as she pushed her sister's hand away. Then she nodded at the Viking. "Yes, I would like more, thanks."

He gave her a small, knowing smile that made Maggie wonder if he was a mind reader. Hell, stranger things had been happening, she thought. Why not?

Nora'd arranged this dinner for Maggie and Quinn to meet. It hadn't gone too badly, actually. The gorgeous giant seemed determined to win Maggie's approval. Which, of course, only made her more suspicious.

The small dining room in the guesthouse behind Maggie's place was lit by the flickering light of a dozen candles. There was a short, squat clay bowl in the center of the table bursting with fall-colored chrysanthemums, and their spicy scent blended with the smell of the lemon polish Nora had used on the table Grandpa had built.

"Isn't he amazing?" Nora's gaze followed the tall man as he left for the kitchen of Nora's house, already clearly at home. He'd been there only since late last night, but appeared to be settling in for a long stay.

There went that little tingle of warning again.

Slanting a glance at Eileen, Nora then leaned in closer to Maggie and said, "He's not a demon, either."

"Uh-huh." Mental eye roll. "And how do you know that?"

"I asked him."

"What?"

"Maggie, please." Nora waved one hand in dismissal of her sister's outrage. "I couldn't lie to him, and I couldn't very well let him stay in the house with Eileen and me if I didn't know about the demon thing, now, could I? Besides, honesty is too important in a relationship."

"I can't believe—"

"Twenty-two percent of all relationships are based on lies."

"Where do you get that stuff?" Maggie asked.

"Quinn is *completely* accepting of other planes of existence and the possibilities of pixies and faeries," Nora told her, smiling and sighing in pleasure at the same time. "He's so open. So ready to explore possibilities." She sighed again. Maybe she was deflating. "A totally supportive guy. I never would have believed that someone like him existed, Maggie. He's like the perfect man."

"Are you serious?" Maggie shot her niece a look and thought that Eileen was way too busy pretending oblivion. But Maggie couldn't stop herself from whispering frantically to her sister anyway, "I can't believe you. Quinn's been here less than twenty-four hours, and already you've dragged him into our little world of horrors without hesitation?"

"Maggie, I love you." Nora patted her hand, then smoothed her own hair, readying herself for the Viking's return, no doubt. "But you don't understand the deep bonds of affection that spring up between people who are *meant* to be together. I couldn't shut Quinn out. Didn't want to, either. And he's willing to help." She sighed. "It's just so sweet."

"Sweet."

"He's totally committed to helping us, Maggie." Nora's mouth firmed. "I'd think you'd be grateful."

"Grateful?" God, she was sounding like a parrot. Or a broken tape recorder. "Nora, we talked about this, remember?" she prompted in a furious whisper. "We were going to look into this together?"

"We still are," Nora told her. "And Quinn will help."

"I don't think Quinn's going to help us check *him* out."

"We won't have to. He couldn't lie to me, Maggie. I would know. I would sense it. When you and I talked the other night I was uneasy because I missed him. Now that he's here . . ."

"Oh, for—"

"I don't think he's a demon either," Eileen said, clearly having listened to every word of their whispered conversation.

"See?" Nora said, beaming at her daughter.

"Why not?" Maggie asked.

"Because," the girl said primly, looking at her aunt, "every once in a while when you breathe out, Faery dust shows up, and it hasn't hurt him."

Maggie jerked back in her seat. *Good God.* She was spewing Faery dust? That had to be worse than garlic breath.

"If he was a demon," Eileen pointed out, "he'd be dissolving already. Bezel told me all about it."

Logic.

From a Donovan.

Scary.

"Wow." Impressed, despite the fact that she now had to think about what she might be breathing on people, Maggie stared at the girl before saying, "you are an amazing human being."

Delighted, Eileen laughed, and Nora reached across the table to grab her daughter's hand.

"You're brilliant, baby. Thank you for proving my point." Then she sat back, gave Maggie a so-there look and grinned before looking at Eileen again. "You do like him, don't you, honey?"

"Sure." Eileen shrugged and pushed a Brussels sprout around on her plate with the tines of her fork. "He's nice, and he doesn't do those fake laughs that guys do when they want you to like them."

"Another good point," Nora nearly crowed. "If he was a demon trying to infiltrate us, he'd be trying too hard."

Before Maggie could point out that maybe there were a few clever demons in town, Quinn walked back into the room carrying a bottle of chilled chardonnay and a soda for Eileen. Thoughtful of him.

Maggie had to admit that Quinn did seem great. She really wanted to believe that somehow Nora had stumbled on a guy who would be good for her. Who was everything he pretended to be. So why, then, she wondered as Quinn refilled her glass, did she have these doubts still rattling around inside her?

"Nora tells me you've been given Faery power."

Maggie choked on her swallow of wine and, coughing, struggling for air, stared at the man with tears streaming from her eyes. Okay, Nora had told Quinn about what had been going on, but did she have to tell him about Maggie's little problem, too?

He gave her an unconcerned smile designed to disarm and simply waited until she had her breath back.

Wheezing a little, Maggie sent a quick glare at her sister—which was totally wasted, since Nora was practically cooing at her Viking lover. "She did?"

"Well, it's fascinating, isn't it?" He ran one hand up and down Nora's arm in a proprietary way. "An ordinary woman plucked from obscurity and set on a path of destiny?"

"Are you a screenwriter or something?" Maggie shifted in her chair and took another swallow of wine.

He smiled again, and she had to admit that he was pretty devastating when he did. Oh, not even close to Culhane, but damn good.

"And now you've been chosen to save Otherworld?"

"Sounds like you and Nora have had quite the conversation." *More wine, Maggie.*

He shrugged. "You're important to her. She's important to me."

Narrowing her gaze on the man, she only said, "Nora's important to *me*, too."

Something in Maggie's tone must have alerted her sister, because Nora turned and frowned at her.

"I understand." Quinn ignored Nora's sudden tension. Locking his gaze with Maggie's, he gave her a nod. "I love my family, too, and would do anything to protect them."

"Well, it's nice that we understand each other."

"I believe we do. So," Quinn asked, kissing the top of Nora's head while keeping his gaze fixed on Maggie, "are you going to help the Fae?"

Good question. "I don't know."

He might have frowned slightly, but the expression was gone so quickly Maggie couldn't be sure.

"Of course she is," Nora said brightly. "Maggie is just that kind of person."

"You'd have to be careful." Eileen spoke up, and Maggie gratefully tore her gaze from the Viking to look at her niece.

"Boy howdy," Maggie said, and since Nora had already filled Quinn in on everything, she didn't bother to hedge her words. "Battling a queen is high up there on my list of 'be careful' things."

"Not just that." Eileen dropped her fork onto her plate with a clatter and reached for the soda Quinn had brought out for her. She took a long drink, then set the can down, cupping her hands around it. "It's going to Otherworld, Aunt Maggie."

"Oh, God. Imagine actually *going*," Nora said.

"Yeah," Maggie agreed with far less enthusiasm.

"You couldn't eat anything when you were there."

"What?" Not eat? Maggie wiggled her fingers in a give-me signal. "What do you mean?"

"I've been looking up Fae and all the other stuff, remember?" At Maggie's nod, Eileen continued. "Well, the stories say that if a mortal eats anything in Otherworld, they'll be trapped there for a hundred years."

"Trapped?" Nora asked.

"A hundred *years*?" Maggie repeated.

"Time moves differently there, remember," Eileen told them, and she seemed to be enjoying the fact that she had the absorbed attention of three adults. "So if Culhane takes you there, remember not to eat."

"This could be a problem," Maggie muttered, glancing down at the empty dinner plate in front of her. She'd eaten everything but the floral pattern.

"So you pack a lunch," Nora quipped with a laugh. "Maggie, you said this Culhane wants your help. It's not like he's going to trap you there or something."

"Hmm . . ."

"Also, the Fae aren't real fond of mortals," Eileen went on. "So they might not be happy to see you in their world."

"Oh, great. Just great." This kept getting better and better. Maggie rubbed the middle of her forehead in a futile attempt to get rid of the headache forming there.

How was she supposed to fight a legendary queen and win if she couldn't even have a snack while doing it?

And where the *hell* was Culhane?

Ever since the night before, when he'd come to her in her studio, Maggie hadn't been able to stop thinking. Remembering. As a girl she'd felt safe with him. As a woman she felt hungry for him.

But at the moment she'd prefer that safe feeling again.

Eileen was talking, though, sharing more information about the Fae and Otherworld, and Maggie told herself to listen up. Bezel might be training her, but so far Eileen was the real font of information.

But when she looked up she caught Quinn watching Eileen, and the flinty coldness in his eyes made every nerve in her body stand up and shriek.

Culhane strode through the palace halls, his gaze hooded, his steps quiet against the cold blue marble streaked with veins of gold. The crystal walls on either side of him hummed with an energy that pulsed with life, light. From somewhere close by music swelled:

pipes, fiddles, drums. But he didn't acknowledge it. He was here to find a friend. To see if the situation in Otherworld was as it should be.

He'd spent too much time on the mortal plane. And, he admitted silently, even when he wasn't there his thoughts were. Even now, as he moved through Mab's palace, his mind raced with thoughts of Maggie, of what she felt like in his arms. What he might do next to make sure she was as invested in her destiny as he was.

"Culhane!"

He snatched his knife from his belt and whirled around so that the edges of the long, dark brown coat he wore lifted into a swirl of motion about his body. In the palace, even when the halls looked empty, treachery lived and breathed and could erupt at any moment. But the taut tension inside him subsided some when he recognized the tall man headed his way.

"McCulloch." Culhane slid his knife back into its scabbard and nodded toward the other warrior quickly closing on him. He'd known McCulloch for centuries, had fought at his side in countless battles, and trusted him, as he did all of his fellow warriors. McCulloch was the one spreading the word to the males of Otherworld, hoping to get them to take part in the revolution that would free them all from the shackles of second-class citizenry.

The other warrior stopped, looked up and down the hall, then leaned in to speak as though the walls had ears. And in this place it was true more often than not. Mab trusted no one—not her warriors, her servants or the women who served at the highest levels.

"I've been waiting for you."

"I've been busy," Culhane told him, his voice no more than a whispered hush of sound.

"As have we all," McCulloch muttered darkly. "So tell me now. Is it arranged?"

"Not yet." Culhane scowled at his old friend, hating that he was forced to admit he hadn't succeeded in winning Maggie over yet. He'd thought to have her trained and ready for battle quickly. But she was proving to be far less malleable than he'd at first hoped. He should have known, though. Even as a child she'd had a fierce will—otherwise she would have drowned in that stormy sea.

And what a waste, he told himself now, that would have been.

"Mab's becoming suspicious."

"Of what?"

"Of your absences." McCulloch scraped one big hand across the small, neatly trimmed beard he was so proud of. "She's asking too many questions. If she finds out about your mortal, you know what will happen."

"I do." He didn't want to think about it. Not only would the hope of Otherworld be gone, but Maggie would die. And that wasn't something he wanted to consider.

He grabbed the other warrior's arm and pulled him farther down the long, empty hall to a doorway. They stepped through into a fantastic courtyard as the door silently closed behind them. Water splashed and rippled in fountains; hillocks of flowers bursting with scent and color seemed to stretch on for miles; and tall trees, their branches heavy with colorful fruit, lined a golden walkway that glittered in the sun.

Culhane ignored the beauty surrounding them and led his old friend a distance from the palace walls. A soft breeze sifted past them, rustling the leaves of the trees, making the flowers dance and spill their scent. When he was sure it was safe to speak again, Culhane asked, "Has there been talk?"

"No," McCulloch said, lifting his chin and whipping his long, reddish-brown hair back from his face. Dark green eyes narrowed. "The warriors would never betray you, and none of them would speak of it to their women. The other males are quietly telling who they can about the coming battle, and we can trust that they will be careful.

"But you know Mab. Where there's a secret, she's like a mortal bloodhound. She will find out what's going on, and when she does . . ."

Culhane swore viciously at the very thought of what the Faery queen would do to Maggie. He shifted his gaze to the distance and blindly stared at the horizon where sky met meadow. He didn't see the beauty of his home, though. Instead he saw the small, silly house where Maggie Donovan slept. His mind drew up countless images of her, laughing, cursing, frowning. He heard her voice in the wind and could almost feel her skin beneath his hands.

He wouldn't allow Maggie to be destroyed.

"Did you hear something?" McCulloch demanded.

Culhane looked at his friend to see the other warrior in a crouch, scanning the sky with a sharp gaze. Instantly Culhane did the same. Male Faeries couldn't fly. But the women could. They couldn't risk a palace female flying past, overhearing their conversation and reporting it to Mab.

"I don't see anything," Culhane finally said, relaxing his guard.

"Nor do I," McCulloch admitted a heartbeat later. "But it pays to be careful."

"Understood."

"Remember when all we had to worry about was battle with the Tuatha De Danaan?" McCulloch asked with a strained laugh. "Warriors aren't bred for palace intrigue, Culhane. And we're not very good at waiting. It's best if you prepare your half-Fae and end this as soon as possible."

"It'll be done when she's ready and not before."

"Maybe," McCulloch mused, "what you need is a little help. What if I were to pay Maggie Donovan a visit? See if I could convince her to—"

Culhane shot him a venomous glare. The thought of another warrior around Maggie filled him with a rage he couldn't explain, even to himself. It was enough that the feeling was there.

"Perhaps not," the other warrior said, clearly enjoying himself as he held up both hands and took a step back. "Want to keep her for yourself, is that it?"

Yet more annoyance. In his long life he'd never felt more of it than he had since Maggie's Fae blood had awakened. It seemed that he was straddling a razor's edge all the time now, and one wrong step in either direction would see him sliced to ribbons.

"She's not a trophy to be kept," Culhane muttered darkly, though he wanted his hands on her badly. "She's a weapon to be used." But even as he said it, he knew that wasn't all there was to it.

"Nothing more?" McCulloch wondered aloud, and then laughed when Culhane glared at him again. "Well, now, this is going to be more interesting than even I believed. The great Culhane brought low by a half-breed."

He scowled at his old friend, though he didn't bother denying the accusation. What would be the point? McCulloch wouldn't believe him, anyway. "That half-breed will soon be full Fae and your future queen, you braying troll."

McCulloch slapped Culhane on the back, a blow that would have sent a lesser man staggering into the bushes. "I may be a troll, old friend, but I don't dally with mortals."

Neither had Culhane.

Until recently.

Faery wars notwithstanding, Maggie still had jobs to complete. Days were ticking past faster than she would have believed, and she was being forced to fight for the time she needed to complete her contracts.

Every moment she wasn't training, Bezel was complaining about her lack of conviction. Well, she had plenty of conviction. But she also liked eating. Thank God Grandpa had left her the house free and clear, so she didn't have to worry about a monthly house payment. But there were still property taxes to pay, and pesky little things like gas, lights and groceries.

"Damn pixie doesn't care what I've got going on. All he's interested in is bitching and eating all of my chocolate." Turns out Bezel had quite the sweet tooth. She'd gone through three bags of Dove milk chocolate in the last week, with no end in sight.

"Who's eating all of your chocolate, and what could they possibly be thinking?"

Carrie Hanover was thirty-five, divorced, with a two-year-old son. And, since coming home to Castle Bay after her marriage ended, she'd been the owner of the diner that Maggie was currently decorating with an idyllic scene of a New England winter, complete with a decorated tree in town square. She was also the woman who made the best chocolate-chip cookies in the universe.

Maggie looked down and grinned. Deciding to ignore Carrie's question, she asked one of her own instead: "What do you think?"

Stepping back to the curb so she could get the whole effect, Carrie pushed her blond bangs off her forehead, crossed her arms over her chest and took a long look. Just when Maggie was starting to worry a little, the other woman smiled.

"I think you work too cheap for being a genius and everything."

"This is why you're my favorite customer," Maggie

said, jumping off the stepladder and giving herself a mental pat on the back. Hadn't floated once all day.

"And I thought I was loved for my cookies." Carrie's smile broadened as she walked up and dropped one arm over Maggie's shoulders. "Why don't you come inside? I'll make you a latte to go with a platter of cookies."

"God bless you and all those you love," Maggie said with a heartfelt sigh. "Let me just put my stuff away and I'm so there."

Laughing, Carrie went back to work, and Maggie did the same. It didn't take her long. She had a system. Folding up the ladder and stuffing it into the trunk of her car, she walked back to gather her paints. They were neatly lined up in a couple of cleaning trays supposedly built to hold household supplies for the over-eager housewife. Plus, she had a couple of buckets of water that she used to mix paint and soak her brushes. Too full to transport, the buckets were easily rinsed out behind the diner, so Maggie picked them up and headed down the short, shadowy alley to the rear.

This is what she wanted: normalcy. Nothing out of the ordinary. Do a job, get paid, eat cookies, go home. Nice. Tidy.

"I've been watching you."

Maggie dropped the buckets, stood up and spun around so fast she made herself a little dizzy. When her eyeballs stopped jittering in her head, she focused on a young guy in torn jeans and a raggedy denim jacket standing just a few feet from her. His hair was black and hanging over his eyes, and his mouth was nothing more than a grim slash across his narrow face.

He looked every inch a thug, and Maggie knew instinctively that she was in trouble.

"Oh, God . . ." Maggie looked around for help, but naturally she was alone back here. *Perfect.* Fear was awakening inside her, closing down her lungs, squeezing her throat shut.

He shook his head a little as he noted her fear. "Oh, please. Don't flatter yourself. I don't want *you*. God, you're *human*. All I want is the power."

His eyes flashed black. The whites were gone completely, giving him an eerie, terrifying look that went well beyond that of a common street thug. He held up what looked like a gold jewelry box—what he was planning to trap her Fae power in—and it looked really out of place in his grubby hand.

Maggie fought for control. Fought to gather in the focus Bezel had been pounding into her head for the last few days. This was her first test, after all, and if she couldn't beat a scroungy demon, how would she last against Mab?

"You know," she said, scuttling along the wall of the diner, "you might want to rethink this whole thing. Remember how I killed a demon to get the power. . . ."

He frowned a little as if considering it, then shrugged. "You were lucky."

"Maybe." Seriously, where *was* everybody? What happened to alley people? Didn't they wander up and down peeking through trash cans anymore?

"Let's see what you got, then," he said, and swept in so fast she could hardly track his movement.

Maggie did the first thing she thought of: She kicked one of her buckets, hard, and it flew straight at the guy, drenching him in pastel-colored water that streamed off his face and soaked into his denim jacket.

Didn't slow him down much, but it did distract him.

"That's it, lady. You're toast." Disgusted, he wiped the colored water off his face with a sneer. Then he reached behind him, pulled a wicked-looking knife from somewhere and held it up so she could admire the gleam of the sharp blade. "One swipe and the dust is mine."

Closer.

Maggie saw her own death in his eyes and knew no one was coming to help. Culhane . . . where the hell was he? And why wasn't Bezel around? Didn't they say they were going to keep an eye on her? Well, where the hell were her stalkers when she needed them?

Wasn't it just like a man?

The demon made a grab for her, but Maggie dropped like a stone, avoiding his grasp; then she rolled over the asphalt and winced as some broken glass bit into her thigh. But she was up again a moment later, really wishing she'd taken some self-defense courses. First thing tomorrow, she promised herself. If she survived, she was going to make *somebody* teach her how to kick some ass.

"Just hold still, will ya?" He sounded irritated. "I don't have all day."

"Fine," she said, suddenly realizing that what she needed to do was get close to the knife-wielding whatever-he-was. It was a risk, because, hello? *Knife.* But what choice did she have? She couldn't run all the way home with this guy on her heels. In the first place she'd never make it. She was way too out of shape. In the second place she wasn't about to take this freak back to her house, where he could get a shot at Nora and Eileen.

So she stood her ground despite the fact that her knees were knocking. Lifting her chin, she stared into those blank black eyes and said, "Here I am. Come and get me."

He smiled. "Wise decision. Don't worry. I'll make it quick."

He would, too. She didn't have much time, but she used what she had to concentrate as furiously as she ever had before. Maggie drew a deep breath and gathered her power, her focus, what was left of her strength. As the smiling demon stepped in and pulled his arm back to deliver a killing blow, she concentrated with everything she had and blew a stream of gold Faery dust into his face.

His scream sliced as deeply as the knife might have if it hadn't fallen from his fist to clatter on the asphalt. Maggie lurched backward, slapped her hands to her ears and hunched into herself as the demon dropped to the dirty ground. Mouth open in a shriek, eyes wide, he stared unbelieving up at her as his body exploded into dust and the wind carried what was left of him down the alley.

The back door of the diner opened and Carrie's chef stuck his head out. "Maggie? Did I hear somebody screaming out here? You okay?"

Now *the cavalry shows up.* "Um, I think it was a cat."

"Big cat."

"You have no idea."

"You sure you're okay?"

"Yeah, Frank," she said, taking a long, deep breath to steady herself. "I'm fine. Thanks for checking."

"Hey, that's what we do around here. Look out for each other, right?"

"Right," she murmured as he ducked back into the kitchen and shut the door.

Gathering up her paint cans, Maggie noticed her hands were shaking. Probably not a good sign. The great chosen one all nervous over fighting a demon? What was going to happen to her when she had to fight Mab?

Would *she* be the one to end up a pile of dust blowing in the wind?

E

"Do it again!"

Maggie did as instructed. She dropped into a crouch

on the back lawn, swung one leg out and around, then jumped to her feet and punched both arms out in rapid succession.

"Congratulations," Bezel called out, and popped another chocolate bar into his big mouth. "First time you didn't land on your ass."

"What does Faery breath do to pixies, I wonder," Maggie mused, giving the ugly little man a dark look.

"Makes me uglier." He hooted.

"Hard to imagine."

"You're doing really well, Maggie." Nora applauded from the sidelines in the backyard. She was perched in a lawn chair with a glass of wine and a plate of cheese and crackers beside her. "Wasn't it wonderful of Quinn to offer to teach you to fight?"

"Yeah." Maggie glanced over at her newest teacher and noted in disgust that the Viking wasn't even breathing heavily. While she, on the other hand, wanted to ice her entire body. Her bruises had bruises. She had so never been meant to be a fighter. An eater, yes. A fighter, no.

But since her narrowly escaped fiasco with the alley demon yesterday, she'd made good on her vow to herself. She was learning how to defend herself. What good it would do her against Mab, who the hell knew? As mean as Bezel was, he just wasn't big enough to teach her any kind of defensive moves, so when Quinn volunteered she'd taken him up on it.

"Not bad," the Viking told her, coming closer. He kicked her feet wider apart, lifted her fisted hands and turned her body until she was standing at an angle to him. Funny, but for a stock market trader, he sure seemed to be good at this hand-to-hand stuff. "Don't open yourself to attack. Protect your body. Tuck your chin in. And remember, you can fly."

"God, I'm an *idiot*." Her hands dropped to her sides

as her jaw fell open. "For chrissakes, I *did* forget I could fly. Or float. Whatever. When that guy came at me I should have just tried to take off."

Nora took a sip of her wine. "Wouldn't that have been something to see? It's a shame Quinn can't teach you to fly, isn't it?"

"Yeah," Bezel chimed in. "But males can't fly—and he's not a Faery, so, hey."

Maggie stared at the pixie, then shifted a hard look to Quinn, who was ignoring all of them.

"Use your opponent's weight against them," he said. "Most won't expect it, and you can use surprise to your advantage." Demonstrating, he braced himself for an attack, thick arm muscles rippling. "Rush me."

"Hah! Right."

"Oh, Maggie, don't be a spoilsport; do it," Nora encouraged with a soft sigh and a smile for her lover. "He's only trying to help."

Looking at Quinn's tall, thick body, Maggie couldn't figure out why anyone in his right mind would ever attack him. But she'd asked for this, right? So with the setting sun blasting into her eyes, Maggie charged at Quinn. She didn't get far. Instantly he grabbed her arms, rolled backward and tossed her over his head to land on her back with a thud that jarred every bone in her body.

"Ooooh, that looked painful. . . ." Nora hurried to her.

"Wine," Maggie said faintly, holding up one limp hand.

Bezel's sharp laughter sliced at the air.

Sheba barked at the new game.

And Culhane stood in the shadows, shaking his head and watching.

"Why don't *you* teach her?"

Irritation raced up his throat as he turned to face the girl who'd crept up behind him. Again. Either Mag-

gie was splintering his attention drastically, or Eileen
Donovan was sneaky enough to be Fae herself.

He took a patient breath and noticed that here, near
the flowers and bushes lining Maggie's yard, the air
didn't taste quite as bad as it usually did. Eileen was
staring up at him, small in her T-shirt and jeans, and
the laces on one of her shoes were undone. She looked
harmless—but he'd already learned that Donovan
women were anything but.

"You move as quietly as the Fae," he told her.

She shrugged and gave him a smile. "You were busy
watching Aunt Maggie. So how come you're not the
one teaching her how to do all this stuff?"

"Because it's better for her to learn from someone
else."

"Why?"

"Because she doesn't trust me."

"Why?"

He blew out a breath, gave her a fierce frown that
had been known to startle Fae children into howls of
despair and said, "Enough questions. You shouldn't be
talking to me, anyway. I don't want the others to know
I'm here."

"Why?"

Culhane's head dropped in resignation. A small
laugh shot from his throat in spite of his best efforts. "If
you had been the chosen one, little warrior, the battle
would already be won."

Eileen grinned, clearly delighted, then walked closer
and stood beside him in the shadows to watch everyone else trying to get Maggie back on her feet. Maggie staggered a little, took a sip of Nora's wine, then
turned, tripped over Sheba and sprawled face-first on
the grass.

"It's not going well, then," Culhane muttered to no
one in particular.

"It would be if you were the one teaching her."

"Is that right, now?" Culhane was still watching the sad show on the lawn.

"Really . . ." Eileen's voice came out thoughtful now, and quiet. "I think you'd be better, because you're a much better Faery warrior than Quinn is. He spends way too much time kissing my mom."

Chapter Eight

*H*er words slammed into Culhane, shaking him down to his bones. How had she . . . ? He dropped to one knee beside her and studied those suddenly solemn Donovan eyes. Was she a seer? Did she have magic of her own? And what the bloody devil was he supposed to do about this new situation? Best to start slow. Find out what she knew and what she was guessing.

"What makes you think Quinn is Fae?"

She sighed, a patient sound and one that sent another ripple of annoyance through Culhane. Could it get worse than a mortal child pitying a Fae warrior?

"Grown-ups are all alike, Fae and human. Did you know that sixty percent of all adults don't pay attention to kids? Not even their *own*?" She shoved her hands into the pockets of her jeans. "Kids see a lot more than you think we do. Sometimes we even see stuff you guys miss completely."

Culhane shifted a look at the yard and couldn't help smiling as Maggie's worthless dog sat itself down on her behind. Maggie yelped, Bezel fell to the ground, rolling and laughing in that awful voice of his, and true to Eileen's description, Quinn was pulling Nora in for a kiss.

Clearly the other warrior was being distracted. Distracted enough that he'd allowed a child to see through his disguise.

But how had this one small human girl identified what was supposed to be a secret plan? What were her too-shrewd-for-her-age eyes noticing? "Tell me then, what do you see when you look, little one?"

She was staring at him when he turned his gaze back to hers. "I see the way Quinn watches Maggie. Just like you do. Like you're hoping she can do what you want her to do, and worried that she can't. Plus, he's big like you, and moves around as quiet as you. And I saw him breathe Faery dust once, too."

Ifreann take him, Culhane thought. A careful plan set in motion, only to be shattered by a bright child. "And have you told your mother or your aunt what you noticed?"

"Nah." She shrugged and stuck out her bottom lip for a brief pout. "They wouldn't believe me, anyway. They think I'm just a kid."

"We know better, don't we?" Culhane said softly.

"Yeah, we do."

She stood before him, proud and sure of herself, and so she should be. She'd seen what he and Quinn had hoped to keep hidden. And now Culhane had another problem: what to do with the child he both admired and resented.

"You, too, are part Fae," he reminded her, his voice hardly more than a whisper on the wind.

"I know," she said with a smile. "Very cool."

"And so, Eileen Donovan of the Fae . . ." He faced her solemnly, his gaze locking with hers. "Will you keep the secrets of the Fae warriors?"

"Why should I?"

A question for a question.

Clever and tricky child.

"For the sake of Otherworld. And for your own. It's

important, Eileen. A task that you alone can accomplish."

"Are you going to hurt Aunt Maggie?"

"I've no intention of causing her harm."

Her lip curled. "That's not really an answer."

"It's the best I have for you."

"And my mom?"

He blew out a breath, and a sparkle of Faery dust shone briefly in the shadows. "Your mother's in no danger from me."

She studied him for a long moment or two, then apparently approved of what she saw.

"Okay, then. I'll keep your secret." Eileen held out one small hand to him.

Culhane took it in a firm shake, according her the respect he would any other brave soul, then released her. "You would make a fine Fae warrior."

Eileen grinned. "Thanks, but I'd rather fly."

That night when the phone rang, Maggie lurched for it, caught her legs in a twist of sheet and slid to the floor. Her already-bruised hip banged into the old hardwood, and she could have sworn she saw stars glittering in the darkness.

"For God's sake—"

It was pitch-black outside her room and in. The middle of the night. The phone rang again, and this time her stomach slammed into her backbone and did a quick turn. Phone calls in the middle of the night were rarely good news.

She yanked and pulled at the sheet to set herself free, even as she wondered frantically who could be calling. If there was an emergency at Nora's her sister would have simply run across the yard and through the back door.

The shrill scream of the phone sounded again. Free

at last, Maggie staggered to her feet, snatched up the phone and plopped onto the bed. "Hello. What?"

"Hello to you too, Mags."

"Claire?" Blinking like a blind woman turned loose in traffic, Maggie reached for the bedside clock, stared at the bright red numbers and yelped, "It's one thirty in the morning. What's wrong? Are you dead?"

"Crap. Sorry about the time. Forgot all about the difference. It's nine thirty in Scotland."

"Oh, well, then, that's okay." Maggie dropped onto the bed, phone still clutched in her hand. "Is everything all right? You? Your parents?"

"We're all fine."

Maggie's gaze shifted to the window and the night beyond the glass. The wind was howling, and the bare branches of the oak where Bezel insisted on sleeping were dancing like pagans at a festival. Across the yard a single light burned in Nora's house, and from the foot of Maggie's bed came Sheba's insistent snore. Everything was good. Quiet. Peaceful.

So she relaxed. Knowing that Claire was fine, too, she could, if she forced her eyes to stay open, enjoy talking to the friend she missed so much. "I think I'm awake now, so tell me everything." She tugged the quilt her grandmother had made higher on her chest and pushed the pillow behind her back. "Start with, When are you coming home?"

Claire laughed a little. "According to my mother, I *am* home. But," she added, "I'll be back in Castle Bay in a week or so."

Since Claire was one of the rare artists who actually made a living with her painting, her time was her own. She had no employer to answer to and no employees to worry about. Maggie envied that in a way, but seen from another light it meant Claire had few ties to bind her to a place. And as someone who was entrenched firmly in her rut of family and home, Maggie didn't know how Claire managed to thrive so far from her own real home.

"Anyway," her friend said, jolting Maggie from her thoughts, "I didn't call just to talk."

"Something *is* wrong." Was that a cold draft of air sighing across her or just a twinge of worry? "What is it?"

"It's you, Mags." Claire's voice went softer. "I called to warn you."

"Warn me?" That cold she'd felt settled down on her now, chilling her skin, seeping into her bones. "About what?"

Claire sighed, and the ripple of it sounded across the phone lines despite the thousands of miles of ocean separating them. "Look, how long have we known each other?"

It felt like forever, but in reality . . . "About ten years."

"And in all that time," Claire said, her Scottish accent rolling softly over the words, "have you ever known me to be crazy?"

"Are we counting the night we got drunk and went to the lighthouse to chase ghosts?"

"No, we're not."

"Then no," Maggie said, trying to ignore the worry in Claire's voice. "You're not a nut. Any more so than any of us, that is." Besides, thinking about how weird her life had been lately, she had a far higher spot on the crazy ladder than Claire could lay claim to.

Still, Maggie hugged the quilt to her now and wished she had an electric blanket. Seriously, the cold she felt kept getting colder. "Just spit it out, okay?"

"Fine. I had a vision."

Maggie frowned. "A dream, you mean."

"No, a vision." Maggie could almost see her friend rubbing her bottom lip, a nervous habit Claire was forever indulging in. "I don't talk about this much, for obvious reasons, but the women in my family have the sight."

What was she supposed to say to that? "Uh-huh."

To someone else Claire shouted, "I'm telling her, Mother, if you'll leave me be. . . ." There was a brief pause. "Sorry. There's only the one phone in the bloody house and it's in the kitchen, and can you get a bleeding moment to yourself? No." Her voice shifted again, and became almost an apology. "Yes, Mother, I know you're only trying to help—"

"Yoo-hoo!" Maggie called into the phone.

"Right. Sorry again. Honest to God," she muttered, "now I remember why I moved thousands of miles away. So, it's the second sight we have," Claire said, talking faster now, as if she could sense Maggie's disbelief and was doing all she could to combat it. "It's a knowing, I guess. Of future events. Of things that might happen."

"You can see the future." One fist tightened on the quilt and held on as if she were in the front seat of a roller coaster, shooting down the tracks.

"Possible futures." Claire's voice was loud now, drowning out her mother in the background.

"Okay . . ." Maggie's gaze drifted to the window again and seemed to hone in on the single lamp burning in one of Nora's windows. A small beacon of light in the black.

"Fine," Claire told her, her voice almost as chilly as Maggie felt. "Don't believe me. Wouldn't be the first time I've lost a friend over this—"

"Who's lost? I'm right here! Didn't say I didn't believe you."

"You didn't have to."

"Claire." Maggie sighed her friend's name. "If you knew what's been going on around here for the last couple of weeks, you'd understand how a psychic pal is *not* going to make the headlines in my life."

"So you do, then . . . believe me?"

"Why not? Trust me. When I tell you what I've found out about me, you'll think I'm the fruitcake."

"What you found out?" Claire asked. "You mean about the Fae thing?"

"*Huh?*" Maggie gaped at the phone in her hand. "The Fae thing? You knew? How did you know and I didn't know?"

"Hello? Visions," Claire said patiently.

"Right. Vision girl." Maggie flopped back against her pillows; then something occurred to her and she bolted upright one more time. "You have *visions*? So did you see when Mike cheated on me?"

"Um . . ."

"Did you know when Todd was planning to up and leave?"

"Now, don't take on so—"

"And poor Joe. Did you see *that*?"

"What about Joe? I thought you broke up with him. You didn't take him back, did you?"

"No, I didn't take him back," Maggie snapped. "He was eaten!"

"Hmm. Didn't see that coming. What? Hold on, Mags." She must have half covered the phone with her hand. "For the love of God, Mother, I'll actually *pay* you to give me five bleeding minutes on the phone all by myself." When she came back, Claire said on a sigh, "Well, call that ten pounds well spent. So. Joe was eaten, you say? Demon?"

"How do you know about demons?"

"Visions."

"Right. But apparently not full-coverage visions, huh? I mean, you would have told me about Joe being snack food if you'd known, right?"

"God, yes. That's just so awful. Poor Joe."

"Poor Joe? Let's have a little sympathy for the inno-cent bystander, okay?" Maggie tucked her quilt tighter around her. "So these visions. There are some things you miss?"

"I didn't say they were perfect," she muttered. "And think about it: If I had told you about what losers Todd and Mike were, what then?"

"Then I'd have had a warning that they were creeps."

"Oh, please. Everyone but you knew that already."

"Nice. You still could have warned me." One more time, Maggie flopped back against her pillows.

"And of course you'd have believed me."

"Hmm." Maybe not. "Good point."

"Look, Mags, we can talk about the other stuff when I get home. I only called because of what I saw. It's about Nora."

Maggie sat up straight, the cold forgotten as the quilt pooled in her lap. "What about Nora?"

The phone went dead.

"Claire? Claire!" Maggie shook the damn receiver as if it would help, then scowled at it when the line remained silent. Stomach pitching wildly now, she fought back a rising tide of panic. "What the hell? Nora? She had a vision about Nora? What'd she see?"

"Maggie."

"Jesus H. Christ!" She threw the phone and shrieked as the air rippled in front of her and Culhane appeared out of nowhere. "*Stop* doing that! If you're trying to kill me, it'd be easier to just hit me over the head or something." She slapped one hand to her chest as if to keep her heart where it belonged.

"I wasn't meaning to scare you, only to talk with you."

"Well, I'm talking to my friend. Or I *was*." She scrambled to retrieve the phone, hung it up, then lifted the receiver to call Claire back. Find out what the hell she'd seen in her vision about Nora. But there was no dial tone.

"Damn it. What's wrong with the phones now?" She glanced across the yard at Nora's little house and thought about sprinting over there to check on her sister and her niece. But it was the middle of the night, and she knew they were fine.

Wasn't Quinn the Viking there? If there was danger, which Maggie didn't want to believe, then he was more than capable of dealing with it.

Unless, she told herself suddenly, *he* was the danger.

On that disturbing thought, she jumped out of bed, brushed past Culhane and grabbed her jeans off the easy chair beneath the window. "No time for you now, Culhane," she muttered. "I've got—"

He simply reached out, grabbed her upper arm and pulled her to him. The air left her in a rush when her chest hit his, and just for a second she forgot her sister, her niece, hell, even her own *name*. Staring up into his eyes she watched as those pale green eyes went even paler than normal until the soft color blended in with the whites and she felt as though she were staring through windows into eternity.

Oh, boy. Now she was getting as crazy as the world around her.

Heat she couldn't deny slipped through her, chasing away the cold that Claire's phone call had built, and for that she was grateful. But, she told herself as she tore her gaze from Culhane's captivating stare, she couldn't fall into a swoon here. She had to check on Nora. Eileen.

Family first, *then* her hormones.

"Let go."

"No." His grip on her shifted, tightened as he wrapped both strong arms around her middle.

Pressed along the length of him, Maggie felt every inch of his hard body, and her own responded instantly to a particularly hard region of his. Yet more heat pooled low in her belly, and need reared up inside her.

Her breath was strangling in her lungs as his big hands smoothed up and down her spine, defining her curves, sliding over the thin fabric of her nightgown.

She looked up at him again. Big mistake, she realized as she found herself lost in his eyes. Even through the haze of what she could only think of as a complete body meltdown, she felt him respond to her nearness. Felt his heartbeat quicken as hers did and knew, when he only strengthened his hold on her, that he was caught in whatever silken vise held her.

Oh, she'd never felt this before, and Maggie, for a moment, luxuriated in it. The fire, the heat, the soul-swamping *lust*.

She wanted him more than she'd ever wanted anyone or anything. But there was something else there, too. Beyond the lust. Beyond the heat. Beyond the yearning. There was a thread of connection that had been there from the moment they'd first met in her kitchen. From the first time he'd appeared in her life and told her that her world was about to change.

She didn't entirely trust it. Didn't know if she wanted it, even. But she wanted *him*. *That* there was no doubt about.

Here was the excitement she'd dreamed of. The man who could make her *feel* more than she'd ever thought to. The shake-up of the very comfortable rut she'd made for herself. And oh, she was ready.

So ready.

"You're beautiful in the moonlight," he said, and the soft music in his voice played on her every nerve ending. "It would be better, easier, if you weren't," he admitted, lifting one hand to stroke her hair back from her face, only to then touch his fingertips to the curve of her ear.

She shivered at the caress, but it was heat driving those shivers now, not the cold.

"I'm not beautiful," she argued. "Nora's the beauty. I'm the creative one."

He smiled, one of those rare actions that never failed to make Maggie's breathing catch in her throat.

"You've no idea what you are. Your beauty is there for anyone with an eye to see it. But it's not only your beauty that pulls at me." He sighed and let his hand drop to her waist. "It's what's in you. What you'll do. Who you'll be."

That stiffened her, made her step back from the heat, away from the want. Locking her gaze with his, she asked, "And if I'm not what you think I am? If I can't do what you expect, then what?"

He shrugged, and she had to admire the slow ripple of muscle. "It's impossible. You are the one."

"I don't want to be the one," she murmured, and her voice was lost in the darkness. Half turning from him, she looked out the window and focused again on that solitary light burning in Nora's window.

Two weeks ago she'd known who she was, what she was. Now that had been stripped away, and she didn't have any idea as to what was left. Was she still Maggie Donovan? Or had the Faery dust already begun turning her into someone . . . something else? And if she wasn't Maggie, then who was she?

"You wonder," he said, moving up behind her, laying his big hands on her shoulders until she felt both the weight and the warmth of him sliding into her. "You wonder what comes after."

She lifted her chin, trying to push her doubts and worries aside. But they remained, niggling at her, tugging at her until she responded the only way she could. "You're the one with the private pipeline to the future—why don't you tell me?"

"Possible futures," he reminded her, using the same words her friend had just a few minutes ago.

Remembering Claire and the phone dying on her and Nora in danger . . . "You have to leave. I have to go see Nora."

"Not now."

"Yes, now. Don't tell me what to do." Maggie pushed her hair back and stabbed her index finger at him. "You may be some hotshot warrior where you come from, but here you're only a guy who shows up without being invited—too damned often—to be a pain in my ass."

"Maggie—"

"Go away." *Please go away*, her brain pleaded. She didn't need to be drawn to him, to the very man who'd tossed her life upside down. She didn't have time for a man in her life, and if she did, she sure wouldn't be picking a guy who could appear and disappear whenever the hell he wanted to. "I mean it, Culhane, go away."

He only sighed. "Your training's begun, and still you don't believe. Your power grows, and still you won't listen. Perhaps it's time you *see*."

Moving for her jeans, she glanced at him. "See what? No, don't tell me. I don't want to know. Go away. I have to get dressed and—"

He didn't listen, simply waved one hand in front of her, and just like that, Maggie was dressed: jeans, dark green sweater, even her tennis shoes were neatly tied.

"Impressive," she finally said.

"It's time for you to see," he repeated. "I should have done this earlier; I realize that. But I wanted you to have time to understand what's happening to you. Now I know you won't truly comprehend it until you've seen for yourself."

"Seen *what*?"

He only shook his head, wrapped her in his arms and tucked her head beneath his chin. Maggie knew she should have tried to push away—for all the good it would have done her. He was huge, after all. Way stronger than she was. Then there was the simple, humiliating truth that she *liked* him holding her. Liked the way he felt pressed along her body. Liked the way it made her feel.

All of those thoughts and more flashed through her brain in an instant as the air around them seemed to shimmer. Maggie's vision blurred as swirls of color and shapes dazzled her eyes. She felt wind sliding past her, and a sense of movement.

Okay, this was new.

Instinctively she closed her eyes, clung to Culhane, and felt his arms around her tighten in response.

Moments later, when all movement stopped, when the wind blowing around them ceased, Maggie cautiously opened her eyes again. She almost wished she hadn't.

"Okay," she said, more to herself than him, "we're *so* not in Kansas anymore."

"Kansas?" He frowned at her.

She gave him a wry smile. "I guess not everyone's seen *that* movie. Never mind. Where are we?"

"You know where we are," he said, his voice low and close to her ear. "*This* is Otherworld."

Culhane hadn't planned to bring her here so soon. And certainly not at this moment. But he'd been watching her as she slept, then had heard the telephone conversation with her friend. He'd had to end it, hadn't he? He couldn't have Maggie interfering with his plans for Nora. Even now Quinn was making the move Culhane had decided was necessary. Soon Maggie would know what the stakes in the battle were.

But he would be the one to tell her, not her friend.

So he'd blanked the phone, tapped the power with his own and shut the blasted thing down. After that he'd had no choice but to adjust his plan. Keeping Maggie with him now was the only way he knew to bring it all home to her. To show her what was needed.

What she was meant for.

Now Culhane looked at his home through her eyes as she turned in a slow, deliberate circle, trying to take it all in. She had no way of knowing that Otherworld was as large as her own. That she couldn't see the whole of it at once.

His gaze slid over what was, to him, the familiar, and he wondered what she thought. Roads paved with silver bricks wound through the heart of the city and shone bright under noonday sunlight. Trees as old as time spread heavy branches out, entwining one with another until bridges were formed, linking the trees and the homes within them. Windows, carved into the tree trunks themselves, marked the homes of both pixie and Faery.

In the distance shining buildings speared up from flower-laden ground, looking like magic wands. In the far distance, dominating all below it, rose the crystal towers of Mab's palace, bright in the glare of the suns.

When Maggie turned toward him, an expression of pure astonishment on her features, he cupped her face in his hands. His thumbs brushed across her cheeks and sparked fires under his skin. As a look of shock and bewilderment crossed her face, he knew she felt it, too.

The feel of her beneath his hands was heat and more. There was magic here. A kind he didn't want. A kind he hadn't planned on. A kind he couldn't—didn't even want to—ignore.

He'd sensed the beginnings of a bond between them even when she was no more than a child. Hadn't he felt the threads connecting them, stretching and pulling, though loosely then? Hadn't he guessed those years ago that her destiny was more than just the saving of Otherworld?

In centuries of living, fighting, protecting his people, Culhane had never felt for a woman what Maggie Donovan incited inside him. She made him want. Made him desire. Made him need.

And he was still unsure what he thought about that.

Brushing those more-than-disturbing thoughts aside, Culhane focused his attention on the here, the now, the essential.

"It's beautiful." She turned in his arms, looked up into his eyes and narrowed her own as she did. "But why am I here? Why'd you bring me here, Culhane? This isn't my world."

"It will be soon." He shook his head. "Frown at me if you must and deny it if you can, but you feel the power growing within you, and that you can't ignore forever."

She stepped back, as she seemed to do more often than he'd like. "I'm not talking about my so-called powers," she said. "I'm talking about you taking me off to fairy-tale land. I don't belong here. This isn't my place. I already have my world. My life. My family. Heck, my *dog*."

"If Mab isn't stopped, what makes you think that family, that world, will be safe from her?"

"Why would she care about us? She has all of this." She swept one arm out to encompass the glimmer and shine of Otherworld. "In my world people don't even know Mab exists. They think of her as a legend. Lucky bastards."

"This place won't be enough for her forever. She knows there are other places, other dimensions. Over the centuries she's grown more and more dissatisfied. Her own greed will spur her on to take what she doesn't already have. And she'll want *all* the worlds under her reign."

Still frowning, still denying, she flattened her mouth into a thin, tight line. As stubborn in her own way as

Mab herself, Maggie wouldn't acknowledge the truth unless it was thrown in her face. Which was why Culhane had had to bring her here.

He grabbed her before she could skip out of reach, and when she tried to pull away he only tightened his grip. Drawing her in close, he stared into her eyes. "You wonder what the future is? Where Mab's ambitions will take her? Then see it now for yourself."

He turned her to one side, waved his hand, and the air shifted, swirled, reality bending. Otherworld dropped away as an assortment of images rose up from the fog and produced other realities.

Here the Faery war bled into Maggie's world. Here people were screaming, cut down in the streets as demons and Fae alike fought for supremacy. The humans didn't stand a chance. The powerful beings from Otherworld slashed and burned and took what they wanted, leaving only charred rubble in their wake.

The scents, the sounds, the images were so clear, so real, Maggie trembled in his arms.

"Oh, my God."

Culhane ended the demonstration and waited until she lifted her gaze to him before speaking. "She'll do it, Maggie. Believe me. If not now, then soon. Mab will eventually want it all."

"How am I supposed to stop a Faery queen, Culhane?" She scraped her hands up and down her arms, a nervous habit he'd noticed her indulging in often. "She's a *queen*, for God's sake. And I'm—" She stopped, laughed shortly and admitted, "I'm no threat to her and you know it. I can't be the one you want. I can't be your destined whatever. If I were I'd know it, wouldn't I? Wouldn't I be stronger or braver or—"

"You are all you need to be, Maggie Donovan. You must trust me that it will be more than enough. You've only to believe. To try."

She blew out a breath and turned her gaze back to the vast, shining sweep of Otherworld. Her voice, when it came again, was tired, soft. "Say I do believe—hypothetically. How do I fight her and win?"

"We're going to work on that while you're here," he said.

"While I'm here? I can't stay here indefinitely. I have to go home. Nora and Eileen . . . not to mention Sheba—"

"Won't miss you."

One dark red eyebrow lifted. "Thanks very much."

Now he smiled. That sharp tongue of hers was never far away. "I meant only that they won't notice your absence. Time moves differently here. You'll be home before they know you've gone."

"Right." She nodded. "Eileen told me that, too." She glanced at one of the closest trees, this one laden with golden fruits that begged to be plucked and eaten. She slid a glance at Culhane, and he could almost see the fast-moving thoughts whirling through her mind. "Eileen also mentioned something about how you can't eat or drink anything in Otherworld or you're trapped here for a hundred years."

Laughing outright, Culhane reached up, tore a fruit from a low-hanging branch and offered it to her, still smiling. "That's as much a lie as pixies being tiny, pretty creatures. Your people know nothing of us. We left your world so long ago that the legends that have survived have been so changed, so twisted, they hardly hold more than a glimmer of truth."

"Well, sure, you'd say that. I eat an apple and boom—your prisoner."

He bit into the fruit himself and chewed while she watched, still unconvinced. After he swallowed, he sighed. "You can starve yourself if you've a mind to, Maggie. You'll decide that for yourself. But the simple truth is, whether you eat or drink means nothing here.

We trap who we wish—for our own reasons. Food has nothing to do with it."

"How do I know that?"

"Woman, do you really believe I need a piece of fruit to trap you? I don't. You're here now. And here you'll stay until I say you leave."

Chapter Nine

*M*aggie stayed at Culhane's side, because seriously, what choice did she have? Not a good thing when
the only soul you know in a place is the man who's just
told you he's as good as kidnapped you.

Unless she could find a way out on her own, she was
pretty much stuck with Culhane.

"Don't stare," he muttered, draping one arm around
her shoulder and drawing her into the shadows of yet
another ancient, spreading tree.

"How can I not?" she whispered just as fiercely. "It's
not every day I see women *flying*, for God's sake."

Or, she thought, herds of pixie children shrieking
and darting through the branches of the trees. Or Fae
men shimmering in and out of existence at the blink of
an eye. How the hell did they keep track of everybody
when they were forever disappearing or launching
into the sky? Childcare here had to be a bitch.

Everywhere she looked, there was something new
to be dazzled or astounded by. Hard to believe that a
completely separate and wildly different world existed
right alongside her own. It made Maggie wish she'd
read more science fiction.

The trees, Fae versions of condo living, were everywhere. Shining silver roads twisted and roped their

way up hills so green and lush it almost hurt to look at them. And at the very crest of the biggest hill was a crystal palace that glistened like polished diamonds in the midday sun.

Make that *suns*.

Plural.

Two suns for Otherworld.

Even the air was different. Cleaner, with a thick, foresty scent. The sky looked different, too. It seemed bigger somehow, and it was a shade of blue Maggie didn't think she'd ever be able to duplicate with paints.

The people—the Fae, she reminded herself—didn't seem all that different from those she knew. Well, except for the whole flying-and-disappearing-into-a-ripple-of-air thing. They laughed, they shopped, they scolded their children.

Which just went to show, she guessed, that people were pretty much the same wherever you happened to find them. Even if they weren't people so much as . . . Faeries.

The problem here was, Maggie told herself, that knowing the Fae were so much like her own family and neighbors made it that much more difficult to turn her back on all of this. How could she tell Culhane to go find himself another chosen one after seeing his world? Now she knew it was real. That it was just as important to the Fae as her own world was to her.

How was she supposed to pretend to not care?

Her stomach churned, and Maggie knew it wasn't the piece of fruit she'd eaten despite Eileen's warnings because, let's face it, she never turned down food, threat or no threat. No, it was sheer terror turning her stomach into a pit of frothing nausea. Dread.

Not to mention a lot of self-doubt.

She was supposed to save not only Otherworld but her *own* world? How in the hell was that possible?

"You're talking to yourself."

"What?" Maggie frowned at him. "No, I'm not. I'm thinking."

"Out loud. Others are noticing."

"Oh, well," she said, drawing those two words out long enough to be their own sentence. "Can't have that. Pixies in trees and Faeries flying are okay, but hey, let's not *talk*. Wouldn't want to look weird or anything."

Beside her Culhane hissed out a breath, and somehow that made Maggie feel better. Hell, if she was going to be in a death-spiral tizzy, then he could be, too. Why should *he* have it easy?

He grabbed her arm, dragged her off the silver brick road—the Wizard of Oz should have had silver; very pretty—and into a narrow space between two of the elm tree condos.

Backing her up against the closest tree, he loomed over her, and Maggie didn't know whether to be pissed or to give in to the lust scratching at her throat. Apparently it didn't matter that he made her mad. She still wanted him. But for now she settled for being pissed.

"Knock it off, okay?" She shoved at his chest with all the success she would have had pushing a train off its tracks. "I've had a rough couple of weeks, and you're not making it any easier."

"It *isn't* easy. That's the point," he said, practically biting off every word. "You can't draw attention to yourself while you're here. If Mab discovers you're in Otherworld, she'll kill you before you have a chance to fight her for the throne."

"Then why the hell am I here?" Maggie threw a couple of frantic glances around her, then remembered to look up, too. Flying Faeries, pixie children scampering through trees . . . God, there was no way to be sure they weren't being overheard. Watched.

Finally she turned her gaze back to Culhane, and when

she spoke again, she kept it quiet. "If it'll be so easy for her to kill me now, what'll make it different later?"

"You'll have more access to your powers. They grow daily."

"So you keep saying. But big deal. Who cares if they're growing? If I don't know how to use 'em, what good are they?"

"You will. You're learning."

"Sure, how to breathe on demons." She pushed at him again, but it was useless. "I'm guessing that's not going to work on Mab."

"No," he admitted, and looked over his shoulder at the crowds of Fae moving through Otherworld. "But you'll have more. Know more." He looked back at her. "Besides, strength alone isn't the only way to win a battle."

"Strange talk from a warrior."

"Warriors more than anyone know that sometimes luck plays the most important part in battle readiness."

Maggie slumped against the tree and didn't even notice how the rough bark scratched her skin through her sweater. "I don't know if you've been paying attention, Culhane, but lately my luck sucks."

&

"She's not what I expected."

Culhane shot McCulloch a hard look. "What does that mean?"

The other warrior's eyes lit with humor, but he was smart enough not to smile. "Only that I thought the chosen one would be big. Strong. Have a face like an ax blade and a body the size of mine."

Culhane didn't know whether to defend Maggie or apologize. He looked out into the main room of his house and watched as she wandered in a slow circle, taking in everything. He hadn't meant to bring her here. Never considered bringing her to his home. Yet here, at least, no one would see her. At least, no one who would tell Mab.

Here in Culhane's rooms at the Warrior's Conclave, Maggie was surrounded by warriors who would defend her presence in the hopes that she might actually lead the revolution they all wanted.

"If you like," McCulloch offered, "while you tend to your duties, I'll see that Maggie is kept . . . entertained."

Culhane shot his friend a look hard enough to drill holes in his body. "She stays here. Alone, if I'm not with her."

"Is that wise?" the other warrior asked. "Isn't it better for her to meet the rest of us?"

"She did meet you all last night." He'd watched her as she laughed and talked with his fellow warriors, and he'd quietly steamed that she never laughed like that with him. She didn't look at the others with the same gleam of suspicion in her eyes. She hadn't treated any of the others as she did him—as if he were the enemy.

McCulloch frowned. "Did she say anything about that?"

She always had something to say, Culhane told himself. And after meeting a roomful of Fenian warriors, Maggie hadn't disappointed him.

"Your friends are gorgeous," she'd said, astonished as the last of the warriors left them in peace. "I mean, seriously good-looking. Aren't there any ugly Faeries?"

"No, we leave ugliness for the pixies."

"Good plan." Then she'd looked up at him and smiled at his glowering frown. "Hey, you're not worried, are you? Well, don't be. You're way better-looking than your friends. Plus, there's the whole sexy frowning thing you do."

Culhane shook his head at the memory and didn't want to admit even to himself that he'd enjoyed her words more than he should have. It had taken the sting out of the fact that she'd seemed to enjoy herself so with the warriors. Though it wasn't important what she thought of him, he thought. The only important matter now was Maggie's training—and the battle with Mab.

"Even though her ears aren't wholly pointed, she's a fine-looking part-Fae," McCulloch mused again.

Gritting his teeth, Culhane pointed out, "What she looks like has nothing to do with the prophecy."

"True enough," his friend agreed with a slow smile, "but for myself, better to have a chosen one who's pleasing to look at. After all, if things go as you planned, she'll be our next queen."

"She will," Culhane said, and even to his own ears it sounded like a vow. One he had every intention of seeing come to fruition. "Once she's on the throne we'll finally have a voice in ruling Otherworld."

"Through you as her consort, of course."

"Of course." That had always been the idea. Rule from behind the scenes. Bend Maggie to his will and see to it that the changes necessary to his world were made. Although now he was beginning to see that "bending" Maggie wasn't going to be as easy as he'd thought when they first went into this. Still, she would listen to him. He was almost sure of it.

It was a good plan.

"Thousands of years we've taken to get to this point," McCulloch said, turning his head to look at the woman eating her way through a bowl of fruit. He shook his head. "Now it's all come down to a mortal woman who talks too much and is always hungry."

"She's not wholly mortal anymore." Culhane watched her pick up a pale blue pear and take a bite. "She's Fae. Or soon will be."

"Will it be enough?"

A question Culhane didn't want to entertain.

⚜

Maggie's stay in Otherworld had so far been pretty boring. Okay, the scenery was nice. And she wasn't talking about the view out the window. Culhane's fellow warriors looked like they could be headliners at Chippendale's or something. Maybe a classier place than that. These guys were impossible-to-describe gorgeous. There wasn't a single ugly Fae warrior in the tree.

Yes, tree.

She was living in a gigantic tree with windows overlooking a fast-moving river and a thick, dark green forest beyond. Probably a pixie housing project. Culhane's rooms were big; round, of course; and furnished with all the comfort of a prison cell.

There didn't seem to be a soft surface anywhere. But then, she thought, big, tough warriors probably weren't interested in *comfy*. But she was. Even the chairs were plain wood, and her butt would have given a lot for a pillow.

Pushing up and out of the chair she'd been planted in most of the day, Maggie walked to where Culhane sat at a table, studying maps.

"Can't we go outside?"

"Too dangerous."

"I'm bored."

"Practice your training."

"Uh-huh." She blew out a frustrated breath. "That'll happen."

When he scowled at her briefly, she pointed out, "We're in a *tree*, Culhane. How'm I supposed to practice flips and falls inside a tree, for God's sake? Besides, I don't have anyone to practice *on*, remember? To practice fighting you really sort of need an opponent. I want to go home. I miss Nora. And Eileen and Sheba. Hell, I even miss *Bezel*."

"You've only been here two days."

"Feels like longer." She turned away, walked back to the window and looked out at the river again. She'd spent a lot of her time the last couple of days doing that. Captivated by the rush and flow of the river, she wondered where it led—and how she could get there.

"Why bring me to Otherworld if all you're going to do is lock me up in your house?"

He leaned one arm on the table. "You needed to meet the warriors who will fight for you once you're queen. You needed to see the world that hangs in the balance. You needed to *know* that this is not a game. Not a choice."

All right, she'd give him that. Up until he'd swept her into Otherworld, Maggie had managed to convince herself that there was still a way out for her. That the world of the Fae had nothing to do with her life. That she could walk away whenever she wanted and reclaim the life she'd once thought so routine.

But the truth was, there was no backing out.

Otherworld was real. And beautiful. Filled with beings going about *their* ruts. How was she supposed to ignore them now that she knew they existed? But damn, she couldn't just sit in a tree for much longer without going ape shit.

Whirling around, she planted both hands on her hips. "Come on. Let's do something."

"You are worse than a pixie."

She grinned. "Good. Insults. At least it's conversation."

He sighed, leaned back in his chair and kicked his long legs out in front of him. "I've never known anyone who talks as much as you do."

She ignored that. After all, he was right. She *did* talk a lot. "So, tell me about this place."

"It's Otherworld. I have told you."

"No," she said slowly and patiently, "this particular place. All of these warriors. Is this a guys-only tree?"

"We live in one place, yes. We train together—"

"Training again."

He ignored her. "We work together."

"But no girls allowed?"

"There are no female warriors," he acknowledged.

"Why not?" She wandered the circumference of his tree room again. "Seems to me that a flying warrior would be a good thing in battle."

"Female Fae don't fight." By the look in his eyes, he was astonished she'd even considered it.

"Have you ever asked them?"

His frown deepened. She wouldn't have thought that possible.

"No, we haven't."

"Never know till you ask." She stopped, looked at a lethal-looking sword hanging on the wall, then moved on. "So how long have you lived here?"

"Since I became a warrior."

"So. Long time?"

"Yes."

"How long?" Maggie tilted her head and looked at him. Culhane might appear to be about thirty-five, but she knew damn well he was older. He was always talking about *centuries*. She'd just never thought about how much older he really was.

"Millennia."

Staggered, Maggie stared at him. "I suck at math, but even I know that's at least a thousand years."

"More."

"My God, Culhane . . ." Maggie shook her head, took a step toward him, then stopped again. "*More?* You're really old. Seriously old."

A sneering smile touched his mouth, then was gone

again in an instant. "Yes and you, in comparison, are hardly more than an infant."

"Yeah?" Maggie walked closer, her gaze on his. When she reached the table she planted both hands on the cool wood surface and leaned in toward him. Just as she'd expected, his gaze dropped to her breasts. "Well, I've seen the way you look at me, old man, so I'm guessing you're what we call a cradle robber."

He looked up into her eyes. "I don't know what you're talking about."

"Sure you don't."

He pushed one hand through his thick black hair, and just for a second Maggie considered doing it for him.

"What are you thinking now?"

"Hmm?" She smiled. "Nothing." Nothing she was willing to admit. Nope. If he could pretend that there was nothing going on between them, then she could, too. Damned if she'd be the first to admit that she *really* wanted to get him into bed. Heck, she didn't even want to admit to *herself* that she liked—okay, maybe more than liked—him. Much easier all the way around to keep this on the level of simple lust.

Besides, she was twisted up into knots only because she was trapped in a tree! What she needed was to get out. To do something. *Anything*.

Abruptly he stood up from the table. "I'll help you with your training."

"You?" Maggie grinned up at him. "The great Fenian warrior is going to train me like a common pixie?"

Steel was in his spine, but amusement in his eyes. "Bezel is no common pixie."

"That's good to know. God, thinking about a whole race of pixies like Bezel is just too much."

"On that, at least," he said with an almost elegant bow, "we agree."

Moving around the room, he pushed his furniture out of the way until the center of the room was bare but for a rug the color of spring grass. "Now we'll train."

Maggie grinned as he came toward her. Lifting both hands, she said, "Then show me what you got, old man."

Chapter Ten

He charged her, coming in low and fast. Caught in his eyes, Maggie waited until he was almost atop her before she shifted her balance, sliding out of his reach and moving to stand behind him.

"Very nice," he said with a brief nod. "But I could have stopped you if I'd wished."

"Yeah." Maggie grinned and kept moving, sidestepping, watching him. "That's what they all say."

His lips quirked slightly. "You think you can outdo a Fae warrior?"

"Took you out with a milk jug, if I remember it right."

He winced. "That was different."

Probably not a good idea to taunt a warrior. But come on. He was just so tauntable. So damn sure of himself in everything. Though, she had to admit, with reason.

He was circling her now like a tiger watching its prey. His pale green eyes were fixed on her as if measuring, judging what move she might make next.

Her insides fisted as Maggie felt the power of his stare slicing through her. His features were flat, expressionless. Impossible to read, and Maggie suddenly realized what a formidable enemy Culhane would make.

Facing him on a battlefield would have been seriously intimidating. Hell, facing him here in a tree, knowing he was on her side, was pretty damn fearsome.

"You're thinking."

"Don't sound so surprised," she quipped, still moving, keeping her position directly opposite him.

"But you're *not* thinking about battle tactics."

"Hello, have you met me? Glass painter. Not exactly a soldier."

"You have to be."

"Oh." She stopped and dropped her fists to her hips. "Okay. Why didn't you say so? I'll just push my mental 'soldier' button and be right with you."

He rushed her in a movement so fast it blurred the air around him. Maggie didn't even think. She reacted instinctively. When Culhane got close enough she reached out, grabbed two fistsfuls of his shirt and let herself drop. She rolled, using her feet against his midriff to toss him over her shoulder and slam him into the wall behind her.

"Wow!" Maggie stood up quickly, looked down at him and grinned like a loon. "Did you *see* that? Did you see what I did there?"

"Yes," he assured her, jumping to his feet. "I saw." He stretched his neck. "And felt."

"You're way bigger than me, Culhane. How did I throw you that hard?"

Irritation flashed briefly in his eyes and warred with admiration. "As I said, your power grows."

"Yeah, but . . . *damn.*"

He rubbed the back of his head. "You hold the power of five slain Fae. As that dust overtakes you, your strength will be much greater than that of the average Fae."

"Stronger than you, too?"

His mouth flattened. "Perhaps."

"Hmm. Not happy about that, are we?"

"Of course I am happy."

"He said with a snarl."

Culhane straightened up to his full, very impressive height and looked down at her. "You did what I'd hoped you would do. The fact that you were able to throw me is a good sign. You're not only coming into your strength, but you're becoming more comfortable with it."

"No, I'm not." Okay, yes, it was cool tossing Culhane across the room. But comfortable? No. She didn't think she'd *ever* be comfortable with what he expected of her.

"It was one lucky toss," she said finally, and, keeping her gaze locked with his, she added, "You said yourself I'll need luck, but that's not going to be enough, and we both know it."

"You'll have what you need when you need it. I'll see to it."

"What? You're going to fix the fight?" Her teasing smile faded as she watched him. "You can't do that, can you?"

"The fight won't be 'fixed,' as you call it. But it will be on even ground."

"Even ground? Is that possible? Me against a queen?" She shook her head, looked around her at his home and then shifted her gaze back to his. "This is a mistake, Culhane, and you know it."

Culhane blew out a breath and told himself to be patient. To remember that she was new to this. But his own impatience for change made that difficult.

She was finally beginning to use her growing strength—as evidenced by the fall he'd just taken. Not that he couldn't have stopped her if he'd wanted to, he assured himself. He'd been taking it easy on her. Wanting her to feel the thrill of victory. Confidence was important. She needed to feel as if she were able to defeat the queen.

An internal voice called him the liar he was. He hadn't expected that she would react so swiftly, so smoothly to his attack. She'd surprised him—as she had since the moment they met.

She was more than he'd thought at first, but, more important, she was more than *she* believed herself to be. If she were to be queen, Maggie would need to feel that she'd earned it. That she was prepared for it. Bringing her to Otherworld was an important step.

Culhane had had to show her this place. Make her realize it was real and just as vital as her own world. She'd had to see the Fae and recognize that in many ways her people and his were much alike. How could he expect her to fight for a place and a people she didn't know and only half believed in?

Now it was time to take the next step in her training. To show her all that rested on her shoulders. To make it plain to her that there was no avoiding any of this. There was nowhere for her to go but forward.

To show her that this was what she had been born to do. Her entire life had been leading her to this time.

She was worried, and he'd noticed that the blue of her eyes darkened when her thoughts were rushing through her mind. She was thinking of the coming battle, of the future that stretched out in front of her, unknown, unseen. And she was mentally pulling back from the confidence she'd only just gained.

Perhaps the answer, then, was to silence her doubts with a distraction. Give her something else to consider. To fill her mind.

Culhane moved in closer, and with every step he took he saw her eyes narrow with suspicion.

"What're you doing?"

He gave her a slow smile. "Something we both want."

"Now hold on a second. . . ."

"You want me."

She blinked. "No ego problems here."

"This is not about ego," he told her, and came close enough to catch her scent. It was the simple truth. Yes, he knew she wanted him, but he wanted her as well. Never before had he been so haunted by a woman. Never before had a female reached him beyond the physical.

Maggie filled him, drawing him in, and in moments everything seemed to change. He'd thought to distract her. To use the heat between them for his own purposes. Now, though, his own want and need had eclipsed his desire to redirect Maggie Donovan's thoughts.

His hands itched to touch her.

"This is weird. Just a minute or two ago I was thinking that . . . Well, never mind. But now? Seriously, Culhane, this might not be such a good idea."

"Probably right," he agreed, knowing that he was already tempting the Fates by having Maggie here in Otherworld. The risk of Mab finding out about her before it was time was a dangerous one.

Here at the Warriors' Conclave, though, Maggie was safe from Mab. The tree was warded, heavy spells concealing the interior from prying eyes—even the queen's. Mab wouldn't find out about Maggie until the right moment—as long as Culhane continued to resist the urge to have Maggie in his bed. During sex their powers would blend, merge, link them together in a soul-deep connection that Mab would sense immediately because of the hold the Fae queen continued to have on Culhane.

He couldn't have her. Not yet. Not completely. Indulging in his fascination with this part-Fae would only be increasing the risk. And yet . . . her hair shone in the pale light of the fire burning in the hearth. Her skin seemed to glow. She backed up a step. Her mouth . . . She licked her lips, and Culhane wanted to follow that action with his own tongue.

"Why do you fight this?" he asked, actually curious. He'd felt her desire for him. Seen the way her eyes followed him. A man—Fae or mortal—knew when the woman he wanted returned that desire.

"It's not that I don't want to. . . ." She glanced behind her as if to make sure she wasn't about to trip on something. "It's just . . . I think there's enough going on right now, don't you? I mean, the whole 'chosen one' situation and, um . . ." She sidestepped, moving closer to the fire until she was backlit and the dark red of her hair shone and burned like an inferno. "I mean, if we, you know, did the hokey pokey or whatever—"

"Hokey pokey?"

"You know. Sex."

"Ah."

"Well, it would only make things even weirder, don't you think?"

"No," he said, still advancing, still watching her eyes, seeing the hunger she fought to deny glittering at him. Though he couldn't have her completely, he could have a taste of what would eventually come.

"Culhane . . ." She looked around as if seeking escape, but there was nowhere to go.

He moved in closer and saw emotions churning in her eyes. Her breath came fast and hard, and he knew her heartbeat was thundering in her chest. As was his.

"I must," he whispered, bending to her, cupping the back of her head in his palm. "I must at least have this, Maggie. *We* must."

"Oh yeah."

She closed her eyes as his mouth came down on hers. Instantly heat jolted through Culhane with the sizzling blast of a lightning strike. His body shook with the force of the desire pushing through him. This was more than he'd expected. More than he ever thought possible. He parted her lips with his tongue and she opened for him eagerly, tasting him as he tasted her. Their breath tangled, their tongues mated and their bodies yearned, pressing together, wanting, hungering.

Need pulsed into life in a desperate frenzy that forced Culhane to draw on every drop of his warrior's strength to resist it. He shifted his hold, wrapped his arms around her, his hands moving up and down her spine. His hips rocked against hers, and she lifted one leg to hook it around him, pulling him even closer.

The kiss became more frantic, more fierce. A groan slid from her throat and fed the flames already consuming Culhane. He was hard and ready and knew nothing would be more satisfying than burying himself inside her. It was all he could think of. All he could want.

And he couldn't have it. Not yet.

"Gods take me," he muttered thickly as he tore his mouth from hers. Body aching, he took a step away from her, as he didn't entirely trust himself to keep his distance. She stood there, her mouth swollen from his kiss, her eyes dazzled with passion and need, and he was forced to call a halt. For both their sakes.

"What?" She lifted one hand, pushed her hair back, then leaned against the wall as if she didn't have the strength to stand on her own. "That was ... amazing."

"For me, as well," he told her, keeping his gaze shuttered so that she couldn't see just how deeply he'd been affected.

"Okay." She nodded, pulled in a deep breath and then let it slide from her lungs again. "Clearly you were right. I do want you."

"I know." He lifted one hand to his mouth and rubbed at his lips gently, as if he could still feel her mouth on his.

"Yeah, I guess it's no secret now," she said. "But more than I want you, I want to go home, Culhane. I need to see my sister. My niece. Feed my dog. Paint some windows."

Impatient that she continued to cling to what she was destined to leave behind, he said, "That life is behind you."

Her eyes went wide. "No, it's not. It's *my* life, and I need to get back to it."

"You can't leave yet."

Now she frowned, and the desire in her eyes was swallowed by a flicker of anger that burned more brightly with every passing second. "See, that's where you're wrong. You can't keep me here."

"And how will you leave?" His gaze met hers for a long, heart-stopping moment, and what she saw in his eyes made her own narrow in response. She was understanding. Good.

"Make no mistake: Here I do as I please." His own desire was draining away as if it had never been, and Culhane could hardly believe that only a moment ago he'd been willing to risk the very future of his world for the chance to bury himself in her body. A Fenian warrior? Defender of the Fae? For centuries only his will, his sense of pride and duty had led him.

Why was it *now* that his own body chose to betray him?

Culhane would not be led around by his cock. He would keep Maggie Donovan in her place. Remind her who was in charge here. That she was in his world now. Until she'd proven herself to be committed to the cause for which she was born, she wouldn't be returning to her world.

Before he could speak, though, there was a soft sigh of sound behind him. Instincts rearing, Culhane spun about, dropping into a crouch before Maggie, prepared to meet whatever attack came. He waited, knife in hand, blade shining with the light from the fire as a doorway magically appeared in the air.

"*Ifreann* take you, Culhane!" Bezel's scratchy voice appeared before he did, and as he stepped through the magically drawn portal into Culhane's home the pixie was still shouting. "You could have told me Quinn was taking Nora today! This is trollshit. What am I supposed to tell the kid? You know I don't like kids. I don't even like my own!"

"Take Nora?"

The pixie stopped shouting long enough to look up at Maggie and then to slant a glance at Culhane's furious face.

"Oops." Bezel made as if to step back through the already closing portal, but Maggie was too fast for him. Pushing past Culhane, she grabbed the pixie by the collar of his green velvet suit and held on despite how he kicked and squirmed.

"What do you mean, Quinn took Nora?"

"Probably went to a movie," Bezel said, giving her a smile that displayed every one of his jagged teeth and in no way appeased her.

"Culhane?" Maggie turned on him.

"Bezel, you cursed excuse for a pixie, why are you here? How did you get into the Warriors' Conclave?"

Bezel waved a long hand at him. "Pixie play. Easy enough to go where I want when I want." His eyes narrowed. "And if you didn't want company, you should have told me what was going on!"

"You knew the plan."

"What plan?" Maggie demanded.

Neither of them looked at her.

"Not when it was going to happen!" Bezel twisted again to get free, but Maggie's fingers dug into the soft material of his jacket so he hung from her fingers as he would from a coatrack. " 'Great Fenian warrior,' my pixie ass! Didn't exactly keep me in the loop, did you?"

"Bezel—"

"What loop? What's happening, and where is Nora?" Maggie gave him a shake, but her fierce gaze was fixed on Culhane.

He still wouldn't look at her. Instead he spoke to Bezel. "They've gone, then?"

"Yeah." Bezel muttered something, then spoke up. "A little while ago. In the middle of the damn night. You know, I need my sleep. Pixies get meaner than drowning trolls when they don't get sleep."

"And usually you're such a ray of sunshine!" Maggie gave him a shake.

"Watch the velvet, okay? My wife made me this suit, and Fontana'll kill me if I let a human tear it. Trust me, you don't want to see my wife mad." Scowling fiercely enough to make every one of his numerous wrinkles become a chasm on his face, he said, "The kid woke me up. Startled me so bad I fell out of the damn tree. Nearly broke my neck."

"*Nearly* isn't good enough," Maggie pointed out. "What the hell is going on here?"

"Oh, for the sake of pixie children, leave me be," Bezel shouted up at her. "Shake me again and I'll barf. On *you*."

"Barf?"

"Heave," Bezel translated for Culhane.

"You're a disgusting little troll," he said.

"Hey, it's not my fault!" Bezel kicked to be free, and that didn't help either, since his huge feet were well above the floor. "Nobody tells me a damned thing."

"Is *someone* going to tell me what's happening to my family?"

Bezel shot Culhane a look that said clearly it was up to him to do the talking. If it weren't for the blasted pixie interfering, Culhane would have had another day or two to introduce her to the rest of Otherworld. To take her to the scholar. To expand her knowledge, her training, before throwing down his ultimatum.

Now there was no choice.

"Nora is with Quinn."

Maggie's eyes narrowed on him and glittered dangerously. "She wouldn't have left Eileen alone, so I'm guessing she didn't go willingly."

He nodded. "Quinn took her, according to my instructions."

Why?" Her eyes were cold. Hard. Like slivers of sapphire flashing with chilly light.

"As leverage," he said, lifting his chin and giving her the stare that had been known to quell uprisings. "We will keep your sister to ensure you do what you have to do."

"You're *blackmailing* me?"

"She won't be harmed."

"And I'm supposed to take your word for that?"

"Hey!" Bezel shouted. "Stop shaking me! Better yet, put me down and I'll get outta here. Sounds like you two need a minute alone."

"Not a chance, Tinker Bell."

"Hey!"

"Where is she?" Maggie looked at Culhane and demanded that he tell her.

"She's safe. For now. Quinn will protect her."

"Protect her."

Insulted, Culhane announced, "Quinn is a Fae warrior. One of my best."

"Uh-huh. So he's a Faery bastard, like you."

Bezel laughed, and the sound was appalling.

"The only one Nora needs protection from, Culhane, is *you*."

Culhane stepped in close, ignored the thrashing pixie, and stared into Maggie's eyes. Only moments ago they'd burned with passion. Now the cold was so deep, so complete, he felt the chill of her stare slide into his bones. Yet this was as it had to be. This was too important to risk Maggie losing her nerve, refusing to fight. As long as they held Nora he knew that Maggie would do whatever was necessary.

"Do you really believe that?" Now that the matter

was out, he decided to emphasize the importance of what was happening.

Keeping his gaze fixed on hers despite the hatred shining out at him, he started talking. "You were nearly killed by a demon."

"That was about me, not Nora."

"There are other demons roaming your world. Rogue Fae, too, walking your streets, preying on humanity. *No one* in your plane of existence is safe."

"My family's not involved in this."

"Of course they are; don't be a fool. By reason of being your sister, not to mention part-Fae herself, Nora is a great prize. What better way to manipulate the chosen one than to hold her family hostage?"

"I guess you ought to know."

Bezel wheezed out a chuckle, and, irritated beyond reason, Culhane pried the little creature from Maggie's fingers and let him go. Turning to him, he ordered, "Go back to the house. Watch over Eileen."

"*Him?*" Maggie's outrage was clear in her shout. "You're sending Bezel to watch over Eileen?"

"I can do it," he said, brushing fussily at the lapels of his coat. "I got teenagers of my own. Said I don't *like* kids, not that I can't take care of 'em. I can handle her."

"What about everything else out there?" Maggie threw a venomous look at both of them. "If Nora's in danger, then so is Eileen."

"Please." Bezel snorted, then stroked his straggly beard with one hand. "Like I can't handle a pesky demon. A little pixie dust. A little magic. Don't worry about the kid," he said. "Looks like you got bigger problems right now."

She turned on Culhane again. "You took Nora to make sure I'd play your game."

He sighed. "Yes. You should be grateful."

"Oh yeah?" Stunned, she gave him a wide-eyed stare. "Why's that?"

"Nora is safer with Quinn than she would be at your home."

"I don't know whether to believe you or not," she admitted, and that barb hit home.

To a Fae warrior there was nothing more important than his honor. To have the woman he wanted question his word was an insult that stabbed at him.

He blew out an exasperated breath.

"Are we done?" Bezel snapped.

"Go," Culhane ordered.

The pixie drew a circle in the air with the tip of one finger, and a pale wash of gold light defined it. The air within the circle swirled and crackled with energy. Bezel tossed another look at Culhane. "Next time don't be so blasted stingy with the information, huh?"

Then he stepped through the portal and it closed up behind him, leaving Culhane and Maggie alone with only a cloud of simmering fury standing between them.

"You shouldn't have done this, Culhane."

"I shouldn't have had to," he corrected. "But with your sister under my protection I know you won't retreat. You'll fight now. And you'll win."

Her mouth flattened into a grim line. "I'll never forgive you for this."

"So be it," he said. Reaching for her, he took her shoulders in a hard, firm grip and loomed over her until she was forced to tip her head back to stare up into his eyes. "Know this, Maggie Donovan: I do what I must to protect my people. It is what I was bred for. What I have known for longer than you can even imagine."

"You had no right, you bastard."

She struggled in his grasp, but Culhane's grip on her was too strong for her to escape him until he wished it. "I make no apologies for doing my duty. I will use whom I must, *do* what I must to protect those who depend on me."

She went still as stone then. "What about Nora? What about me? We don't get your protection?"

"You do. You already have it. Nora is in no danger as long as—"

"I do what I'm told?" she finished for him.

He nodded. "You're angry."

"Damn straight."

"Good. Feed the fire of your fury. Lock it down deep inside you. Hold it close and allow it to burn."

"No problem." Reaching up, Maggie carefully peeled his hands from her shoulders. When he was no longer touching her, she turned her face up to his and looked into those pale eyes that were at once both familiar and strange. She'd thought the two of them were getting closer. Even half thought she could seriously fall for this Fae warrior with no sense of humor and a bad attitude.

Now, though, she knew the truth.

There was nothing between them.

Probably never had been. A part of her was sorry for that, because despite knowing what he'd done, what he *would* do, Maggie would miss what might have been.

"You hate me, I know," he said, and even the music in his voice sounded bitter to her now. "Use that hatred of me to help you find the strength to end this."

"I will," she promised, closing her heart to him, refusing to listen to the clamoring in her blood or the pounding of her heart. "Oh, and Culhane, if hatred is power, then let me tell you—I'm strong enough right now to defeat Mab without breaking a sweat."

"He's not as bad as you think."

Maggie forced a smile for McCulloch. The man was almost as tall as Culhane and nearly as gorgeous. His shoulders were broad, his dark red hair was practically the same shade as Maggie's own and he wore a neatly trimmed goatee. His dark green eyes were filled with understanding as he watched her.

As Culhane's friend, he obviously felt bound to defend him, but nothing he could say would take the sting out of what had happened.

"You're right," she said. "He's probably worse."

"Females," the warrior mused, "are ever a mystery to me." He walked with her through the garden toward a splash of sunshine breaking through the shade of the trees. "You know what his burdens are, yet you refuse to forgive him for doing only what he must."

"Y'know," Maggie said, stopping suddenly and forcing the warrior to do the same, "not really interested in his pain right now. Still too pissed to do anything but hope he's miserable."

"You have your wish." McCulloch gave her a half bow, took her arm and steered her once again toward that golden light within the dark shade of the forest. "He is torn between what he knows is right and what he desires."

"Still not making me feel any better." But then, nothing could. She hadn't seen Culhane since the day before. He'd left her in his rooms after their argument, and she'd had nothing to distract her from her thoughts, her worries, her fears. The damn Faery had lied to her. Kidnapped her. Stolen her sister. Was she supposed to be Saint Maggie or something and say, *All is forgiven*?

Well, screw that.

He wasn't forgiven. How could she forgive him when she knew that Nora was off somewhere with the Viking, and Eileen was alone with only a crabby pixie to watch out for her?

He'd screwed with her life. Messed with her family. Twisted her up inside until she spent every night wrapped in hot, erotic dreams of him, thanks to that spectacular, bone-searing, hormone-igniting kiss.

In spite of everything, she *missed* him, damn it.

She kicked a rock on the path and heard it scuttle off under the bushes. Then she turned a dark look on the warrior walking beside her. "Where are we going, anyway?"

"Sanctuary."

"What's that?"

"You'll see that soon enough."

"Cryptic. You're all so freaking cryptic. What is up with that?" Frustrated, Maggie demanded, "None of you can give me a straight answer. Is it a Fae thing or a warrior thing?" She paused. "Never mind. Probably a *male* thing."

His eyebrows lifted.

"How come you're the one taking me to this sanctuary, anyway?"

He shrugged, a simple motion that had his broad shoulders lifting and falling like Mount Everest during an earthquake. Seriously huge, these guys.

"It's easier for me to take you." He shot a guarded look about them, as if searching for hidden enemies. Apparently reassured, he continued. "Culhane is the leader of the warrior race. When he goes out he's noticed. And anyone he's with is noticed. No one is paying attention to where I go and what I do."

"Uh-huh. You believe what you want to. But the bottom line is, you're telling me that Culhane was too afraid to face me." Small consolation, but all things considered, she'd take it.

"A Fae warrior," McCulloch said, lifting his chin and firming his mouth, "fears nothing." He thought about it for a moment, then added, "Except perhaps for his woman."

That brought her up short. She pushed her hair out of her eyes and turned her face into the wind. "I'm *not* his woman, and how caveman does that sound, anyway?"

"Caveman?" He shook his head. "No matter. You are his woman, Maggie Donovan. Whether he knows it or not. I can see it in him."

"Then you need your eyes checked, big guy." Disgusted, she continued. "The only reason he wants me is because he needs me to fight Mab."

"That is only a part of it, I believe."

"Right." Her voice dripped sarcasm. "Culhane's crazy about me. That's why he's so nice. So understanding. So freaking *honest*."

"I've known Culhane from the beginning," McCulloch said softly.

"Beginning of what?"

He shrugged. "Beginning of all."

She couldn't prevent one word from slipping out. "Wow."

"As you say. It is a long time. I've never, before this, seen him concern himself with the feelings of others. Not even those he defends." He looked at her and said, "Always, his duty has been clear to him. This time, though, there's something else pulling at him. Making him hesitate to do what must be done. And I can only guess that something is *you*. He doesn't want to hurt you, even though he knows he may have to. You are . . . important to him."

If she was so freaking important, he wouldn't have set her up like he had. Wouldn't have used her own hormones against her. Hell, he was *seducing* her into being the Chosen One he wanted so badly. Then, just in case his seductive powers were a little lacking, he kidnapped her *sister* as a backup plan.

Oh yeah. Fae in love. Watch out.

"Oh, well, aren't I special." Maggie snorted. "Culhane's concerned that his kidnap/blackmail victim is upset. He's so worried that he's hurt me, he's holding my sister hostage. Wait. I feel a tear coming on. A Faery with a heart of gold, that's what he is, all right."

He laughed, and the booming roll of it thundered around her like a sudden storm. "You are just what Culhane needs, Maggie Donovan. He's spent too many millennia seeing nothing but fear and awe in the eyes of others."

"Fear and awe?" She poked McCulloch's chest with her index finger. "None of that here, let me tell you. And just so you know, I'm not interested in being what Culhane needs." *Liar, liar.* "The only thing I want from that no-good, lying Faery bastard is . . ." Problem: She didn't know what she wanted from him.

Well, not entirely true. She wanted to kick Culhane where it would hurt him for a century or two. And she wanted to yell at him some more. Then there was the fact that she just plain *wanted* him. Could that be more annoying?

Still chuckling, McCulloch said, "Ah, it's good to laugh again. There's been too little of it in Otherworld these last years."

Maggie didn't want to care; she really didn't. But she'd met the warriors, she'd seen the people, and damn it, she was getting drawn into this whether she liked it or not. Grumbling under her breath, she heard herself ask, "Is it really that bad here?"

He sighed. "Not if you're female. Queen Mab uses her warriors to fight her battles, but once the war is won she has no use for us. Other Fae males have no place at all in our society." His voice went to steel. "It must change."

"And I'm supposed to accomplish all that?"

McCulloch looked down at her and smiled. "You have only to complete your destiny. The rest will come."

There was more. There had to be. But just like Culhane, this warrior knew how to keep secrets. Seemed like she'd never get just a straight answer out of anybody.

Worse, even if they gave her a straight answer, she couldn't be sure she could believe them. What the hell kind of upside-down life had she toppled into?

This was all Joe's fault.

Dating a man-eating demon. Ending up a snack. What had he been thinking?

"Are you ready?"

She snapped out of it, looked up at the warrior and frowned. "Do I get a choice?"

"No."

"Then I'm ready."

He smiled as if he were enjoying himself, and hey, it was nice that *somebody* was. Then he drew a golden circle in the air, just as Bezel had to return to her world. The inside of the circle shuddered and shook, and the wind blowing from it was warm and smelled of lemons and flowers.

"Come, then. To Sanctuary. Perhaps you'll find your answers there."

She doubted it. McCulloch held out one hand to her, and Maggie glanced back over her shoulder at the tree where the warrior band lived. Culhane was probably there. Maybe he was even looking out his window to watch her disappear into a portal.

Well, if he was, she told herself, he wouldn't see her hesitate.

Taking McCulloch's hand, she stepped into the unknown.

Again.

&

"But where's Mom?" Eileen sat on the floor next to Sheba and Bezel and kept her gaze locked on the pixie. The house was dark but for one lamp and the flickering light of the muted television set. It was the middle of the night, and Eileen was a little more scared than she wanted to admit.

Her mom was gone, and so was Aunt Maggie, and they *never* left her alone. She glanced around, checking the shadows in the corners of the room as if to make sure there were no monsters about to spring out at her. Then she reminded herself she was almost thirteen and she shouldn't be acting like a baby or something.

After all, she wasn't *alone*, alone. She had Sheba. And Bezel.

"Quinn took her somewhere," the pixie said gruffly.

"Why?"

"Because." He didn't sound very happy about her questions, but Eileen knew that if you didn't ask, you never found out anything.

"Quinn's a Faery, too, isn't he?"

"Not much gets past you, does it?"

"Where'd he take Mom?"

"What am I?" Bezel demanded. "Answer pixie? I'm sitting right here with you. How the *Ifreann* do I know where they went? Does anybody tell me anything?"

Sheba whined and cuddled closer to him, and Bezel's long fingers stroked through the dog's fur, unconsciously soothing.

Eileen nodded in sympathy. "Nobody tells me anything, either."

"You're a kid." Bezel snorted and tugged at his wispy beard. "Nobody tells kids anything. Why would they? But I'm two thousand and seven."

"Really?" Eileen's eyes went wide as she was momentarily distracted. "You don't look that old."

Bezel preened a bit. "Well, I work out."

"Is Maggie with Nora, too?"

"No," Bezel said, clearly irritated. "She's with the 'Great Fenian Warrior' Culhane."

"Well, how come I don't get to go somewhere cool?" Her fears were slowly sliding away. After all, Bezel was here. It wasn't like she was completely alone. Plus, she was in her own house.

"How do I know?" He leaned back against the couch and crossed his big feet at the ankles.

"Well, it's not fair, that's all," she muttered, plucking at the hem of her cotton nightgown. "Thirty-three percent of all children who have their dreams quashed turn out badly."

"What?"

She sighed. "Mom and Aunt Maggie get to do things, and I'm stuck here."

"Welcome to my world."

"How long will they be gone?"

"Probably be back before morning," he grumbled.

"Really? Oh yeah. Time moves different for Faeries, huh?" The knot in her tummy started to go away as she realized everything was going to be okay. Her mom and Aunt Maggie would be back really soon. Maybe if they didn't come back until late tomorrow morning she wouldn't have to go to school. And since they weren't around now, they couldn't tell her to go back to bed. So she'd get to stay up as late as she wanted. That was good, too.

"Smart kid." Bezel pushed himself to his feet and held out one hand to the girl. "Look, I'll tell you what I know while we get something to eat, okay? Your mom buy some more of those cookies with the chocolate and marshmallows?"

"I think so." Eileen took his hand and stood up, then looked down at the pixie. "We can have cookies and milk."

"Ugh. Bovine lactation?" He shivered.

Eileen laughed, and the rest of that knot inside her dissolved. "Okay, you can have a Coke."

"Sounds good."

"Bezel?"

He sighed. *"What?"*

"If they're not all back by morning will you take me to Aunt Maggie?"

He scratched his chin, tipped his head to one side and considered the request. Finally he smiled. "Yeah, I can do that. Serve Culhane right for screwing with a pixie."

E

Sanctuary was a castle in the clouds.

Literally. There was no ground under it, which was enough to make a person uneasy at first. But after a few minutes Maggie got used to it. Pretty much.

"So, no ground at all?" she asked, looking out one of the wide windows that were kept open so that sweetly scented air could pass through the long halls lined with more books than she'd ever seen. Leaning out the window, Maggie stared down, down, *way* down, to the suggestion of green far below them.

"None," a voice that wasn't McCulloch's said from behind her.

Maggie whipped around fast, almost lost her balance and grabbed hold of the window jamb to keep her balance.

A tall, lean man with long blond hair and pale blue eyes smiled at her. "Best not to fall out the windows. It's quite a drop."

"Yeah," she said. "I noticed. Where's McCulloch?"

"Gone back to Otherworld."

"Fabulous. More disappearing Faeries. No wonder Mab hates those guys. Can't depend on 'em to stick around. Hey, wait a minute. Aren't we *in* Otherworld?"

"We're in Sanctuary," the man said, walking closer with a slow, easy grace that told Maggie he was completely comfortable with who and where he was.

He wore black slacks, an open-at-the-throat longsleeved white shirt and soft shoes that made only a whisper of sound on the silver-veined marble floor.

"You are Maggie Donovan," he said when he was no more than a foot away from her.

"That much I know," she said, a little hesitant at being dropped into yet another unfamiliar spot. "Who are you?"

"My name is Finn. I run Sanctuary."

He was gorgeous, too, which Maggie was beginning to expect. Every male she'd run into since falling down the rabbit hole was the stuff female fantasies were made of. His features were clean and sharp, his eyes thoughtful and his mouth moved easily into a smile.

Yes, very nice to look at, but there was none of the tingling sense of expectation that happened to her when she looked at Culhane. *Damn it.* Would have made her life easier if she'd been able to be attracted to someone else. *Anyone* else. *Blasted Faery.*

"Are you a warrior, too?" she asked, though she doubted the answer would be yes. He wasn't built like the other warriors. Though his shoulders were broad, he was more leanly muscled than the Fae bred to fight.

"No," he said, and smiled again as if he were reading her mind, which she really hoped he wasn't. "I'm a scholar and a wizard."

"Of course you are." She blinked up at him and shook her head a little. No point in being surprised. If she allowed that, she'd wander around with her mouth hanging open all the damn time. Faeries, pixies, demons and now *wizards.* "Well, you look way better than Dumbledore."

He grinned and gave her a brief bow. "Thank you. Wonderful books, those."

"Yeah, my niece, Eileen, loves 'em." So did Maggie. Of course, she'd always considered them *fiction.* She glanced out the window again and was nearly mesmerized by the soft, swirly movement of the wispy clouds sliding past. "So, Mr. Wizard, where exactly are we?"

"Everywhere and nowhere. Sanctuary exists out of normal time and space."

"Oh, good. Even more cryptic."

"Not at all. If you'll come with me, I'll explain what I can."

Well, where else would she go? Out the window? Maggie started moving and walked alongside him as he headed down the long, pale hallway. The walls were marble, too, but they weren't cold. Instead warmth radiated from them, welcoming. She caught the scents of lemon and flowers again and spotted vases filled with staggering bouquets of brilliantly colored flowers. And the lemons? She was willing to bet the smell came from the polish that had the miles of bookshelves gleaming in the soft light.

"Sanctuary's open to all and haven to all," Finn was saying, and Maggie reined in her thoughts and listened. "When the Fae enter Sanctuary, their powers are stripped from them and not returned until they leave again. No powers exist here but mine, so you're safe."

"I'm safe? With no powers?"

"In Sanctuary, yes. No one can harm you here."

Now that he mentioned it, Maggie did feel different. Lighter somehow, as if something had slipped off her shoulders. Apparently, that something was her powers. Shouldn't she be more pleased about that?

"I'm supposed to take your word for it that I'm safe from *you*?"

He grinned, and Maggie had to envy the Fae women. So far, every male in Otherworld was heart-stoppingly dazzling.

"You don't have anything to fear from me," Finn assured her. "You're here at Sanctuary to learn. Culhane asked me to show you the breadth of your powers and the depth of our need."

"Oh, man." She stopped and stared at him. "You, too?"

"I am male. Is it so hard to imagine where my sympathies would lie?"

"No, I guess not. Guys always stick together."

"True enough," he said, and led her into a cavernous room with a ceiling that had to be fifty feet high.

Across that ceiling spread a mural of such rich and deep colors, Maggie was caught in the sheer beauty of it. It depicted Otherworld, of course—the land, the people, the magic. Her artist's heart ached and in spite of everything she wished she were holding a paintbrush in her hand. She wanted to paint everything she'd seen. The warriors. The trees filled with windows. Sanctuary, surrounded by clouds.

But here she wasn't an artist.

Here she was expected to be a savior of some sort.

God help them all.

"These books," Finn said as she looked at him, "and the others in Sanctuary, hold all the knowledge of all the worlds."

"All?"

"Did you think there was only your plane and Otherworld?" He laughed. "No, there are many dimensions, many levels of existence, and each of them is peopled by beings as diverse as you've already seen."

She turned in a slow circle, examining the towering shelves of books. Of varying sizes and shapes and color, there were hundreds of thousands of books, and just thinking about reading them all made Maggie tired. "You expect me to read these? All of them?"

"Of course not. I'll give you the volumes you need. You'll study. You'll learn. And when the time is right you'll save Otherworld."

Confidence was good, she supposed. "Pretty sure of yourself, aren't you?"

"Sure of you, Maggie Donovan. I've seen the future.

What can come of it. You are at the heart of whatever change comes, good or bad."

"But no pressure." She rubbed her hands up and down her arms and, despite the warmth in the room, felt a bone-deep chill snake along her spine. How was she supposed to do this? How could any one person be responsible for so many?

Still smiling, Finn waved one hand and a dozen or more books, scattered all over the room, floated through the air and settled onto a long, polished table. He waved again and one of the bright floral chairs at the table slid out in welcome.

"Sit. Read. See for yourself what you are and what you can become."

*

After two days—Faery time, that is—in Sanctuary, Maggie felt as though she'd been in school for a century. Finn was determined to teach her as much as possible in whatever time they had.

"Mab has reigned unchallenged for more than three thousand years," Finn was saying as Maggie watched him. "In the beginning she was a fair enough ruler. She's always favored the female Fae, but that was to be expected."

Maggie's head was pounding. She braced her elbows on the tabletop and watched as Finn strode around the room. He should have been wearing a cloak or a pointed hat decorated with stars or something. A wizard in jeans somehow lacked . . . authority.

"Sometime into her reign, though, she changed." He stopped, fixed Maggie with a hard look and said, "She thought only of bolstering her own power. But for her warriors she surrounded herself only with females. Fae males were slowly pushed into the background until finally even they can't remember a time when things were different."

"So why'd they let it happen?"

"What could they do? Their own queen had declared them to be unimportant. Soon they began to believe it, as well." He walked faster, his strides long, powerful. Shoving his hands into his pockets, he shook his head in disgust as he talked. "Mab decreed that no male would hold a position of authority. She was the only law. And any who dared disagree with her were tossed into a demon dimension to fend for themselves."

"Nice." Maggie shifted uneasily on her chair. Was that what she could expect if she couldn't beat Mab?

As if sensing her thoughts, Finn walked across the room and stopped just opposite her. "You will be a better queen. I've seen it."

"Uh-huh. Have you also seen that I don't really want to be a queen?"

"Yes," he told her, smiling. "But destiny is not something you can ignore."

Maggie wasn't so sure.

Chapter Eleven

"Concentrate on the act of drawing your power from your center and directing it through your fingertips."

"Thought I didn't have power here." She grinned as she teased him.

"You don't." Finn sighed as if he were as exhausted as she felt. "I'm . . . lending you some of mine so that you can practice, remember?"

Maggie stared at Finn for a long moment. He was practically unteaseable. If she were teasing Culhane like this, he'd have been shouting at her by now. Strange that she missed that.

Letting her thoughts of Culhane go, she paid attention to Finn again. With her borrowed power she'd already learned how to peek into possible futures, and how to fly—well, almost. She had the floating thing down; it was steering that was giving her problems. Finn had also shown her how to throw blasts of energy from her fingertips—like tiny lightning bolts—and how to direct a flow of Faery dust with her breath so that another demon wouldn't be getting the drop on her anytime soon.

He was a better teacher than Bezel; that was for damn sure. Finn didn't lose his temper and call her names for motivation. And God knew, he was easier to look at.

But thoughts of Bezel brought on thoughts of home. Of her family. Nora was never far from her mind, and Maggie tortured herself daily by wondering what sort of prison Culhane had locked her in, the no-good bastard Faery from *Ifreann*.

Which was exactly where she hoped Culhane was at the moment, in Faery hell, frying his Faery ass.

"You're not listening."

"What? Oh. No, guess I wasn't." As usual Culhane had been up front in her brain. Even furious with the damn Faery she couldn't stop thinking about him. How nuts was that? Shaking her head, Maggie sat up straight, focused on Finn and said, "Totally here now. Really."

He gave her a pleased smile, teacher to recalcitrant student. "All right, then. To draw a portal, you have to concentrate not only on focusing your power but on where you want to go." To demonstrate, he sketched out a golden circle in the air, and instantly it was filled with that swirl of crackling power and air. "This one, for example, leads to Otherworld. But portals can open anywhere. That's why it's important that you focus."

"Wait a minute." Maggie frowned as his words echoed in her mind. Then she stood up, came around the table and stopped in front of him. "You're telling me that if I don't concentrate on where I'm going I could end up anywhere?"

"Do you not use a map when traveling?"

"No," she said, surprised at the question. "If I get lost, I stop for directions."

His head bowed in defeat, but it was only momentary. He closed the portal before looking at her and spoke patiently. Again. "Magic takes focus. Power isn't to be treated lightly. Having your destination fixed surely in your mind is the only way you can reach that destination. You wouldn't want to find yourself in a demon world, would you?"

"Hell, no," she said quickly. "But how'm I supposed to concentrate on my power and my destination and, oh, say, not floating away, all at the same time? I can multitask with the best of them, but that's insane."

"It will get easier the more you do it."

"Assuming," she pointed out with a lot of snark around the edges, "I don't land in a demon dimension on my first try and get eaten."

"You won't. I'll help you."

"This just gets crazier and crazier." Muttering under her breath, Maggie started walking. Didn't matter where she went; she just needed to move. She was here in Sanctuary to learn. To supposedly get more accustomed to the feel of power. To embrace the Fae within, so to speak. Instead she felt as though the weight of all the worlds were crashing down on her shoulders and threatening to crush her.

"You're not going to draw a portal, are you?"

"Now?" She glared at her teacher from across the room. "I'm not exactly in a 'concentrating' state of mind, you know?"

"There's not much time, Maggie," Finn told her in that patient tone that was sooo beginning to grate. "You must learn all you can."

"You know what? I'm full up," she declared, coming to a sudden stop. "That's the problem. You guys keep stuffing me full of more and more information, and I can't hold it all, okay? I mean, seriously, disk full already. No more information. No more training. No more practicing for a fight I don't want to have and am in no way ready for. No more kidnapped sisters and nasty pixies. No more patient wizards and hunky Faeries."

"Maggie, you're overwrought."

"I'm over-, under- and around wrought," she shouted, just managing to keep from yanking at her hair. "If I don't get out of here and go home fast I'm going to explode, and it won't be pretty; trust me on this." She jabbed her index finger at him from across the room and was surprised to see a tiny bolt of blue-tinged lightning flash from that finger. "Sorry; forgot about that. And *see*? All these powers aren't making me safe! They're making me dangerous!"

"If you'll only calm down," Finn said, brushing at the burned spot on his white linen shirt, "you'll see that you had excellent aim, at least."

"Stop being so PATIENT!" She felt her already stretched-tight nerves go that one extra notch that had them snapping inside her. "God, don't you ever shout? Get pissy? Get flat-out, kick-a-wall furious?"

"What purpose would that serve?" He sounded genuinely curious, and Maggie knew they would *never* be close.

"That's it." She laughed and heard the vague tinge of hysteria in the sound. "I'm done. I can't stay here. I can't do any more than I have. That's it, Finn. You're a nice wizard and everything, but I don't even want to look at you anymore."

"Culhane said that—"

"*Culhane?*" Just the sound of the Faery's name made her want to scream again. Why wasn't he here to be yelled at? Why was she left with only a too-patient wizard to dump on? Finn wasn't the source of her anger; she knew that, despite the fact that if she had to listen to that condescending, patronizing tone of his for much longer she was going to wring his wizard neck. "Do you really think I care what Culhane has to say?"

"I think we should take a break," he said carefully, keeping one eye on her as he moved toward the door. "Perhaps tomorrow we might—"

"No tomorrow!" She took a few steps toward him, fists clenched at her sides, and noticed that the great and powerful Oz backed up real quick. "No tonight. No yesterday or next week or next year . . . School's out, Finn. Until I see Culhane, in person, we don't have anything else to talk about. *Capisce?"*

His calm, even features went tight momentarily, and Maggie wondered if he might actually yell. Then the moment passed.

Finn pulled in a deep breath and whipped one hand through the air. A portal appeared just to the right of him, and even from across the hall Maggie felt the power streaming from it. The air rushing from its heart was warm and smelled of the forest.

"There. A portal to the Warrior's Conclave. To Culhane. Go," Finn urged, his eyes a little wild. "Speak to the warrior, and when you're ready to finish your lessons, return."

"Finally." Maggie didn't hesitate. She didn't even spare the wizard another look as he left the room like a man running for his life. "Culhane, you blasted Faery, ready or not, here I come."

E

Culhane's sword clashed with another warrior's, and he felt the sting of the blow race up his arm. Metal rang against metal, making the kind of music a warrior lived for. Sweat streamed into Culhane's eyes, blurring his vision as he advanced and parried and advanced again.

Wind blew over the training grounds, and the other warriors gathered together roared their battle cries. Hundreds of swords were wielded by the most fearsome fighters in Otherworld. Dust kicked up from the ground, and from the trees came the shouts and hoots of pixies watching the warriors battle-test each other.

The practice field sat behind the Warriors' Conclave, and a high wall surrounded the area. Here the Fae warriors honed their battle skills and waited for the call from their queen.

Here Culhane had buried himself since Maggie had

left for Sanctuary. Here he'd driven himself and his men to the brink of exhaustion. They worked, they practiced, they trained so that Culhane would have no time to remember the look of betrayal in Maggie's eyes when she learned that he'd had her sister taken from her.

He refused to be swayed by the echo of her fury replaying in his mind. He'd done only what he'd had to and would do again. She must see that his devotion to this plan, to the future that only she could ensure, was unwavering.

He'd buried himself in the world he knew and tried to forget about the world she'd introduced him to. A world where he wanted a part-Fae woman enough to risk the future he was counting on.

A crackle of sound blew up, and light speared into his eyes as a portal opened in front of him. Culhane had barely registered the fact that Maggie was stepping over the threshold when he realized that the blade of his training partner's sword was slashing down toward her.

He shouted a warning she didn't catch and threw himself at her. Culhane covered her body with his as they hit the hard-packed dirt, and the violent jolt of their landing slammed through them both. He felt the swish of air as the blade sailed harmlessly past them and knew how close they'd all come to killing the very woman they needed.

From the trees pixies applauded as if they were watching a play. But around Culhane the warriors went silent and battle play ceased. Fury and relief tangled inside him, and Culhane stared down into Maggie's eyes and shouted, "By the halls of *Ifreann*, you could have been killed!"

Even through the red haze of anger, Culhane was only too aware of her lying beneath him, her breasts crushed against his chest, her legs and hips wiggling as she tried to escape, her hair spilled across the dirt in a dark red blanket. Her eyes snapped with all the fury he felt charging inside him, and her hands shoved at his chest.

"Get off me, you damn Faery!"

"Woman, you don't step into a portal without knowing where you're going!"

"Yeah, so Finn told me." She shoved again, and though it had no effect on him, Culhane moved anyway, getting to his feet and pulling her up to join him.

She brushed dirt off her jeans and out of her hair, and winced a little as she stretched her body, checking for broken bones. "He's the one who drew up that little energy-doorway thing. So blame him for sending me here. I told him I needed to see you, and here I am. I didn't expect a damn sword to . . ."

Her voice trailed off as she looked around, past Culhane's hard, cold features to the faces of the warriors surrounding her. The wind tossed her hair into her eyes, and she reached up to pluck it free. Then she shifted her gaze back to Culhane and her eyes narrowed. "I need to talk to you."

"Finn shouldn't have sent you." He glanced around the enclosure, uneasy with her presence. If Mab were to discover her . . .

"No," she agreed, stabbing at him with her forefinger. "Oh, sorry. Not used to the lightning-bolt thing yet." She patted out the flames on his shirt, then gave him an extra slap for good measure. "This is your fault, Culhane. You tricked me. Lied to me . . ."

Someone whistled. Someone coughed. Then the other warriors began drifting away silently, as if loath to remind her of their presence. Culhane spared them all a hard glare. Brothers in arms indeed.

"Come with me." He grabbed her arm and started for the Conclave.

She dug in her heels and yanked back, pulling herself free of his grasp. She looked surprised, but probably no more than he was. Her power and strength were growing.

"Not a chance. Not until we've talked."

"We will talk inside. Not out here."

"Why not? I *like* it here!" She jutted her chin out at him, and Culhane gritted his teeth in response.

Had he really been thinking that he'd missed her? Had he really been tempted at night with dreams of her? With recollections of the kiss that had served only to make him even hungrier for her than he had been before? A more infuriating woman he'd never met, *Ifreann* take them both.

His voice dropped as he moved in close to her. "You could be seen here by more than the pixies already enjoying the performance you're providing them."

She spun around and glanced at the high branches of the trees outside the walled field. Dozens of pixies, shouting, laughing, calling names, lined the limbs of those trees like needles on a cactus.

When she turned to face him again, he saw that she'd calmed somewhat. "Fine. Inside."

He grabbed her, held her close and shifted before she could change her mind again. In the blink of an eye they were standing in the center of Culhane's home, staring at each other.

His arms were around her, his mouth only a breath from hers. The taste of her was still rich and thick inside him, tempting him to taste again. To feel the pull of what lay between them. She looked up at him, and Culhane imagined that those eyes went soft with desire, with pliancy. Then she kicked him.

He let her go and moved back, refusing to give in to the urge to rub his shin. "What was that for?"

"Take your pick!" She folded her arms across her chest and tapped the toe of one shoe against the hardwood floor. "For taking my sister? For lying to me? For dumping me in Sanctuary with a wizard who's so patient it made me insane? For not caring enough to see how I'm doing, to even bother to check in?"

"You told me you never wanted to see me again," he reminded her, enjoying the fire of her outburst. By the gods, he'd missed her.

"*Now* you listen to me?" Walking up to him, Maggie locked her gaze with his, and Culhane saw fire in those sapphire depths. When she was close enough she fisted her hands in his shirt. "No more lies, Culhane," she said, her voice as tight as the grip on his shirt. "No more bullshit or evasions or half-truths. From now on I want to know everything, got it?"

"I can't make you that promise." He almost wished he could. But if a lie was needed, then he would use it. Culhane lived life by his own code. He couldn't change who he was—even if he wished to, not even for her. He covered her hands with his. "I do what must be done, Maggie. I can do no less."

Her shoulders slumped and her grip on his shirt loosened up a little. "Yeah, I get that. I don't like it, but I get it. And I'm getting that I have to do that, too. But damn it, how am I supposed to trust you if you keep lying to me?"

"Maybe trust is too much to ask," he said, his gaze moving over her features like a starving man surveying a food-laden table. He'd wanted her. Missed her. Now here she was.

"I'm asking anyway," she told him. The blue of her eyes darkened as she stared at him, and Culhane watched emotions flash and shift across their surfaces. "I want to trust you, Culhane. I want—"

"I want that, too," he admitted, his voice a hush in the quiet of the room. "I want . . ."

Maggie Donovan was the chosen one.

But she was more to him than that.

She was—

"Aunt Maggie!"

"*Ifreann!*"

Eileen's delighted voice shattered the intimate atmosphere and had Maggie pulling away from Culhane's grip to run to her niece. Arms empty, body burning, he watched the emotional scene and put his own needs, once again, aside.

Grabbing Eileen up in a hug, Maggie squeezed tight and grinned. Her niece's hair was wild and windblown, her eyes sparkling with excitement and her mouth turned up in a wide grin. The girl had never looked more beautiful to Maggie. "It's so good to see you, kiddo. But how'd you—"

Bezel jumped through the portal next and sent her an evil grin.

"Oh." Maggie looked at the pixie. "Of course."

"Did we interrupt something?" he asked with a cackle of glee riding just below his words. Sliding his glance from Maggie to Culhane and back again, he was clearly enjoying himself.

"What are you doing here?" Culhane's teeth were gritted tightly enough that his jaw muscles flexed when he spoke.

Bezel shrugged narrow shoulders. "I told the kid I'd bring her if you weren't back by morning."

"It's not morning yet in her world." Culhane's voice was soft and dangerous.

"Yeah. But we got bored. We ran outta cookies, and there's nothing new on TV."

"Maggie, it was so cool," Eileen was saying. "The world got all blurry and there was wind and a kind of roaring noise—"

"That was me," Bezel snapped. "You were pulling my hair."

"Oh. Sorry. Woooowwww . . ." The girl dragged a

single word into five or six syllables as she did a slow turn, looking around Culhane's home. "You live in a *tree*?"

"Take her back," Culhane ordered.

"This is awesome," Eileen said, wandering the room, staring out the window and shouting, "Look! More pixies! Hello!"

"Take her back now," Culhane muttered.

"Oh, are those guys warriors, too? Like you and Quinn? Do they know where my mom is? Hey, you guys!" Eileen leaned out the window, waving one arm. Maggie raced across the room to grab hold of her.

"No can do, oh Mighty Fenian Pain in My Pixie Ass." Bezel tugged at the lapels of his velvet suit, then smoothed one gnarled hand over his silvery hair. "Got a chance to see the wife and I'm taking it. Going to spend some *quality* time with Fontana while I'm here," he said, his eyebrows wriggling on his forehead like silver snakes. "Been gone a long time now, if you catch my drift."

"Ew." Maggie made a face, dragged Eileen back from the window, then looked at Culhane. "I'll take Eileen home. And I'm going with her."

"You can't."

Maggie stared up at him and read a hunger in his eyes that she shared. Despite what he'd done, what he'd been to her, she was still drawn to him like metal shavings to a magnet. Or maybe it was more like a mosquito to a bug zapper.

He was dangerous. Untrustworthy. With his own agenda.

And he made her feel things she'd never known before. Made her want to feel more. Which was exactly why she needed to go home. She'd just had a big, hairy sign dropped on her head. Maybe she should listen to it. "You're a big believer in fate, right? Destiny?"

He nodded, still scowling, his features tight.

"Then think about it. Eileen and Bezel showing up. Now. Just in time to stop us from—"

"From what?" Eileen demanded.

Bezel snorted.

"Never mind," Maggie told her niece, deliberately ignoring the pixie. "The point is, fate stepped in. Signs like that are pretty hard to ignore. We're not supposed to be . . . you know. At least, not now."

"You mean sex?" Eileen prompted. "I've had the health course, Aunt Maggie, I'm not a kid."

"Speaking of sex . . ." Bezel murmured.

"No one's speaking of sex," Maggie told him.

"I am. Fontana's gonna be glad to see me," he assured her.

"Someone should be," Culhane muttered.

"Funny, Fenian."

"Did you know that twenty-two percent of all children who don't learn about the facts of life from their parents end up in halfway houses?"

"WHAT?" Maggie just stared at her. "You just said you took the health course!"

"Yes, but families should talk about sex openly," Eileen said, sliding an interested look at Culhane. "It's much healthier."

"You're healthy enough," Maggie told her, and made a mental note to talk to Nora about this. If Nora ever came home. If Maggie got home in one piece. If Mab didn't kill her and take over the world.

If, if, if . . .

"Don't go," Culhane said. "Not yet."

"Yeah, let's stay, Aunt Maggie. If we're not going to talk about sex, you could show me Otherworld."

Culhane sighed as his chin hit his chest. "Very well. I suppose you might as well go now, after all."

"Tough luck for you, Culhane." Bezel patted the other man's arm until the warrior snarled at him. "Hey, at least one of us is getting lucky."

"Pay no attention to him."

"I never do," Culhane assured Maggie.

"Good. And I'm sorry things went a little wonky here in the last few minutes."

"Hah!" Bezel shook his head.

"Don't you have a wife to go visit?" Maggie demanded.

"I'm in no hurry. Things're just getting entertaining around here."

"Eileen, go look out the window," Maggie said. "Take Bezel with you. And no leaning!"

When her niece and the pixie were safely across the room, Maggie moved in close to Culhane. He looked so cute. And frustrated. Which she really understood. *God.* She was thinking nice things about him again, and she wasn't entirely sure she was through being mad at him. Oh, it was really time to leave. But before she went . . .

"Answer me one question," she said, cutting off whatever he might have said. "Is Nora safe? Be honest with me about this, Culhane, or I promise you when I am queen I'll make your next millennia a living *Ifreann.*"

"She's safe," he said. "And will remain so—"

"As long as I do what I'm supposed to."

"Yes."

"Forty-two percent of blackmailers end up getting shot in alleys, you know." Eileen wandered back from the window.

"Where does she get this stuff, anyway?" Bezel demanded.

"I need a few days, Culhane. Am I going to have to fight you for them?"

The silence in the room pulsed with life—animosity and curiosity, heat and need. Finally, though, Culhane spoke up and shattered it. "No. You can go."

He lifted one hand to open a portal, but Maggie stopped him with a grin.

"Wait," she said. "Let me do it."

"You can do one, Maggie?" Eileen moved in close. "Ohmigod, that's so amazing. Can I learn how to do it, too? Because I've been doing research on genetics, and since I've got Fae blood—"

The portal opened, and the air shifted and again streamed with the crackle and hiss of energy. Maggie turned to Culhane with a victorious smile on her face. "See? I'm learning."

"Oh yeah. Impressive as male Fae flying," Bezel said with a groan.

"What?"

"It's a portal to Netherworld," Culhane said with a sigh as he closed the pulse of energy and opened a new one. "You must concentrate, Maggie. Or all will be lost."

"Netherworld—what's Netherworld?" Eileen was still talking when Maggie gave her a gentle push through the doorway.

"I can learn to concentrate, Culhane," Maggie told him just before she went through after her niece. "Can you learn to tell me the truth?"

Then she was gone, and the light went with her.

Culhane stared at the spot where the portal had been, a frown twisting his mouth.

"Gotta admit," Bezel said, "the girl asks good questions."

"Get out."

"Gone."

&

"Is Mom in Otherworld?"

"I think so." Maggie sat on the edge of the bed and smoothed Eileen's hair back from her face.

"You think she's okay?"

Looking into her niece's worried eyes, Maggie forced a smile. "Yeah, I'm sure she's okay. They're just protecting her, really."

Eileen gave her an oh-please look. "I'm not stupid, Aunt Maggie. I was actually there when you were talking to Culhane about this. I know they took my mom to make sure you'd do what they told you to."

Maggie blew out a breath, leaned in and planted a kiss on the girl's forehead. When she straightened up again, she said, "You hear too much."

"Forty-five percent of all information is discovered while eavesdropping."

She smiled. "Is that right? So did you 'discover' anything else interesting lately?"

She flopped over onto her side, tucked her right hand under her cheek and looked thoughtful. "Not really. I mean, before Mom left, I heard Quinn telling her that Mab was getting suspicious about Culhane being in our world so much."

"Really?" Did Culhane know that? Of course, he'd have to know. So what did that mean for Maggie? Was Mab more likely to pop over here and investigate why one of her warriors was spending so much time with mortals? Would that bring the big fight on sooner?

And if it did, was Maggie ready?

Um, no.

"You're gonna do what Culhane wants so Mom can come home, right?"

Maggie pushed her troubling thoughts aside and looked down at her niece. Eileen was so smart, so together, sometimes Maggie forgot that she really was just a little girl. And right now that child was worried about her mom. Who could blame her?

"Course I am," she said. "You think I'm going to waste all this training Bezel and Culhane have been putting me through?"

"Can you beat her?" Eileen asked.

Hmm. Sometimes honesty wasn't the best policy, Maggie thought. For all of her bitching at Culhane to tell the truth, she knew she couldn't tell her niece that she was scared shitless about fighting Mab.

"You bet I can," she said, and gave Eileen a smile that was filled with all the confidence she wasn't feeling.

The girl sighed, sat up and wrapped her arms around Maggie for a big hug. Then she whispered, "You're not a very good liar, you know?"

"I'll work on it." Laying Eileen back down, Maggie reached over, turned off the bedside lamp and said, "Try not to worry about this stuff, okay? I'm going to take care of Mab, and your mom is okay. I'm sure of it."

Nora screamed loud enough to rattle the windows carved into the walls of the tree.

"Oh, my God, that was incredible." Body still shuddering with the force of her climax, Nora dropped onto Quinn's bare chest with a heavy sigh.

Propping herself up on her elbows, she looked down into her lover's eyes and smiled. "I think it was even better than the last one."

"It's all you, my love." Quinn reached up, smoothed Nora's short, choppy hair with his fingers, then drew her head down to his for a kiss.

"Mmmm . . . I really shouldn't be enjoying myself so much. I *am* a hostage. But maybe it's that Norwegian syndrome thing. . . ." She paused, thought about it for a second and asked, "Norwegian? Swedish? Doesn't matter."

She drew one hand down his chest, defining Quinn's sculpted muscles with the tips of her fingers. The Faery was truly a work of art. And a magician in bed. Nora'd never experienced anything like what happened to her during sex with Quinn. And she couldn't seem to get enough of him. All she wanted to do was touch and be touched, to taste and be tasted, to—

Guilt reared its ugly head and took a huge bite of Nora.

"Oh, God. I'm a horrible mother. I'm here, in Otherworld, having incredible sex with my very own personal Faery, and my *daughter* is at home with a pixie. What does that say about me? My life?" Her forehead hit Quinn's chest, and she felt the rumble of a chuckle roll through him. "You think this is funny?"

"No, I think you are adorable."

She lifted her head and blinked back a sudden, unexpected sheen of tears. "You do?"

He caught her face between his palms and stared into her eyes. "I do. You are a wonderful mother. You are raising a bright, happy child. You have been kidnapped and held hostage, and yet your concerns are for her."

"Well," Nora said grudgingly, "I haven't exactly been tortured, have I?"

"That is still to come."

A tingle of expectation swept through her and disappeared in another rush of guilt. "I should be furious with you. Taking me away. Leaving Eileen behind . . ."

"It is safer for her to be at home than here in Otherworld. The more humans here, the greater the chance of Mab discovering your presence. That would mean danger for all of us."

"Fine, fine." She'd heard those arguments when he'd first taken her through the portal. Though it still bothered her that Eileen was in one world while she was in a different one, what he said made sense. On a level that didn't even touch the guilt factor.

She squirmed a little and felt Quinn's body, still locked deep within her, stir to life again. Nora sighed, trying to ignore the building heat inside, and said, "You're *sure* she's safe?"

"The little one is fine. Didn't we look into a portal only a short while ago? The child is with Bezel, who will protect her with his life, or answer to the Fenian warriors."

Nora chewed at her bottom lip. "There is that. But it's been days and—" She stopped. "Time. It moves differently here, so really, I've only been gone about an hour or two, right?"

"Yes." He smiled up at her and lifted his hips.

Nora groaned softly, closed her eyes and swallowed a gulp. "So really, my being here is no worse than me going on a date at home and having a sitter come in to be with Eileen."

He skimmed one hand down the length of her back and over the curve of her bottom. His fingers kneaded her soft flesh, caressed her Faery tattoo, and a fresh bolt of need shot through Nora so fast it stole her breath.

"Precisely."

"Okay," she said, sighing now as Quinn stroked his big hands up and down her spine, "then I'm not going to worry. For a while."

"Good. The little one is fine; I promise you." Quinn braced his hands at her hips and pulled her into a sitting position atop him.

Nora sighed, arched her back and let him fill her completely.

"Now, my hostage," he murmured, "I fear it's time to search you for weapons again."

"Really?" Nora's eyes brightened. "But you just searched me a few minutes ago."

"I might have missed something," he said, eyes gleaming.

She swiveled her hips against him and watched his eyes flash with heat. "Well, then, it's best to be thorough."

"I am devoted to doing my duty," he said, and sat up to take one of her nipples into his mouth.

"Mmmm . . . I do love a man who loves his job."

Quinn flipped her suddenly onto her back and drove himself deep. Then, smiling, he whispered, "Work, work, work . . ."

Chapter Twelve

*A*fter getting Eileen settled into bed, Maggie went to her own room and stretched out on the mattress. God, it was good to be home again. But how could she sleep? Thoughts of Culhane, and Mab and Nora, and Bezel—and Culhane, mostly—kept stomping through her mind. There was too much to think about.

Damn him, anyway. This was all Culhane's fault. She'd never asked for a destiny. Hadn't she been happy before? Painting her windows, enjoying her rut? Scowling, Maggie had to admit that, damn it, the answer there was a big *no*. She hadn't been happy. Not completely. There'd always been something missing in her life.

Not like there was a big, gaping hole or anything. Maggie'd done fine, despite her lousy taste in men and the fact that she couldn't make a living as an artist or that she'd dug herself into the aforementioned rut. It was just, at odd moments, she'd sometimes felt like she'd forgotten something. Put a piece of herself on a shelf somewhere and couldn't remember where she'd tucked it. Like a missing piece of a jigsaw puzzle, that nagging something was there.

It didn't ruin the picture—or her life—but if that missing piece fit into place, then everything would have been whole. Complete.

But until she'd met Culhane she hadn't had a clue what that missing piece was.

Now she was really afraid she knew.

She missed hearing Culhane's voice. Seeing those rare smiles. The feel of him. The touch of his hand. The way his gaze landed on her with the power of a caress.

Damn him, anyway. She sat up, punched her pillow into shape, then flopped back onto it again. Irritated at Culhane and furious with herself, she muttered, "He kidnapped you, idiot. He's got your sister holed up God knows where with a Viking Faery, and Eileen's all alone with a pixie."

Anger surged, then receded.

He was doing what he had to; she knew that. What he believed was important, not just for him, but for his world. She'd learned enough in her time at Sanctuary to know that Culhane and the others hadn't lied to her, at least about this. For centuries male Faeries had been treated like boy toys by the females. They had no say in their councils, and unless they were married—or, as they put it, *joined*—they might as well be invisible.

The warriors were a little better off, which only made Maggie sort of admire Culhane a bit—which she wasn't happy about, either. But she had to admit, he didn't *have* to fight for the other males of his race. He could have had his life and the rights warriors enjoyed and never given the others a thought. But he wouldn't.

He was risking everything to help all Fae males.

"No matter who he has to use," Maggie muttered thickly, and turned off the lamp at her bedside.

Shadows drifted into the room. Outside her window night crowded close and the stars glittered brightly. She wondered if Culhane was looking at the sky, too, then told herself to stop being a romantic idiot.

Still furious with Culhane and even angrier with herself for giving a flying damn about him, Maggie surprised herself by dropping into sleep. Then the dreams came.

"You're still angry." Culhane came close, smelling of the forest and leather and pure male.

The scent of him surrounded her, his heat reached out for her and Maggie swayed toward him. She didn't want to. Had promised herself that when she met up with him again, she'd be cold. Hard. No better than he deserved.

Yet one glance from those pale green eyes of his and she felt herself yearning. Damn it.

"Yes, I'm still angry," she said, despite the way her body was beginning to heat and tremble. "You lied to me. You used my family against me."

"I need you, Maggie."

"You need me to be what I'm not."

"No," he said softly, reaching out to drag the tips of his fingers along her cheek. "That's not what I'm talking about. I need you. Your touch. Your warmth. My body aches for yours. Has for longer than I care to admit. That kiss we shared haunts me. I hunger for the taste of you in my mouth again."

Oh, God, she wanted that, too. It didn't seem possible, but even more heat swamped her, pooling in her center, making her wet and achy and so damn ready for him her knees shook.

"I don't want to need you," she said, lifting her gaze to his.

Around them candles leaped into life, tiny, bright flames dancing and swaying in a wind that neither of them could feel. Behind them a lush bed with a mountain of pillows lay waiting, and overhead a sweep of stars blanketed the sky.

"But you do," he whispered, his fingers now moving over her lips gently, tenderly.

"I do," she said, leaning into him, feeling her breasts press against his chest, her nipples hard and sensitive to the slightest touch.

"Then take me, Maggie," he said, bending down, lowering his mouth to hers. His breath brushed across her face; his eyes seemed to swallow her in their pale, pale depths. "Take me, and let me take you."

She felt him. Felt the nearness of a kiss she'd hungered to experience again—

And the dream changed, images fading, Culhane slipping away from her as new images rose up in her mind and had her twisting on the tangled bedsheets. Her dreams became nightmares in the space of a single heartbeat, and even in sleep, Maggie fought to get free of them.

Fae invading her world, destroying what they couldn't take, driving humanity underground, where mortals huddled in fear and hid from beings they couldn't understand. Strangers fell away then and became something else.

Something more horrifying.

Nora, lying still in the backyard, eyes sightlessly focused on a deep blue sky. Eileen, kneeling beside her mother, wailing in grief and fear.

Maggie's tears slid down her cheeks as the nightmares gripped her. Her panic was real, her heartbeat pounding in her chest. She knew that if she could only wake up, everything would be all right, but she couldn't find her way out of the dream.

Suddenly the images changed again, and a different future showed itself.

Nora, happy, with a baby in the curve of her arm as she smiled down at Eileen.

A bustling city where humanity went blithely on its way, completely oblivious to any threat from the world of Fae.

Finally Culhane, smiling at Maggie as he pulled her down atop his naked body and buried himself deep inside her. She could feel him. His skin. His strength. The invasion of his body into hers, and she quivered on the brink of release, knowing that it would be more fulfilling, more spectacular than anything she could have imagined.

Her body arched; her head fell back; Culhane called her name—

And she woke up.

"What the hell?" Bolting upright in her bed, Maggie

gasped for breath and looked blindly about the room.
The nightmares had already bled away, leaving only
that last, lingering image in her mind. Culhane.

It always came back to Culhane.

She could still feel his hands on her. Feel her climax
trembling just out of reach. "How is it fair that I wake
up just before the good part?"

Shaking, she pushed her hair out of her face, tried
to stop thinking about the fact that her body was still
humming and concentrate instead on her family. Yes,
the nightmares were vicious and terrifying, but they
were only nightmares.

Eileen and Nora were safe. Maggie knew it. Felt it.
Besides, no way would she even *consider* another pos-
sibility.

She swung her legs off the side of the bed, walked
across the quiet, shadow-filled room to the open window and stared out at the night. Clouds moved silently
across the sky, like ghost ships sailing across a black
sea, making the stars seem to wink in and out of existence. The quiet was overwhelming, broken only by
Sheba's whine as she slept.

It was as if she were alone in the world. She didn't
like it.

Glancing over her shoulder at the empty bed behind
her, she ached for Culhane.

"Just dreams. That's all." Saying it sort of helped,
but she still felt confused and scared, and so damned
sexually frustrated she wished heartily for that shower
massager she'd been planning to buy.

But even as she thought it, she knew that wasn't true
either. She didn't want *just* an orgasm.

She wanted a Culhane-driven orgasm.

Despite the fact that the man had lied to her, ordered
her around and kidnapped her family, she wanted him
so badly she could hardly draw a breath.

"Maggie, you are such an idiot," she whispered. "You

can bet Culhane's not lying in bed dreaming about you. So get over it. Get past it. Just do what you're supposed to do so you can finish this and forget all about Faery warriors with pale green eyes."

She sighed and leaned her forehead against the cold window glass. "Yeah. That's gonna happen."

By morning Maggie had pushed the memories of her dreams and nightmares into a tiny corner of her mind, then barred and locked the door behind them. She got Sheba fed, Eileen reassured about her mom's safety, then off to school, and was halfway through her second painting job of the morning before the next disaster struck.

If she did say so herself, the Bank of Castle Bay was looking damn good. She had wreaths on the double doors, and pine boughs dripping with ornaments decorating every window. She'd painted a layer of snow across the bottoms of the windows, and was just going back in to add candles when she heard the voice come from directly behind her.

"I've come for the power."

"Damn it." Maggie tensed, every bone and muscle and nerve in her body on red alert.

Rather than turning around, she stared into the window glass and caught the reflection of an older woman standing behind her. About fiftyish, the woman had short, stylishly cut white hair, sharp blue eyes and was dressed in one of those elegantly styled business-type suits.

Okay, not what she was expecting.

Then Maggie focused on the red lights flashing in the eyes of the "woman." Definitely demon.

She turned around carefully, still holding her jar of lemon yellow paint in one hand and a thick sable brush in the other. Running her gaze up and down the woman, Maggie said, "You're not exactly dressed for fighting."

"Oh," the demon woman said, idly checking her— let's face it—great manicure, "this shouldn't take long."

"Okeydokey, then." Maggie glanced at the street, crowded with shoppers and cars idling while waiting for a parking spot to open. "I'm guessing we don't do this here."

"No, I think not." She smoothed the tip of her finger over her eyebrow and glanced toward an alley. "We should step in there. I wouldn't want anyone to watch me kill you and get the wrong idea. I'm meeting a friend for lunch at the diner in twenty minutes and don't have time to waste making up explanations."

"Good plan." Maggie's mind was racing, and she had half a mind just to stand where she was. Clearly the woman wouldn't risk a confrontation in front of witnesses, so if Maggie just stayed put she'd have nothing to worry about. *On the other hand*, a voice in her head whispered, *if you don't fight her here, she'll only show up somewhere else. Maybe at home.* Nope, couldn't have that.

Besides, if she were going to have to fight demons and, oh, say, a Faery queen, she might as well get used to it. Waving one hand out in front of her, Maggie said, "After you."

"Well, thank you. Courtesy is really a lost art these days, don't you think?" The woman minced her way into the alley with tiny steps, moving carefully to avoid getting any grime on her spectacular taupe heels. "I remember when people actually said *hello* on the streets. Or held doors for you." She glanced over her shoulder at Maggie and kept walking. "Good manners don't cost a cent, you know."

Hmm. Emily Post for the demon set.

The alley was shadowed and smelled of rotting garbage and something else Maggie would just as soon not identify. Puddles of dark liquid ran down the length of the narrow passage, and she made a mental note not to fall down.

"This is just awful," the woman said, turning to face Maggie. "Someone should call the city."

"I'll get right on it."

"Oh, not at the moment, dear. I really think you should just save yourself the pain and give me the powers now. I've got my receptacle right here." She lifted one arm to show Maggie a gold charm bracelet with a dangling gold ornament. When she flicked the clasp the bauble opened, ready and waiting to accept all Faery dust.

"I don't think so. I'm going to be needing it, and besides, it's *mine*."

"Only because you killed Theodora," the woman said, wagging a finger and *tsk*ing at her. "And really, Dora's mate is just furious with you. Trust me when I say that surrendering your power to me is by far the better choice for you."

Maggie sniffed and wrinkled her nose. "If it's you or Dora's husband taking the power, I'm still dead."

"Well, yes. But I'll be quick. He won't be."

Her stomach doing a quick spin, Maggie swallowed back the fear clawing its way into life inside her. She hadn't asked for any of this, but here it was. The woman across from her, who could have been any well-dressed Junior Leaguer type, made a fast move and lunged at Maggie, those beautifully manicured nails up and aimed like ten sharp knives at her face.

"Hey! A little warning!" Maggie ducked beneath the woman's claws and sprang up a couple of feet away.

"Why would I warn you, you stupid bitch? I'm trying to *kill* you."

"Good manners?"

The demon grinned, and just for a second her human disguise fell away to reveal a dark complexion riddled with scars and open sores. Then her mask was back in place and she leaped again, this time trying to hook one arm around Maggie's neck.

Moving just as quickly, Maggie spun around, swung one leg out and knocked the demon to the ground. The woman shrieked, and Maggie wasn't sure if it was because she'd been thrown or because she'd landed in the muck. Didn't really matter, she told herself, taking a deep breath, preparing to blow a stream of Faery dust at the woman's eyes.

"Oh, no, you don't. I want the dust, but I'll take it my way." Pushing Maggie over, the woman jumped on top of her, straddling Maggie's midsection. One hand held the bauble up close to Maggie's mouth; the other wrapped around her throat. "Now, as you die, the dust will fill the receptacle, and it'll all be over."

Her vision blurring at the edges, Maggie struggled for air that wouldn't come. The old demon woman was going to take her, and how embarrassing was that? She was going to die in an alley and never see her family or Culhane again. The male Fae would still be slaves, and her world would be up for grabs.

All because Maggie was a lousy fighter.

"You see? I promised you it would be quick."

Too furious to be scared anymore, Maggie grabbed the demon's hand and ripped it off her throat. Lurching fast to one side, she tossed her opponent into a pile of cardboard boxes, then jumped to her feet. "You almost had me," Maggie told her, rubbing her sore throat as if strong fingers were still clasped around it.

"I do have you." Crawling out from the mess, the woman tugged her skirt down to her knees and stood up, a piece of rotting lettuce stuck to the top of her head like a dark green hat. "You're nothing."

Maggie stabbed a finger at her, and a lightning bolt shot across the alley, lighting up the shadows with a pearly blue glow just before it slammed into the woman. She shrieked again and slapped at the flames eating away at her jacket.

"You bitch!"

"I'm not finished." Another bolt, and another, blue flashes erupting in the shadows, slamming into the demon again and again. She couldn't keep up with the flames, couldn't stop them.

Maggie ran at the woman, letting her rage, her frustration, bubble up and over. Fear was gone, and in its place was a steely determination. She was through running from her "destiny." She'd use what she'd learned and then learn even more. She'd take out demons who tried to kill her, and she'd fight the stupid Faery queen and win, damn it.

Her punches were solid, her kicks magnificent, and in a few minutes it was all over, and what was left of the snotty demon was blowing away down the alley, coating the trash with a sooty residue.

Brushing her hands together, Maggie left the alley to go back to work. "You know, she was right. I think I will call the city. Tell them to take out the trash."

*

"Where have you been?"

In the palace of Otherworld Culhane bowed deeply, then straightened and looked into the eyes of his queen. Mab stalked a wide circle around her throne, casting withering glances toward him.

She was tall, lithe and beautiful. Her long golden hair hung like a thick, rich cape down to the middle of her back. Her features were delicate, but her dark green eyes were shrewd as she fixed them on her warrior.

"As always," he told her, "I train with my brothers."

The throne room was enormous, with crystal walls gleaming with a soft inner light. The windows were wide and always open so that Mab could take flight whenever she wished. They were warded, though, to prevent any other Fae from slipping inside unnoticed.

The great room had been built specifically for the parties and celebrations Mab had once been known for. But that time was long past. She no longer trusted her subjects enough to allow them easy access to the palace. To her. Now this room, like the rest of the crystal stronghold, lay empty but for the queen and a handful of trusted servants.

Culhane remembered long-ago days when he'd been honored to serve his queen. When he'd taken his place in this room, stood with his brother warriors and proudly watched over the Fae she ruled. His loyalty then had been unquestioning, his duty clear.

And so it was now, though the object of that duty, that loyalty, had changed.

Mab sat down on the sculpted silver throne. Her long fingers caressed the polished round gems that decorated the elaborate chair. Light flashed off the silver, shimmered in the hearts of the rubies, sapphires and emeralds. Mab's mouth pursed as she studied him and slowly crossed her legs. "Ah, but it's not only warrior training that's kept you away from me this long, is it?"

"My queen?" Centuries ago Culhane might have been on edge having this private, personal interview. Having Mab's complete attention. But he was accustomed to the politics of the palace now, and that knowledge had never served Culhane better than at that moment. His features were blank, his gaze holding only his question to her.

Hopping up from the throne again, as if she couldn't bear to sit still, Mab took the three steps to the marble floor and crossed the room to him. Her shoes, with their needle-thin heels, tapped against the floor like nervous fingers on a tabletop. Standing before him, she locked her gaze with his as if trying to read his thoughts.

He was thankful that even Mab couldn't accomplish that particular task. Her face looked as though it had been carved from ice: pale, hard, cold. Culhane had been in service to his queen long enough to know that she was in a dangerous mood.

"You've been in the mortal world."

"As I am wont to do," he agreed. "It pays to always know what is happening in the other planes."

"You've been spending much time there," she mused, walking in a slow circle around him, her heels clicking, clicking. She lifted one hand and dragged it across his shoulder blades. Culhane stayed perfectly still. "A curious queen would wonder why."

"My queen is more clever than that," he said easily, as she came around his right side to stop in front of him again. Flattering Mab was always a good idea. Culhane noticed her eyes shining with the compliment he'd paid her, even as suspicion remained. "My queen understands that as a Fae warrior, it is only my duty to keep track of possible problems."

"And have you found some that I should know about?"

"None." He inclined his head slightly on the lie. "I would, of course, tell you immediately were that the case."

"Of course."

Mab studied him for another moment or two, then turned and walked from him to a bank of windows that overlooked the palace gardens. Through the open windows the heady scents of roses and lupine and a dozen other types of flowers rushed in. From a distance came the sounds of laughter and the faint musical lilt of pipes.

"There is word of a demon feud in the mortal world," Mab said softly.

"Is there?"

She didn't look at him, only kept her gaze fixed on

the scene beyond the glass. "It appears a demon was killed and the power of the Fae it held stolen."

"I will look into it myself," he promised with another bow. How had word reached her already? Who did Mab have on the other side watching, collecting information? And why hadn't she come to him for that chore? Was it possible she already suspected him of treachery?

No, he told himself, even as his features remained calm, unconcerned. Mab was not a queen known for her generosity of spirit. If she had even a hint that Culhane was no longer her man, then she would have dealt with him already.

Finally the queen turned from the window, walked back to him and linked her arm through the curve of his. "Yes, Culhane. I think that would be wise. Go back to the mortal world. Find out who killed the demon, who took the Faery dust, and return it to me."

"And if another has already merged with the dust?"

She shrugged as they walked from the throne room into the wide, empty, glittering hall. "Kill whoever it is, collect the dust and bring it to me."

"Yes, my queen."

Chapter Thirteen

𝒯aery time might be flying past, but in Maggie's little corner of the world the days were dragging. While Nora was off somewhere being a hostage, Maggie was trying to soothe her niece, take care of day-to-day stuff—painting, shopping, oh, and in her spare time training to kill ugly-ass demons. The usual.

"If you don't move your butt faster than that, you're gonna lose it." Bezel stalked a circle around her in the backyard, glowering at her from under beetling brows. It was as if he were trying to make himself even uglier than usual.

"In case you hadn't noticed . . ." Maggie paused for air and briefly held up a hand to indicate that she'd get back to him in a minute. Bending in half, she set both hands on her knees and took long pulls of sweet mother oxygen. She still felt like she was dying, but at least she had enough air to snap at Bezel, "I *am* moving my ass, you little troll."

"Troll!" He snorted. "I'm too tall to be a troll, and too damned pretty besides."

"Dear God."

He wheezed out a laugh. "Wait'll you have some time to look around Otherworld. You're gonna be remembering my handsome face with fondness.

Some of those freaks over there are enough to turn *my* stomach."

This from a pixie known to mix tuna and Hershey's syrup.

Maggie was still struggling for air, so she used this chance to stall her mini–drill sergeant long enough so she could take a break. "I was there, remember? The Fae are gorgeous."

"Some of 'em," Bezel allowed. "But my mother always said pretty don't mean shit."

"A lovely sentiment. Look, I'm all teary."

"Hey, she knew what she was talking about. Some of those gorgeous Faeries are nastier than trolls. And that's saying something, believe me."

"Great. So Otherworld is a mess, and even if I become queen I've still got problems." As pep talks went, this one pretty much sucked. For three days she'd been working hard, devoting whatever time she could to being at Bezel's mercy. The pixie was tireless when it came to running Maggie ragged. But she was determined. She was going to be stronger, faster, more powerful than even Culhane expected.

Already she felt the difference inside her. It was just as Culhane had said: The longer the Faery dust was a part of her, the more it seemed that it always had been. She could feel strength running through her like a river. She hardly floated unexpectedly at all anymore, and once this battle was over she really did want to work on the whole flying thing. Her portals were being drawn more easily and looked a lot less shaky than they had only a few days ago.

So all in all she was coming along fine. Would it be enough? God, she hoped so.

"I just thought that Mab was the real problem," she said, not really wanting to focus on all the other crap lining up in front of her like ugly department store lines on Christmas Eve.

Bezel dropped to the lawn beside the dog, smoothed out the wrinkles on his velvet suit and said, "Mab's the worst, but once you get past her there're plenty of other things just waiting to take a shot at you."

"Fabulous."

"What? You were expecting rainbows and puppies?" He stroked one hand down Sheba's head. "No offense, pooch. Otherworld's just like anywhere else. Nice folks, crappy folks, strange folks, psycho folks."

"Stop." She lifted one hand to shut him up. "You're not making me feel any better, thanks. So if this is your idea of cheering me up, do me a favor and quit while you're behind."

"Why would I be trying to make you feel better? Not my job, lady. I'm here to make sure you don't get your clock cleaned."

"Feel the love."

"Look, gods know I hate to admit it, but Culhane's right. You *are* needed there. That's not saying you'll be *wanted*. And it don't mean everybody's gonna throw you a damn parade or something."

"What am I knocking myself out for, then?" Maggie straightened up, pushed her hair back from her—dear God—*sweaty* face and glared at the pixie. "I've been damn near killing myself these last few days, getting ready for a battle I don't give two shits about, while my sister's off somewhere in fairy-tale land, and Culhane hasn't even bothered to show his face!"

"You doing this for him or for yourself?"

"I'm having a rant here, not really looking for logic."

"I said you'll be *needed*, didn't I?" He shook his head, and his silvery hair lifted in the wind.

"Yeah?" Maggie looked at the nice cool lawn, the soft grass, the patch of shade, and thought wistfully about stretching right out and taking a nap. Not proactive girl, but definitely happier girl. But true to the vow she'd made to herself, she dismissed the lovely thought of rest and instead threw punches. "*Fae* need *me*."

"I just said that. You don't listen. Don't you have any sense at all? Culhane's told you that the Fae males are pretty damn sick and tired of being walked on."

"And? So? Yes?"

His mouth screwed up as if he were chewing something nasty. "*And* your coming in to shake things up will probably kick off a civil war. So yeah, they're gonna need you to put a stop to it."

"Huh?" Arms tired, Maggie started doing the kicks Bezel had shown her earlier. She felt like a sad, sad, way less flexible copy of Buffy, but what the hell. "If my involvement starts a civil war, how is that better for anybody?"

"Change isn't always easy."

"Wow. Very Zen. Thanks." Frowning, she muttered, "A civil war. And I'm supposed to head that off at the pass?"

"Otherworld has been the same damned way for thousands of years. It's ripe for exploding. Fae hate pixies; pixies hate Fae. Dark men go after Gray men. Gray men are just creepy."

"Hold it." Maggie held up a hand. "Gray men? What're they?"

Bezel shuddered and his lips curled back. "There's lots more terrible things than them, but Gray men give me the trots."

"Oh, crap."

"Exactly." Still shuddering, Bezel said, "They're all gray and misty, like fog, but alive. They can be solid if they want, but usually they just stay all misty, damp and cold, and when they attack they sort of slide into you, making your insides all slick, like mossy rocks. . . ."

Now it was Maggie shivering as the images rose up in her mind. She rubbed her hands up and down her arms to chase away the chill, but it didn't help.

Bezel shook himself. "Anyway, there's lots worse than a Gray man out there, so why worry about them?"

"Sure. Why worry?"

Bezel took a breath. "So anyway, back to what I was talking about. Female Fae have all the power, and male Fae are sick of it. So, yeah, things are getting tense back at home, and you as the new queen are gonna have to deal with it. Otherworld's gonna need you."

"Wow," she said, taking another breather, since her legs were screaming at her to sit down. "You paint such a lovely picture of life in Faeryland."

"It ain't pretty, but it's home."

"Why the hell am I killing myself to get in shape to take on all that trouble?" Maggie tipped her face into the wind, letting it blow past her, through her, surround her. As a kid she'd loved the wind. It had always made her feel powerful, strong. Yet now she still felt unsettled.

Bezel pushed himself to his feet, waddled over to her and said, "Because. Destiny picked *you* as the lucky lottery winner. Otherworld needs a kick in the ass, and you're just the human to do it. Some back home figure a mortal's got no place in Otherworld. Me, I figure you've gotta be better than Mab."

Amused in spite of everything, Maggie said, "Thanks for the vote of confidence."

He tipped his head back, stared into her eyes and grudgingly admitted, "Yeah, well, you don't suck so much anymore. You're learning."

"Enough?"

He rubbed his beard.

"Aunt Maggie!"

"Training here!" Bezel shouted.

Ignoring him, Maggie turned to watch Eileen jump off the back porch. "What is it?"

"I just talked to Mom!"

"What?" Maggie started toward the girl already sprinting across the lawn. Eileen's grin was bright as daylight, her eyes were shining and her dark red hair flew behind her like a victory flag. "Is your mom here? At the house?"

"No." Eileen stopped and grinned even wider. "She's in Otherworld, but Quinn opened a portal and I could see her. I saw him, too; he was right there with Mom, and the room was so pretty. All these crystals were shining in the sunlight and throwing rainbows around." She paused. "They must have been prisms, not crystals, I guess. Anyway, it was *way* cool, and wait until I tell Amber. She's gonna be so jealous that she didn't see it—"

"Aw, troll spit," Bezel muttered.

"Tell Amber? You can't tell her about any of this, sweetie." Maggie panicked a little. Bad enough her life was screwed. She didn't want Eileen's friends thinking she was a weirdo. There was absolutely nothing in the known universe that could be as cruel as a kid to one of their own. "Secret, remember?"

"Not from best friends," Eileen told her. "There's a whole best-friend-only rule. Besides, Mom said you told Claire."

"That's different." Maggie caught the mutinous look on Eileen's face, but couldn't come up with anything to defeat it on short notice, so she went for distraction. "What'd your mom say?"

Eileen sniffed. "She said she's fine and I shouldn't worry and she'll be back as soon as you kill the queen."

"No pressure."

"Now that the hugging portion of the day's over, can we get back to training?" Bezel glared at both of them.

"She didn't say anything about where she is?" The question was for Eileen, since it was clear Bezel wasn't interested in chatting.

"Nope." The girl dropped to the grass and smiled when Sheba shifted position enough to lay her head in Eileen's lap. "She only said she was fine and I shouldn't worry and I should remind you to actually cook vegetables sometimes."

"My *cooking*?" This was what her sister's message was? *Remember to make Eileen eat vegetables?* She shook her head, bit back anger that wouldn't do any good, because Nora was who she was. That wouldn't change. Instead she asked, "Did Quinn have anything helpful to add?"

"Not really." Eileen shrugged. "He just kept looking at Mom and smiling a really dumb smile."

Unexpectedly Bezel laughed. "This is great. Donovan women are mowing down the Fenian warriors. Something even the Tuatha couldn't do."

"Who?"

"Oooh." Eileen turned on Bezel. "I read about them. Tuatha De Danaan."

Maggie only looked at her, stupefied. "How do you know this stuff?"

Eileen gave her a proud smile. "It's in my Faery research." Then she turned to look at Bezel again. "But the legend says the Fae *are* the Tuatha."

"Oh, please." Bezel rolled his eyes so high in his head, all Maggie could see were the whites. Very creepy. "Your people get it wrong all the damn time," Bezel said with a scowl. "You'd think they could manage to write down a damn legend or two, but no . . . ancient vocal storytellers." His voice went singsongy and sarcastic. " 'We don't need to write it down. We remember. It's what we do.' Idiots. The Tua came to Ireland a long time ago and tried to roust the Fenians— the Fae—but Culhane and his boys drove the Tua underground."

Maggie's head was reeling. Every time she thought she'd caught up, new information came her way.

"But the legends say that the Fae moved underground and—"

"Why in *Ifreann* would the Fae want to live underground? What? We don't like sunshine? Do we look like moles to you? The Tua went under because they had no choice. It was go underground or die. They eventually became Bog spirits." Bezel's long, wrinkled nose wrinkled even further, like he was smelling something disgusting. "There they stay. They live under the bogs in Ireland, and they're always plotting ways to get out. Which ain't gonna happen as long as the Fae are around—" He stopped, tipped his head to one side and studied Maggie thoughtfully. "Hmm. Just another reason for you to take over in Otherworld. Mab's bored with the whole Tua problem, and one of these days she's not going to send the warriors to push 'em back into their peat pits. Then they'll get out and—"

"And what?" Eileen was leaning in toward him, eagerly soaking up everything the pixie had to say.

"Don't really know," he admitted. "But it won't be pretty."

"This is fascinating. My research tells me that—"

"Hey," a voice called out from the back of the house, "is this a private confab or can anyone join in and— *Jesus Christ!*"

Maggie turned and saw Claire MacDonald stop dead in the yard, her gaze fixed on Bezel, her mouth hanging open and her eyes wide enough to swallow up most of her face. She lifted one hand and pointed a shaky index finger at Bezel. "What the *hell* is that?"

E

"Time is getting short."

Culhane turned around, tearing his gaze from the lighthouse just offshore to look at the warrior beside him. He glared the other man into silence. "We all know that, O'Hara. That's why we're here."

O'Hara stepped uneasily from foot to foot, his giant frame rippling with the movement. He threw a quick glance over his shoulder, as if half expecting to see Mab herself striding up behind him. "We should be meeting at the Conclave. We have wards there. Magic to keep us from being overheard. Meeting in the mortal world is risking too much."

Several of the other warriors murmured in agreement, though none of them was willing to say it aloud. Culhane knew how they felt, though. Meeting here in Castle Bay was a risk. But a calculated one. He wasn't willing to hold a meeting at the Warriors' Conclave until he was sure of all of his brothers' loyalty again. He never would have guessed that a day would come when he wouldn't trust his men. But these were dangerous times.

His gaze swept the beach, but he barely noticed the few humans dotting the sand. The ocean was gray and frothing with a coming storm. A cold wind blew, scattering sand in its path, and when the first stray drops of rain spat from the sky, the few hardy souls walking the shoreline ran for home.

But the humans didn't worry him. He scanned the area again, more carefully this time, searching futilely for a shimmer of power. A hint that Mab's spy, whoever he was, was watching the warriors meet. But there was nothing, and he had to wonder if there actually was a spy at all. Or was Mab simply using what power she had to reach out with her mind to try to catch her warriors in something?

Shaking his head, he pushed those thoughts aside, strengthened the wall of Faery power that kept him and his men hidden, then looked at each of the six warriors he'd summoned in turn. "We meet here because Mab's grown more suspicious. She knows about Maggie Donovan."

"What? How? Mab hasn't been on this plane, and

when Maggie was in Otherworld she was at the Conclave." McCulloch's voice was deep and rumbling, just below the roar of the ocean.

"She doesn't know of Maggie herself," Culhane explained. "Only that the Fae power was released from the amulet and claimed by someone else. She's charged me with killing Maggie."

McCulloch grinned. "Then she's safe."

"For now," Culhane hedged. "How Mab knows, I'm not sure. She is either keeping a closer watch on us herself, or—"

"There may be an infiltrator among us." Riley looked disgusted at the very thought. "Has it come to this, then? Warriors turning on warriors? Isn't it enough that our own queen treats us no better than bridge trolls? Must we now guard our words from our own brothers?"

Another rumble of outrage and anger rippled from the gathered men, and Culhane felt the strength of the connection among them. He and these six men had been together for millennia. They'd served in the Tuatha wars together, had stood side by side and back-to-back in more battles than he could count. He trusted each of them with his life. What was more, he trusted them with Maggie's life.

But there were over a thousand Fae warriors, and Culhane wasn't as sure of all of them. Eyes narrowing, flickering with the cool rage he felt within, he said only, "If there is a traitor in the warrior ranks, we will find him. There's no place in the Conclave for a brother we cannot trust."

"I don't believe it," Muldoon muttered. "Warriors won't turn on each other."

"I hope you're right," Culhane told him. "Until we know for certain, though, all we can do is be on our guard. Be wary."

Curran shifted a look at the others, then said, "We

have something else to consider here. There's talk of revolution among the males, even if Maggie Donovan fails in killing Mab."

"She won't fail." Culhane knew it. He'd been waiting centuries for Maggie's arrival. According to the words of the prophecy he'd first read so long ago, he knew that she would do exactly as she'd been destined to do.

"There was a riot in the streets last night," Curran told him. "The warriors were called out to halt it, and we ended having to guard the palace half the night from the crowds shouting for Mab to show herself."

It was all coming to a head now, and there was no way to avoid it, even if a small part of Culhane wished that he could do exactly that—not for his own sake, but for Maggie's. The thought of her fighting Mab filled him with dread as with the expectation he'd been nourishing all these long years.

He didn't want to see her hurt. And could think of no way to prevent it. In the final say, Maggie would have to win or lose on her own. Culhane had never before felt helpless, not in centuries of life. But now knowing that he couldn't stand before her made him half wish that he'd never heard of Maggie Donovan. That the prophecies were a lie. That he could leave her here to live out a life that wasn't filled with the promise of risk and danger.

He couldn't stop fate, though. No one could. It was Maggie's destiny to fight. He could only do what he might to assure that her destiny to *win* became reality.

"Go back," he said, taking the time to meet his brother warriors' gazes one by one. "We don't want Mab getting even more suspicious. Be watchful. Be ready."

As each of the men shifted back to Otherworld, leaving him alone, Culhane shifted, too. But he didn't return home. He went instead to Maggie.

∮

"What is *that*?" Claire repeated, her gaze fixed on Bezel.

"Just watch who you're calling a *that*!"

"He's a pixie," Maggie said, grinning at her best friend. Claire's long black hair was wind ruffled. Her brown slacks and soft yellow shirt were wrinkled, and that—on a usually impeccably groomed Claire—more than anything told Maggie that her friend had come directly from the airport.

Underneath the surprise at finding a hideously ugly pixie in Maggie's backyard, there was a shine of worry in Claire's eyes that explained why she'd rushed home. Still, Maggie asked, "What're you doing here early? I wasn't expecting you back for another few days, at least."

Still staring at Bezel, who was giving her a hard stare back, Claire crossed the lawn to Maggie. Her brown heels sank into the soft grass so that every step was labored. She cleared her throat as she walked a wide berth around Bezel.

"Yeah," she said, the roll of Scotland in her speech. "Couldn't stay there any longer. My mother was driving me insane, and besides, I couldn't stop thinking about you and Nora and— Oh, hi, Eileen. Didn't see you."

"Don't worry about Mom. She's fine. I just talked to her."

Relief swept across Claire's features. "She's here, then? No problems? Thank the goddess. I was so sure that it was going to be—"

"She's in Otherworld," Eileen said matter-of-factly. "But she's okay. Quinn's there, too, and—"

"Otherworld?"

"Long story." Maggie hugged her friend and took a second to enjoy having at least one thread of normalcy back in her life. She'd really missed Claire, and somehow seeing her again made all the other craziness a little easier to take.

"I'll bet," Claire said, "and I'd love to hear the whole story at some point, but you have to know"—her voice dropped to a whisper—"I'm still getting images of Nora in danger. Of *you* in danger."

"A witch?" Bezel spat out that last word, and his face scrunched up with disgust. "You let a witch in here?"

Claire whipped her head around to pin him with a glare. "What's wrong with witches, you nasty little imp?"

"Imp?" He fired a hot look at Claire. "I'm no house imp, you eye-of-Newt eater. Do I look like I'm small enough to live in a flour bin? Do I look like I'd *want* to?" That glare slid to Maggie. "Nice friends you got."

"Witch?" Maggie paid no attention to Bezel, instead staring dumbfounded at Claire. "You didn't say you're a witch. You said you were psychic."

"I am," Claire countered with a lift of her chin. "I'm also a witch."

"Cool," Eileen whispered.

"So why's there a nasty little imp in your yard?" Claire fired a look at Bezel.

"What's an imp?" Eileen asked.

"I'm no imp, you blasted cauldron stirrer!"

"Cauldron?" Claire sniffed.

Maggie had clearly lost control of the conversation.

"You think Culhane's gonna be happy there's a witch in the mix?" Bezel shot his question at Maggie.

That got her speaking up. "You think I care what Culhane thinks?"

"Culhane. He's the Fae warrior?" Claire ignored Bezel and spoke to Maggie.

"Why would Culhane care about witches?" Eileen tugged at the sleeve of Bezel's jacket.

"Yeah, he is," Maggie said, looking at Bezel herself, and wondering. "Speaking of Culhane, where is he? Three days now . . . that's how long in Fae time?"

Bezel stood up and shifted uneasily on his oversize

feet. Rubbing one hand over his beard, he fixed a hard look on Claire before turning his gaze back to Maggie and clamping his lips together pointedly.

"How long?"

"Not in front of the *witch*."

"This isn't about Claire," Maggie told him, stepping away from her friend to close in on Bezel. "How long?"

He finally shrugged and blew out a disgusted breath. "A few months is all."

"Months? It's been *months* and he hasn't bothered to check in? I thought I was the Great Fae Hope or something."

"That and five bucks'll get you a latte," Bezel muttered.

Behind her Claire laughed shortly, then choked off the sound. "Sorry, sorry."

Good, because Maggie wasn't amused. *Months* it had been for Culhane. He clearly wasn't missing her. Probably hadn't even given her a thought in all this time. That damn kiss they'd shared had set her insides into an eternal flame, keeping her hot and eager every damn minute of the day. But he could go *months* without even seeing her. *Way to go, Maggie. You can really pick 'em.*

Damn Culhane—he was always in her thoughts; asleep or awake, there he was, his image, his voice, tugging at the corners of her mind. She'd believed in his passion for his "cause," and for her. Yet he hadn't even bothered to look in on her in all that time.

"I can't believe this."

"Maggie," Claire said, laying one hand on her arm, "it's only been a few days."

"For *me*, not for him."

"You mean Mom's been in Otherworld for months?" Eileen's voice sounded a little worried. "What's she been doing?"

"I'm sure she's fine," Maggie said.

"Yeah, but . . ."

It was a subject Maggie really didn't want to get into. Months alone with her Viking Faery? Maggie knew exactly what Nora had been spending her time doing. And so, she thought as Bezel started whistling, did the pixie.

The eerie, off-key sound issuing from Bezel's ugly mouth seemed to chip away at what was left of Maggie's control.

"Forget about Nora for a minute," she demanded of the pixie trying to be invisible. "What's Culhane been doing?"

"You mean *who*," he muttered just loud enough for Maggie to catch it.

"What do you mean, *who*? Which *who* are you talking about, and why don't I know about this *who*?"

"I don't mean anything," he said, clearly regretting opening his mouth.

Well, it was too late now. A few long steps ate up the distance between her and Bezel, and once she was there Maggie grabbed the lapels of his velvet jacket and lifted him right off the ground. Feet swinging, arms wheeling, he shouted, "Hey, put me down!"

"Not until you tell me where Culhane is."

"None of my business," he said, frantically looking down at the ground below him. "Warriors don't tell pixies what they're doing, you know. And I've been here with *you*, haven't I?"

She shook him. Hard. "You know something, so spill it."

"You rip this suit and Fontana's not gonna kick just *my* ass."

A female pixie? The least of her worries. She gave him another shake just so he understood that. *"Where?"*

Overhead, storm clouds scudded across the sky. The first few drops of rain pattered on the lawn, and one drop hit the pixie dead in the center of his forehead, only to roll down the length of his nose.

Bezel's pale eyes met hers, and she felt the chill in them even before he spoke up. She could see he didn't want to tell her. Could see that he wished to hell they'd never started down this conversational road, but they'd gone too far along it to stop now.

"Mab, okay?" he finally blurted as Maggie gave him another shake. "Culhane's with Mab."

Chapter Fourteen

"Well, he is a warrior," Eileen said. "Why wouldn't he be with the queen?"

"Uh-oh," Claire whispered.

"*With?*" Maggie dropped him, and Bezel landed with a thud.

"Oh, that's nice!" The pixie stood up, brushed his butt off with both hands and mumbled under his breath.

"With Mab?" Maggie repeated as the edges of her vision swam with red. "*With* with?"

Still dusting himself off, Bezel looked up at her with disgust. "What the hell do you think I mean? Of course *with* with."

"Okay, that's our cue to go. Private conversation." Claire grabbed Eileen's hand, plucked her off the lawn and started for the house. "How about you and I go have a snack? I didn't even eat on the plane."

"But I want to hear . . ." Eileen half turned around, but Claire kept dragging her along.

Maggie spared them only a quick glance. Then she turned the full focus of her hot stare on the pixie.

"He's with Mab," she said, every word ground out like it was sliding across broken glass. "He's signed me up to fight the bitch he's *sleeping* with?"

"They probably don't sleep much."

Maggie shot him a look that should have fried his pixie ass, and Bezel automatically backed up a step.

"Hey, don't kill the pixie messenger." He held up both hands, long fingers wiggling as if he could ward her off.

"I don't believe this." Maggie couldn't decide exactly how she was feeling—besides the fury, that is. That was really clear and, at the moment, pumping fast and thick through her veins like liquid, bubbling tar. But the undertone of that fury was betrayal.

Culhane had lied to her. Well, okay, he'd never actually said he *wasn't* sleeping with the freaking *queen*. But he hadn't told her the truth, which was more or less the same damn thing, she assured herself.

"It's not like he had a lot of choice, you know."

"Oh," Maggie said with a sarcastic sneer, "was the poor man tied down to a bed? Was he forced to have *sex* with a *queen*? Did she take advantage of the poor Fae warrior?"

Now it was Bezel's turn to sneer. "You're not entirely wrong."

"Please." Maggie started walking, quick, short steps that took her in a tight, angry circle around the pixie keeping a wary eye on her. "How dumb do you guys think I am, anyway?"

"Well . . ."

"That was rhetorical." The words were snapped out along with another icy glare. "He's using me, romancing me, and all the time he's—"

"The queen's consort."

"Nice name for it." Her steps stumbled a little, but she recovered quickly enough. "Consort. Male whore. Whatever."

"Nice mouth you got there." Bezel only frowned when she threw him another hard look. "Culhane's the head warrior. It's his job to be at the queen's beck and call, and believe me, she becks and calls a *lot*."

"Oh, that's very comforting. Thanks so much."

"Not here to comfort," he pointed out. "Two hundred years Culhane's been dancing to Mab's flute. You think it's easy for a guy like him to do that? To take all of her trollshit on a daily damn basis?"

But Maggie had stopped listening. "Two *hundred* years? He's been with Mab for two hundred years?"

"*Ifreann* take me," Bezel muttered, and kicked at the ground, sending up a shower of pebbles and dirt.

Maggie didn't notice. Her mind was too busy. Two hundred years he'd been with the queen. Hell, Maggie hadn't been able to make a relationship work for longer than six weeks at a stretch. And the lucky winner who'd made it to six weeks had traded her in for a demon and been gulped down like a Happy Meal.

The wind whipped around her, tearing at her hair, her clothes. Above her the sky roiled with dark clouds scuttling in off the sea. The naked branches of the oak tree rattled and grumbled like a group of old men, and still she walked. She couldn't stand still. Couldn't get a grip on what she was feeling, thinking. Betrayal, sure. Fury, no doubt.

Jealousy . . . okay, some.

Damn it. All the time she'd been dreaming of Culhane, imagining his hands on her, what it would be like to be touched by him, wanted by him . . . he'd been giving his best to the queen he claimed to *hate*!

Then one completely off-the-track thought sputtered through the turmoil in her brain.

Mab had kept Culhane in her bed for two hundred years.

He must be *really* good.

Not the point, Maggie. So not the point.

"Look at it from his side," Bezel said, and this time his words got through.

"I thought I was."

"Women. Pixie, Fae, human—you're all alike. You

get stuck on one thing and we couldn't blow you out of it with a rocket launcher."

"He's been lying to me!" Why she bothered to explain, she didn't know. Bezel was bound to be on Culhane's side. Not only were they both from Otherworld; they were both *male*. Right now that made them both the enemy.

"Yeah? Well, whatever he's done is working. Take a look at your hands, you idiot human."

She did and noticed for the first time that streaks of blue and white fire, bursts of energy, were slashing from the tips of her fingers like illuminated daggers. The jagged pieces of lightning were bigger and stronger than they'd been in Sanctuary, too. Along with her fury, her power was crackling inside her.

"You think you could have done that without him? Without Finn? Without me?"

"Maybe not." She took a calming breath and watched as the bolts of energy slowly faded away. "But he didn't have to lie to me. Didn't have to make me think—"

"For the love of pixie children, think about this yourself for a troll-blasting minute!"

Maggie stared at him. As long as she'd known him, Bezel had been snide, condescending, rude and downright mean. But this was the first time she could remember him being really pissed.

"What? What should I be thinking about?"

"Culhane's a warrior. As much as I get sick and tired of hearing him remind me that he's an all-powerful, pain-in-my-sweet-ass Fenian, that's the blasted truth." His lips twisted into a grimace. "He is who he is and can't be anything different. Not for Mab. Not for you.

"He's old. Older than your time can understand. He's fought more wars and battles than the history books can list, and he's still standing." Bezel moved in close, tipped his head back and fixed his ice-chip eyes on hers. "And here's *why*: Because he's smart—though if you tell him I said that, I'll deny it to *Ifreann* and back. He knows how to win. Knows how to use what he has to get what he needs."

"That's supposed to make me feel better?" Maggie countered. "To know he's using me?"

"Of course he's using you, you stupid human. Why in *Ifreann* wouldn't he? Your arrival was written in the prophecies a thousand years ago. He's been waiting for you. Is he really *not* going to use you when you finally show up?"

"Still not making it better."

"You've used him, too," Bezel told her flatly. "To teach you. To hand you over to those who would train you, so you'd be able to stay alive. So what's that make you?"

Even as her rage began to fade into a hot, simmering bubble in the pit of her stomach, Maggie had to admit, grudgingly, that the damned pixie had a point.

Bezel sighed. "Culhane's a warrior, trained to protect and defend his people any way he can. And you're his newest, finest weapon."

"Well, don't I feel *special*?" There was the rage back again. "What am I? His shiny new dagger? How long till my blade gets dull and I'm tossed aside, huh?"

"What the . . ."

She shook her head, dismissing the pixie and all he represented. Earlier she'd been missing Culhane. Now, if he popped into her yard at this moment, she knew she'd kick his Fae ass all over Castle Bay and back to Otherworld.

She had half a mind to open a portal and go face the lying Faery bastard on his turf. Let him know just how she felt about being the weapon of the month.

But even as she considered it, Maggie let that thought go. She wouldn't turn to him. Not even in the heat of anger. She was going to do what she'd been doing: She was going to keep training. And she was going to learn. But she wasn't doing it for *him*.

She'd do it for her world. For her family.

Culhane, that mighty Fenian warrior, could kiss her ass.

Breath huffing in and out of her lungs, Maggie fought for control over the myriad emotions raging inside her. So she was his weapon? Oh, that realization stung somewhere deep within—almost as deeply as the knowledge that Culhane was tying her up in sexual knots while he was off screwing the queen he purported to hate.

But a quiet voice asked from out of the tumult, *Is a weapon all you are to him? Is that all he sees in you? Or is there more? Does he want as you want? Does he need as you need?*

That, she thought, was the real trouble. She had no idea what Culhane was thinking, wanting.

The hard part was realizing that—damn him—she wanted to know.

&

An hour later the storm was raging.

Rain.

It almost never rained in Southern California, but when it did the world rolled to a stop. People huddled in their homes as if afraid they'd melt from the unexpected showers. Stores closed the doors that usually stood open in welcome, and even the few tourists stayed locked in their hotel rooms.

Maggie couldn't paint windows in weather like this—and a good thing, too, since she was in no mood to be painting happy, shiny scenes.

She tucked her hands deep into the pockets of her jacket and trudged on. Claire was still at her house, wanting to talk, but Maggie wasn't ready for some best-friend bonding time. Not yet. Anger and betrayal still bubbled in her stomach and frothed through her veins, so it probably wasn't a good idea to talk to anyone. Not for a while, anyway.

After listening to Bezel, she'd needed some time alone. Some thinking time. Some pissing, whining and wailing time. She wanted to kick something. She wanted to punch something until her knuckles bled.

And that thought startled Maggie right down to the bone. She'd never been a fighter. Had never felt the urge to smash and bash. One liners were her weapon of choice, and she'd been known to slice a snotty cashier or repair person to ribbons with her gift for sarcasm.

But punching?

"God, I am changing." She felt it, of course. For the last three days she'd been training hard. Working her ass off . . . well, not literally, unfortunately, but even she had to admit that she was changing on some basic level.

Culhane had been right: She did feel different now. It was as if that first promise of power from the Faery dust had finally become a part of her. Or at least, more a part of her, sliding into every cell, sparking a strength and an energy she'd never known before. And finally the unexpected floating was down to a bare minimum.

Strength, energy, endurance. All good things. But this urge to fight had her worried. "What the hell else is that damned dust doing to me?"

Her words were snatched by a furious wind and tossed aside as if her question didn't matter even to the heavens. Why that should surprise her, she didn't know. It had already been made completely clear that Destiny was in the driver's seat here. And Maggie was more or less along for the ride.

Which was just one more thing she didn't like. She preferred control. Making her own decisions. Deciding who and what she was going to be. Suddenly being turned into something less than—or was that *more* than?—human was definitely not something she would have chosen for herself.

She stopped briefly on her walk to the beach and tipped her face back, letting the wind and the rain wash over her skin. Raindrops slid like tears across her cheeks, and the cold wind brushed them aside almost as quickly as they fell. Probably better that way, she told herself as she started walking again. She already looked like a crazy person out for a stroll in a winter storm. No sense looking like a *crying* crazy person on top of it.

Passing familiar stores, Maggie nodded through rain-streaked windows at the people within, and idly noted how many of her decorated windows she passed along the way. There was another painter in town, but she hadn't really made much of a name for herself yet—and if she couldn't figure out how to make a *jolly*-looking snowman, she never would—so Maggie's own Christmas decorations were the majority of what she spotted.

It made her feel better, more settled, to look at the bright, cheerful holiday decorations she'd created. It was normalcy. It was *hers* as this Faery power could never be. These things she'd brought out of herself, from her mind, her imagination, her talent. This she'd *made*. The Fae thing had been done to her.

She stopped at the signal on the corner of Main and Pacific Coast Highway. Waiting in the pelting rain for the light to change, Maggie thought about just darting across the wide road, light or no light. But she wouldn't. This was who she was, too, she realized. She was a person who would wait for the walk signal even if it were two in the morning. Even on a day like today, when there was no traffic and she was slowly turning into a wet ice cube, she would wait. Because it was the law. Because it was right. Because she couldn't do anything else.

"Play by the rules, don't you, Maggie?" she muttered as an errant raindrop sneaked beneath the collar of her jacket to roll down her spine like the tip of a cold finger. "And what does that get you, exactly? It gets you into the middle of a Faery war and feeling like you can't back out, that's what."

She should have been a rule *breaker*. Should have walked on the wild side. Maybe then she'd have been too unpredictable for the Fates to screw with. With that thought in mind she actually stepped off the curb, ready to go crazy against the red light.

Naturally the light turned green almost instantly. Grumbling about that, she trotted across the street. Then she hit the sidewalk, made a quick right turn and walked toward the rock-lined jetty.

It didn't even surprise her to realize where she was headed. Growing up in Castle Bay, Maggie had always gravitated toward the lighthouse. Maybe it was because of that day she'd nearly died here. Maybe it was the draw of that fine line she'd almost crossed that kept pulling at her. And, she thought now, maybe it was really the memory of Culhane saving her that drew her to this place subconsciously. But whatever the reason, this was where she came when she needed to think. To be by herself.

To just . . . be—and how New Agey and like Nora that sounded—she headed here.

The rush of the sea and the slap of waves against the rocks soothed her. The salt spray lifting into the air as wave met stone was like perfume, and the cold wind was an icy embrace. She'd always felt more powerful here, more sure of herself than anywhere else she'd ever been. Now, with all this newfound insight she was experiencing, she realized that the power she felt came from that day when she'd saved herself. When she'd refused to surrender and quietly die.

"Funny I never considered that before," she whispered, hunching her shoulders against the wind that pushed her one step for every two she made forward.

Now, with the Fae strength rushing through her system, that sense of power cresting inside her was incredible. She took long, purposeful strides down the concrete path that wended its way to the lighthouse, and as she walked the sea charged at her from both sides. Whitecaps churned on the water's surface, and black clouds huddled overhead as if concentrating their attack. Thunder rolled like a freight train, needles of rain poked at her and lightning shone from behind the clouds.

The stone base of the lighthouse was right in front of her, a bright red door with a heavy brass lock at its center. She couldn't get into the building itself, but that wasn't what she needed. She needed to be out here, in the center of the storm, because nature's rage so closely mirrored the storm inside her.

Here, with the wind and the sea howling, she felt free enough to shout out her own frustration without worrying about being overheard. Facing the ocean, the boiling clouds and the misty fog beginning to rise and twist around the rocks, she called out fiercely, "Damn you, Culhane. You should have told me."

"Yes," he said from right behind her. "I should have."

Chapter Fifteen

"*W*hoa!" Maggie spun around so fast her sneakers squeaked on the wet cement, and she would have lost her balance completely if Culhane hadn't stretched out one hand to grab her.

Quickly she shook him off and threw her wet hair out of her face. "I don't want your damn help, you bastard. You're sleeping with her. You're Mab's lover and you never bothered to *tell* me?"

"I wanted to."

"Right. What stopped you? Oh yeah. Can't really romance the new queen if she knows you're diddling the old one!"

"That's not why." He sounded patient, damn him all the way to Faery hell and back again. What right did he have to be patient with her?

"Didn't you think I deserved to know?" She gave in to the urge crowding her and slugged him in the stomach. For all the good it did. He didn't even flinch. Apparently her power hadn't grown strong enough to hurt a Fae warrior. "What am I to you? Just the pet human you need at the moment? Is that it? Is that all I am?

The rain didn't touch him. He stood opposite her in the teeth of the storm, and it was as if he were standing under an invisible umbrella. The rain fell around him, beside him, but he wasn't even damp.

Maggie felt her sodden hair hanging in strings around her face and thought she could have punched him again just for the fact that he looked so damn good, while she looked like a shipwreck survivor.

"Pet human?" He shook his head, and his black hair lifted as if from the kiss of the wind. Then his gaze settled on hers again, and Maggie was caught by the power in those pale green depths. "That's what you believe? What you feel when we're together? What I've *shown* you in the last week or more?"

"Oh, don't get on your high Fae horse with me, buddy. What am I supposed to think?" It was a challenge. A demand for the whole truth and nothing but. She wanted to know, damn it. She didn't want to guess anymore. Didn't want to have to pretend that he didn't matter.

That what they could have had if he hadn't been a lying, cheating bastard didn't matter.

He stared at her. His expression didn't change; his eyes didn't leave hers. All around them the storm raged on, but between them there was a stillness, an eerie calm that Maggie was in no condition to enjoy.

"I was at your house," he said abruptly, and it wasn't what she'd been expecting. "I overheard Bezel tell you. Saw your reaction and felt your pain."

"What do you want? A medal for eavesdropping? A prize for staying in the shadows and saying nothing? *Again?* Besides, I wasn't in pain," she lied. "I was pissed. Still am."

"As you should be," he acknowledged, which only pissed her off further. "But you should also realize that I didn't tell you everything for a reason."

"Oh," she said, folding her cold, wet arms over her chest. "This should be good."

"I have been trapped by my oath to the queen for

two hundred years." His voice was thick with an emotion that sounded a lot like bottled fury. "It is not by choice that I became Mab's lover. She chooses a warrior to serve her when she likes. And it's not by choice that I have stayed."

She swallowed the knot in her throat and fought to stand there, to hear him out, though it was harder listening to him than she'd thought it would be. Unbidden, images of him and Mab together, limbs tangled in the night, came to her, and she brutally shut them down. "Then why?"

He shrugged. "She is queen. She commands. We obey. It's always been this way. But it doesn't have to remain so."

"Which is where I come in." Her voice sounded bitter, even to her. "So when I'm queen, do you do your duty by me? Is that the reason for the slow, hot looks? For the whispers, for the *seduction*? Are you getting used to the idea of having to sleep with me? Working up to it slowly so it won't be a task you hate? Because let me tell you, that just turns a girl on to know that a guy's put her on his to-do list."

Anger flashed across his features, and his eyes burned with a darkness she'd never seen there before. Reaching for her, he grabbed hold of her shoulders, gave her a shake, then loomed over her so that she had to tip her head back to meet his gaze.

"Do you really believe I *don't* want you? You can say that to me? When you know what you do to me with a look?" His hands tightened on her. "Do you not remember what we felt with that kiss? It haunts me. *You* haunt me."

Maggie squirmed in his grasp, fighting to get free. She didn't want to be sucked back in by sweet lies or soulful looks. She wanted to hang on to the rage that was choking her.

"Don't you know that I have spent your lifetime waiting for you?"

She finally wrenched free, though she knew it was only because he released her. Pushing sodden hair out of her eyes, she demanded, "What's that supposed to mean?"

"It means I've watched over you—watched you— your whole life. You know about that time here."

When he'd pulled her from the water the day she nearly drowned. "Yes . . ."

His voice dropped so low that it was nearly lost in the pulsing roar of the sea. "We've met other times. Other places."

She shook her head. She understood why she hadn't been able to recall him on that day she'd nearly died; the shock and fear alone were enough to jumble memories. But other times? No. She would have remembered him. Would have remembered the feelings that dazzled her body whenever he touched her.

"When you were a girl," he said, as if sensing her disbelief, "you took a trip to Ireland."

Frowning, Maggie nodded. "Gran and Grandpa took Nora and me there when we were teenagers. I was fifteen. But what's that got to do with anything?"

Sighing now, Culhane lifted one hand and, when she would have stepped back, frowned at her to hold her in place. Then, gently, he touched her forehead with the tips of his fingers.

Images flew into Maggie's mind as if they'd been hiding behind a locked door that had suddenly been thrown open. They flooded her senses, stole her breath, and she was helpless to do anything but stand as an observer and watch.

County Kerry. That was where they'd gone, where Gran had once met the Faery lover who had started this whole Donovan family saga. One day her grandparents had taken

Nora into Tralee for some shopping, but Maggie had stayed at the cottage they'd rented for the month.

She took a walk across fields so green and rich the color was almost alive. In the bright sunlight she sat beside the circle of tumbled stones that Gran had shown her the day before.

"Here," she'd said, "is where we met, where he found me." And so Maggie had gone there, and her teenage heart had longed to find magic herself.

That was when she saw him: a boy about her age, with long black hair, pale green eyes and a smile that stripped her of breath even from a distance. He'd come out of nowhere and walked through the Faery ring to her side as if nothing else in the world existed.

Heart pounding, breath held, Maggie watched him, and when he was close enough he reached down for her hand and pulled her to her feet. The Irish wind caressed her as he smiled, and everything inside her exploded with light.

"I knew you'd come," he said. "I've waited."

"Who are you?" She couldn't tear her gaze from him. Didn't want to.

He didn't answer, only smiled again. His fingers stroked her cheeks, as if he needed the touch as badly as she did. Then he dipped his head, claimed one sweet, soft kiss, and whispered, "Someday."

She came up out of the memories feeling as shaken as she had that long-ago day. Maggie hadn't thought of that morning-bright kiss in years. She hadn't wanted to remember, because for years no other guy had been able to hold a candle to that Irish boy with fire in his touch and summer in his smile.

Now she looked up at Culhane and saw the face of that boy in the features of the man. "It was you."

"It was," he told her. "I'd waited for you and then you were there, with sunlight in your hair and meadow flowers all around you. I had to speak to you. Touch you."

Shaken, Maggie stepped back and away from him. "I don't even know what to say to that."

Culhane felt her confusion and thought that it was far better than her anger. As the storm continued to grow around them he saw only her. Just as he had then. "I've been near you since your birth. Keeping you safe. Watching you grow. Waiting for your time to come. For the prophecy to be fulfilled. The time is here, Maggie, and we must work together or none of us will have a future."

She scraped her hands over her face, rubbed her eyes, then scooped her fingers through her soaking-wet hair before looking at him warily. "I'm still mad at you."

"I know."

"That's it?" she countered. "Just 'I know'?"

"What more would you have me say?" Culhane felt a stirring of anger himself and thought, not for the first time, that Maggie Donovan was the only female he'd ever known who could inspire such wild swings of emotions within him. "I can't change my past, not even for you, and even if I could, I wouldn't. What I've done has made me who I am. Made you who *you* are."

"You're still having sex with Mab."

He sighed. "I don't *want* Mab. I want only you."

She whirled around, tearing her gaze from his to stare out at the storm-tossed sea. "I don't know if that helps or not."

He moved up behind her but didn't touch her. Couldn't risk it. He wanted to taste her again, as he had so long ago. Wanted to lose himself in the scent of her, in her touch, her body. But he couldn't risk that. Not yet. Not when they were so close to their goal.

"This is your destiny, Maggie."

"I don't want it."

Her words were faint, sliding just beneath the sound of the storm. "You would be foolish if you did."

She glanced at him briefly, then looked back to the sweep of sea and storm clouds.

"Neither of us has a choice in this, and I will do everything I can to see that you succeed. Your destiny and mine are intertwined. As you were meant for this, so were you meant for *me*."

She laughed shortly. "I don't know that I want that, either."

Now he smiled, though she couldn't see it. "Yes, you do." He laid his hands on her shoulders and felt the rush of power inside her. "We are a team, Maggie, you and I."

"Some team," she said, narrowing her eyes as she looked over her shoulder at him. "You lie to me and just expect me to fall in line."

"I explained that."

"Doesn't change the facts, Culhane. Where's Nora?"

"What?" The abrupt shift of topic threw him for a moment. "You know where she is. Otherworld."

"With Quinn."

"Where she will stay until this is done."

"You mean until I do what you want."

"Know that Nora's safer where she is than she would be here. If Mab finds out about you she won't hesitate to kill you, as well as your sister."

She opened her mouth to ask a question, and he answered it before she could.

"Remember, Eileen is safe. I have told you, even Mab doesn't approve of killing children."

Maggie blew out a breath. "So the Evil Queen has standards. Okay, good to know. But Nora's been with Quinn for months in your world. How do I know she's safe? Or happy?"

A half smile pulled at one corner of his mouth, but there was no answering smile on her face.

"It's Quinn you should be concerned about," he said, hoping to take that flash of worry from her eyes. "He's half in love with her and forgets about his duties as a warrior to spend more time with Nora. And," he added, to get a spark of interest out of Maggie, "as for her being happy, I've been told that sex with a Faery is an amazing experience for a human."

Something flashed briefly in her eyes. Then she swallowed hard and said, "Uh. Great. Good for Nora. Glad somebody's having a good time."

Fog twisted and slithered up across the rocks, lifting from the sea, writhing with the wind, covering the stones, the path and reaching out for the two who stood together, yet separate. Seconds ticked past, the sea and the storm crashing around them as the cold crept closer.

A sense of something dark, cloying, caught Culhane's attention, and he turned to see the fog rising, stretching, solidifying. "Maggie . . ."

She looked, too, and inhaled sharply as a being materialized from the wisps of fog. Black holes where eyes should have been and a skeletal suggestion of a face stared at her with a hunger that was raw, undeniable.

"A Gray man," Maggie whispered, remembering what Bezel had told her about them. The pixie hadn't even come close to describing what she felt being this close to it.

Culhane moved instinctively to stand between Maggie and the threat.

But she stepped out from behind him, rain sluicing down her face, her body. Her eyes were cold and hard, though, her features set in unforgiving lines as she stared at the Fae that twisted and writhed in the wind. "Bezel told me about them," she said softly. "Said they were creepy."

As if in answer, the fog-shrouded creature shimmied closer to her, reaching out with wispy tentacles that looked all the more menacing for their fragile appearance. The closer it came, the colder she felt, a bone-deep iciness that crept through her veins, settled in her soul and seemed to leach out every drop of warmth inside her.

"You," it whispered, and the voice was as thready as the body. "I come for you."

Maggie's heart raced in her chest. Her mouth went dry, and the cold wrapping itself around her made her feel as if her bones were brittle enough to snap.

"Go," Culhane told it, his strength, his authority ringing in his tone. "Go now and live."

He seemed unaffected by the Fae, and Maggie was desperately jealous. But, she reasoned, if Culhane could withstand this thing's powers, so could she. She focused, calling on all of the bits and pieces she'd learned over the last couple of weeks. She remembered Bezel's taunts, Finn's quiet teachings and Culhane's absolute belief in her.

"No," Maggie told the warrior beside her, never taking her gaze from her enemy. "No, it came for me. Let it try."

It did, sweeping across the few feet of space separating them like mist in a nightmare. No substance. No sound. Just a nameless threat and the deepening cold. It spilled across the jetty, wrapping itself around the rocks, reaching for her as the black eyes in the mist glittered eerily in the darkness. Needles of rain hammered at them, yet the mist survived, and a sly sigh of sound became whispered threats that rode just above the thunder of the sea.

"I won't let you win," Maggie said, stepping away from Culhane, her gaze fixed on the insubstantial creature stalking her.

In the dark, rain-shrouded air, the wisps of its arms shredded, came together and faded again. Each time it was closer to her, and Maggie held her breath, preparing for the moment when the thing would actually touch her.

Culhane stood nearby. Watching.

Maggie was determined to prove herself. She'd fought demons and lived. Trained to fight a queen. If she couldn't fight and win against a Fae, then she stood no chance at all against Mab.

In the embrace of the wind she lifted her arms. Her gaze locked on her enemy, her mouth tight, she allowed those gray threads to touch her, to wrap themselves around her.

That icy touch was a living nightmare as Maggie's mind shrieked away from the sensations pouring into her. Terror. Emptiness. Death. She swayed with the impact of the emotions slamming into her and held on to the tattered edges of sanity with a tight grip.

This was worse than a fight. This was more than pain. This was the end of everything. Mind shattering, soul draining, she felt the Gray man's triumph and fought her way back from the edge of madness. The soft sigh of a disembodied laugh whispered into the wind, and Maggie answered.

She struggled to find her voice, her will. Locking her knees, she stiffened her spine and forced herself to meet the black gaze that was like a void. "You won't win. I won't let you."

Surprise flashed briefly in those empty depths, and Maggie knew she'd already beaten it.

"You won't scare me off, fog boy, and you won't kill me, either. Not tonight." She pulled her power to her, wrapped it around the cold within and smothered it. Lightning erupted from her fingertips, and she let the power flow. Bolts of blue and white shone and flashed with a near-blinding brightness. Those bolts stabbed at the ethereal creature, and it twisted in on itself before fighting back. Energy pulsed darkly, radiating off the Fae in shades of gray and black that were swallowed and shattered by the light pumping from Maggie's fingertips.

It slid farther away then, trying to slink back into the foggy mist atop the water.

But Maggie followed, moving in, never hesitating. Again and again she used her power, her strength, her confidence to beat back the threat, and pride filled Culhane's throat and heart as he watched.

When a reedy scream echoed out around them and the last of the fog dissolved, Maggie stood like a warrior at the edge of the sea. The wind tore at her, the rain drove at her, yet she stood as steady as the rocks beneath her feet.

It was then Culhane knew she was more than even he'd thought she could be.

Maggie slowly turned her head to look at him. She dragged in a breath, blew it out, and said, "I'm a little shaky, Culhane. But I'm still standing."

"You are," he said. "You did well."

"I did, didn't I?" She turned to look out at the ocean and added, "I'll probably never look at fog the same way again, though."

"You fought past your fear." Culhane moved closer but didn't touch her. He sensed her fragility despite the aura of strength still clinging to her. "I know what a Gray man can do. The welling pool of emptiness they can open inside you."

"It was awful," she whispered, not looking at him. "I actually thought about screaming, *help!* But now I'm glad I didn't." Finally she turned to meet his gaze as she said, "I think I needed to prove something to myself—and to you."

Culhane understood. "You did. Now you see what you can do. What you are destined to do."

"So why," she asked, "aren't I filled with satisfaction?"

"Maggie—"

"The Gray man is Fae."

He nodded. "Yes."

"So, lots of different-looking Fae," she said.

"As in any race," Culhane admitted, "the Fae come in many forms and sizes."

Something suddenly occurred to Maggie. "How'd that thing know to attack me? If he knows, doesn't Mab?"

Culhane shook his head. "No. Not yet. The Gray man was here when we arrived. He only sensed your power because you were nearby."

Nodding, she swallowed hard and said, "Okay. That's good. You know, Bezel did warn me that some of the Fae wouldn't be happy to see me in Otherworld."

"He was right. There are some Fae who remain loyal to Mab no matter what."

"And there are more like him? It? Whatever?"

"Many more," he said softly.

"So basically," Maggie said, as that jittery feeling she'd had while fighting roared to life again in the pit of her stomach, "I'm not going to know whom I can trust, right?"

"Me, Maggie," Culhane said. "You can trust me."

She looked at him, and though her heart screeched at her to walk into his arms, her mind held her back. If she was going to get out of this, she would need Culhane's help, she knew. But she was also going to have to stand on her own two feet. Make some hard calls on her own and hope they were the right ones. She wanted to trust him—but that was all she could give him for now.

&

"Where've you been?" Nora rushed to Quinn the moment he shifted into his apartment in the Warriors' Conclave. She'd been alone for what felt like hours. And she didn't like it. Alone, she had too much time to think. To worry. To realize that it had been *months* since she'd seen her little girl.

It didn't matter that Quinn kept reminding her that only days had passed in the mortal world, and that Eileen had hardly had time to notice she was gone. For Nora it was months. And she missed Eileen desperately. Yes, fine, having an amazing Faery lover keep her captive in his fabulous tree-house apartment had its appeal. But she was a *mother*, for God's sake. And it was time she got back to it.

"I'm sorry," he said, wrapping his thick, strong arms around her and holding her close. "There was a battle in the streets. We were called out to stop it."

"Battle?" Every other thought was pushed aside momentarily as Nora stared up at him, running her hands up and down his chest, his arms, as if looking for wounds. "Are you okay? Who were you fighting? You're not hurt?"

He smiled, and everything in Nora turned over and shook itself silly. "I am unhurt, Nora. I'm a warrior. This is what I'm trained to do. And the Fae are immortal, remember?"

Yes, she did. They'd had plenty of time to talk . . . well, when they weren't in bed . . . and he'd told her a lot about the life of the Fae. "Yes, you're immortal. Unless someone comes along and chops off your head or something."

"That won't happen."

"Even if it doesn't, you could be hurt. Injured."

"But I wasn't."

"Who were you fighting?"

"Male Fae were protesting in front of the palace. Mab's women came out to drive them away and the war raged." He shook his head as if he still didn't believe what he'd seen himself. "Never in all my years have I seen a male Fae take arms against a female."

"Were there casualties?"

"Nothing serious," he mused. "But Mab's female guard was almost outmatched. They were so surprised, I think, that they delayed in countering the attack. Then, too, some of the females changed sides midbattle and stood with the men."

"Really? That's great. Isn't it?"

"For our purposes, yes. Mab will not agree." He moved away, walked to a cabinet on the far side of the room and opened it. Reaching for a crystal bottle containing a honey-colored liquid, he poured two glasses full and walked back to Nora. Handing her one, he said, "Otherworld is in turmoil, more than it's seen in centuries. As a warrior I will be called on to help more often now. That means I won't be with you as much as I have been."

"I guess I knew that was coming," she said, taking a sip of what he'd told her was nectar—a honeyed wine that tasted like summer. "But, Quinn, when you're gone it's so hard to be here alone. I don't see anyone. Don't speak to anyone. I don't have any idea what's going on out there, and when I know that you're fighting . . ." Nora sat down on one of the four chairs in the room and felt the soft swell of the material reach up to hold her. "I was worried. And because I'm *stuck* in this tree—"

"You didn't leave the Conclave, did you?" Quinn stood in front of her, staring down, meeting her gaze as if trying to see into her mind, her heart.

Why was it, Nora wondered, that he could look at her and everything in her became wild and alive as it wasn't when he was gone? Why had she finally found the man for her, only to discover he was Fae and didn't even live in the same dimension? And why did her heart ache so at the thought of leaving him?

"No," she said, and he nodded grimly. "But, Quinn, I can't just stay here. As nice as your home is, I feel like I'm in a cage."

"But you cannot leave." He tossed back the rest of his nectar, set the glass down, then crouched in front of her so that they were eye-to-eye. "Nora, you are part-Fae."

"I know, but—"

"And in the time we've been together," he said, his gaze locked with hers, "we've shared ourselves. Joined on so deep a level that your Fae blood is awakening."

"What?" That she hadn't expected. That she hadn't been prepared to hear. A part of Nora was thrilled at the prospect of finally becoming what she'd always secretly wanted to be. The other part of her worried at what this change would do to the rest of her life. There was Eileen to consider.

"Power has swelled from my body into yours. It's not strong yet, but it will be."

"Then that should make me safer here, shouldn't it?" Nora reached for him, cupping his face between her palms. "My Fae blood will make me fit in here. I won't stand out in a crowd, right? This is better?"

He covered her hands with his own, then turned his face and kissed her palm. "As the Fae within you awakens," he said softly, "your mortal blood is defined by the difference. If anything the danger is greater for you here now than it was before."

"Danger."

Standing up, Quinn pulled her from the chair and held her closely to him. "The Conclave is warded with strong magic. No one but warriors and those few we trust are allowed to enter, and so you are safer here than anywhere else in Otherworld. Leave this tree and your mortal blood will sing out to anyone you encounter."

"And then?"

"Then Mab finds you." He tipped her chin up with the tips of his fingers. "She would kill you if she found you. She doesn't allow the Fae to blend with humans."

"She'd kill me." She swallowed hard, felt a trickle of fear slide through her and then curled against Quinn's broad chest again. So much was happening so quickly. "Then send me home," she said. "I miss my daughter. I need to see her, Quinn. I need to be with her."

"I can't, love," he told her, and she heard the unspoken apology in his voice. "To send you back to your home now would be even more dangerous for you than staying here. If Mab discovers Maggie she would use you to stop your sister."

"But Eileen—"

"Is safer without you at her side, drawing Mab's interest. Only wait awhile longer," he promised, bending his head to kiss her gently. "Be strong for just a little more time, Nora. Soon this will be over and you can return to your life."

Return to her life. Go back to Castle Bay. To Eileen. To Maggie. And leave Quinn behind? God, she would miss him. Miss what she'd found with him. How would she ever live the rest of her life not seeing him, feeling him? Yet maybe he didn't feel the same.

"Are you so eager to be rid of your hostage?" She whispered the question, half-afraid of his answer.

"I've never been less eager about anything in my far too long a life," he told her.

She smiled. Knowing that he cared for her didn't solve anything, but it made her feel a little better. "This is such a mess, isn't it?"

He tucked her head beneath his chin and stroked her back with his strong hands, soothing, reassuring. But Nora's mind whirled on.

How could she leave Quinn? How would she survive losing him? But she couldn't stay with him, either. Eileen shouldn't grow up in Otherworld. She deserved a normal life. And Nora wanted to give it to her. As much as she cared about Quinn, Eileen had to be her priority.

But until she went home again . . . Reaching up, she wrapped her arms around Quinn's neck and pulled his mouth to hers. When he kissed her the doubts, the fears, the worries slid from her mind in a river of fire so deep and hot, Nora felt as though she were combusting.

After several long moments, she pulled her head back, looked into his beautiful eyes and said, "Why don't we go to bed and you can make me just a little more Fae?"

"Good idea." He swept her up into his arms, and as he carried her to his bed Nora let herself believe that there would somehow, some way, be a happy ending to all of this.

*

"So that's the story," Maggie said a couple of hours and a bottle of wine later. She drained the last drop or two of chardonnay, then carefully set her glass down onto the coffee table and glanced at Claire. Her friend looked a little blurry.

"And quite the tale it was." Claire took the last swallow of her wine, leaned back against the couch and stretched her legs out in front of her, jostling Sheba. "Sorry, you lazy dog, you."

"Yep, everybody's sleeping but us. Eileen's asleep in her bedroom, Bezel's curled up in his tree, Sheba's practically unconscious, and snoring to boot, and Culhane? Probably sleeping in the arms of his bitch queen. The bastard."

"All men are dogs," Claire said with the careful diction of the quietly drunk.

"The thing is . . ." Maggie stopped, fought the fuzz in her brain, then scowled, trying to remember what she'd been about to say. Then it came to her. "The thing is, I still want the Faery rat bastard, you know? I mean, he's lying to me and dragging me into a huge mess and I still want to crawl up onto his lap and—"

"Take pity on the celibate," Claire pleaded. "No word pictures, if you don't mind."

"Right. Celibate. Too bad you're not Catholic. You could be a nun."

"I don't think they take witches."

"Probably not. What the hell am I going to do?"

Claire reached out from her spot on the floor, set her empty glass beside Maggie's, then patted her friend's hand. "You're going to fight Mab and become queen."

"In one version of the future, sure," Maggie said, wishing suddenly that the fireplace her grandfather had built was actually a working one instead of being a hidden wine refrigerator. On a stormy night a fire would have been more comfort than the clank and moan of an ancient furnace. Yet having extra wine handy was its own kind of comfort.

She looked at Claire then and voiced her real fears. "But what about the other futures I've gotten glimpses of? The ones where I lose and everybody dies? God, the images are so real they terrify me."

"I know. I only caught a glimpse or two, and they did the same for me."

"Oh yeah. I forgot you can 'see.' "

"Isn't that nice?" Claire murmured, licking a stray drop of wine from the rim of her glass. "See? You're not acting different around me now that you know. . . . You're a good friend, Mags."

"Yeah, I'm the best. Just ask the pixie sleeping in my tree." She laughed suddenly, worry dissolving in a happy mist of wine. "I've got a *pixie* sleeping in my tree. How weird is that?"

Claire rested her head against the couch cushion. "Strange indeed. But couldn't you have found a nice pixie?"

"Are there nice pixies?"

"How the bloody hell should I know?" Claire giggled, snorted, then waved her empty wineglass. "I think I need some more."

"Good call." Maggie crawled over to the faux fireplace, yanked on one of the decorative irons, and a panel slid open to reveal the minifridge stocked with white wine. Because, really, who needed red?

She pulled out one of her favorites, closed the panel, then scootched back to her spot on the floor. Then all she had to do was wrestle with the bottle opener, struggle with the damned cork and splash more wine into her and Claire's glasses.

"Mission accomplished," she said, and grabbed her own glass to take a healthy swallow. If only the other mission she faced were as easily dealt with.

"See, the whole problem is . . ." Maggie paused for a fresh gulp of wine. "It all comes down to me, Claire. Win or lose, it all comes down to me. How is it fair that I'm in charge of what happens to the world?

"If I win, there're still problems; I get that. But if I lose . . . I see people—my family, even—dying in those dreams. That future could happen, too."

"It won't." Claire sighed a bit, took a sip of wine and added, "I saw danger for you, Mags. You and Nora and everyone else. But I didn't see death."

"Doesn't mean it's not there." God, could she be more depressing? "This seriously blows. I hate being depressed."

"Let's see if I can just get another peek." Claire closed her eyes, took a deep breath, and silence purred into the room as Maggie waited. And waited. And waited.

Finally she shoved her best friend. "Hey, no falling asleep while I'm in a depression!"

"I'm not sleeping, you silly cow," Claire told her,

eyes still closed. "I'm reaching for a vision. Looking for a sign."

"Oh. Okay. Good. Search away." She let her gaze wander the living room, the familiarity of it all sliding into her like a virtual hug.

Hug. Culhane. Sex. *Damn it.* Even when she was allowing herself to wallow in self-pity and depression it didn't take long for thoughts of her sexy Faery to rise up. *Ooh. Rise up. There's an image*, she thought, and smiled at her mental picture of a fully risen Culhane stretched out across her bed.

"God, I'm a slut," she muttered.

"True, but keep it down, will you?"

"Right, right." Maggie took another drink. "The Great and Powerful Claire needs silence for the hocus-pocus." She frowned. "Why is that, do you think? If you need quiet, why aren't witches born deaf? Wouldn't that make it easier? Or are earplugs enough?" She swirled the wine in her glass and watched it shine in the lamplight. "Good thing I'm only destiny's bitch and not a witch—rhyming!" She grinned to herself. "Because it's never quiet around here."

"Truer words," Claire mumbled, eyes still closed.

"Right. Sorry." Maggie clamped her lips shut, but then she couldn't drink her wine, so that didn't last long. Still, she managed to keep quiet for another minute or two. Then Claire broke the silence herself.

"It's not clear."

"Hmm? What's not?" Maggie blinked at Claire, willed her familiar face into focus and then held her breath. Her best friend's eyes were open and the normal blue was gone. Now those eyes churned with silver, sparking with some inner light Maggie'd never seen before. Just another spot of weird in a life that was suddenly way too full of it. "Claire? Did you know your eyes are silver?"

"I can see, but the way's blocked. The images changing." Her voice had changed, too. Going soft, with a thread of steel underneath. "You can win, but not as they think you will. Not as you fear you will. There's a battle. There's pain. There's ..."

Her eyes snapped back to normal.

"There's *what*?" Maggie demanded.

"I don't know. Visions ended. Ooh. More." Claire took her glass and drank a long gulp of chilled white wine.

"Well, what kind of crappy vision is that? Just the trailers? Not the end?"

Claire shrugged. "I told you, it's not like I've got satellite reception or high-def or something. I get what I get when I get it."

"Very helpful."

"Hey, at least in my vision you *lived*."

"True." Maggie's stomach released one of the tension knots. Didn't make a huge difference, but at this point she'd take what she could get.

"Y'know, Mags," Claire was saying between chugs of wine, "if it's okay with you I think I'll stick around. Stay here with you and Eileen till this is done."

"Okay, but why?"

"I'll feel better if I'm close. And maybe perx ... pox ..." She stopped, rubbed her tongue across her front teeth and tried again. "*Proximity* to you will bring more visions."

Outside, a storm raged in the night, wind buffeting the glass, rain slapping against it like eager fingers tapping. There'd been more winter storms in the last couple of weeks than Maggie could remember seeing in years. Coincidence? She didn't think so. But the cold and the wet were outside. Inside she was warm and half-tipsy, sitting with a friend who was willing to put her own life on hold to help Maggie.

"Thanks," she said, resting her head on the couch

cushion behind her again. "I appreciate it, though Bezel won't be happy."

"Another plus," Claire said with a laugh as she lifted her glass in a toast.

"I suppose, all in all," Maggie agreed, clinking her glass to Claire's, "it could be worse."

Chapter Sixteen

Naturally, Maggie'd jinxed herself.

She had tempted the Fates with that it-could-be-worse shit, and now worse was here.

The morning had started off all right, considering that Maggie had a headache the size of Oregon. But most of the storm was gone, leaving only a cold wind and a few black clouds behind as a reminder.

Bezel, of course, was in top form, ordering her around, making her practice until her fingertips were singed from the thousands of lightning bolts she threw. She'd run what felt like hundreds of miles, doing circles around the yard. She'd punched and flipped and kicked until every square inch of her body was pleading for rest.

And that was when all hell broke loose.

"Oh, let her sit down for a moment, you ugly pixie," Claire demanded from the sidelines.

"I don't hear witches," Bezel retorted, covering his big ears as he made a *la-la-la-la-la* sound to illustrate.

"But if Maggie's tired, how can she fight?" Eileen asked, enjoying her unofficial break from school.

What with the Gray man showing up the night before, Maggie was too nervous about her niece's safety to have Eileen anywhere but home. Although maybe she'd be better off away from Maggie completely. But Maggie couldn't stand the thought of that, so until this mess was over one way or the other, as far as the school knew, the girl had the flu.

"You think Mab's gonna give her a time-out?" Bezel countered. "Culhane's gonna owe me big for this. Kids and witches and part-Fae pains in my butt. My life sucks."

"*Yours* sucks?" Maggie asked between gasping breaths.

"Fifty-five percent of all heart attacks in women are caused by overexertion," Eileen said.

"Huh?" Maggie looked at her and slapped one hand to her chest, as if she could stop a heart attack before it started.

"She's not having a heart attack," Claire soothed.

"Let's see some fire bolts," Bezel ordered.

"Twenty-seven percent of all heart attacks go unnoticed. Until it's too late."

"HUH?" Maggie was wheezing now and seriously rethinking the whole keep-Eileen-at-home thing.

"It was *you*."

A new voice. From behind her. Deep. Dark. Gravelly and filled with menace. Maggie's blood turned to ice in an instant, and the chatter in the yard dropped away as if it had never been. She so didn't want to turn around.

"Ah, crap." Bezel scuttled closer to Maggie. "It's a demon. A big one, too. Don't go nutso on me now. Just kill it so we can get back to training."

"Get away, pixie," the big voice said. "This is between me and the bitch who killed my mate."

"Oh, fabulous," Claire muttered.

"He's a *demon*?" Eileen asked.

"It wasn't my fault," Maggie said, and turned to face an absolute giant of a guy lumbering toward her. Seriously big. Seriously mean-looking. And seriously pissed. *Just perfect.*

"You killed her," he said, and as he came closer he allowed his human mask to slip a fraction.

Maggie had the sense of gray skin, yellow teeth, and claws that looked as sharp as razor blades. He was big, and he was determined to kill her. Her life just kept on sucking.

"I had to. She was eating my ex-boyfriend and about to eat me."

"She stops on her way home for some fast food and dies for it?" He shook his head and bunched his fists together, slamming them against each other at the knuckles. "I don't think so. I gave her that Fae power for our anniversary. You took it; now I'm gonna get it back."

Good God.

He charged. Maggie pushed off the ground, floated high enough to clear his head, then landed again. *Excellent.*

"You've learned to use it," he said. "Good. Makes this more interesting." Then he pulled a gold ball from one of his pockets and flipped open the catch. "I'll trap the power here when I'm done with you."

When she was dead, he meant. *Well, hell.* No way was she going to die in her backyard in front of Eileen, for God's sake. Hadn't she just blasted a bad Fae the night before? Hadn't she stood there, proud and triumphant, basking in her own sense of pride and Culhane's admiration? She was Maggie, hear her roar.

But just in case, she sent a quick, silent prayer to whatever gods might be listening. Never hurts to cover all your bases.

The demon smirked at her, then sent a quick look at everyone else in the yard. "Stay out of this, all of you, and you might not die." Pausing, he tasted the air and smiled grimly. "I can smell power that isn't the pixie. . . ." He focused on Claire for a long moment, then sneered. "Witch. Pixies and witches and wannabe Fae.

This'll be easier than I thought. You bunch stay put, and I'll let you live."

"Big talk from a walking dust bunny," Bezel called out.

"Way to go, you little tree rat," Maggie told him. "Piss him off some more, why don't you?"

"Kill it already," Bezel shot back.

Claire didn't say a word, just pulled Eileen behind her and gave the demon a glare to match his own. Then she glanced at Maggie. "Do it, Mags. For all the worlds. For yourself. Prove you can do it."

Easier said than done. But what choice did she have, really?

He ran at her again, and she dipped out of his reach, but she wasn't fast enough to avoid the scrape of his claws across her shoulder and upper back. Pain erupted just beneath her skin and fed the flames of anger building within. "Damn it, that hurt!"

He grinned at her, a broad smile that held no humor but plenty of malice.

"And my shirt's torn!" The soft cotton fabric was flapping in the wind, and she waved her arm to demonstrate. The scrape on her back stung, her shirt was ruined, and Eileen was probably terrified. Anger churned through her, and Maggie let it build. *Use what you've got, Maggie,* she told herself, *and take this creep out.*

So she focused. She concentrated. She dredged up everything she'd used the night before and reached for more. Then she threw herself into the fight.

Dropping into a crouch, Maggie swung out her leg, knocked his out from under him and felt the earth shake when he landed on his back. But he was fast as well as big, and in an instant he was back on his feet, looking a little less cocky. Then his eyes narrowed on her, sparks of red jittered in their centers and he growled as he reached for her.

Maggie let him get close enough that he thought he was going to win. She could see it in his eyes. He was already doing a private victory dance, thinking he had her. He was going to turn her around so she couldn't breathe on him; then he was going to kill her and steal the Fae power. Or, at least, she guessed that was the plan.

But while he was celebrating she ducked under his beefy arms, slashed out with her left hand and sent blue-and-white bolts of energy flashing at him. He shrieked as flames tickled his shirt, burned into his skin, and while he worried about the fire Maggie came in even closer, drew on everything she had inside her and sent a stream of Faery dust at his eyes.

The demon knew what was coming in the instant before those golden flecks of power reached him. He made a last-minute grab for the receptacle, wanting to hold it up, to catch the dust and save himself, but he was way too slow. Way too late.

His eyes went wide and horrified and he pulled in one last breath before releasing it in a scream that scraped the air like knives on metal. Then he burst into a cloud of dust that the wind picked up and carried out of the yard in a gritty haze. He was gone. She was alive.

Good times.

"Oh, my God!" Claire was the first to reach her, and wrapped Maggie in a hard hug as she jumped up and down in excitement. "You did it. You killed him. And you're not even hurt!" She checked Maggie's shoulders and winced. "Well, all right, some scratches, but I can heal those for you. Maggie, you were wonderful."

She was still reeling. Still feeling the adrenaline coursing through her, mingling with the Fae power, making her a trembling bundle of Maggie. But Claire was right: She'd done it. Actually done it. Yes, she'd fought a couple of demons before this, but she'd won those matches as much through luck as skill.

The Gray man had been different, too, she told herself. Culhane had been there, and despite the fact that she'd fought the Fae on her own, a part of her had known that the warrior was close enough to depend on if things went badly.

But here she'd truly been standing on her own two feet. She'd had to face the fact that those she cared about were in danger and still manage to keep her head. She'd had to remember, to concentrate, to think and feel her way through powers that she hadn't had nearly enough time to get used to yet. And she'd done it. Despite Bezel's doubts. Despite her own doubts—Maggie had proven herself.

"You really were great, Aunt Maggie." Eileen's eyes were shining with pride and admiration. "It was *awesome*."

"I did it," Maggie muttered, breathing hard but smiling. She could look into the faces she loved and realize that she had saved them. Protected them from the things her nightmares had been showing her. She'd faced the beast and she'd survived again. On her own. Because of what *she* could do, she'd saved them all.

"Yeah, yeah." Bezel interrupted and pushed both Claire and Eileen aside. When he was in front of Maggie he looked up at her, his gaze hard and clear. "Big deal. You beat a pissed-off demon."

"Here, now," Claire argued. "Give her her due, at least, you miserable little troll. She won."

"Yeah," Maggie said, offended that Bezel couldn't take one stupid minute to give her a damn pat on the back. "Don't I get a little time to 'whoopee' a little? 'Yay, me' and all that? Isn't this what I've been working my ass off for? Hell, Bezel, you've been training me night and day; aren't you at least glad I was listening?"

"You don't get it, do you?" He shook his head viciously, and his long silver hair flew in wild wisps. Bending down, he grabbed a handful of dirt from the edge of the garden and stood up again. "See this?" He let the soil drift from his hand as he said, "*This* is what you fought." Then he pointed to the mountains in the distance. "*That* is what you face."

The glow of victory inside Maggie flickered and died as she stared at the mountains. He was right, blast him to his own version of hell and back. She hated that he was right. Hated that she'd lost the certainty in her own abilities that she'd had just a second ago. Hated that fear was creeping back in.

This demon, though big and horrifying, was nothing compared to the battle still waiting for her. She hadn't learned enough to match powers with a Faery queen, for God's sake. She was the one who was going to be slapping at licks of flame rippling across her shirt when she faced Mab. If she was *lucky* that was all Mab would do to her.

The queen had centuries of practice dealing with her powers. She no doubt had *more* power than Maggie, too. There was just no way this was going to turn out well.

"You think Mab's gonna be taken care of with a few energy bolts?" He snorted in disgust. "What? *She* doesn't have 'em? Come on!"

"She'll do it," Claire sniped. "I've *seen* it."

"Oooh." Bezel shuddered. "The witch speaks. I'm so scared. Save me."

Maggie glared at him. "Thanks for the pep talk, Coach." Then she hobbled toward the house, looking for some aspirin.

℮

The dreams came again that night, moving through Maggie's mind at lightning speed. The images changed, distorted, shifted and swirled, blending together, then drifting apart again.

She saw Nora happy, and in the next instant her sister was dead. Before she could so much as scream, though, the dream changed again, and Maggie saw herself as queen of the Fae, with warriors bowing to her—then she saw herself dead at Culhane's feet.

She twisted anxiously in her sleep, trying to escape. Trying to find a way out of what was coming. When she woke with a start, gasping for air, she knew, bone deep, that there was no way out. No way to avoid the confrontation that was headed at her with the single-mindedness of fate.

Pushing her sweat-dampened hair back from her face, Maggie sat alone in the dark and replayed all of the disturbing images in her mind again. Which future was real? Were any of them? Was the future set in stone already, and all of this nothing more than an exercise in futility? Or could the future be rewritten?

"Even if I can rewrite it," she murmured, needing to hear a voice, if only her own, "how do I do it? And if I die, what happens to Nora and Eileen?"

God, she wasn't ready to die yet. There was way too much she wanted to do. She wanted to see Europe. Wanted to walk down quiet streets in Paris or sit in a café and look out at the Alps. She wanted to taste wine in Tuscany and go back to Ireland and paint all the magic she'd seen there as a kid.

"But none of that's going to happen until you get through this, Maggie," she told herself firmly, despite the quaver in her voice. "Because like it or not, destiny's in charge here. So get on board already. Because anybody standing in the way is going to get crushed."

Culhane and the warriors were as ready as they could be. There was really nothing more they could do until Maggie finally faced Mab.

The rumbles of Otherworld were louder, he thought, stalking down a long silver road leading from the palace to the closest village. There were fights among the Fae now, as people chose sides and declared their loyalties. Male Fae were already beginning to rebel against their women, which was making for even more trouble, as females suddenly were faced with mates who were no longer willing to take orders.

The scent of flowers hung in the air, and he narrowed his gaze, squinting into the glare of the suns. Light flashed off the crystal and silver, shimmered on the leaves of the trees, slanted off windowpanes with a beauty that was familiar. Still, he felt the undercurrent of an ugliness that had been building for centuries.

Mab, though, didn't see it. Or chose not to. He'd left her only moments ago and he could still hear her.

"Why haven't you found the stolen Fae power yet? It's mine by right," she said, giving him a haughty look that she'd perfected over the centuries. *"I am your queen, and I expect better from my warriors."*

"Yes," he said, hoping to appease and at the same time keep her unaware of his divided loyalties. *"But, my queen, there is unrest in Otherworld. The warriors are being called on to settle disputes in the streets and can't be expected to roam the mortal world searching for stray power."*

Mab narrowed her glorious eyes on him in a fit of temper that had sparks lifting from her fingertips. "I didn't ask the warriors to get me that power, Consort. I commanded it of you."

"You did. And I will find it and bring it to you." He didn't add, of course, that when he brought the power to her, that power would be within the woman he hoped would defeat the queen. *"But I cannot leave the problems here for my warriors to handle alone."*

"Then they are incapable of action without your guidance? What pitiful warriors I find I have."

"No, my queen," he said. "I thought only to be here where I'm needed."

She stood up from her throne, stepped off the podium and walked toward him. "I tell you where you're needed, Consort."

"I am, as always, at your command."

Mab tilted her head to one side, her long blond hair falling in a thick wave off her shoulders. She stared up into his eyes and wondered aloud, "Are you? Are you still my loyal consort, Culhane? It's been some time since I've called you to my bed."

For that he was grateful. He would do what he must, but Culhane had no wish to join with the queen when his body wanted only Maggie Donovan. But he couldn't say that much aloud. So he fell back on the courtly responses he knew Mab expected. "It has been too long, my queen."

Lifting one hand, he touched her waist, let his fingertips caress the curve of her hip. She smiled as if satisfied, then stepped back and away from him abruptly.

"I find I'm much too busy to satisfy you at the moment, Consort. Get you to the mortal world." She fixed him with a stare that was filled with impatience and greed. "Find the power and bring it to me at once. If your warriors are so clumsy, so inadequate to the task of controlling Otherworld while you're gone, then there will have to be unrest until you've returned."

Culhane nodded and gave her a brief bow. "I will go immediately."

"Good." Her voice stopped him before he could leave the throne room. "And, Culhane, I grow impatient. Do not keep me waiting."

&

Maggie'd rather face another Gray man than vacuum. But despite the fact that she had windows to paint, demons to fight and a queen to kill, life went on. Clothes had to be washed, vacuums had to be run, groceries had to be bought.

"Screw fighting demons," Maggie muttered as she hovered five feet off the floor, scraping off a layer or two of grime off the top of the damned entertainment center. "Dusting will kill you."

She hated housecleaning more than any other thing in the known universe. She'd always thought, *What's the point? It only gets dirty again.* Seemed like a massive waste of time and effort to her, but on the other hand, she hated a mess, too.

Naturally, being a sensible woman, Maggie had hired a cleaning service to come in twice a month to do most of it. In between times Maggie did the decluttering and putting away of stuff. But she'd been a little distracted the last couple of weeks, and now she had no choice but to clean before the maids arrived the next day and discovered what a slob she was.

Watery sunlight spilled through the open living room curtains, and a slight breeze skipped in through the partially opened windows. The scent of the sea filled the old house, and Maggie started humming to keep herself company. With the place empty, it felt a little weird to be all alone. She'd been surrounded by people and action for the last couple of weeks. Hearing herself think was a novelty.

"What are you doing?"

"Jesus!" Maggie grabbed the top of the entertainment center, whipped her head around and glared at Culhane, floating right alongside her. "To answer your question," she said, choking back her heart, currently lodged in her throat, "I'm having the crap scared out of me by a Faery. You?"

"I meant, why are you wasting time with menial tasks?"

"How should I be wasting my time, then?" She

dropped to the floor, picked up the vacuum and turned it on, hoping to drown him out or make him leave. Either one would do. But the high-pitched whine coming from the machine told her she'd probably sucked up one of Sheba's chew toys.

"Perfect." She snapped off the machine, flipped it over and began digging past the roller. "This is just freaking perfect. Why are you here?"

He dropped to the floor beside her, then crouched so that he could look her in the eye. His scent wafted around her, and Maggie drew it in deeply with every breath. The forest, leather, *him*.

The damn Faery was a walking temptation. Or, as the nuns used to say, *an occasion of sin*. Hell, he *was* sin. Maggie had lain awake most of last night—after the nightmares drove even the thought of sleep out of her mind—thinking about . . . well, everything. She'd come to the conclusion that the only way she was going to keep her head on straight through the rest of this was to stop thinking about Culhane. About the way he made her feel. Want. She needed desperately to be able to concentrate on the little things, like . . . staying alive.

Wouldn't you know he'd show up as if to test her newfound resolve? Why the hell did he have to smell so good?

"I've come to take you with me back to Otherworld."

Of course he had. Watch her kill a Gray man, disappear for a few hours—how long was that in Faery time? And now he shows up to whisk her off for more show-and-tell in fairy-tale land. She glanced at him from beneath her lashes and felt her stomach lurch and her mouth go dry.

His eyes, so pale, so clear and sharp, were fixed on her. His mouth lush, and so damn kissable she could almost taste him. His jaw strong and hard, and set now as if it were stone. A welling tide of attraction and desire rose up inside her and stole what little breath she had left. The man was too big a distraction. One she couldn't afford right now.

"Can't." There. She'd said it. Yay, her. She turned her gaze back to the upended vacuum and kept digging past the roller that still had tinsel wrapped around it from *last* Christmas. Damn stuff. They ought to make cars out of tinsel. It was indestructible. "Sorry. Kinda busy at the moment."

"With cleaning tasks? Maggie—"

"Culhane, don't. I've got a life to get back together. I don't have time for another visit to the tree house." She didn't have the endurance for it, either. It had been hard enough before, being shut away with him in his house in the forest. Now, though, that much togetherness time would only result in sex, and then she'd be even more scattered than she was now. She so didn't need that.

Finally she found the obstruction behind the roller, yanked it out and scowled down at a green-and-gold button. "Not Sheba's. Bezel's. Off that ugly suit he's always wearing."

She tossed the button onto the coffee table and stood up. Looking down at Culhane, she whipped her hair back out of her face and told him, "I appreciate the offer of a field trip, but I've got to finish this cleaning, do some laundry, then, when Claire and Eileen get back from the grocery store, put all of that stuff away."

Culhane stood up, his movements slow, deliberate. He grabbed her hands, and she felt the heat and sizzle of his touch dart up her arms and settle in her chest. God, she so didn't need this right now. Yet everything in her yearned for it.

"This isn't your world anymore, Maggie."

It was the one thing he could have said to shatter the

little spell she'd felt being woven around her by his nearness, his touch. She didn't *want* to lose her world.

"You're wrong," she said, and tugged her hands free. "This is my real world. This is my reality. A water heater that's on its last legs. Painting jobs piled up and waiting for me. A niece who's worried about her mom and flunking math. A friend who's worried about me and trying not to show it. A crabby *pixie* living in my oak tree and eating all my damn cookies. It's a life that sometimes includes fighting the stray demon. It's *not* the other way around," she said, getting a little hot as she defended her right to have a normal life. "I won't be what you want and try to squeeze in what *I* want in my off hours. I can't live like that, Culhane. I *need* normal."

"Your life has changed," he told her, moving in so close that Maggie could see only him—nothing behind him, around him, only Culhane. Only his eyes. "Normal for you now is what others will never know."

"I don't want your normal. I want my own." Stubborn, she knew it, but couldn't stop. She heard the near whine in her voice and couldn't silence it. "God, when all this started I actually thought, *Okay, cool. Break out of your rut, Maggie. Get out there. Have some excitement in your life.* Well now, that rut's looking pretty damn comfy, I can tell you."

He smiled, that gorgeous mouth of his curving at the edges, his eyes softening as he watched her. "You are a wonder to me, Maggie Donovan. Though I'd felt our connection before, I didn't expect this. You talk too much, eat incessantly and argue even when you know it will do no good. You were an irritation to me at first, and now you are simply essential."

Hard to believe that he'd gotten to know her so well in such a short period of time. But then, he'd been watching her all her life, hadn't he? He'd known her for freaking ever, and she—

"Irritation?" She planted both hands on her hips and gave him a look designed to fry his Faery ass. "Well, thanks very much." Then the rest of what he'd said settled in, and everything in her melted.

"Oh, God." *Essential?* How many big, strong men were willing to say that to a woman? To admit to a need that deep? How many women were ever lucky enough to hear that from the man they . . . *Nope. Not going there.* She stopped herself from even thinking the L-word. She couldn't drag that into the middle of this now. Weren't things unsettled and confusing enough?

His gaze moved over her face like a caress. He lifted one hand to smooth her hair, then traced his fingertips down along the curve of her jaw. Smiling a bit, he swiped his thumb down her nose and rubbed his fingers together to get rid of the dust he'd just cleaned off her skin. "I find I think of you far too often," he said, "and not only for what you can do for Otherworld."

She blew out a breath and took in another one, drawing the scent of him deep within. Maggie's insides were jumping, and her heartbeat was crashing like thunder in her chest.

She'd been so sure last night that the only way to survive what was coming was to separate herself—emotionally, at least—from Culhane. Now she realized in a blast of understanding just how dumb that decision had been. She couldn't do this without him. More—she didn't want to. He'd become such a part of her life, she couldn't imagine him *not* there anymore.

And wouldn't you know she'd be having this über-romantic moment when she looked like the dregs of hell? Here she stood, staring up into the eyes of the Fae she lo—never mind—covered with dust and grime and . . . Oh, who cared?

"I woke up today determined to avoid you," she admitted, and saw his lips quirk. "I figured the best way for me to handle what I feel when I'm around you was just not to be around you." Maggie sighed and felt her own surrender in the action. "There's so much going on that I thought keeping you out of my head and my heart would make it easier to deal with all the other shit. But I was wrong. Keeping you in my head makes it easier."

"And your heart?" he asked, his voice a hush.

"You're already there. I don't think I can get you out now."

"Good. As I don't want you to." He cupped her face in his palms, and heat slid down and through her, rushing like a river cresting its banks. His thumbs stroked her cheekbones; his gaze met hers. "I, too, thought to keep myself from you. To somehow look at you and see only the future of Otherworld. But you're more, Maggie Donovan. You're my future as well, Goddess help us both."

Maggie held her breath as he leaned in closer, closer. His breath brushed her face; his warmth radiated out to her, wrapping itself around her, drawing her in. She moved in, no longer interested in avoiding him, ignoring him. He was all she wanted. She wanted to feel the magic of his kiss again, feel the heat and the need and the passion. When his lips covered hers, sensation coursed through her, pumping thick and hot and delicious. Everything in her swelled as if every cell within was blossoming.

His mouth moved on hers, deepening the kiss, parting her lips with his tongue, and Maggie moaned, giving as she took. Her slight hitch of sound made him tighten his hold on her, yanking her hard and flush against his body. Maggie did what she could to get even closer. Clinging to him, she lifted both legs, wrapped them around his hips and clung even harder, exposing her jeans-clad core to his rigid body.

She was so ready for this. Tiny explosions of want and greed sizzled inside her, and she ground her hips against his as if she could fight her way through their clothes. Feel his skin, his body against hers, inside hers.

Maggie tore her mouth from his, desperate for air. Her head fell back, and his mouth came down on her throat. He whispered in a language she didn't understand as he kissed and nibbled and licked until she thought she would lose what was left of her mind.

Why hadn't she done this before? Why had they waited? Torturing themselves and each other with the waiting? There was so much to be discovered. To be felt. Experienced. And she wanted it all. Now. Now, before her world dissolved again, or something else disgusting and cruel showed up to try to kill her. God, she didn't want to die without knowing what it was to be with Culhane.

"You're everything," he whispered, locking his lips on the pulse beat at the base of her throat. "All and more, it's you, Maggie. You and only you."

His voice was a caress that sighed through her mind, her heart. Time came to a stop. There was no world beyond this room, beyond this man. Her warrior.

He slid one hand between them to the waistband of her worn jeans. Quickly he undid the button and pulled the zipper down. Maggie gasped as his fingertips smoothed over her skin in a touch that was both featherlight and full of fire.

Her legs slipped from his hips even as she locked her arms around his neck. His gaze held on hers, he watched her as his hand slid farther down her body. His long, clever fingers dipped beneath the wispy elastic band of her panties and reached for her heat.

Maggie swayed into him when he cupped her, her skin humming, her body rocking into his touch. God, she felt as though she'd been waiting all of her life for this moment. For this man. He stroked the hard, sensitive bud at the very heart of her and Maggie whimpered a little, her fingers clutching at his shoulders. Then he dipped his hand lower still, and pushed one finger and then another into her wet heat. "Oh, God, Culhane!"

She'd never known anything like this. A simple, intimate touch from him was so much more than she could have expected. His breath on her face was warm and sweet. His touch was like fire, searing her skin, burning her bones, driving heat deep inside her to pool in her belly and spill through her veins.

He stroked her, in and out, his touch driving her toward a climax that hovered tantalizingly just out of reach. She stared into his eyes and could hardly see him through the haze of need nearly blinding her. But he watched her with such wonder, such tenderness, she gave herself up to the moment and ordered her whirling mind to be silent.

This was about feeling, experiencing, knowing what it was to have his hands on her at last. Her blood was hot, too hot for her veins, and she felt as if it were boiling just underneath her skin. Every breath she managed to drag into her lungs was charged with lust and need.

Culhane dropped his head and took her mouth in another out-of-control kiss, devouring her, allowing himself to be devoured in turn. Her hips rocked into his hand. His fingers continued to stroke and delve, drawing her closer and closer to the edge of a precipice. Maggie couldn't breathe and didn't care. All she wanted was this. His hands on her body. His mouth on hers.

"Shatter for me," he whispered against her lips. "Let me give that to you."

She *was* shattering. She felt it as her body trembled on the brink of something amazing. It was too much, she thought. She couldn't possibly survive if he kept this up. But how could she even think of asking him to stop? Then he rubbed that one spot that was the center of the storm raging within her, and her body erupted into a wild, frantic orgasm that spiraled on and on and on. Maggie shuddered and surrendered to what only Culhane could give her.

Chapter Seventeen

Seconds, minutes, hours, hell, *days* could have passed before Maggie's body stopped pulsing like a broken neon light.

God, she thought, if a kiss and a stroking could create that kind of orgasm, what would a full-body one be like? It might actually kill her, she decided wistfully, and wondered idly if this was the planet-shifting thing Nora had talked about.

Maggie dropped her forehead to Culhane's shoulder, struggling for air, thinking that oxygen was really overrated, anyway. A moment later, though, she lifted her head again and, smiling, looked up into his eyes. The instant their gazes locked, everything changed.

She gasped and tightened her grip on Culhane as images spilled from his mind to hers. Shattering, splintering slices of color and shape twisting into faces, places that sped by so quickly, Maggie couldn't identify them all. He stared at her, clearly as amazed at what was happening as she felt.

"Ah, blast. Do you see?" he asked, his voice hardly more than a strained whisper.

"I do, Culhane. What's—" She broke off when one crystal-clear image solidified in her mind: a blond woman who could only be Mab, jumping to her feet from a silver, jewel-encrusted throne, throwing her head back and screaming in raw fury. Then the image blinked off as if Maggie had hit the power button on a TV.

"Damn me to *Ifreann*." Culhane reacted instantly. He took a step back and away from Maggie. "I shouldn't have touched you so intimately. This is why I've held back from you, Maggie. To keep Mab from finding you before it was time." He shoved one hand through his thick hair and stalked a wide circle around her, his movements jerky, his steps long and hurried.

Maggie had gone from warm and fuzzy to tense in a split second, and she was reeling from the shift. She zipped up her jeans and watched him as her lover dissolved into the fierce Fae warrior she knew so well.

"There's a connection between us. Mab and me, I mean," he told her, speaking quickly now, words tumbling over one another as he rushed to explain. To make her see.

Maggie watched his face as she spun in a tight circle, keeping her gaze locked on Culhane. His features were etched with worry, his eyes flashing with a knowledge as old as time.

"Because of that connection to Mab she can feel what I'm feeling. Sense, if she's a mind to, what I'm doing. She rarely uses this gift, since nothing in this world or any other matters to Mab more than herself." Disgusted, he stopped dead, stared at Maggie and said, "I knew that if you and I came together, the bond between us would be enough to alert Mab. Now she knows, senses what I feel for you, and knows I'm no longer her man." He scraped one hand across his jaw, the back of his neck.

Maggie rubbed her hands up and down her arms, half expecting the Faery queen to burst into the living room with a flaming sword. "What does this mean, though?"

"She hasn't known about you—you personally—until this. She's been aware of the Fae power being stolen, going missing, but she had no idea that it was you who'd claimed it or that you're training to use it."

Maggie swallowed hard, nerves tangling in the pit of her stomach as she realized what Culhane was saying. Even the pale wash of sunlight sliding into the room seemed somehow dimmer, and the air felt so much colder. "Now she knows."

"Yes." He reached for her, then folded his fingers into fists to keep himself from touching her again. "She knows. And knowing will make her move. She won't wait until we're ready, Maggie. I'd hoped to delay this. To give you more time to feel your way into your new world, but the time is over. Ended. Mab will decide the time and place now, and it won't be in our favor." Jaw tight, eyes hard as flint, he said, "Maggie, you must—"

He jerked his head up and around, as if sensing something that Maggie couldn't feel.

"Culhane, what is it?"

"No!" He shouted the word until it echoed off the walls and ceilings and speared into Maggie's heart like a dagger. He fired one last, frantic glance at her.

Then, in a blink, he was gone.

Apparently they were out of time.

⚜

"I'll watch out for the kid," Bezel told her a half hour later. "And the damn witch."

"Thanks." She spared the ugly little man a quick smile that she didn't feel. Since Culhane had disappeared, Maggie'd been able to think of only one thing: getting to Otherworld and settling this. If she just hung around, waiting for Mab to make her move, she'd be forced to meet the queen on her own turf. And no way would that turn out well. Maggie would be no better off than poor Joe had been what felt like a lifetime ago—Creature Chow.

So she'd come up with her own plan—one she hoped like hell had a chance of working. She'd taken a shower, washed her hair and changed her clothes, because frankly, if she was going to die, she wasn't going to do it covered in dirt and dust.

So she wore a long-sleeved red T-shirt, faded blue jeans and a pair of boots she hadn't worn since the last time Claire had conned her into hiking in the woods. They were sturdy and heavy, and hopefully would do more damage in a good kick than her tennis shoes would.

Standing in the backyard now, beneath the tree Bezel had claimed for his own, Maggie took a long look around. Chrysanthemums blooming in the flower bed, Sheba snoring on the patio, a fence that needed painting and a lawn that needed mowing. It was all so normal. So everyday. God, she wanted to come back to it.

She wanted to be here for Christmas so she could string around the house the damned lights that were always a tangled mess. She wanted to be here in the spring to see if the stupid bulbs Nora had insisted on planting upside down actually bloomed. She wanted to go to the art show in Laguna this summer and maybe sell some of her paintings.

Hell. She just wanted to be here.

"Hey!" Bezel kicked her and jolted her out of the little pity party she was throwing for herself. "This is no time to go all weepy. If Mab pulled Culhane out of here like you said, then he's locked up tight. The bitch queen of the universe isn't gonna let him get near enough to you to help, so you're gonna be on your own."

"I know." God, she hoped she wasn't going to throw up.

"I'd help, but pixie magic ain't gonna be enough against Mab, anyway."

Surprised and a little touched by the offer, Maggie smiled. "Who are you, and what have you done with Bezel?" She paused and added, "Seriously, thanks for the thought."

"Plus, I don't want to get your nasty human blood all over this suit Fontana made me." He flicked a long finger over his lapel. "She'd kill me."

"And you're back to normal." *Good. Better.* A nice pixie would only make her as weepy as he'd already called her. Didn't really need that right now. What she needed was a bazooka. A tank, maybe. Oh, and a happy little battalion of soldiers to stand between her and the queen.

But since she wasn't going to get what she needed, she'd do what she had to instead. "Okay, I can do this." Nodding to herself, she called up her concentration, fought for focus past the mind-numbing fear, then closed her eyes and sketched out a circle in the air.

Within that circle color swirled and a warm breeze rushed out to ruffle her hair. Maggie took a deep breath to steady herself, then looked at Bezel. "Did I get it right?"

He glanced inside the golden, shimmering circle, then back at her. "Yeah. You did. Too bad you're gonna be meat right when you're starting to get the hang of this."

Maggie gave him a withering smile. "These little chats of ours always help so much."

"Quit stalling," he sniped, and stabbed one finger at the portal.

"Right. Okay, then. Wish me luck." Maggie took one more glance around the yard—hoping it wasn't her last—and stepped into the portal.

Just before the circle closed behind her, she thought she heard Bezel say, "Luck, kid. You're gonna need it."

Finn was there waiting when Maggie stepped out of the portal and into Sanctuary. He didn't even look surprised to see her, which made her wonder if maybe he'd been keeping an eye on her, too. Didn't matter really, either way.

"Culhane's gone," she said.

"I know. Mab's on a tear, but she can't get to you while you're here. As I told you before, I am the only one with power in Sanctuary. See?" Finn pointed to a wide shelf that lay bare but for one small bubble of gold dust that swirled in a tiny tornado, trapped behind a barrier Maggie couldn't see.

"That's your power," the wizard said. "Stripped from you the moment you stepped into Sanctuary. It won't return to you until you leave."

"Good." She stared up at the power that had so changed her life and found she didn't really hate it as much as she'd thought she would. "That's part of the reason I'm here."

"Really?" His eyebrows quirked as if he were intrigued, but Maggie spoke again before he could ask her for more information.

"Do you know where she took Culhane?"

"Yes. Word is already spreading." Finn took her arm and steered her down a long corridor toward the main library, where she'd read so many of his books. "Mab has him in a cell in the palace."

A twist of something cold and hard jolted through her system, but Maggie swallowed it back. In jail, but alive. With her mind full of thoughts of Culhane, she hardly noticed the beauty of the place that had so stunned her on her first visit. "At least she hasn't killed him." She grabbed Finn's arm. "*Can* she kill him? Aren't Fae immortal?"

"Yes, they are, and yes, she can kill him." Finn frowned at her frown and admitted, "I know that sounds contradictory. But cutting off Culhane's head would certainly kill him, and I wouldn't for an instant put it past Mab to do it."

"Oh, God." Maggie rubbed the base of her own throat and let Culhane's image rise up in her mind for a long moment. Only a half hour ago she'd been clinging to him tighter than Saran Wrap on a plate of Christmas cookies. Now he was in prison being held by a crazy queen, and Maggie was in Sanctuary preparing to put her possibly really bad plan into play.

They stepped into the cavernous library, and Maggie's gaze naturally swept the floor-to-ceiling shelves filled with hundreds of thousands of books. The windows lining the walls were, as always in Sanctuary, open to the sky beyond and the warm breezes that swirled through the room. In that sky, white clouds swept majestically past Sanctuary and looked so damned peaceful, Maggie almost resented their very existence.

She'd give a lot at the moment for a little peace in her life. But she wouldn't get that until she got past *this*.

"The queen will be in no hurry to kill him, at least," Finn said, and Maggie was sure he meant that to be reassuring. "She'll want to make him suffer for a century or two first."

"God, she's a piece of work, isn't she?" Maggie thought of Culhane, the fierce warrior, locked inside a cell, and everything inside her closed up. It would kill him to be shut into a cage. Kill him slowly, eating away at who he was, who he'd been, inches at a time. Her heart hurt for him, and hardened even further toward the queen who would do that to a warrior who had been not only her lover, but her loyal defender for centuries.

Maggie listened to the silence for a minute or two, drawing what strength she could from it. Okay, it wasn't much. But soon she was going to need all she could get. Plus, the moment she started talking, telling Finn why she was there, there would be no going back. So pardon the hell outta her for delaying a minute or two before setting out on the dead-end road ahead of her.

"Why have you come to me?" Finn asked quietly, and she turned to look at him. "Are you looking for a place to hide from Mab? Because even if you are, you can't stay here forever, Maggie."

His blue eyes were shining, and his features were taut yet blank, as if he were waiting to hear what she had to say before deciding how to feel about it. Good idea, actually.

"No, I'm not here to hide." Although her inner chickenshit whimpered and said, *Oooh. Good idea. Let's do that.*

"I have a plan," she said, shutting down that internal voice and locking her knees to keep them from knocking.

"I'm eager to hear it." Finn smiled at her, and on a purely feminine level she had to admire the man's gorgeousness. But right now all she needed was for him to listen to her without bursting into howls of laughter.

As she outlined her half-baked plan, Maggie felt a little better when Finn not only didn't laugh, but gave her a look filled with admiration.

"It could work," he said when she was finished.

"Your mouth to God's ear," she told him, repeating something her Gran used to say all the time.

"You've a courageous soul, Maggie Donovan. Destiny chose well."

"Let's hope so." Maggie took a breath and held it.

"It's a daring plan," Finn said. "One no Fae would have come up with."

"Well, then, let's hear it for the human." Maggie sat down in one of the library chairs and pretended it was because she wanted to. The truth was, she wasn't sure her legs were going to hold her up much longer.

It was fine and good to come up with a plan when you were at home and pissed off and desperate. It was something else again to be standing in Sanctuary about to make it happen. Still . . . the words *no choice* echoed through her mind, and she inhaled sharply, hoping to ease the swarms of butterflies currently going nuts in her stomach. It didn't help much.

"When will you go to her?"

"Now," Finn said. "No point in delaying this if you think you're ready."

Ready? Who was ready? Not Maggie. What she was really ready to do was run screaming from Sanctuary and pretend she never heard of Fae or pixies or wizards with kind eyes. Unfortunately, not an option.

"As I'll ever be." Her mouth was dry, and when she licked her lips nervously, Finn seemed to understand.

He waved one hand in the air and produced a tall crystal glass filled with water and lemon slices. "Drink this. I'll be back as soon as I can."

She hadn't even nodded before he blinked out of existence. How strange was it, she wondered, that she was sort of getting used to all of the popping in and out?

Carrying her glass of water, she sipped at it as she made herself stand up and wander around the inside of the library. Most of the floor space was empty, the bookshelves being stacked along the walls. The marble floors veined with shining silver glittered brightly in the light streaming in through the open windows.

The scent of fresh flowers flavored the air, and if she tried, Maggie could almost convince herself that she was in some great European museum, and any minute now a docent would come strolling in, leading a pack of camera-clicking tourists.

But the illusion didn't last. It kept slamming up against reality. She really hated reality.

"It's done."

"CRAP!" She spun around, sloshing her water across the floor as her heart jumped into her throat. "Just when I think I'm getting used to the way you guys travel, one of you scares the hell out of me."

"Sorry." The wizard walked up to her, took the glass of water and tossed it into the air. It disappeared as if it had never been.

Easy to do the dishes around here, anyway.

"You saw Mab?" Maggie asked. "What did you say? What did *she* say?" Why was he just standing there smiling at her?

"I saw the queen. I gave her your message, told her that you were waiting for her here in Sanctuary."

"And?" She waved her hand, urging him to hurry up already and tell her what was what.

"She was amused."

"Fabulous," Maggie muttered.

"But she agreed."

A rush of something that might have been fear-tinged relief swept through her. "Okay. That's good. I think. No, I know. It's good." She fisted her hands at her sides and nodded again.

Nerves scattered through her at the thought of finally coming face-to-face with the woman destiny had chosen her to defeat. She couldn't win against Mab on her turf: The woman was far too powerful, and Maggie was a novice. There was no way she'd be able to stay alive, let alone win a fight while trying to match her puny powers against those of a centuries-old queen.

But here, she thought, it was different. In Sanctuary they were on even ground. Here Mab wouldn't have her powers any more than Maggie would. Here it would be the two of them on more equal terms than Maggie would be able to find anywhere else.

"This is where I have the best shot," she murmured.

"True." Finn waited until she looked up at him to continue. "But even without her power Mab has millennia of experience to call on. She's still a formidable enemy, Maggie. Don't forget that."

"Man, you and Bezel with your pep talks. You really know how to get a girl all charged up."

He smiled faintly and laid one hand on her shoulder. It felt warm, strong and solid, and she appreciated the effort to reassure her.

"You were meant for this, Maggie. I believe that. As does Culhane."

Culhane.

Maggie's mind filled with his image, and a thread of steel snaked along her spine. He thought she could do this. He'd seen to it that she'd been trained. Had learned enough to think that she at least had a shot at this. And because he'd believed in her, he'd been snatched away by his queen and tossed into a dungeon somewhere.

So now it was up to her to convince everyone that he hadn't been wrong.

And the sooner the better, as far as she was concerned. Much more waiting and she'd be wound so tight she wouldn't remember a thing she'd learned. "So she's coming. When?"

"Now."

A soft voice that rang with authority filled the room, and Maggie turned to watch as Mab, queen of the Fae, walked into the library.

Maggie'd gotten only a glimpse of the queen in the moments before Culhane was pulled away. And that quick look hadn't been a flattering one.

Now, though, Mab looked every inch a regal Faery. Her features were delicate, her skin as pale as fine porcelain. Her long blond hair swung behind her as she walked with a confident sway. She was tall and thin and looked as fragile as a butterfly. But her eyes told a different story. There Maggie saw strength and a cool deliberation that convinced her she might be in even bigger trouble than she'd thought.

"*You* are the one who stole the Fae power?" Mab asked, sparing barely a glance at Finn as she honed in on Maggie. "If I'd known how unprepossessing you were, I'd have gone after the power myself and saved my warrior the effort."

Frowning, Maggie said, "Aw, you're just saying that to be nice."

Mab ignored her. "Now you've come here. To my world. Why, I wonder? Do you seriously think to conquer *me*? You, who are nothing more than a mote of dust beneath my feet? You, who are merely human, with a gift you don't understand? I have ruled for generations. I am Mab, queen of—"

She kept talking, but Maggie sort of zoned out. She'd somehow expected Mab to step into Sanctuary geared up and ready to fight. Instead she was wasting time tossing insults and trying to impress Maggie with how important she was, which wasn't really working. Maggie was far too nervous, too tangled up inside to be awed.

". . . I am eternal." Mab was still talking. "I am feared and respected across the mortal globe. I am—"

"Culhane keeps telling me that I talk too much," Maggie interrupted, because she'd really rather get this fight over with. "But you haven't shut up since you walked in."

Mab's face flushed with a sudden spurt of temper, and Maggie was glad to see it. If the queen could get pissed, she could be distracted. Hey, any rope you could grab when you were falling was a good one.

"You would dare to speak to me like this?" Mab sniffed, narrowed her eyes and lifted a delicately pointed chin. "You're nothing. Less than nothing. Why Culhane bothered to linger with you at all is beyond me."

"I'll bet a lot of things are beyond you, Mab."

She hissed.

So she was nothing, huh? Maggie felt her own temper spike and was grateful for it. She liked mad way better than terrified.

"Like, for example," Maggie taunted, "I bet you missed the fact that you came here all set to squash me like a bug, but didn't seem to notice that your power got zapped out of you the minute you walked in."

Startled, Mab flinched visibly for an instant, then recovered as if that slip had never been. Her mouth worked tightly as she started to move in a circle around Maggie. It was as if Finn had disappeared. Neither of the women so much as acknowledged his presence.

This was about the two of them. And Maggie began to move counterclockwise opposite the queen.

"Forgot about that, didn't you?"

"Do you really believe I would need power to crush you? I don't."

Probably not, Maggie thought, but it was good to know she didn't have the extra bells and whistles.

"Well, I don't know," Maggie said, continuing to move, stalking the queen as she herself was being stalked. "I figure if you really could crush me all that easily, you would have already started."

To one side of them Finn moved into the light streaming through one of the dozen or more open windows. Neither woman so much as glanced at him.

"Why would I rush this?" Mab walked with small, deliberate steps, still every inch a queen—until she stepped into the water Maggie had spilled, and Mab slipped just enough to ruin the effect. Recovering quickly, she frowned. "You've gone to so much trouble to get me here, it seems only right that we should make this encounter last."

"Uh-huh." Maggie grinned, and that annoyed Mab, too. She could see it. That one small slip in the water on the floor had made the queen seem less omnipotent. Less . . . royal, somehow. So Maggie played Mab's game, walking in an ever-decreasing circle as her mind raced, trying to remember all the moves Quinn had taught her.

"Culhane's brought you to this, hasn't he?" Mab asked, clucking her tongue in feigned sympathy, surprising Maggie enough that her concentrations wavered a bit. Mab saw it and shook her pretty head. "To a fight you don't want and can't possibly win. I should have stopped him—for your sake, if nothing else. He's gone rogue, you see. Can't be trusted."

"But you can?" Sarcasm dripped off every word.

"I'm a queen."

"And they're always benevolent," Maggie countered with a laugh.

"Silly child. A queen rules not with benevolence but with authority. Strength. Fear. But between us there doesn't have to be a battle. Don't you understand? Culhane brought you to this for reasons of his own. Fostering revolution in my kingdom. Turning the Fae against one another. But he's been stopped. Jailed." Her eyes hardened and looked like two flat emeralds, devoid of light. "His cause is finished. So you waste your life by coming to me."

"You came to me, remember?" Maggie smiled. "Besides, jailed or not, he's still Culhane."

"Yes, I suppose he is." Mab stopped moving, waved one hand and, when nothing happened, hissed out a complaint.

"Oops," Maggie said with a laugh.

"No matter." Mab turned to Finn and snapped out an order. "You still have your power. Open a door to the cellar of the palace. Let her see the 'throne' her warrior's earned with his treachery."

"Jeez . . . are you always this melodramatic?"

Finn glanced at Maggie as if he'd rather not comply with the queen's command. Then he lifted one hand, and a window into another place opened. This was no portal. This was different. There was no swirl of energy. No blast of heat or cold. This just *was*. A hole in the room without substance, but still there. Still real.

Maggie looked into it and saw Culhane pacing in a cage with silver bars. A huge man trapped in a too-small cell, and Maggie could feel his raging frustration.

"For crimes of sedition and working with a human against his queen," Mab said, loudly enough that Culhane apparently heard and stopped pacing to look through the window at them, "the Fenian Culhane will rot in that cell. Eternity spent in a cage."

When she stopped speaking, Culhane grabbed the bars of his cell and shook them hard enough that the silver clattered—but held. "Maggie!" His voice—loud, frantic—came through clearly, and Mab frowned.

"No call to me? Your queen?" She pouted prettily. "Two hundred years you lie with me, and now you call for your human whore? This is the great Culhane? This is the Fenian warrior of legend?"

She laughed, and though the sound of it was as musical as bells ringing, there was no humor in it. No warmth.

Maggie'd had enough. She moved in behind Mab while the queen was distracted calling insults at her trapped warrior. "You really do talk too much," she said.

Mab whirled around, and Maggie threw a punch with everything she had. Her fist connected with Mab's nose, and Maggie felt it give. Her hand hurt, but blood was flowing from the queen's pretty little face, and her look of horrified shock was priceless.

"You *strike* me? You would *dare*?"

"Oh yeah." She threw another punch and caught Mab's chin. That had the queen spinning around, a less than dainty move, as she stumbled in an ungainly move.

"I am a queen," Mab shouted as her arms wheeled to regain her balance. Then she lifted one hand to her nose, clearly dumbstruck to see blood. Her own blood. "You don't lay hands on me."

"Gonna be a short fight that way," Maggie countered, and moved in again. Her only hope was to get in as many strikes as she could before Mab recovered enough to fight back.

This was what she'd been hoping for by luring Mab to Sanctuary. Her only chance at winning was in a physical match. Mab had been using nothing but magic and Fae powers for centuries. She'd probably forgotten how to fight. To really get into it one-on-one and try to hurt somebody before they hurt her.

Then Mab's fist connected solidly with Maggie's jaw and she saw stars. Okay, maybe the queen hadn't forgotten as much as Maggie had hoped.

"Foolish human." Mab tossed her hair back and sneered. "Do you think I'm less without my powers? I'm still Mab. I've fought more battles than you can imagine. I've reigned as queen for two millennia. I am the one the legends speak of. I am the one humans fear when they step across a Faerie circle in the dead of the night. I am—"

"Mab. Right. I got it. You gonna talk me to death?"

Mab screamed her rage and raced at Maggie, eyes wild, fingers curled into talons set to swipe at her eyes. But Maggie was ready, and when the queen got close enough Maggie grabbed her filmy, pale green blouse, planted one booted foot in Mab's belly and let herself roll over onto her back. She flipped Mab as easily as she had Culhane not too long ago, and hearing the crazy-ass queen's fragile little body slam into a wall was just wonderful.

Maggie was back on her feet an instant later, and though already her body hurt and places she hadn't even known existed were now singing with pain, she felt . . . charged. A part of her still heard Culhane's shouts of encouragement, the rattle of the silver bars on his cage as he fought and strained to escape.

Another part of her knew that Finn was close but staying out of range. But mostly Maggie focused on the enemy, coming to her feet and wobbling just a little.

Mab gave her a reluctant nod. "Strong for a human. And sneaky with it. I approve."

"Well, don't I feel loved."

"You and I don't have to be at odds, girl," Mab said, walking toward her with slow, mincing steps. "We could work together. This doesn't have to end badly for you."

"Have you checked your scorecard lately?" Maggie asked, grinning. " 'Cause I think you'll find that my team's winning."

Mab chuckled. "So it would seem to a child."

Maggie wasn't going to let herself be distracted, and that was all this was. Mab would talk and talk, get Maggie off guard, then come in fast to get the upper hand. Well, Bezel might not have taught her how to fight, but that talkative, annoying little pixie had *really* shown Maggie how to avoid hearing irritating conversations.

"If you change your allegiance to me, we two could do great things," Mab was saying, her voice practically a coo now, tempting, alluring.

Even with a broken nose, a bruise already blossoming around one eye and her hair a tangled mess, Mab, queen of the Fae, was regal.

And not to be trusted, Maggie reminded herself.

"Your power grows," Mab said. "Even now I sense it welling within you. There is much for you to learn."

"I'm doing fine, but thanks for caring," Maggie said, stepping back carefully for every step forward Mab took. Thank God the library was empty but for a few chairs and that long table on the other side of the room. Nothing to trip on. Nothing to fall over.

"I could teach you more than Culhane or Finn would ever be able to."

"Right," Maggie snapped. "What would we call those classes, I wonder? How to Fuck Up a Kingdom 101? How to Turn on Your Warriors and Let Otherworld Go to Hell for Beginners? Thanks, Professor, but no, thanks."

Mab moved unbelievably quickly and slapped Maggie's face with her open palm. The smack was hard enough to make Maggie see stars, and the pain sizzled like fire on her skin.

"Who are you to say these things to me?"

Mab pushed, shoved, then delivered a solid punch to Maggie's jaw that had her stumbling backward with the force of the blow. *Okay, seriously underrated Mab,* she thought. Even without her power the queen was managing to more than hold her own.

Culhane had been right, she thought as she straightened up and looked into the cold green eyes of a mad queen. Luck on a battlefield was sometimes more important than strength.

She just hoped she had some good luck waiting for her.

"Don't you realize what I offer you, you stupid human? I offer you eternity at my side."

"Uh-huh," Maggie said, tossing a quick glance behind her before fixing her gaze on Mab again. "Or until you get tired of me. Then what? A cage beside Culhane? Do you have one all set up for me? No, thanks, Queen of the Damned."

Another hiss of outrage from Mab. Then she shouted, her voice echoing over and over again, sounding like a chorus of pissed-off Mab: "Culhane forged his own fate! Two hundred years he was my consort! And still he turned on me. You think he would be different with you?" She shook her head and gave Maggie a pitying stare. "You're more foolish than even I thought. You are nothing more than a tool to him. He will use you, then discard you. I offer you a way out of such a fate."

Despite Maggie's best efforts, Mab's words got through, and she wondered frantically if the queen was right. Was Culhane only using her? Was what they felt when they were together nothing more than Faery magic? Was he seducing her into trusting him so he could do whatever he wanted and she'd sit by like a good little Stepford wife and nod her head?

No.

Mab was only trying to distract her, and damn it, it was working.

"Forget about it, *Mara*," she said, deliberately using the nightmare name for Mab that Eileen had discovered on the Internet.

The queen's head whipped back, and her eyes went wide in surprise at the little jab.

"Yeah," Maggie said, nodding. "I know about you. How you like to spend your off-hours dropping nightmares into humans' minds. Ooh. Scary. But you're not going to tempt me to the dark side, Darth Faery. I'm here to kick your ass, and that's just what I'm going to do."

"Idiot." All pretense at gosh-let's-be-best-friends instantly dissolved. The queen was once again haughty, unapproachable and terrifying. Her cold green eyes glittered in the sunlight washing over the room, and her mouth, when she smiled, looked just as hard as the marble they stood on. "So we end this here. Now. While your warrior lover is watching." She spared a quick, amused glance at the captive Culhane and listened to his shouts of rage as if they were music.

"Fine by me." Hey, Maggie could do bravado as well as the next really crazy person.

"Before I finish you, let me tell you your future," Mab said, walking again slowly, deliberately closer to Maggie. "You will die. Painfully."

"I figured." She didn't sound scared, did she? Good for her.

"Then I will kill your sister."

Maggie's eyes narrowed on an indrawn hiss of breath.

"Did you think I didn't know about the whore my warrior Quinn is hiding in Otherworld?" She laughed again, and this time it sounded deadly. "I haven't bothered with her yet, but that time is gone. When you're gone, she's next. Then her whelp."

"Eileen," Maggie whispered, and ice coated her insides.

"She's a child now," Mab said, her voice soft, somehow gentle despite the venom in her words. "But the moment she comes of age she dies. Your line ends today," Mab swore, running one hand under her broken nose and wincing at the resulting pain. "Then I will allow Culhane to watch me throw open the gates of Otherworld. The Fae will stream into your dimension. Your world will worship me. And after yours"—she paused for effect—"all the worlds."

"That is trollshit," Maggie said, and slammed her fist into the bitch queen's pretty face. Mab jerked, surprised, and Maggie took advantage.

Slamming blow after blow into the queen, Maggie zoned out, hardly feeling the pain in her hands, her arms. The burn of fatigue pulling at her. She fought because she had no choice. Because she had to win. To lose meant losing everything, and that she wouldn't risk. Mab had to be defeated.

But the queen didn't give up easily. Her punches and kicks were sloppy, but there was strength behind them. So she wasn't used to fighting with her hands, but her eagerness for battle made up for that.

When Mab took her down to the floor, Maggie felt her teeth rattle as she landed hard on the unforgiving marble. Mab's fragile hands linked around her throat with surprising strength, and Maggie frantically went for the only move she had left. Grabbing a hunk of Mab's glorious hair, she yanked it viciously until the queen shrieked and pulled away.

Chick-fight moves. Humiliating but effective.

The fight was taking a toll on both of them as they wobbled and weaved on unsteady feet, still circling each other. Each of them bloodied, looking for a weakness to exploit. Each of them wanting this ended and over.

Maggie knew she couldn't last much longer. Then a soft breeze blew through an open window at her back, and an idea flew into her mind that she could only hope would work. Maybe, she thought wildly, when you needed luck the most, you had to make your own.

Mab gathered her strength and ran at her. Maggie did the whole fall-back-and-flip-her move again, her heavy boots punching into Mab's belly. Maggie smiled grimly at the sound of the high-and-mighty queen slamming into the floor, but she didn't pause to enjoy it. Instead Maggie was up and running before Mab had recovered. Grabbing the queen, she dragged her up, then bent her back over one of the open windows.

The wind lifted Mab's hair like a blond flag, whipping it wildly behind her head. Wide emerald eyes got even wider as she fought to get a grip on Maggie, to hold on to the window jamb, anything that would help her regain her balance.

But there was nothing she could do but whisper something that brought a smile to her eyes even as Maggie gave her one last shove.

With a scream that seemed to last for centuries, Mab fell through the window of Sanctuary. Maggie planted both hands on the windowsill to help hold herself up, then leaned out to look, while her lungs heaved in gulps of air. The wind blew at her face, and she was forced to squint to see the Faery queen falling through what seemed like eternity. Satisfaction rolled through Maggie in a thick wave.

"Ding-dong, the bitch is dead," she whispered, trying to push Mab's last words out of her mind. Trying to hold on to the fact that she had survived. She had won.

Nora, Eileen, her world, were safe.

"Oh, man," she muttered, sliding to the floor in a bruised and exhausted heap. "I'm so whipped."

She leaned her head back against the wall and could only watch as Culhane stepped out of his cell and into the window Finn had drawn what seemed like a lifetime ago. He raced to her side, dropped to one knee and cupped her bruised cheek in his palm.

"Ow!" Everything on her hurt.

He smiled, glanced over his shoulder at Finn and said, "Nectar, if you will."

"Right away."

"What's nectar?" She stared up into Culhane's pale green eyes and felt all of her tension drain away. The fight was over, he was here and it looked like she wasn't going to die anytime soon after all.

"A kind of wine," he said, smoothing her hair back with the gentlest of touches.

"Oh. Good for me."

"You were magnificent," Culhane told her, bending now to place gentle kisses on her forehead, her cheek, her lips. "I feared for you. Watching you fight, being unable to help, nearly killed me."

"I know," she said, and a warmth like nothing she'd ever known before slid through her as she basked in what was shining in Culhane's eyes.

He grinned. "It was a brilliant stroke, bringing Mab here."

"Yeah." She smiled, and winced when her split lip sent a zip of pain to her brain. "I'm feeling real clever at the moment."

"You won, Maggie." He kissed her carefully, and the zing of that was worth the little bit of pain. "You fulfilled the prophecy more gloriously than even I expected. You defeated Mab."

"I didn't kill her, though," she told herself, then thought about it. "Or did I?"

Finn walked back into the room, carrying a crystal glass filled with a pale gold liquid. Maggie realized he probably could have just used magic to get the wine, but he'd purposely left her and Culhane alone for moment. *Smart wizard.*

He handed her the glass, and as she took a sip and sighed, Finn said, "No, you didn't kill her. Sanctuary is out of time and place, remember? She fell, but she can't land. There's nowhere and nothing for her to fall to."

There was probably some kind of weird magic logic in there somewhere, but Maggie was just too beat to try to understand it. "So Claire was right," she muttered, more to herself than to the two Fae bending over her. "She said she saw Mab defeated, but not dead. Huh." Then she focused and looked up at Culhane. "You mean she just keeps falling? Forever?"

Finn shot Culhane a look over her head, and the warrior answered her question for her. "She'll find a way out. Eventually."

"So it's not over." Maggie thumped the back of her head against the wall. "It's like those crappy-ending movies on the Sci Fi Channel. You think the bad creature's dead, and then in the last scene you see an egg breaking open and you know it's all gonna start up again."

"What?" Finn frowned at her.

"Never mind." She was just too tired. She'd worry about Mab getting out of free fall some other day. For now she wanted to finish her wine, go home, take a shower and fall face-first on her bed for a day or two.

Lifting her gaze to Culhane's, she looked into those

pale green eyes that had come to mean so much to her, and asked, "Not that I'm not glad to see you, but how'd you get out of your cell?"

"When Mab was defeated her power to hold me ended."

"Yeah?"

"Yes." Finn stood up, glanced at Culhane, and then the two of them each took one of Maggie's arms and pulled her to her feet. She swayed a bit, gripped her wine and locked her knees. She wasn't going to end this fight by fainting.

She had some pride after all.

"As I told you, power is stripped from your body when you enter Sanctuary."

"Yeah, but Mab left." So to speak. "So didn't she get her power back?"

"No." Finn led the way as Culhane helped Maggie into the entry of Sanctuary.

There, high on the shelf behind the barrier, rested three spinning vortices of Fae power. One was Maggie's, one was Culhane's and the other, largest one . . . "Mab's?"

Finn bowed. "To regain your power you must leave the way you came. Mab didn't."

"No shit." Maggie chugged the last of her wine and handed the empty glass to Finn, who made it disappear. "So what happens to her power now?"

"It's yours." Finn smiled. "To the victor . . ."

Culhane turned her to face him. "It's as I told you, Maggie. Mab is defeated and *you* are queen."

A staggering thought. So, she not only wasn't going to lose her own burgeoning power, but she was getting even more of it. Was that a good thing? Probably. If she could figure out how to use all of this new power, maybe she could be ready by the time Mab finally showed up again.

Because she would. Maggie knew it deep down to

her bones. There was just no way Mab was going to stay away. She'd come back, and when she did, this little fight was going to feel like a cocktail party in comparison.

But those were worries for another day. Right now she just wanted to celebrate being alive.

"Well, all in all," Maggie said, wincing as fresh pains began to make themselves known, "I guess it's good to be queen."

Epilogue

Being the newly crowned Fae queen didn't get her windows painted.

Maggie still had forty scenes to slap on glass in the next two weeks. Then she'd have to deal with Thanksgiving-dinner prep, since Nora was too caught up in her Faery warrior to be trusted around a stove.

Holding her cup of coffee, Maggie stood at the back door and looked out into her yard. Everything was normal. Sort of. Nora was home, and Quinn Terhune was bopping in and out, dividing his time between Nora and his duties in Otherworld. Nora and Eileen were happier than Maggie had ever seen them, so she supposed having a Faery warrior for an almost-brother-in-law wasn't so bad.

Although, now that Nora was becoming Fae—or, as she so delicately put it, *I'm Fae by injection*—Maggie had to keep an eye out for her sister floating at inconvenient moments. Not to mention the fact that Eileen seemed to think that her aunt the queen should be able to make *her* Fae, as well.

"Probably trouble coming from that quarter real soon," Maggie muttered to herself, watching Eileen sit beneath the tree, stroking Sheba's fur.

Nora and Quinn were locked in an embrace near the

flower bed, and Claire was sitting in front of her easel, painting in the bright winter sunlight.

Claire was spending a lot more time at Maggie's place these days, and Maggie knew that part of the reason for that was the easy acceptance of the world of magic she found there. The secret she'd kept had been gnawing at her for years, and now that it was out, Claire's smiles came a lot more easily.

Although, Maggie thought, some of those smiles probably had something to do with the Fae warrior McCulloch, who just happened to pop in whenever Claire was around. More romance coming? She chuckled. "Pretty soon there'll be little hearts and birdies circling over the old Donovan house."

Still smiling, she took a sip of her coffee, letting the hot black brew slide through her system. The jolt of caffeine was good, but her smile lasted only until she heard Bezel's crabby voice raised in complaint.

"Would *you* want a house made up of crappy wood? I don't think so!"

The pixie was in the oak tree, ordering everyone around while he built himself a more permanent home. It seemed that his wife, Fontana, had tossed his ugly ass out for spending too much time with humans. So until she could find a way to get rid of him, Maggie was stuck with the little troll.

"Hey!" Bezel shouted, hanging from a tree branch to glare down at Culhane. "I'm using magic here. Do I look like I need a troll-spitting hammer tossed at me?"

Culhane laughed, and the sound of that rich, deep voice sent a swirl of something hot and wicked pumping through Maggie.

"Then get it done, you miserable little hobbit!"

"Hobbit!" Bezel snarled at Culhane, and the two old friends dropped into an insult contest that Bezel would no doubt win.

Maggie muffled a chuckle and watched her own

personal Fenian warrior as he harassed his tiny friend. She and Culhane still hadn't made it to bed, but Faery kisses were wearing her down fast. Still, there were other considerations, as well.

The civil war Finn had predicted was fast brewing in Otherworld. Culhane had tried to convince her to move to the palace permanently, but Maggie wasn't ready to give up her life just yet. She'd be queen—on her terms. Which meant she lived here and stepped through a portal a couple of times a week.

Culhane had vowed to help her all he could, and she was going to count on that. He knew way more about Otherworld than she ever would.

She sighed, leaned against the doorjamb and watched as Culhane spotted her. When he came toward her, smiling that breathtaking, hormone-enhancing smile, she kept her gaze fixed on him. That long black hair, the pale green eyes, the lithe, muscled body. He was quite the package. Just looking at him had her heart jittering in her chest and her palms itching to touch him.

He'd stayed with her for two days as she recovered from her fight with Mab. He'd taken care of her, held her while she slept and awakened her with kisses that urged her to heal faster. He'd been there. Every time she looked for him, there he was.

She wanted to turn to him. Wanted to revel in him. But she couldn't help remembering what Mab had whispered just before she fell through the window in Sanctuary. . . .

"What is it?" He came up beside her, dropped a kiss on her forehead and smiled down into her eyes. "You look worried."

"No," she lied, because she wanted it to be the truth. "Just thinking."

"Ah, well, then. Since your thoughts don't seem to be making you happy, why not come out and help me torture Bezel instead?"

He was right. No point standing here torturing herself.

"Now, that sounds like fun." Maggie smiled up at him. He dropped one arm around her shoulders, pulled her in close to his side and kissed the top of her head.

Maggie felt the solid, hard warmth of him and tried to shut out that last, lingering memory of Mab. Tried to close her mind and her heart to the sound of the defeated queen's voice.

But she couldn't. She heard that voice nightly in her dreams, and now, as Culhane walked beside her into the sunlight, Mab's vicious little muttering came again.

You think you've won . . . but just so you know, when Culhane whispers to you in the night . . . he lies.

After Maggie Donovan defeats the former queen
of the Otherworld and assumes the throne,
she'd give almost anything to return to the
familiarity of her old life. But a certain sexy
Fae warrior has much more exciting things
planned for Maggie.

Read on for a sneak peek at
Maureen Child's next
Queen of the Otherworld novel,

BEGUILED

Coming in August 2009 from Signet Eclipse

*B*eing a queen wasn't the thrill ride Maggie Donovan had expected.

Where were the jewels? The crown, for God's sake? Where were the adoring crowds, simpering minions and life o' luxury? Where was the fun? Shouldn't she have a mall named after her at least?

So far her responsibilities as the newly crowned queen of the Fae had been a royal pain in the ass.

Sure, only a couple of weeks had passed since Maggie had tossed the former queen, Mab, out a window to another dimension. But come on. No way was Maggie going to spend every freaking day of—oh, let's see—*eternity* listening to a bunch of whiny Faeries.

Which was why she was back in her own world doing something important.

"I need more snow, Maggie. It has to look really Christmassy, you know? And don't forget the wrapped presents under the tree. Oh, and the rocking horse. Remember the rocking horse."

"I know, Barb," Maggie said, forcing a smile at the older woman who owned Barb's House of Beauty.

Every year Barb paid Maggie to paint Christmas scenes on the front window of her beauty shop. And every year Barb wanted to outdo Sam's Hardware. Which was no small feat.

Sam's windows had been painted for two weeks already, so Barb had had plenty of time to study what Maggie had given him and think up ideas for one-upmanship. Always a good time in Castle Bay, California.

A tourist stop on Pacific Coast Highway, Maggie's hometown was small, familiar and just the antidote she needed for the *bizarreness* that had become her life. The town was slow, except in the summer when tourists clogged the streets and made cash registers ring. During the winter it was no more than a rest stop on the road, as tourists hit the bigger towns farther north such as Monterey and Carmel. And that was fine with Maggie.

She liked Castle Bay just the way it was. Here, she was plain old Maggie Donovan, artist and glass painter. Here, Maggie was known as Nora's sister and Eileen's aunt. She was a tiny part of the community, not some mythic queen expected to ride herd on the weird inhabitants of Otherworld.

Barb went back inside. Maggie picked up a white paint–laden brush, leaned out from her ladder, touched the glass and shrieked like an idiot when Culhane, Fae warrior, would-be lover and current pain in her ass, popped into existence beside her.

"Damn it," Maggie shouted, glancing through the window into the shop to make sure Barb hadn't noticed the tall, dark, gorgeous hunk of hormone happiness appearing out of nowhere. Barb hadn't.

Leaning against her ladder, Maggie looked down at him and instantly knew she shouldn't have. Seriously, the man was perfect eye candy. Six feet five inches of completely amazing male. He had sharp features, a strong jaw and green eyes so pale that they looked like windows into another world. His shoulder-length black hair gave him the look of a pirate, and the white shirt, dark green pants and knee-high brown leather boots he wore completed the picture nicely. On any other guy that outfit would have reduced most women to giggles. On Culhane it made him look like a walking, breathing invitation to sex.

Also, he had a great mouth, a nasty disposition and the ability to drive Maggie crazy in a heartbeat.

"I cannot believe you have come back here to paint pictures on glass." He set both fists at his hips, widened his stance and gave her a look that said he was ready to do battle. "You are expected at the castle. Maggie, you must return to Otherworld," he said, as if issuing a damn command.

That's what being the head Fae warrior for two hundred years will do to you. Make you an immortal, arrogant bastard.

Culhane had been ordering her around since he pushed his way into her life nearly a month ago. Claiming that Maggie's destiny was to defeat Mab and rule Otherworld in her place, he'd pretty much orchestrated everything to make sure his *prophecy* came true.

Plus, the whole time, he'd made Maggie crazed with lip-sizzling kisses, and the promise of a Fae-driven orgasm that had her strung so tight, the wrong word might snap her in two. He was probably doing it on purpose, she thought. Keeping her all stirred up and achy with need just so she'd go along with whatever the hell he wanted her to do. So far it had been working. If this was her eternity, there was just no way she was going to make it.

And damned if she'd be done in by her own horniness. So she was going to cling with both hands to however much *normal* she could get. An ocean breeze slid past her, ruffling her short auburn hair and carrying the scent of the sea, just two blocks away. At the skate park across the street, kids were riding the cement slopes on their boards and shoppers were juggling for parking spaces.

All blissfully normal. All quiet. All ordinary. Except for the fact that she had a damn Faery practically snarling at her.

"I can't go to Otherworld right now," she told him. "Busy here. See? Actual work."

He snorted. "You are a queen, Maggie. You do not have to work."

"Hah!" She turned to the window and laid a brush-load of white paint down into the first of several snow-drifts. "Seriously? Being queen is a boatload of work. Listening to all of you guys whine about what needs changing and what shouldn't be changed and how I should do it and how I'd better not do it. How'm I supposed to know who to listen to?"

She paused for breath, added more snow to the window and then kept talking. "I've been queen for like two weeks, okay? I don't know anything about Otherworld—"

"I can teach you."

"—and I don't want to know," she added, giving him a quick glare over her shoulder. "I didn't ask to be queen, you know. You guys came to *me*."

"You were the one who killed the demon and claimed the Fae power."

"That demon was eating my ex-boyfriend, remember? And then tried to chow down on *me*. And I didn't mean to kill her, anyway, and believe me, if I knew then what I know now . . ."

"What?" He laughed shortly. "You would do something different? You would allow the demon to kill you instead?"

Well, he had her there. Damn it.

"Okay, no. I still would have done what I did, but then I would have given the power to Mab. She was such a bitch that she deserved to have to be queen." Remembering how she'd tossed Mab out the window, Maggie sort of regretted it now. Of course if Mab were still alive, then she'd be trying to kill Maggie, which would just be a whole *different* sort of problem. Guess it was better to be queen than dead.

But that didn't mean she didn't have to paint windows, pay bills, buy groceries and, you know . . . be a person.

Culhane blew out a frustrated breath. This, Maggie was used to. She got it a lot from Culhane and the nasty-ass pixie Bezel, who was still living in the oak tree in her backyard.

How did her life turn into a paranormal soap opera?

"It is your destiny."

"Right. Well, destiny can get in line," Maggie snapped, stepping off the ladder and walking to the array of paints she had lined up neatly against the building. Culhane was always pulling out the destiny card. "I've got sixteen more windows to do before Christmas, and in case you didn't know, Thanksgiving is next week and I'm gonna have to do that, too, because Nora's got some kind of weird flu, which I think your stupid Fae warrior Quinn gave her."

"The Fae do not get sick."

"They're just carriers?" Maggie frowned, picked up another brush, swirled it into the blue paint and stood up again, still frowning as blue tempera paint slid off the brush and onto her hand.

Her sister Nora had been sick for days and refused to go to a doctor—which was probably just as well because she was having so much Faery sex lately that Quinn's powers were sort of overtaking her, and Nora kept floating at odd moments. How would they explain *that* to the doctor? So, with Nora sick, her daughter Eileen had been spending more time with Maggie because if Nora had some weird Faery plague, they didn't want Eileen getting it. Which meant that Maggie was getting to listen to play-by-play descriptions of life in middle school and which boy was the cutest and which girl had it in for Eileen.

Not to mention she had a crabby-ass pixie eating all of her damn chocolate.

God, even thinking about everything going on in her life made her tired. "I *sooo* don't have time to be queen."

"Time or not, you *are* the queen, Maggie, and nothing can change that. You must come with me."

Culhane grabbed her arm. The minute his hand touched her, Maggie felt a blast of heat that shot straight through her system and down to her hoo-hah. Energized with expectation, her hormones did the little clog dance of happiness and started to make her ache with a need that she knew wasn't going to get answered any time soon.

Fabulous. Because what she really needed to make this day complete was feeling so horny it hurt.

"God, Culhane, go bug somebody else, will ya? I'm busy here."

He ignored that. Big surprise.

"The Banshee contingents are insisting on speaking with you."

"Banshees have contingents? I thought they just went around screaming when people died."

He smiled and damn, that quick grin had a way of making her knees wobble. "They do. They want a wider territory. They've been in Ireland for millennia. They want to move to the New World."

"The *New World*? Who're you, Columbus? It's not the New World, Culhane."

"It is to us."

"Fine," she said, pulling free of his grip, though she hated to disappoint her hormones, who were now wearing party hats. "Let 'em leave Ireland. What do I care?"

"Maggie, you must learn. The Banshee cannot leave Ireland for here. If they do, it will create a war with the Cree-An."

"The *who*?"

Grumbling under his breath, Culhane shook his hair back from his face and said, "The Cree-An have been haunting on this ground for centuries. If the Banshee invade, the war will spill into the world of human dreams and the nightmares they cause will follow them into the waking."

"Freaking nightmare faeries now?" Maggie groaned and looked up and down the suddenly deserted street as if searching for an escape. She didn't find one. Though it made her wonder where in the hell everyone had gone. She didn't even hear the low rumble of skateboard wheels on cement anymore. Weird.

Shaking her head, she demanded, "What the hell am I supposed to do about all of that?"

"You must *listen*," he said for what had to be the twelve millionth time in the last couple of weeks. "Make compromises. Give the Banshee England. The Cree-An do not like the British. They think them unimaginative and old-world."

"Fabulous. Faery prejudice."

"I know this is a lot," Culhane said, moving in close to her, crowding Maggie enough that every breath she took, she drew in the scent of him.

Damn, he smelled good.

"But you will learn, Maggie. You will be the queen that destiny has named you."

"What if I don't wanna be?" she countered, held her breath and risked looking directly into his eyes. Oh *God*, he really was way too gorgeous. "What if all I want is to be me, Maggie Donovan, failed artist and glass painter extraordinaire?"

His hands moved to cup her face, and Maggie felt that touch right down to the soles of her feet. Oh, that probably wasn't a good sign, she thought. Why did it have to be Culhane who could turn her into a puddle of needy goo? Why couldn't she have fallen for a nice plumber? Why did it have to be a Fae warrior who made her want to toss her panties into the air?

"You are so much more than *just* Maggie Donovan. It is in your blood, your heart, your very soul." He bent his head, and his breath brushed her cheek. "You are the one, Maggie. The only one—"

"You are *not* gonna believe this, Mags."

Maggie looked past Culhane to see her sister, Nora, leaning up against her Fae lover. Great. More people popping in and out. Pushing away from Culhane, Maggie walked to her sister. "Nora? What's wrong? What's going on?" She looked up and down the street again and demanded, "And where the hell did everybody else go?"

"They did not go anywhere," Culhane grumbled, glaring at the other Fae. "Quinn has enchanted the street, blocking us from being seen and from seeing anyone else. Which he should not have done. Using magic in this world is always dangerous."

"Enchantments. Great. Fabulous. What next?" Maggie asked.

"Better than having people watch me float," Nora muttered, and swallowed hard, lifting one hand to her mouth. "Oh God, my chakras are *sooo* out of alignment."

"What the hell is going on here?" Maggie looked from Nora to Culhane to Quinn. "If I'm the damn queen, somebody *talk* to me."

"Get off my back, your freaking *majesty*," Nora snapped. "I'm feeling puky and pregnant right now, so back off."

"Pregnant?" Maggie shook her head and blinked at her sister. "You're *pregnant*?"

"I am proud," Quinn announced.

"I'm sick," Nora moaned.

"I'm speechless," Culhane added.

"Well, I'm not," Maggie yelled, turning on him. "If Fae sperm is that fast-acting, you can just keep your sexy Fae body far, far away from me!"

About the Author

Maureen Child is the award–winning author of more than one hundred romance novels and often says she has the best job in the world. A six-time RITA nominee, Maureen lives with her family in Southern California.